autumn

the human condition

autumn

the human condition

David Moody

The right of David Moody to be identified as the author
of this work has been asserted by him in accordance with
the Copyright, Designs and Patents Act 1988.

This is a work of fiction. All of the characters,
organisations and events portrayed in this novel are
either products of the author's imagination
or are used fictitiously.

First published in 2005 by Infected Books
'Home' first published in 'The Undead' by Permuted Press (2005)
and 'Extreme Zombies' by Prime Books (2012)
'Joe and Me' first published by This is Horror (2012)

This edition published in 2013 by Infected Books

A CIP catalogue record for this book
is available from the British Library

ISBN 978-0-9576563-0-7

www.infectedbooks.co.uk

Cover design by Craig Paton
www.craigpaton.com

www.davidmoody.net
www.lastoftheliving.net

INTRODUCTION

I originally envisaged **Autumn** as a standalone novel, but when I'd finished writing the first book back in 2001, it occurred to me that as I'd destroyed pretty much the entire population by the end of the first page, there would no doubt be many more stories left in my dead world to tell, if anyone wanted to read them. Fortunately, they did. Through the four subsequent novels I've been able to take my survivors way beyond the early days of the infection, right into the *post-post-apocalypse*. The problem was, the more I thought about the end of the world, the more I found to write about.

Back in 2005, when I first thought I'd wrapped the series up, I released the first edition of this book, describing it at the time as 'part companion, part guide book and part sequel'. But things change, and the acquisition of the series by Thomas Dunne Books meant the story continued after **Purification**. More than a year has now passed since the release of the final novel, **Aftermath**, and it seems the perfect time to revisit and update this collection and bring the series as a whole to a close.

The stories you'll find here fall broadly into three categories. Briefest are what I originally called **Autumn: Echoes** – snapshots of the lives of people caught up in the throes of the apocalypse (*where were you when the world ended?*). Some are recognisable characters from the novels, others are minor bit-players who had interesting back stories to tell. You'll find a 'who's who' at the end of the book.

The second batch of stories focus largely on what happened before or after events described in the novels. For example, in **Breaking Point**, you'll read what happened to Michael and Emma between **Autumn** and **The City**. In **Beginning to Disintegrate**, you'll discover how the group of survivors we meet in **Disintegration** came to be stuck with each other.

Finally, there are numerous other shorts here which are self-contained and take place well outside the main story arc. I came up with a number of scenarios which were too interesting to forget about, but which didn't fit naturally into the novels. For example, in **The**

Garden Shed, a proud man refuses to leave the home he's worked so hard to own, and in **Office Politics**, we meet a man whose coping strategy is enviably simple: complete denial.

I hope you enjoy this collection, and that you've enjoyed the rest of the Autumn series. In closing, I wish to record my enormous thanks to everyone who has been involved in the series in one way or another over the last decade: to the editors, artists, and publishers who've worked behind the scenes, but most importantly, to the readers who've supported the books from the beginning. I'm indebted to all of you.

David Moody
June 2013

BEFORE

JAKE WILSON

Eight months ago, Jake Wilson packed up his family and emigrated to Canada from the United Kingdom. A regional manager for a global finance house, Jake agreed to move overseas for a well paid, two year posting. He, his wife Lucy and their two children settled quickly into their new surroundings. The people who found it hardest to adjust were those they'd left behind. Even after more than half a year, Polly Wilson – Jake's well-meaning but highly strung and over-sensitive mother – still finds the distance between her and her son difficult to deal with. Mrs Wilson and her husband made their first visit to Canada several weeks ago, but it did little to reassure her. If anything it's made her even more neurotic. Jake has grown to dread the weekly telephone calls from home. It's now the early hours of Tuesday morning.

'Jake? Jake, is that you?'

'Mom? Bloody hell, do you know what time it is?'

'Are you okay, love?'

'Apart from being woken up in the middle of the night I'm fine. Why shouldn't I be?'

'Haven't you heard?'

'Heard what? Bloody hell, Mom…'

'There's no need for the language, Jake, we were just worried about you, that's all.'

'Why?'

'Are you far from Vancouver?'

'It's on the other side of the country. It's thousands of miles away, why?'

'Because something's happening there. I don't know what exactly. I don't think anyone knows. Your dad and I saw it on the news and—'

'You're not making any sense. Look, Mom, I'm really tired.'

'I'm sorry, love. It's just that you're all so far away and we worry about you.'

'I know, I know… What are you doing up so early, anyway? It's before seven there, isn't it?'

'Your dad couldn't sleep. You know what he's like once he's awake. And once he's up and about I can't relax. He woke me up with his shuffling and his moaning so we both got up and came downstairs. We were watching the news, and when we saw they were talking about Canada we thought we should call…'

'So what exactly is supposed to have happened in Vancouver?'

'They're not sure. No one's saying much. No one seems to know.'

'So you've woken me up to tell me that no one knows very much about what's happening in Vancouver? Come on, Mom, I've got an important meeting first thing tomorrow and I can't afford to—'

'No. Listen, son, something's definitely happened there but they don't—'

'Well was it an accident or a bomb or…?'

'I don't know.'

'Mom, you've got to stop this. I know you mean well, but this isn't little old England. This place is huge. Just because something's happening in the same country, it doesn't always mean it's going to affect us.'

'But this sounds serious, love. They say the city's gone silent.'

'What's that supposed to mean? Vancouver is a massive city for Christ's sake. There are thousands and thousands of people there, millions even. You don't lose contact with millions of people just like that.'

'I know, but—'

'You can't lose contact with a whole bloody city, Mom.'

'I know, but they have.'

'What channel are you watching? Are you sure it's genuine? It's not just a film or one of those drama-documentaries, is it?'

'Jake, your father and I are not stupid. I know what I'm watching. It's the news and it's real. We're sitting in front of the television right now. I'm only telling you because we're concerned about you, Lucy and the boys.'

'So tell me again, what exactly is it they're saying?'

'Your dad says to put your TV on, son. You're bound to have some news where you are. You're much closer than we are.'

'Okay, give me a second.'

'What can you see?'

'Hold on, that's strange.'

'What is?'

'I can't get a picture on some of the channels. Cable must be down. Sometimes this happens when...'

'What about the radio? Try your computer, son. Try the Internet.'

'Hang on, here's something.'

'What are they saying?'

'Christ, Mom, it's just like you said, they've lost contact with the area around... Hold on, you said Vancouver, didn't you?'

'Yes, why?'

'Because the station I'm watching here is talking about Winnipeg. That's miles away. And Seattle, and Portland. They're talking about a massive part of the country. Bloody hell...'

'Are they saying anything about what's happened, Jake? Do they know why—'

'Christ, Mom, they've put a map up. It looks like it's spreading out from the west.'

'What is?'

'I don't know. Nothing... Just nothing... They're not explaining anything, they're just...'

'Where are Lucy and the boys, Jake?'

'Lucy's here in bed with me, the boys are asleep.'

'You should lock your doors. Don't answer the door if anyone comes.'

'What's the point of locking the door? This isn't anything...'

'Jake... Jake, are you still there? What's the matter, son?'

'Nothing. Thought I heard something.'

'What?'

'Thought I could hear...'

'Jake? What's happening?'

'Mom, I'm going to put the phone down. Listen, I'll call you back as soon as I—'

'What's wrong?'

'Something's happening on the other side of the river. There's a fire. It looks like something's gone into the front of one of the buildings on the waterfront. I can't see much from here… Hang on a second and I'll try and… Shit, that's all I need, the kids are awake now. Bloody hell. Lucy, could you go and…? Lucy? Honey, what's wrong?'

'What's the matter, son?'

'Lucy? Don't struggle, honey, lie back and I'll get you a—'

'Jake…? Jake, love, are you still there?'

Over five thousand miles away and completely helpless, Mrs Wilson listened to the muffled sounds of her son, her daughter-in-law and her two grandsons choking to death.

Their heartbreak was short lived. Within hours both Mrs Wilson and her husband were dead too.

DAY ONE

Amy Steadman is a twenty-four year old graduate. After joining the company on an accelerated training programme, she now manages the lingerie department in an exclusive women's fashion boutique located in a busy out-of-town shopping outlet. She lives on her own in the town of Rowley in a small one bedroom flat above an antiques shop on a narrow road just off the main high street.

It's five-thirty in the morning. Amy's alarm has gone off, and she's just dragged herself out of bed after a miserable night's sleep. This morning Amy has to make her quarterly sales presentation to the company's senior management team. She dreads these meetings. She doesn't have a problem with standing up and justifying her performance to these self-important, grey-suited people, but she detests the way they stare back at her. They are smarmy, lecherous men and she can feel them undressing her with their eyes. She hates the way they don't listen to anything she says, the way they joke and taunt her and make lewd, inappropriate comments. She finds their cheap, double-entendre-laden conversation offensive but she puts up with it. It's all part of the job, others have told her.

In Amy's line of business appearance is everything. She walks the shop floor as a representative of the store and the numerous designer labels it stocks. She knows that she must be perfectly coiffured and immaculately presented at all times. Customers directly associate her with the products she sells. The better she looks, the more chance she has of making a sale.

After a quick breakfast (she doesn't feel like eating much this morning) and a lukewarm shower (she needs to get her landlord to sort out the plumbing), Amy dries her hair and sits down in front of the mirror to apply her make-up. An exercise in precision application, this is crucially important to her. Far more than just another part of her perfect appearance, it is a mask. She is painting on her work personality and her customer-facing smile. In fifteen minutes she creates a character far removed from the real Amy Steadman: the girl who sits in front of the television on her own most nights, eating chocolate and relaxing in her pyjamas and baggy jumpers. She hides behind the mask. The senior managers who stare and leer at her see only the fixed smile, the perfect white teeth and the flawless complexion. They are unaware of the contempt she feels for them.

Less than an hour after getting out of bed, Amy is dressed, psyched-up and ready to go. She leaves her flat and crawls through the early morning traffic in her wreck of a car, arriving at work in just under fifty minutes. It is almost eight o'clock, and the store will shortly open its doors to the first customers of the day.

'These shoes are killing me,' Lorraine moans.

'Well what do you expect?' I tell her. Do we have to go through this every morning? Lorraine (who's had more nips, tucks, false tans and hairstyles than the rest of us put together) is a total slave to fashion. 'Bloody hell, girl, those heels would be enough to cripple anyone. You're almost on tiptoe!'

'You're all right, you've got the height you lucky cow,' she says. 'Short buggers like me need all the help we can get.' She stops talking and looks over my shoulder. 'Oh, hang on, here they come.'

I turn around and see that the first of our overpaid visitors from Head Office has arrived. My heart sinks. I smile through gritted teeth as the area manager makes his entrance with his entourage. What a vile and odious little shit Jeff Brent is. 'Morning, Mr Brent.'

'Morning, Andrea,' he grins, getting my name wrong as he always does. 'Looking more beautiful than ever!'

'And you're more of a fucking creep than ever,' is what I want to say back to him but, of course, I don't. Instead I just smile politely, force out a little laugh and then relax when Maurice Green appears at my side to take Brent through to the back offices.

'Excuse me, Miss,' a quiet little voice says from somewhere behind me. I turn around and see an elderly man clutching a negligee, looking more than a little bit uncomfortable. It's an odd choice of nightwear. He's either married to a gold-digger or he's a transvestite.

'What can I do for you, Sir?' I say, looking around for one of the others. Lorraine has disappeared the way she always does when customers need serving. This isn't fair. I have to get to my meeting. I haven't got time to be dealing with customers today.

'I bought this for my wife's birthday last week and she doesn't like it,' he says. Judging by the age of the customer in front of me, if she isn't a gold-digger then his wife could be anywhere between sixty and eighty years old. Can't imagine I'll be wearing underwear like this at that age.

'I see,' I say, taking the negligee from him and holding it up. There isn't much of it. Definitely not to be worn in winter. 'Didn't she like it? Do you want a refund?'

He shakes his head.

'No. Actually I was wondering whether you had it in any other colours,' he says, taking me by surprise. His face turns lobster pink with embarrassment. 'She doesn't like black,' he explains, 'says she'd rather have red. Says it makes her feel more… you know.'

I'm going to be late for the meeting. I'll have to hand this old gent over to a colleague, but there's never anyone about when you need them. I start leading him over to the customer services desk when something catches my eye over by the main doors. I can see Gary Bright, the area finance director, down on all fours. He looks like he's being sick. Is he choking? His laptop's on the floor and there are confidential papers blowing all over the place. I look for Jenny Clarke who's the duty first aid officer but Christ, someone else is down now. A woman just to the left of me has collapsed against the customer service desk. Bloody hell, she looks like she's suffocating. She's clawing at her neck and her face is bright red, eyes bulging.

Shit, Shirley Peters from sportswear is on the floor at the bottom of the escalator now. Her skirt's caught in the mechanism. She looks as if she's just—

Oh God, what's that?

I can feel something at the back of my throat, like I've got something trapped. I try to clear it but I can hardly swallow and the more I cough, the worse it gets. Something's scratching the back and sides of my throat and I can't clear it. I need to get some water. It's still there. It won't go. Stronger now, getting worse. Christ, it feels like someone's got their hand around my neck.

Need to get help. Jesus it hurts.

It's stinging and burning. Bloody hell, I can't swallow. I can't breathe.

11

Calm down. Calm down. Calm down.
Oh fuck, I can taste blood in my mouth.
Just don't panic. Slow down. Try and breathe. Try and—

Starved of oxygen, Amy fell back into a rail of designer dresses, pulling half the display down on top of her. She gagged and retched as blood dribbled down the inside of her inflamed throat. Unable to focus, she was momentarily aware of frantic, terrified movement all around her.

She clawed at her neck and began to thrash about as the remaining oxygen in her blood stream rapidly disappeared. Already numb, she felt no pain when the back of her head thumped against the hard marble floor.

Her mouth and chin now covered with blood, Amy tried to stand but couldn't. The world became dark and the screams around her became muffled, then fell silent.

Less than two minutes after infection, Amy Steadman was dead.

JIM HARPER

I'm in big fucking trouble. I can't believe what I've just done. Christ knows how I'm going to get myself out of this one.

There are mistakes and there are mistakes. There are minor indiscretions you can brush under the carpet, and there are fucking huge mistakes that you know are going to cost you big time and haunt you for the rest of your life. This is the biggest of all the fucking huge mistakes I've ever made. This is the worst thing I could have done.

I'm in a hotel room. It only took me a couple of seconds to get my bearings after I woke up. I'm here on a course from work. This is only day two of five but the way things are going it could well be my last day in the job. It's a quarter to eight and the first session of the morning starts in less than an hour. I've missed breakfast but that doesn't matter. I couldn't eat anything. I feel sick to my stomach. Problem is, this isn't *my* hotel room.

I'm keeping as still as I can, lying on my side and looking out of a crack in the curtains at a dull and rainy morning outside. I'm trying to work my way back through the events of last night, trying to remember everything that happened. We're here for the week – Monday through to lunchtime Friday. There are seventeen of us from different outlets up and down the country. We had a formal meal last night to break the ice and get to know everyone, then we moved into the bar. And that was where we stayed. I got talking to a couple of lads from up north, then I ended up with two girls who work in my area. I'd met one of them before, but I didn't recognise her friend. Turns out she was Helen Hunter – the daughter of Bill Hunter, my area director and one of the nastiest bastards you could have the misfortune to come across. My missus, Chloe, works in his office.

And here's where things get really, really fucked-up. I haven't plucked up the courage to look yet, but I'm ninety-nine per cent sure this is Helen Hunter's bed, and I'm equally certain that Helen Hunter is in it with me. Whoever it is lying next to me, she's just wrapped her arm around me and she's kissing my neck.

Don't react. Keep calm. Just keep calm and get things in perspective. Am I completely sure it's Helen? I'm having trouble remembering last night clearly. I remember sitting in the bar with the two girls, drinking hard. I was starting to get to the stage where you know you've had a few and your body's trying to tell you to stop. Sometimes the beer plays tricks on you: the alcohol sort of waits for a while, then creeps up and rushes you all of a sudden. I'd been fine all night but I knew having another drink would have been a mistake. Thing is, I know I stayed for at least two more pints after that. One of the girls went to bed and I remember being left there with the other. It was definitely Helen. The rest of our group were long gone and we were the only two left in the bar.

We were having one of those conversations where you start discussing things you know you shouldn't be talking about, but you can't stop. She started telling me about her relationships and sex, then moved on to her likes and dislikes in bed (concentrating more on the likes). I started to get more and more uncomfortable and, at the same time, more and more turned on. She was flirting with me (okay, I was flirting with her too) and I remember thinking I was going to have to try and be a bit more distant in the morning because we've got a whole week to get through together and I didn't want to give her the wrong impression. Problem was, by then I'd already done more than enough, and what happened next was inevitable.

I remember us finishing our drinks and leaving the bar. We walked through the lobby together and went up to our rooms. We walked down the same corridor and I started to get jumpy because I thought she was following me. I stopped outside my room and took out my key and she did the same with the room next door. She made some cheap comment about fate and coincidence and destiny or something and I just mumbled because my brain had stopped functioning properly. I remember thinking that I should just go into my room, shut the door and go to bed but I was having one of those moments where my brain was trying to stay in control but the booze and my dick had long since taken over.

Helen Hunter is a cheap (but fucking gorgeous) tart with a reputation for being a marriage-breaker and sleeping around. I kept telling myself to turn and run but instead of walking away from her I walked towards her. She wrapped her arms around my neck and whispered something filthy in my ear, can't remember what. I remember smelling her perfume and the booze on her breath, then feeling myself getting hard. We kissed. One kiss, then another, then another and another until we were practically eating each other's faces. My hands started to wander. I grabbed her backside and pulled her closer. One thing led to another and... and that's why I'm in trouble now.

It has to be said though, what I remember of last night was damn good. She lived up to her reputation. She was half-undressed by the time we'd made it onto the bed and I was completely undressed seconds later. The lights were full on and the curtains were open but neither of us cared. All I could think about was fucking her senseless. There was no hint of passion, just sheer lust. It felt like minutes, but I remember looking at the clock on the bedside table at one o'clock, then again at two and then three. At some point one of us had turned the lights off and we'd finally fallen asleep.

Despite the fact what I've done is wrong whichever way you look at it, it was bloody good. Just lying here thinking about what she did last night is making me feel horny again...

'It's ages yet until the course starts, Jim,' she says from behind me, her breath tickling the nape of my neck. She starts dragging her nails over my skin, just enough to hurt. Christ, she's barely done anything but she's really turning me on. I should try to be strong and tell her no, but what's the point? The damage has already been done. Might as well lie back and enjoy it 'cause the shit's going to hit the fan later...

Helen rolls me over and I look up into her face. She's fucking beautiful – an absolute gem. For a second it's easy to forget that I'm married and that the woman I'm in bed with is my boss' precious daughter, because I can't think straight. All I can do is react to what she's doing to me. Now she's sliding down underneath the covers, biting my chest and licking me and she's not stopping there. She's going lower. I put my hands behind my head and lie back. Might as well make the most of it.

Quarter past eight. It's over. The sudden frenzied excitement and lust has gone and all I feel now is panic and regret. What have I done, and why have I just done it again? Helen's grinning at me like an idiot but then, compared to me, she's got nothing to lose. Chances are I've already lost everything. How the hell am I going to be able to look Chloe in the face now? After the last time I promised her this would never happen again. I mean nothing to Helen. This has just been a bit of fun for her. I'm another one of her victims, another conquest, another notch on the bedpost, and some other poor bastard will probably be taking my place in this bed tonight. I should have known better. I knew what she was like. She'll walk away from this without a bad word being said, and I'll take all the flack. If Bill Hunter finds out then I've fucking had it. I've probably just thrown away my marriage, my house and my career for one night of sex. What a fucking idiot.

What do I do now? She's out of bed and I'm left lying here on my own, looking up at the ceiling and trying to work out how I'm going to blag my way out of trouble. Easiest thing would be to grab my stuff from the room next door and do a runner, but I know I can't do that. I can't believe I've been so stupid *again*. This is definitely the worst yet.

She's in the shower. Despite the fact that we've just spent the night together and I've already explored every available inch of her naked body, I feel embarrassed now because she's undressed. I try not to look but I can't help myself and she knows it. She's flirting again. She knows I'm watching, and she probably knows what I'm about to say. She's doing everything she can to put me off.

'Look,' I say, clearing my throat, 'we need to talk.'

She doesn't answer. I don't know if she can hear me over the noise of the shower. Most of the course delegates' rooms are on this floor so I don't want to shout but I don't have any choice. This won't wait.

'Listen, I'm going back to my room now. I had a great time last night, Helen, but what we did was wrong…'

She peers around the side of the shower curtain, making sure she shows more than enough bare flesh to make me lose my train of thought.

'I'll see you later,' she says. 'Play your cards right and your whole week will be as good as last night.'

I try to protest. 'You were great last night, but I made a mistake.

I'm sorry. We should just pretend it never happened and...'

She's shaking her head. 'Too late for that,' she says, grinning. 'You're going to learn more in this little room than you will on the course. I'm going to do things to you that are barely legal. You're mine for the rest of the...'

She stops talking.

The expression on her face changes.

'What's the matter?' I ask. Bitch is just playing with me again.

She's rubbing at her neck, 'I... I can't...'

She massages her throat with one hand and grips the shower curtain with the other to keep herself steady. Christ, she's suffocating. She's trying to breathe in, but it's like she can't get any air. She's looking at me with wide, frightened eyes and I don't know what to do. I just stand there. I can't move. I want to help but I don't know what to do.

Her legs buckle and she falls, pulling the shower curtain down with her. Her head hits the faucet with a soft thud that makes me feel sick. Now she's lying in the bath, shaking and choking, and there's blood pouring out of a deep gash on the side of her head. It's washing down the plughole, mixing with the foam and running water like something out of *Psycho*. I turn off the shower. Christ, there's blood everywhere. I need to get help.

I run to the bed to get my trousers. My legs are wet from the shower and I can't get them on. I trip over, then crawl around the room. I grab the phone and ring Reception to get them to call an ambulance but there's no answer. No one's picking up.

I'm standing in the bathroom door again now, half-dressed, and Helen's not moving. I can't bring myself to touch her. I have to do something, but Christ, I think she might be dead.

'Helen?'

I must be a real spineless bastard. For a split second I actually feel relieved because I realise now I might have a chance of salvaging something from this mess. I can tell them I was in the room next door and I heard her fall down so I came into help and I found her like this...But hold on, isn't that going to make things worse? My clothes are in this room. And it's not just my clothes, there will be hairs and fingerprints and God knows what else all over the bed and probably all over and inside her too. Fuck, what if they say I did it? What if they think I pushed her over in the shower to keep her quiet about what we'd done together?

Got to get out of here.

I grab my things and run to the door. I try to leave the room but then I see her body again and I stop. I have to help her, but I'm too fucking scared. I run out into the corridor, then stop because there's another body. Jesus Christ, it's a porter. I don't want to get any closer to him. I can see his face and it's all twisted and contorted with pain and there's blood on the carpet around his mouth.

There's another body further down, just outside one of the rooms. It's Steve Jenkins from the Southampton branch. I sat opposite him at dinner last night. And there's another on the stairs... one of the course tutors, I think.

I can't handle this. I go back into my room and pace around the bed, trying to make sense of everything that's happening.

I can't hear anyone outside.

I try the phone again but no one answers. Same with my mobile. I'm really fucking scared now. I'll wait for a couple more minutes, then I'll go and find help.

James Harper hid in his hotel room like a frightened child for hours before finally plucking up courage to go out and look for help. The smell of burning forced him to move. The hotel kitchens were on fire and the fire was spreading down the building.

He searched the rest of the hotel but he was the only one left alive.

SHERI NEWTON

Of all the shift patterns I work, this is the one I hate most. I can handle starting early in the morning and working through the day, I don't even mind starting in the afternoon and working through the evening, but this shift I just can't stand: sat here from midnight until nine in the morning. It's not too bad at weekends because there's usually plenty going on, but mid-week like today the time drags.

The graveyard shift has been worse than usual today. There should always be two of us in on late-lates but Stefan called in sick last night so I've been sat here on my own for almost eight hours. There's been nothing to do and hardly anything to see. Between two and three o'clock the pubs and clubs were clearing out so there was some activity on the streets for a while, but after that everything went quiet until around seven-thirty. That's when the office-workers started to arrive in dribs and drabs.

This job is arse-backwards: I want to be busy when I first come on duty, not when it's close to clocking-off and I'm too tired to concentrate. By this time my eyes are starting to get heavy. Okay, so this job's not physically tiring, but sitting in front of seventeen screens watching CCTV footage of a shopping centre, an office block and the surrounding streets is enough to put anyone to sleep. Still, as I keep reminding myself, it just about pays the bills. It's easy money really. I don't have to do anything much. Even if I see something suspicious all I have to do is call the police or security and let them do all the dirty work. I just stay here and watch.

This has been the slowest shift I can remember. Hardly anyone's out and about on Monday night, fewer still during the early hours of Tuesday morning. I've seen absolutely nothing tonight. I watched a drunk get arrested in the high street about two hours ago but bugger-all since then. The only screen I've watched with any interest is my phone. I can't even text anyone, though, 'cause they're all asleep.

It's just after eight now, and here we go. At last. First sign of trouble for the day.

The cameras cover all the public parts of the shopping centre, as well as the access roads, main delivery entrances, and the reception area in the office block. There's a driver unloading around the back of one of the electrical superstores. He's just fallen out of the cab of his truck, clumsy sod. Bloody hell, what's the matter with him? He must be drunk. The bloody idiot can't even get up. Christ, how can these people let themselves get in such a state and then get behind the wheel? Don't they have a conscience?

Hold on, he's moving again now. He's trying to pick himself up, but he's grabbing at his throat like he's choking on something. Is this for real? I can't see anyone else around to help. I've got a direct line to the loading bay. I'll try and get someone to go see to him...

No one's answering. Come on, someone pick up.

The line's ringing out but no one's answering.

Wait, there's someone else out there with him now. Another man walks out of the shadows, but before he gets anywhere near the guy on the ground, he collapses too. He's crawling along the ground on his hands and knees, spitting up.

Will someone answer the bloody phone?

Shit, on screen seven one of the cleaners working outside the main department store has just collapsed. What the hell is happening here? The two screens I'm watching are showing feeds from cameras at opposite ends of the complex. I was starting to think it might have been exhaust fumes or something like that causing the problems in the loading bay, but how could the same thing affect three people so far apart, all at the same time?

Wait, there are more...

Camera twelve is fixed on the public walkway between Alldays and Brothers Furniture. Oh Jesus, what's going on? I think that's Jim Runton, the assistant manager of Alldays. He's throwing up in the middle of the walkway. That's too dark to be vomit. Is that blood?

No one's answering this damn phone. I hang up and try one of the emergency lines linked direct to the police.

There's Mark Prentiss, the head of mall security. He's running back towards the offices. He'll know what's happening.

Oh no. Christ, now Mark's slowing down. He's not going to make it back here. Bloody hell, his legs just went from under him and he's gone down like all the others.

No one's answering the emergency phone either. That's not right: the emergency phone should *always* be answered. There has to be someone there... I'll try and get one of the security team on their radio. One of them will answer me...

The truck driver around the back of the superstore isn't moving now. He's just lying there, facedown on the tarmac next to his truck. It looks like he's dead but he can't be, can he? The other man near him isn't moving either. The cleaner outside the department store has stopped moving too.

All I can hear is static on the radios.

Jim Runton's body has been shaking since I first saw him go down, constantly convulsing, but now he's still. Mark Prentiss isn't moving either. There's a pool of blood spreading out around his face. It looks black on the CCTV screen.

I can move camera fifteen. That's the camera covering the main entrance and the pedestrian approach. I use the joystick to turn it almost a full circle. There should be crowds of people moving towards the mall from the station now, but bloody hell... all I can see are bodies. Dead bodies everywhere. The streets outside are filled with them. Hundreds and hundreds of them... It's like they've all just fallen where they were standing...

Nothing's moving on any of the screens now.

Sheri Newton got up from her seat behind the control desk and ran out into the small security office. There she found the body of Jason Reynolds, her colleague who'd been due to relieve her, sprawled across the floor in front of her, his wild, frightened eyes staring hopelessly into space. Further down the corridor, Adam, a security guard, was slumped dead in a half-open doorway. She stepped over him, tripping over his outstretched leg, then ran through the ghostly quiet building until she was out on the street.

Sheri walked another few metres before fear and shock overwhelmed her. She fell back against the wall of the nearest building, then slid to the ground. For more than an hour she remained sitting on the pavement, as still as the huge crowds of dead bodies which surrounded her.

SONYA FARLEY

Her pregnant belly wedged tight behind the steering wheel of her car, Sonya Farley stared at the never-ending queue of barely-moving traffic stretching out in front of her and yawned. This was the third time in two weeks that she'd driven this nightmare journey for Christian. Generally she didn't mind; he worked damn hard and he was doing all he could to get everything ready for the imminent birth of their baby. It wasn't his fault he'd been needed at the firm's Scottish office, and she didn't blame him for any of this. He'd finally finished the last design at the weekend and she'd agreed to deliver them to the central branch to save him the inconvenience. Each design had taken many, many hours to complete and she fully understood why he wasn't prepared to leave it to some two-bit courier firm to deliver them. But regardless of the reasons why and the logical explanations for her being stuck out on the road for hours on end, she was struggling. At this stage of their pregnancies, all of Sonya's friends were at home with their feet up, being pampered and getting ready for the birth. And where was she? Going nowhere fast in the middle lane of one of the busiest motorways in the country during the peak of the morning rush hour. And where did she want to be? Just about anywhere else.

Focus on tomorrow night, she told herself. *Tomorrow night Chris will be home and we can finally spend some time together. No more work. No more Scotland.* It would probably be their last chance to relax together before the baby came. They'd planned to go out for a meal then catch a movie, making the most of their freedom, well aware of the massive upheaval they were about to experience. The last few weeks had been hard. Sonya just wanted a few calm days before the birth. *A nice warm bath and an early night tonight is what I need*, she thought. She'd really missed Chris. She hated it when he wasn't there, especially now. She couldn't wait to see him again.

Something was happening up ahead.

Struggling to move her cumbersome bulk and still keep control of the car, Sonya peered into the near distance where she could see the relatively uniform movement of the traffic becoming suddenly more random. Brake lights flashed bright red up ahead and her heart sank. An accident. Shit, that was all she needed. She was miles from the nearest exit and if the traffic backed-up she'd be stuck. She couldn't face sitting her for hours on end, with her swollen belly and swollen ankles. She'd been joking with Chris on the phone last night that if he kept making her do this drive, she'd end up giving birth in the back of the car on the hard shoulder. That didn't seem so funny now...

More brake lights, burning bright against the grey gloom of early morning. Noises too now. Even over the sound of her own car's engine she could hear strained mechanical whines and squeals as drivers struggled to avoid sudden collisions. *Shit*, she thought, *this is serious*. Almost immediately the screaming brakes and straining engines were replaced with grinding thuds, violent smashes and heavy groans as vehicle after vehicle after vehicle slammed and crashed into the one in front, literally hundreds of them forming a vast, motionless, tangled carpet of twisted metal in just a few bewildering seconds.

Sonya had no time to react. Forced to slam on her own brakes as the vehicles immediately ahead of her ploughed into those ahead of them, she braced herself for the inevitable impact. She didn't know what she was going to hit, what was going to hit her or even from which direction the first impact would come. All around her every vehicle seemed to be going out of control as if their drivers had simply disappeared. Just ahead, in the rapidly disappearing void between her car and the mayhem filling the road, countless cars, vans and lorries were swerving and crisscrossing the carriageway. The first collision came from the right as a solid, four-wheel drive vehicle smashed into the rear wing of her car, its buffalo bars caving in the metalwork and shattering glass, the force of the violent impact sending her car spinning round through almost one hundred and eighty degrees so that she now found herself facing the rest of the traffic. Shock immediately gave way to terror.

An expensive-looking executive's car was heading straight for her. Unable to do anything, Sonya watched the driver of the car thrashing about wildly. He was clawing at his neck with one hand, scratching and scraping at it desperately as he struggled unsuccessfully to hold onto the steering wheel with the other. His face was red and his eyes wide with pain. He looked like he was being asphyxiated.

Thrown to the side as her car was rocked by another collision from the left, she shielded her face from flying glass then looked through what was left of her passenger window. A tanker had smashed into a van which had, in turn, smashed into her. The driver of the van had been hurled through his windscreen and was sprawled facedown over the crumpled bonnet of his vehicle, stopping just a short distance from her. She looked away in disgust, inadvertently staring straight into the tanker driver's face, which bore an expression of absolute agony. Dark red blood dribbled down his chin.

The executive's car ploughed into Sonya's at speed, sending her flying back in her seat and then lurching forward with equal force. Consumed by a sudden wave of nauseating pain as her distended belly and her baby were momentarily crushed again, she lost consciousness.

In the brief time Sonya was unconscious, the world around her changed almost beyond all recognition. She cautiously half-opened her eyes. Slumped forward with her face pressed hard against the steering wheel, she pushed herself back and struggled for a moment with the weight of her unborn child. Her own safety was of no concern. She remained still and closed her eyes again, running her hands over her bruised and tender belly, concentrating hard until she was sure she felt the reassuring movements of the baby inside. Her split-second feelings of relief were immediately forgotten when she lifted her head again and looked around.

Apart from the occasional hissing jet of steam and the smoke and flames coming from several vehicles which were burning, the world was completely silent and still. Nothing moved. Where she had expected to hear the cries and moans of the injured, or the approaching sirens of the emergency services rushing to the scene along the hard shoulder, there was nothing.

Sonya tried to open the door to get out but it was wedged shut and she was unable to open it more than a couple of centimetres. Every exit was similarly blocked, the sunroof her only safe escape route. Shivering with shock and feeling ice-cold, she lifted a hand

and opened the sunroof. Every noise she made sounded disproportionately loud in the oppressively silent vacuum that the morning had become. The tinted window above her slid open then stopped with a heavy thud. Slowly lifting herself up, she guided her head and shoulders out through the restrictive rectangular opening. She cautiously stood up, one foot on either of the front seats, then wriggled her toes, water retention having swollen her feet and ankles. She lifted her arms up out of the car and then eased and squeezed her pregnant stomach through the rubber-lined gap. Her arms weak with nerves, she put the palms of her hands flat on the roof of the car and slowly pushed herself up and out. A few seconds more grunting and straining and she was sitting on the roof of her wrecked vehicle. For a while she just sat there in silence and surveyed the devastation. The carnage appeared endless, the motorway completely dead in both directions. Sonya shuffled around so that she was looking back towards the city she had driven through less than an hour earlier. For as far as she could see the traffic on the motorway was motionless. She deliberately tried not to look too closely at any of the wrecked vehicles although it was hard not to stare. Their drivers were dead. Some remained in their seats like blood-streaked shop window dummies. Some were burning. Many other corpses were on the road, lying in the gaps between the wrecks of their cars, tankers, lorries, bikes and vans.

A cold autumnal wind blew along the length of the road, prompting Sonya to get down from her exposed position. Overcome by the incomprehensible scale and speed of what had happened, and unable to think about anything but the safety of her unborn child, she carefully pulled her feet out of the car then slid down the windscreen and onto the crumpled bonnet. Using the wrecks of other vehicles as stepping stones, she crossed to the hard shoulder. It was a little clearer at the very edge of the road, and she began to walk back towards the city. Dark thoughts filled her mind: *How far has this spread? Is Christian okay? I need to call him. Need to let him know I'm all right and the baby's safe. Don't want him worrying if he hears about this on TV.*

The city, more than four miles away, was dying too. She could clearly see it beginning, even from this distance. Random explosions ripped through buildings. Fires began to spread and quickly take hold. She could see smoke pouring into the early morning air in thick, steady palls; a dirty, grey smog.

With her swollen feet already sore, and the birth of her baby ominously close, Sonya dragged herself back towards the city in search of someone – *anyone* – who could help her.

HARRY STAYT

Given the choice, if they didn't need to get up and go to work, school or whatever each day, most people would probably prefer to spend their mornings in bed. Harry Stayt is not like most people. Harry is up, washed, dressed and ready to run by eight o'clock at the very latest, usually much earlier. Harry does not enjoy being cooped up inside. He is an outbound activities instructor, qualified to teach (amongst other things) rock climbing, abseiling, caving, rafting, canoeing, kayaking, mountain biking and hill walking. The summer holiday season has just ended and he has no lessons booked for the best part of the next three weeks. For the first time since early summer he now has some time to himself. Harry being Harry, he intends to spend much of this time doing most of the things he's usually paid to teach.

Harry loves to run. He rents a small cottage in a village which is nestled on the banks of a large, man-made lake. A single, continuous road of some eight miles in length encircles the lake, and this road is his daily running route.

Harry sat on the front step of the cottage and tied his laces. He looked out over the stunning view which greeted him. There could be no better way to start each day, he decided. The world was silent save for bird song, the rippling of the water on the surface of the lake and the occasional distant rumble of farm machinery. And if this was his favourite time of day, he thought, then early autumn was his favourite time of year; a brief, quiet interlude between the busy summer holidays and winter snow and ice.

This morning was picture perfect. The sky above him was clear, uninterrupted blue, and the lush greenery all around was just showing the first signs of beginning to turn. The shades of green which had been present all summer were about to disappear and be replaced by yellows, oranges and brittle browns. And the air… Christ, even the air tasted good this morning. Cool but not too cold, dry but not parched, and with a very gentle breeze which blew at him from across the surface of the water.

All around Harry, the population of the small village were beginning their morning rituals and daily routines. As he locked the door of the cottage and zipped the key into his pocket, he looked around at the few houses and shops nearby and smiled inwardly. What was it about human nature that made people so desperate to restrict themselves with routines like this? He didn't understand it. He'd moved as far away as he could from the city to escape the relentless boredom and monotonous familiarity of the rat-race, but even here, out in the middle of nowhere, people still seemed to crave these ritual-like patterns of life. All around him the same people did the same things they always did: Gill Rogers was opening the village store, putting the same goods out on display in exactly the same place as yesterday. Her husband was taking the usual delivery of bread, milk and papers. The school gates were open and children were beginning to arrive. It was happening everywhere he looked. In some ways he was no better, he had to admit. He often ran the same route at the same time of day and he always performed a well-rehearsed stretching and loosening exercise routine before going out. Although he wanted to believe otherwise, maybe he was as regimented as the rest of them.

Warm-up complete, Harry checked the door was locked, then started his stopwatch and then began to run. He moved slowly at first, knowing that the first few footsteps were crucial. He'd had more than his fair share of avoidable injuries over the last couple of years. It suited his body to start slow and gradually build up to something resembling a decent pace. This was just a simple training run. He didn't intend overdoing it.

He jogged out through the village, acknowledging a couple of bemused folk as he passed them, then ran across the dam and began his usual clockwise circuit of the lake. He'd done this many times and knew it was more sensible to run clockwise because the majority of the children who attended the school lived on farms and in other villages to the east. The timing of his run today had been carefully considered so that he wouldn't reach the busiest stretch of road until the school traffic had been and gone. The rest of his route would be quiet. Harry didn't expect to see more than a handful of people while he was out, and that was how he liked it.

*

Three miles in, and the village had long been lost in the distance. A heavy canopy of trees bowed over the road, giving Harry shade from the cool but relentless sunlight. The branches changed the sounds around him, muffling the very distant rumble of village noise and traffic, making every birdsong and animal noise seem directionless, and amplifying the constant thud of his feet pounding the ground. Even his breathing seemed inordinately loud now.

The peace and tranquillity was disturbed momentarily. The sound of a car's engine (which could have been anywhere between half a mile and a couple of miles away) was abruptly and unexpectedly silenced. Harry then thought he heard the crack and spit of splitting wood. It could have been anything, he quickly decided, but it was probably nothing. One of the local farmers working their land on the steep banks of the lake perhaps? An off-season sightseer? He ran on regardless.

The lake was roughly quadrilateral in shape. He had already run along its longest side and had just followed a sharp bend in the road around to the right. He was now running along the lake's shortest edge and the dense forest of trees to his left, the grey tarmac ahead and the glare of the sun bouncing off the water's calm surface to his right were all he could see. His foot scuffed against something un-expectedly and he looked down and saw that the ground here was covered with debris. Slowing down but not stopping, he kicked his way through the tangled branches of a sapling that had been felled and dragged across the road. Hit by a car? A few metres further still and he saw long, dark, arc-shaped scars which stretched ominously across the tarmac, then more debris where something had churned up the mud and gravel at the side of the road. To Harry's right now was a steep bank which dropped down towards the water. The tyre marks ended there. He knew what had happened before he'd seen it.

Slowing down to walking pace, he neared the edge of the bank and cautiously peered over. Some five metres or so ahead and be-low him, wedged tightly between two sturdy trees as if it had been caught, was the wreck of a small red car. Panting with the effort of his run but still in full control, Harry carefully clambered down the bank, knowing that he had to help. He hadn't seen anyone else in the last half hour and chances were it would probably be as long again before anyone else passed by. It was down to him alone to try and help whoever it was who had crashed. As he made his rapid descent, it occurred to him that there didn't seem any obvious reason why the accident had happened. There were no other vehicles around. Had it been a mechanical failure? Swerving to avoid an animal wandering across the road? Had something happened to the driver? A heart attack perhaps? Whatever the reason, it wasn't important. Dealing with the aftermath was all that mattered.

The driver's door had been wedged shut by the awkward angle at which the car had come to rest. The windscreen was shattered (it had been pierced by a thick, low-growing branch) and he pushed the remaining glass out of the way and peered inside. The driver was dead. The same branch which had smashed through the window had impaled the chest of the stocky, grey-haired man. The appalling injuries suffered by the driver were so extreme that, for a few seconds, Harry didn't even notice he had a passenger alongside him. A woman of similar age, she was dead too. Harry looked into her lifeless face and tried to work out why. She was still anchored into her seat by her safety belt, and had no obvious wounds other than traces of blood around her mouth. Perhaps her injuries were internal? He leant across and checked for a pulse. Nothing.

Harry's options were limited. Did he stay with the bodies and wait for another motorist to pass (which would likely be some time) or did he try and get back to the village to get help? Although harder, the second option was clearly the most sensible. The people in the car were dead; there was nothing to be gained from stopping with them. Harry quickly scrambled back up to the road, brushed himself down, then started running again, continuing his clockwise circuit of the lake.

What started as a gentle training run had become something far more difficult. As well as having to contend with the shock of what he'd seen, Harry also now needed to get his body working again. He'd only stopped running for a couple of minutes, but that had been more than long enough for his muscles to begin to tighten. He forced himself to try and maintain a steady pace, but his head kept telling him to run faster.

Finally another sound disturbed the overwhelming silence. Harry could hear a plane in the distance. He rounded a gentle corner at the bottom of the lake and began to run the relatively straight two and a half mile stretch of road back up into the village. The sunlight flickered through the trees, blinding him intermittently. The run was getting harder. He was beginning to feel cold and the ends of his fingers and toes had begun to tingle. Had the temperature dropped, or was it shock? He'd run this route many times before and he knew he was more than capable of completing the distance, but now he was beginning to doubt himself. And the plane's engines seemed to be getting louder and louder.

At the side of the road a twisting mountain stream tumbled down the hillside, disappearing under the road and trickling into the lake. That was Harry's two mile mark. If he pushed hard he knew that he could be home in around fifteen minutes now, but it would take every scrap of energy he still had to do it. His legs were hurting, and Christ, that plane sounded low...

When the noise from the plane's engine became so loud that he could feel it in his belly like an earthquake, Harry stopped running again. It didn't sound like one of the military jets that often flew down the valley or even one of the smaller civilian aircraft that frequently passed over. The aircraft was moving in the same direction as he was, coming from behind and flying along the length of the lake towards the village. He could see it above the trees now, and he saw that it was far lower than any plane he'd seen here before. At this point the slope of the bank down to the lake was relatively gentle and he jogged down to the water's edge to get a better view.

The plane passed overhead, dropping fast. It was no more than fifty metres from the surface of the lake and it was falling rapidly. As Harry watched, its nose and starboard wing drooped down as if it was simply too tired to keep flying. The inevitable seemed to take an eternity to happen. The rapid descent continued until the tip of the plane's wing clipped the water, then the aircraft somersaulted forwards, flipping over and over and breaking into several huge pieces which landed in the lake with a series of massive splashes, vast plumes of water shooting high into the air.

Harry didn't connect the two crashes he'd seen until he found a third. Kenneth Hitchcock, the local postman, was dead in the middle of the road next to his motor-scooter. Letters were blowing casually like leaves on the breeze. Harry picked several of them up before realising there was probably no point.

By the time he arrived back at the village, he knew that something terrible had happened.

By the time he made it home, the wreck of the plane had sunk beneath the surface of the lake and the water appeared deceptively calm.

By the time he arrived back at the village, everyone else was dead.

JACOB FLYNN
Part i

Jacob Flynn is serving a prison sentence for manslaughter. Like pretty much every other inmate being held here, he'll protest his innocence relentlessly to anyone who'll listen. The fact of the matter is, however, that Flynn caused the death of a seventy-three year old pedestrian through his reckless driving. He'll tell you the old man was at fault as much as he was. He'll give you any number of entirely plausible reasons why he feels his case was handled badly, and why the judge had something against him, and why his solicitor let him down, and how, if it hadn't been for the fact he'd caught his lying bitch of a girlfriend in bed with his best friend, he wouldn't have been driving at almost twice the speed limit down a narrow residential road at just after two-thirty on a quiet Thursday afternoon in late November last year.

Whatever Flynn might tell you, the fact remains he was travelling too fast when he lost control of his car around a tight bend. He mounted the pavement and mowed down Eddie McDermott as he walked back to his house after a lunchtime drink with friends. The fact remains that Flynn's driving was the sole cause of Mr McDermott's untimely death, and in the eyes of the law he is being punished accordingly.

Flynn shares his small, rectangular cell with two other men; Suli Salman (minor drug trafficking offences and assault) and Roger Bewsey (corporate fraud). According to his mental records, he has now been locked up for five months, three weeks and a day.

It is just after eight o'clock in the morning and he has been awake for hours.

I hate this place more with every second I spend here. I don't know how the rest of them handle it. There's some that've been banged-up longer than I've been alive, but I don't know how I'm going to last another week. Every morning I wake up and wish I hadn't got into the car that day. Every morning I wish I'd never found Elaine with that bastard Peters or that I'd never even met the bitch in the first place. We'd only been together for just over a year, and look how much it's cost me. I'll spend more time in here alone than we spent together. I know there's no point thinking like this but I can't help it. The hours are long inside, and there's nothing else to do.

It's the stench that always gets to me first. Even before I've opened my eyes I can smell the disinfected emptiness of this fucking hell-hole. Then I hear it – the relentless noise from the scum in the cells around me. No matter what time it is, it's never quiet in here. There's no escape. *It never bloody stops.* I keep my eyes closed for as long as I can but eventually I have to sit up and look around this concrete and metal hell.

I shouldn't be here.

Maybe if I'd gone a different way that day or if I hadn't gone around to see her then I wouldn't be here now. I'd be out there where I should be. Because of that fucking slag I've lost everything, and I bet she's bloody loving it. She's out there with him, sleeping in the bed that I paid for, wearing the clothes and the jewellery and the perfume I bought her. Bitch.

Bewsey's snoring again. He amazes me. I don't know how he does it. There's a man you'd have put money on cracking up by now. He's in his late fifties, he's overweight, has a stutter, constantly gets picked on by the mentally-challenged thugs in here and, as far as I'm aware, he'd never been in any trouble before he got himself wrapped up in the mess that eventually wound him up inside. Salman, on the other hand, the guy in the bunk above mine, is a cocky little bastard. He's only here for another couple of weeks. He's in and out of these places all the time and has been for years. He'll be out and back in again before either Bewsey or I are released.

The mornings here are hard. Some days there's work to do, but most of the time there's nothing. Most days we spend virtually all of the time sitting in here, locked up. That's when it really gets to me. I've got nothing in common with the rest of the foul shite in here. I've got nothing in common with Salman or Bewsey except the fact we share this cell. I don't have anything to talk to them about. I don't even like them. They both irritate me. Sometimes I wake up and I can't imagine I'll last 'til the end of the day. I feel like that now. To-night seems forever away. Next week feels like it'll never come. And

I've got years of this to get through…

Here we go, first fight of the day. I can hear trouble a few cells down. Someone's screaming. Sounds like they're being strangled. This kind of thing used to shock me, scare me, even, but you get used to it quick and now it doesn't bother me. You can't go longer than a couple of hours in here without someone trying to—

Jesus Christ!

Bewsey just scared the hell out of me. I thought he was asleep. Shit, he just sat bolt upright looking like he's seen a ghost or had his parole turned down again or something. Bloody hell, his face is ashen white. Something's not right with him.

'What's up, Bewsey?'

He doesn't answer. He just sits there, looking at me with this dumb, vacant look on his face. Now he's starting to rub at the side of his neck, like he's hurt or something.

'You okay?' I ask again. Being in this place has made me suspicious of everyone, no matter how harmless they might make themselves out to be. I don't trust him. He's either trying to trick me into getting closer or he's gonna have a full blown panic attack. Either way I'm stopping over here, right out of the way.

'I can't…' he starts, still rubbing the side of his neck. He's looking into space, but his eyes dart up to look above me. Salman's trying to get down from his bunk. He's half-tripping, half-falling down. Now he's doubled-up with pain on the floor and he's coughing and wheezing like he can't catch his breath. He's dragged himself over to the toilet. Christ, he's puking up blood. What the hell is going on here? Now Bewsey's on his feet, still grabbing and scratching at his neck.

'What is it?' I ask but he can't even hear me, never mind answer. He's not faking. This is for real. The cell is suddenly filled with noise, both of them coughing their guts up, trying to scream for help.

Bewsey can't breathe. Bloody hell, the poor bastard can't get any oxygen. He's up on his feet and he's trying to take in air but his throat is blocked. I have to do something. I jump up and push him back down onto his bed. He tries to get up, then collapses onto the mattress. His body starts to shake and he tries to fight but all his strength has gone. I can hear Salman moaning and coughing behind me and there are similar noises coming from other cells around this one. I look back over my shoulder just as Salman falls to the ground. He smacks his head against the wall, knocking himself out cold.

Bewsey's convulsing now and it takes all my strength to keep him down on the bed. His eyes are full of panic – as wide as fucking saucers and staring straight at me like whatever's happening is my fault. There's blood on his lips. Shit, there's a dribble of blood trickling down his cheek from the corner of his mouth.

He's stopped shaking now. Bad sign.

Fuck! He grabs my arm and he's squeezing it so bloody hard I think he's going to break it. Another silent scream. More spitting blood. He arches his back, then crashes down onto the bed. And now he's not moving at all.

I just look at him for a second, then touch his neck and check for a pulse.

Can't feel anything.

He's dead. Jesus Christ, he's dead.

I stare at Bewsey's body for so long I almost forget about Salman. I turn around and I can tell by the way he's lying that he's dead too. Like Bewsey, there's blood trickling from his mouth and there's more pouring out of a deep gash on his forehead.

And now I realise I can't hear anyone else.

The whole bloody prison is silent. I've never known it like this before. I'm scared. Jesus Christ, I'm scared.

'Help!' I scream, pushing my face hard against the bars and trying to see across the landing. No one there. 'There are men dead in here. Help! Please, someone, help!'

Shit, I'm crying like a bloody baby now. I don't know what to do. This cell is on the middle floor. I can see the bottom of the staircase which leads up to the top landing. One of the officers is sprawled out over the bottom steps. I don't know whether he fell or whether what killed Salman and Bewsey got to him too. Even from a distance I know he's dead.

For more than an hour, Jacob Flynn stood in the corner of the cell in shock. He pushed himself back hard against the wall, trying to get as far as possible from the bodies of his cell mates. It was a while before the initial panic began to subside and his brain was able to function with enough clarity to start trying to make sense of the situation. What had happened to the men who shared his cell? Why was the rest of the prison silent? Why did it feel like he was the only one left alive?

A few minutes later and Flynn's logical thought progression helped him arrive at the cruellest realisation of all. If everyone else really was dead, then he was trapped. He dropped to the ground and began to sob uncontrollably, knowing there would be no exercise or work sessions today. There would be no meals, showers, or classes or counselling sessions. If he really was the only one left, then this was it. The cell door would stay locked forever.

As the day wore on and no one else came and nothing changed, Flynn realised that, without warning, the term of his comparatively short prison term had been dramatically extended to life. No parole, no early release... life. Paradoxically, he also knew that without food or water, that sentence would only last for days, not years.

All he could do was sit and wait.

BRIGID CULTHORPE

Brigid Culthorpe yawned, rubbed her eyes and squinted at the spray-paint-covered sign at the end of the street, trying to make out the name of the road they were in.

'It's like a bloody maze round here,' she grumbled to her partner, PC Marco Glover. 'Don't know how you can tell one road from another.'

Glover grunted and nodded as he slowed the patrol car down and coaxed it gently over a speed bump. 'You get used to it. Believe me, Brig, you'll spend plenty of time down here.'

'Get much trouble here then?'

'Virtually *all* the trouble we get starts here,' the more experienced, grey-haired policeman sighed. 'Every town has an estate like this. It's a dumping ground. It's where the scum and the unfortunate end up, and they don't think twice about preying on those folks who can't look after themselves. And even if the trouble doesn't start here, wherever it kicks off it's usually people from round here who start it.'

'Great,' Brigid said as the car clattered over another bump. Glover turned left.

'Right, here we are, Acacia Road. Sounds quite nice, but believe me, it ain't.'

He stopped the car. Brigid got out and looked up and down the length of the street. Ten or twenty years ago this might have been a fairly decent area, she thought, but not anymore. It was desolate. Weeds sprouted through cracks in the pavements and overgrown front lawns had spilled out over collapsed walls and broken fences. The battered wrecks of old, half-stripped down cars sat useless outside equally dilapidated houses. Uncollected black sacks of rubbish had been dumped in piles waiting for an overdue council collection. Acacia Road was a grey and depressing scene.

Brigid's throat was dry. She wasn't long out of training. Her stomach churned with an uneasy mix of nerves, adrenalin and anticipation.

'Which number was it?' Glover asked.

'Forty-six.'

'Come on then. Let's get it done.'

Glover began walking down the road and Brigid followed. They started at number four (which, as it sat between house numbers twenty-two and twenty-six, was most likely actually twenty-four) then increased their speed. Thirty-eight, forty, forty-two, forty-four, and then they were there. Number forty-six. The number had been daubed on the wall in off-white emulsion paint next to a boarded-up window. Even from the end of the path they could already hear the argument inside. She saw the remains of a large piece of furniture and a liberal sprinkling of broken glass in the middle of the overgrown lawn. The front bedroom window had been smashed and a pair of thin, mustard-yellow curtains blew in and out in the early morning breeze like dirty flags. It didn't take a genius to work out what had happened.

'What gets me,' Glover moaned as he forced the garden gate open (the bottom hinge was broken and it scraped noisily along the ground) then walked up the path, 'is the fact that these people are even awake at this time. You know, most of them are usually off their faces on booze or drugs and they don't open their eyes before mid-afternoon. Bloody hell, these people shouldn't even be conscious yet, never mind up having a domestic.'

'Probably still awake from last night,' Brigid suggested.

'I'm sure you're right,' Glover agreed. 'Dirty bastards. More bloody trouble than they're worth. Don't know why we waste so much time here. Should just build a bloody brick wall around the estate and seal the lot of them in, let them fight it out amongst themselves…'

Brigid smiled to herself. Glover was a far more experienced officer than she was, but even after just a couple of days working with him she'd learnt to read him like a book. The closer he got to an incident, she'd noticed, the more he seemed to chatter and swear. She, on the other hand, became more controlled and focused as they approached potentially dangerous situations like this. It was the idea of conflict that she didn't like. Once she was in the middle of the trouble, actually doing something about it, she could handle herself as well as the next man. In fact, she could usually handle herself better than the next man.

'What's this bastard's name again?' asked Glover, nodding towards the grim building they now stood outside.

'Shaun Jenkins,' Brigid replied. 'The call came in from his partner, Faye Smith. Said he was threatening her and the kids.'

'And how many kids was it?'

'Three,' she replied as she reached up and banged on the door. 'Open up please, Shaun. It's the police.'

No answer. Brigid hammered her fist on the door again. She could hear something happening inside now. A child crying, then several sets of heavy footsteps, racing each other to the door. Then a collision and a muffled scream. Jenkins, it seemed, was having a last ditch attempt to sort out this domestic without police involvement.

Glover leant forward and shouted through the letterbox. 'Open up, Shaun. I'll kick the door down if I have to.'

'Fuck off,' an angry voice spat back at him from inside. Glover glanced at Brigid, then stepped back and kicked the lock. They could hear more struggling inside the house now. Something slammed against the door – Faye Smith, presumably – then it opened inwards. Brigid barged through and grabbed Jenkins who had his partner in a neck lock, trying to drag her up onto her feet so he could kick her down again. Brigid grabbed the junkie by the scruff of his scrawny neck and hauled him into the nearest room, then threw him onto a grubby-looking sofa. A large, solid woman, she had a weight advantage over most people and this scarred, drug-addled excuse for a man didn't have a hope. Even if he'd been lucid enough to fight back, he still wouldn't have had a chance.

Brigid glanced over her shoulder at Faye Smith who lay on the threadbare hall carpet in a sobbing heap. 'I've got this one,' she shouted to Glover, 'you get the rest of them sorted out.'

Faye Smith limped towards the room at the far end of the hallway. The policeman could just make out the shape of a child hiding in the shadows of the kitchen door. He saw two more – both boys, both half-dressed – standing at the top of the staircase, peering down through a hole in the broken wooden bannister.

'It's all right, lads,' he said, 'your mom's okay. You stay up there and get yourselves dressed and we'll be up to see you in a couple of minutes.'

Glover glanced over to his right and saw that Brigid was in complete control in the living room. He had to admit, she was turning out to be bloody good in situations like this. He was happy for her to take the lead, despite her relative inexperience. She towered over Jenkins, and the wiry little man squirmed on the sofa.

'Are you going to tell me what's been going on here, Shaun,' she asked him, 'or should I—'

A sudden spit of crackling static from her radio interrupted her. Distracted she grabbed at it, keeping one hand tight around Jenkins' neck. She couldn't make out what was being said through the white noise and interference. It sounded like whoever it was was struggling to speak...

A sudden movement from Jenkins immediately refocused her. 'Look, Shaun,' she said, 'we can do this here or we can...'

The drugged-up expression on Jenkins' face began to rapidly change. He became more alert, and Brigid tensed and reached for her baton, sensing he was about to kick-off. Jenkins tried to push himself up, but then stopped and fell back down. The expression on his face changed again. His features began to twist and contort with pain.

'What's the matter, Shaun?' she asked, still cautious. Jenkins grabbed at his throat and she relaxed her grip slightly. His breathing changed, becoming shallow and irregular. She could hear his lungs rasp and rattle. Was he for real? Christ, what should she do? She hadn't covered this in training. Did she risk trying to help him or should she call Glover and... and the colour in his face was beginning to drain. Bloody hell, there was no way he was faking this. Was this a seizure or some kind of fit brought on by whatever he'd taken, or was it something she'd done? Had she used too much force? Jenkins' eyes, already wild and dilated, began to bulge as he fought for breath. He threw himself back in agony and began to claw at his inflamed throat. 'Glover!' Brigid shouted. 'I need help! Get yourself in here!'

She had to take a chance. She grabbed Jenkins' flailing legs and tried to lay him out flat on the sofa. He arched his back in pain, his willowy frame beginning to convulse furiously. Pressing down on his bare chest with one hand, she tried to hold his thrashing head still with the other and clear his airway. Suddenly motionless for the

briefest of moments, the odious addict then let out a tearing, ago-
nising scream of pain which splattered the police officer with blood
and spittle. Repulsed, she staggered back and wiped her face clean.

'Shit. Glover, I've got a real problem. Where are you?'

Still no response from her partner. Jenkins began to convulse
again. It was her duty to try and save his life, much as she knew it
was barely worth saving. She leant over him, but by the time she'd
decided what she needed to do, he'd already lost consciousness. Now
he wasn't moving at all.

'Glover!' she yelled again. Now that Jenkins was quiet she could
hear more noises echoing around this squalid house. Her heart
thumping, she stood up and walked towards the door. From the
kitchen came a sudden crashing noise as a stack of plates and dishes
fell to the ground and smashed. Brigid found Glover, Faye Smith and
one of her three children lying motionless on the sticky linoleum,
surrounded by broken crockery. The three of them were dead. By the
time she returned to Jenkins, he was dead too. Upstairs, she found
two more corpses. One of the boys was in the bathroom, wedged
between the base of the sink and the toilet pan as if he'd died hiding,
the other was lying on the carpet next to his bed. Both of the distress-
ingly thin children were white-faced but with traces of dark crimson,
almost black blood dribbling from their open mouths.

Brigid reached for her radio again and called for assistance. The
familiar sound of hissing static cut through the silence, reassuring
her momentarily.

But no one answered.

PETER GUEST

I keep going over the conversation in my head again and again, and every time I see Joe's face it hurts me more. I've come close to screwing things up before but I know I've really done it this time. I've made a huge mistake.

What happened at home this morning had been brewing for weeks, but I don't know what I'm supposed to do about it. Sometimes I feel like I'm trapped and I don't have any control. I'm trying to do my best for everyone but no one can see it, and at the same time everyone blames me whenever anything goes wrong. I'm starting to think that whichever way I turn and whatever I do I'll end up pissing someone off. It's always me that pays the price.

I can't stop looking at the clock. It's almost eight. Jenny will have Joe ready for school now. He kept telling me it didn't matter but I know it did. He kept telling me it was all right and that there'd be another time but there's no escaping the fact that I've let my son down again. The trouble is, how can I justify sitting in a school hall watching a class assembly when I should be at the office, closing a deal that's taken months of effort to bring to the table? I know that in financial terms there's no competition and the office has to take precedence, but I also know that on just about every other level I should be putting work at the bottom of the pile. But it's hard. The directors are putting me under unbearable pressure, but that pales into insignificance in comparison to this gnawing, nagging emptiness I'm feeling in the pit of my stomach right now. I think I might have just paid a price that can't be measured in pounds and pence.

It wouldn't be so bad if this was the first time. It wouldn't even be that bad if it was only the second or third time either. Truth is, because of work I seem to have missed just about every notable event in Joe's short life so far. I missed his first day at playgroup because of an off-site meeting and I missed his first morning at nursery because I was in Hong Kong on a business trip. I missed his first day at school. I missed his first nativity play and his first proper birthday party with his friends. And why did I miss all of those things? I did it all for Jenny and Joe. I just want the best for them, and if that means I have to work long hours and be dedicated to my job, then so be it.

Jenny doesn't see it that way.

She really laid into me last night when I took the call and told her I was going to need to be at the office early. She started hurling all kinds of threats around, telling me we were getting close to the point where I was going to have to make a choice between my career and my family. She's said things like that before, but it felt different last night. I could tell that she meant every word. I tried to explain I'm only doing this for her and Joe but she wasn't listening. She asked me if I could imagine a time when I didn't work for the company and I told her I could. It might be a long way off, but I know I won't be there forever. Then she asked if I could imagine being without her and Joe. I said I couldn't and that I didn't even want to think about it. She said that was the choice I was going to have to make. She said if my family was more important to me than work, why did I keep choosing work over them?

Bloody hell, I know she's right and I know I should be stronger, but the company's got me by the balls.

Traffic's really bad this morning. God, that'd be ironic, missing the meeting because of traffic delays after all this grief. It's been bumper to bumper since I left home. It's not unusual: this is the main route into town. A lot of commuters will turn off for the motorway soon, leaving the last mile or so to the office relatively clear.

I'm finally at the last major intersection. I might be sitting at these lights for the next ten minutes but, once I'm through, I'll be at the office in no time. I'll get this meeting done and I'll see if I can't get away a little earlier tonight. I'll find a way of making it up to Joe and Jen. If we get the deal closed this morning we all stand to pocket a decent pay-out next month. I'll take them out for dinner tonight and put it on the credit card. I'll take them for a pizza or a burger, Joe'll love that. Maybe we could go to the cinema if he's not too tired? Perhaps I'll wait until the weekend. Maybe I'll just get them both something from town at lunchtime. But I don't want it to seem like I'm just trying to pay for—

Bloody hell, what was that? As I pulled away from the lights just then I saw a car going out of control on its way down the bypass. There's no way I can turn back. There are plenty of other people about and there's probably nothing I could do anyway. The police watch all these roads on CCTV and they'll be on the scene before anyone—

—*Jesus Christ!* I've just seen two cars plough into each other at the top of the slip road I'm heading down to get into the Heapford tunnel. It happened so fast I didn't see what happened. There was a blue-grey estate and it veered off and smacked into the side of another car. They both went spinning across the carriageway. Thank God I missed it. I hope everyone involved is okay and I don't want to sound completely uncaring, but I can't afford to be delayed today. A minute or so later and I would have been stuck in the tailback and chaos that rush-hour crashes always leave in their wake.

The light becomes electric and the sounds change as I drive deeper into the tunnel. The signal on the radio disappears and the sounds of the city get muffled, snuffed out by the noise of car engines echoing off the close walls. The road ahead bends away to the left and I can see the bright red glow of brake lights up ahead. Drivers are always having to brake hard at the end of this tunnel. They don't anticipate the filter system. Everyone drives too fast down here without thinking and… and there are a stack of cars backing up now. Christ, I hope it is just the filter and nothing more serious. I'm cutting it fine as it is. To be stuck this close to the office would be unbelievable.

The noises around me are starting to change again. Brakes squealing. Engines straining. Hang on, the traffic's stopping, grinding to a halt. There must have been another accident up ahead. Christ, three in one morning, and all in the space of less than a mile… what are the chances of that?

Shit, what the hell is going on here? It's a bloody pileup. A load of cars have smashed into each other at the mouth of the tunnel. They're wedged together and… and I've got to stop before I hit them. I slam on my brakes but I'm going too fast to stop in time. The car behind me isn't slowing down, and neither is the one to my right. The guy on my right hasn't even got his hands on the wheel. What the hell's wrong with him…? I'm going to hit something or something's going to hit me. I try to keep hold of the steering wheel and find a path

45

through the chaos but I'm just—

Less than a minute later, Peter Guest woke up. The world around him was completely silent. Disorientated, he gently pushed himself upright in his seat and gagged as blood trickled down the back of this throat from his broken nose. The first thing he thought was that he was going to be late for his vital meeting, and he struggled to get out of his seat, unbuckling his belt and disentangling himself from the now deflated airbag. He had to get out of here and get to the office. He had to let them know what had happened. Surely they'd understand if they knew he'd been in an accident...

Peter slowly focused on his dull surroundings. The end of the tunnel up ahead allowed a certain degree of grey morning light to seep across the scene. The yellow-orange strip lights in the ceiling above provided a little more illumination, enough to see that his car was wedged between the tunnel wall on his left and the wreck of a black taxi cab to his right. He tried to open his door but could move it no more than an inch or two. He lifted up his aching body, clambered over the dash, and crawled out through what was left of the shattered windscreen. He rolled over onto his back on his car's crumpled bonnet and just lay there, looking up. The effort required to move just that short distance had been immense and he had to psych himself up before moving again. He waited a moment or two longer to let a sudden debilitating wave of nausea subside, then stood upright on his car and leant against the grubby tunnel wall for support.

For as far as Peter could see both ahead and behind, the tunnel was filled with an unprecedented tangle of crashed traffic. Some vehicles had been forced up into the air by violent impacts. A few cars behind where Peter was standing, a once pristine bright red, two-seater sports car lay on its roof, straddled widthways across two other vehicles, its driver and her passenger crushed.

Apart from him, he realised that nothing and no one else was moving.

Peter began to edge forwards, clambering over wreck after wreck, using them like stepping stones to get him out of the tunnel. He was in pain but he had to keep moving. He needed daylight and fresh air. He needed help.

After dragging himself over the boot, the roof and then the bonnet of another car, Peter was faced with a short jump onto the boot of another. Pausing to compose himself and bracing for impact, he jumped onto the second vehicle and lost his footing, slipping down onto a small triangular patch of clear road. He fell awkwardly against another car door, causing the body of a woman to slump over to one side. Her head thumped the window with a heavy, sickening noise, and he realised he hadn't thought about the other drivers. Struggling with his own situation, he'd only been concerned with his safety and trying to get out of the tunnel as quickly as possible. But now he'd stopped to think about the others, they were suddenly all he could see. He scrambled to try and help the nearest person but it was no use, the poor bastard was already dead. The woman in the van beside him was the same, as was the next one he found, and the next, and the next. He kept looking, refusing to accept the illogical truth that he was the only one left alive.

Everywhere Peter looked now he saw bodies: battered and bloodied faces smashed against windows and limp corpses hanging out of half-open doors. And the longer he stared, the more he saw. In the low gloom he saw broken bones, pools of dripping, crimson-black blood, ruptured skin, gouged eyes, twisted limbs and smashed faces. Shock numbed his pain and he began to move again, adrenalin driving him forward until he was finally out in the open air.

But the carnage and devastation wasn't limited to inside the tunnel. All around him now it continued, endless and inexplicable.

Peter walked along silent streets, finally reaching his office almost an hour later. There, amongst the corpses of the colleagues and business associates with whom he should have been meeting and negotiating, he sat and tried to make sense of the nightmare his world had suddenly become.

It was late afternoon before I made it back home. I walked most of the way, and took a bike the rest. The roads were impassable. When I got there the house was empty, just as I'd expected it to be.

I ran the half-mile to Joe's school. Once or twice I nearly stopped and turned back, almost too afraid to keep going. By then I'd already seen hundreds of bodies, possibly even thousands, but they were faceless and nameless without exception. As I neared the school I began to see people I recognised. I walked amongst the bodies of people I had known: Joe's teachers, the parents of his classmates, Jen's friends… I knew that somewhere in the school building I'd find them.

Joe was in his classroom. I found him underneath his desk, curled up in a ball like he was trying to hide. Jen was in the assembly hall, lying next to an upturned chair, buried under the bodies of other dead parents. I carried my wife and my son into another room where the three of us sat together for a while longer.

If I'd listened to Jen I would have been there when it happened. I might not have been able to do anything to help them, but if I'd listened to her I would have been there when they needed me most. My wife and child died frightened and alone.

I don't know what to do now. I don't even know if there's any point trying. I lost everything today.

WEBB

'I ain't interested, mate,' Webb says, even though he knows it's a mistake to piss Crawford off. Crawford throws the car around the corner.

'Don't remember sayin' you had a choice.'

'I don't do stuff like that anymore. I told you, I ain't getting involved.'

'You're fucking useless, Webb,' Crawford yells at him, flicking his cigarette butt through the half-open window. 'It's safe as houses, this is. You ain't going to get no grief, and you ain't giving me no grief either.'

'You said that last time. Look what happened then.'

'Wasn't my fault. That was Kenny. Nothing to do with me.'

'Kenny was stitched-up. It was everything to do with you I heard.'

'Then you heard wrong.'

Crawford cranks up the volume of the stereo to drown out Webb's noise. It also drowns out the sound of the car's knackered exhaust that makes it sound more like a bike. The windows are rattling with all the noise, vibrating in time to the relentless thumping bass. They stop at a red light. Some old woman looks at Crawford and shakes her head despairingly. He gives her the finger and yells at her to fuck off.

'Thing is,' he shouts at Webb as they start moving again, 'if you don't do this then Al's gonna get really fucking mad, and you know what Al's like when he's mad. It ain't gonna be my fault if he comes knocking at your door asking why you let him down…'

'Al's got better things to do. He ain't gonna knock at my door.'

'You're right about that, mate. He won't knock, he'll kick the fucking thing down. You heard about what happened to Marky when he pissed Al off after that fight at The Gallery last week? I seen his brother down the precinct. He said Smith still can't feed himself. They don't know if he's gonna… Shit!'

'What's up?' Webb asks, nervous. Crawford's looking in the rear view. Webb turns around and sees a police car hanging on their back bumper. 'Just take it easy,' he says, 'you ain't done nothing wrong, have you?'

Crawford's sweating. 'This is one of Al's cars.'

'And?'

'Well Al don't buy his fucking cars, know what I'm saying?'

Webb looks around again as the blue lights on the roof of the police car start flashing. 'What you gonna do?' he says. Crawford looks scared. Big man's not so brave now. 'What you gonna do?' Webb shouts at him again. There are sirens now.

At the last second, Crawford crosses from the inside to the outside lane, squeezing through a gap between two cars moving at different speeds. He turns right, then does a U-turn across the other carriageway, doubling-back on himself and leaving the police car stuck in traffic. All they can do is watch Crawford disappear.

'Nice one,' he says under his breath, feeling smug. He puts his foot down again and really starts to move. The streets are busy. He weaves around parked cars and pedestrians and almost knocks a cyclist off his bike. The cyclist shouts something at him but he's long gone.

'They're still following,' Webb says. He can see the blue lights behind them. They're not giving up. They're way back but they're getting closer, fast. Crawford's fighting his way through the traffic but it's moving out of the way for the law and the gap between them is getting smaller by the second. 'What you gonna do?' he asks for a third time.

'Back to Al's.'

'Fuck off,' Webb says, sounding scared. 'I'm not going to Al's.'

'Looks like you are.'

'He's gonna be pissed if you turn up there with the law behind you.'

'I'll lose them.'

'You won't. Fuck off, Crawford. Let me out!'

'What, you want me to pull over and drop you off? Prick.'

'Yes! Fucking let me out.'

'With the fucking police right behind me?'

'Yes!'

'Fuck off!' he says again.

The police car is close behind, blue lights filling their mirrors.

Crawford's trying not to panic. He can't think straight. Does he head back to Al's or keep going into town and try losing them? Does he just dump the car and run? There's another gap in the traffic. He swerves left and takes a fork in the road and drives up and over a fly-over which leads right into the heart of the city…

…and the backed-up, rush-hour grind.

'You fucking idiot,' yells Webb. 'You'll never get away from them now. Traffic's too heavy. They're gonna have your bollocks, mate…'

'*Our* bollocks, mate,' he says as they begin their descent. Down through a short tunnel, under a busy interchange, then back out into daylight. They hit the centre of town and the snarling queues. Half-way down Temple Street and the already crawling traffic has slowed to a stop. Crawford slams on his brakes, over-revving the engine and nudging forward as he looks for a way through.

Webb panics.

He gets out of the car and starts to run along the pavement, crashing into people. Everyone else seems to be walking the other way and he has to fight his way against the tide. Crawford goes to follow him but stops. There's a sudden pain in his throat. A sharp, searing pain like someone's slicing him with a knife. He starts to cough. He can't breathe… and now the police officer hammering on his window isn't his biggest problem. He's choking now. He can taste blood in his mouth…

The policeman turns around and looks back at his colleague who's just fallen out of the patrol car. He's lying in the middle of the road, writhing around in agony. A couple of passer-bys start to move towards him but, before they can do anything, they're both sudden-ly grabbing at their own throats, feeling intense, inexplicable pain. Both police officers are down now. The first has rolled into the gutter, his body convulsing, oxygen-starved.

Webb keeps running until the people around him start dropping to the ground. He slows down but keeps going, weaving through the ever-increasing carnage, side-stepping the bodies as they fall, not knowing what else to do. He looks back over his shoulder and sees that everyone else is down. Crawford's not moving and neither are the police. Neither is anyone else. He's the only one still standing.

Webb stops running and his bottom lip starts to tremble like a kid that's just been shouted at by the hardest teacher in school. All around him people are dead or dying. Cars are crashing. The world is falling apart, and none of it makes any sense.

He smells food and his belly starts to rumble. He's standing next to a burger bar. Everyone's dead inside and the food in the kitchen is starting to burn. He's fucking terrified but his mouth is watering and he needs a drink. Maybe it'll help calm his nerves, he thinks. Maybe it'll help him think straight. He goes into the burger bar, picks up a tray and helps himself to everything he can find behind the counter that's cooked. He steps over dead and dying staff as he grabs a load of burgers, fries and drinks. He leaves the restaurant, shaking with nerves but still trying to look cool as a fucking cucumber, then walks back to Crawford's car, looking up at the buildings on either side of the street so he doesn't have to look down at the bodies. He puts the tray of food on the passenger seat then shoves Crawford's body out and gets behind the wheel. He can't drive but it doesn't matter. He doesn't know where he'd go if he could. He shuts the doors and locks them then winds up the windows and turns the music up so fucking loud it hurts. For now, the food and the noise stop him thinking about anything else.

JACKIE SOAMES

Jackie Soames opened one eye, then closed it again. It was late. Too late. She should have been up hours ago. More to the point, George should have woken her up. Bloody man, he was absolutely useless. She didn't ask much of him; she ran the business and looked after the punters, all he had to do was keep the home running and keep her happy. It was an unusual arrangement but it had worked well for more than twenty years now.

Jackie opened one eye again and double-checked the clock. Quarter-to-eleven! Christ, how could she have slept in for so long? She needed to get ready to open up. She'd never missed opening time before – not even on the day her father died – and she knew she'd get some stick from the regulars if she was late unlocking the doors today. More importantly, she couldn't afford to waste time like this. Time was money. The pub was only just breaking even as it was.

In this trade, Jackie often told anyone who'd listen, you live and breathe the job. You're never off duty. She worked from the crack of dawn until the very end of each day, and she couldn't believe that George had let her sleep in for so long. Where was he? She remembered him getting up when the alarm went off just after six o'clock, but she didn't remember him coming back. Strange, she thought, he usually brought her up a coffee before eight and left it on the bedside table. There was no cup there today.

Last night had been hard going. Monday nights were usually difficult, but Jackie always tried to put on something special to pull in a decent sized crowd. She'd tried quiz nights and theme nights and cheap drinks promotions but her traditional, dyed-in-the-wool punters were hard to please. Last night they'd had a band on, and bloody awful they'd been too. Nice enough lads, but they were all noise and no talent. She'd come across plenty of similar acts trying to make a name for themselves over the years. *Crank the sound up loud enough*, they seemed to think, *and no one will know we can't play*.

They should have been here to pick up their stuff a couple of hours ago but she hadn't heard them. The bedroom was right over the bar, and anything happening down there would surely have woken her up. Christ, she must have been in a deep sleep. Maybe she was coming down with something? She couldn't afford to get ill. She couldn't risk leaving George in charge.

The band hadn't gone down well last night. The Lion and Lamb was a traditional British spit-and-sawdust pub with traditional spit-and-sawdust locals, and halfway through their set, the heckles from the crowd had all but drowned out the noise of the band. The drummer had given up straight away, sitting behind his kit and drinking, no longer playing. The others kept going for another song and a half before admitting defeat. Trying to make the most of a disappointing night without leaving the boys in the band out of pocket, Jackie had locked the doors after closing time and kept everyone drinking through the early hours of Tuesday morning.

Christ she was really paying for it now.

Finally managing to prise open both eyes, she picked herself up out of bed, stumbled to the bathroom and threw up. That was better. Once the acidic taste of vomit and the booze-induced disorientation had passed she began to feel herself again. As a regular drinker of admirable capacity and many years standing, Jackie was hardened to the effect alcohol had on her system. It was a well rehearsed routine now: she got drunk, she fell asleep, she woke up, she threw up, she felt better. And the next day she did it again. It was all part of the job. The first cigarette of the day helped settle her stomach.

Where the hell was George?

'George?' she yelled. 'George, are you down there? Do you know what time it is?'

When he didn't answer she quickly got dressed (no one ever saw her in her nightwear except her husband) and went out onto the landing. Nothing. No sign. Cursing her husband under her breath, she stormed back to the bedroom. He must have gone out. That bloody man had gone out and left her fast asleep. And the lads from last night wouldn't have been able to get back in and get their stuff, either. With just over half an hour to go before opening time, Jackie was close to losing her temper on a massive scale. God help George when she got hold of him. He was probably down the betting shop, he decided, flittering away the money she'd earned on horses and

could see that Westwood Garage was on fire. There were crashed cars all over the place and, for as far as she could see in every direction, hundreds of people lay dead.

This looked like it had happened hours ago. For a moment she was too busy wondering how she'd slept through it than to wonder what had happened and why hadn't it affected her.

What do I do? Where do I start? Where do I go?

Too sober to think straight, Jackie turned around and disappeared back into the Lion and Lamb where she poured herself another gin.

'All right, Tuggie,' Keith Meade shouts across the carpark. The sun's bright this morning. I have to cover my eyes with my hand to see him.

'Morning, Keith. Good day for it?'

He looks up and around. 'Just about perfect, I'd say,' he says as he walks towards the office.

He's right, it's a perfect day for flying. It's days like this that make me glad everything worked out the way it did between me and Sarah. If we were still together then I wouldn't be here now. I'd still be living in our cramped terraced house in the middle of the city, spending long hours stuck in traffic and even longer hours stuck at the office. Most of the people I used to work with are probably still there, too scared to leave. And while they sit at their desks and follow orders and struggle to hit targets, I'm out here in the fresh air, sitting on my backside and occasionally flying. I'm making it sound like I don't do anything around here, but I do – I work damn hard when I have to – but the thing is *I enjoy it*. It doesn't feel like a job.

Shame we had to part on such bad terms, though. Everything happened within the space of six months. I had no idea. She went off with our financial adviser (who advised her he was worth a lot more than I was) and then, just as I was getting back on my feet, the bastards made me redundant. I had nothing to stay in the city for. We sold the house and I took my share and what was left of my redundancy payment and packed my bags and moved to the other side of the country. I got my pilot's licence (it was something I'd always wanted to do) and then managed to get myself a job here at the Clifton Gliding Centre, towing gliders two thousand feet up into the air, then letting them go so they can drift back down to the ground. Easy. Life is good now. Simple, but good.

Three cars, identical in all but colour, pull into the car park. The sound of their wheels crunching the gravel shatters the quiet of the morning. This must be today's visitors. There's supposed to be eight or nine of them I think, sales reps from a company in town, sent here on a team building exercise. Noisy buggers. It's only just turned eight and all I can hear now is them laughing and shouting. Why can't they talk quietly? It's probably just nerves. It's good sport watching blokes like this – blokes like I used to be. They act all cool and relaxed on the ground, but I know they're nervous as hell inside. As soon as they're strapped into the gliders and they're ready to go up, they change. All that bravado and macho bullshit disappears. When there's just the fuselage of a flimsy little plane and two thousand feet of air between their backsides and the ground they shut up and drop the act. I hate all the corporate bullshit and pretence. To think, I used to be a part of that.

As the group disappears into the office to sign in and be briefed on the rules for the day, I get the plane ready. I can still hear the voices of the seven men and two women from the hangar. I climb into the plane, shut the cockpit and fire up the engine, drowning out their noise. I taxi out onto the airfield (which literally is a field here – no concrete runways for us) and move into position. Once we're ready I stop the engine, get out, and walk over to where some of the other staff are standing in front of the hangar.

'Do me a favour,' I say to Willy who's one of the regular glider pilots.

'What's that?'

'Give them a fright, will you? Scare the shit out of these buggers.'

He smiles knowingly. We have a mutual dislike of overpaid businessmen. 'No problem. Anyway, Tuggie, five minutes of being dragged up behind you with your flying is enough to scare anyone! I'll be shitting myself, never mind them!'

'Cheeky sod!' I laugh and Willy walks away, cackling at his own pathetic joke.

Willy and Jones (one of the ground staff) stand and wait for Ed (Willy's lad) who's towing the gliders out of the hangar and out onto the airfield. The tractor he's driving fills the air with its chugging and clattering and clouds of thick black fumes. I head back to my caravan to make a cup of coffee and wake up properly before the flying starts.

We move quickly while the weather's good. It's not even nine o'clock and three gliders are already up.

This is a simple job. The glider's attached to the back of the plane by a cable. I take off and drag it up until we've reached around two thousand feet, then the glider pilot releases the cable. If conditions are right they go up, and I go back down. They usually stay up for anything between twenty minutes and half an hour. The flights might last a little longer today. The clouds are good and the sun is bright. There should be plenty of thermals to keep them up in the air.

We try to have four or five gliders up in the air at the same time. Ed's just attaching number four to the back of the tug plane. I watch the lads getting the glider ready in my mirrors. Ellis (the pilot) nods to Jones who gives me a hand signal and I start to move slowly forward until the cable becomes taut. Another hand signal and I stop. Behind me, two ground hands steady the wings of the glider. A final signal from one of them tells me they're ready to fly.

And we're off again. The plane bumps along the uneven grass for a couple of hundred yards before I give it a little more throttle, pull back the stick, and start to climb. The rumbling beneath me is silenced as the wheels leave the ground. Now the glider's up too and we're on our way. I can see the faces of the two men in the plane behind me. Ellis is talking ten to the dozen but his passenger isn't listening. He's bloody terrified! Idiot's got his eyes shut! Bloody wimp.

Christ, the sun's bright up here. It's blinding, and there's no escaping it when you're in flight. It's hot too, and it's not like you can pull down a blind or open a window – you just have to put up with it. You know it's not going to last for that long. A few minutes flying and then you can—

—Shit, what was that? Turbulence? Not at this altitude. No, I didn't like that, something's not right. I'm looking at the controls in front of me, but there's nothing wrong with my plane. Everything looks normal. Shit, it's the glider. Something's happening behind me, but I can't see what.

Oh, Christ.

Jesus Christ, Ellis is losing control. We're not even a thousand feet up yet and he's lost it. I can't see what's happening and I don't know if he's—

—Oh, God, the glider's rolling to the side. He has to release. If he doesn't he'll drag me back with him and… and I can't see Ellis now.

Bloody hell, I can see the passenger though. He looks like he's trying to get out. He's banging against the sides of the cockpit. Is he having some kind of panic attack?

The glider's tipping again. We have to separate. I don't have any choice, I have to pull the emergency release. If I don't we'll all be going down…

There, done it.

Had to do it.

I'm free again and I've got back control. I bank and climb and look down below me as the glider rolls and dips and begins to spin towards the ground.

I can't watch. I don't know what happened in there, but I know those two men don't have long. It'll be over in a couple of seconds. The difference between a plane crash and a car crash, my instructor used to tell me, is you've at least got a chance of walking away from a car crash. I just hope Ellis can try and get control and level out before he—

—Jesus Christ, what was that? What's happening now? Fuck, another glider just dived right across the front of me. It could only have been a hundred yards ahead. Shit, another couple of seconds later and it would have hit me and I'd be heading down there with Ellis and…and what the hell is going on here?

For the love of God, no.

The planes are dropping out of the sky all around me. The four gliders we put up this morning are all either down or out of control. Keith Meade – a man who's been flying these things longer than I've been alive – has lost control of his glider too. The plane is spiralling towards the hangar. I don't want to look but I can't turn away and I see the flimsy aircraft smash through the roof, its wings and body crumpling on impact.

My heart's thumping. Sweat's pouring down my face. I can't think straight. God knows how I'm managing to keep flying. My legs are shaking with nerves and I can hardly keep my wings level. I've got to keep going. I'm approaching the airfield from the wrong direction but it doesn't matter. There's no one else left up in the sky. I can't see anyone moving down there. Surely someone should have been out to help by now?

I have to leave my landing later than I'd like – what's left of Ellis' glider is strewn across the middle of the landing strip – and it's a struggle to bring the plane to a stop in time. There are pieces of plane and God knows what else scattered all over the place. I can't risk hitting any of the debris. I hit the deck hard and bounce back up but I manage to put the plane down in half the distance it usually takes. I kill the engine and sit and wait for the propeller to stop. I don't want to get out.

But I know I can't sit here all day. I climb out of the cockpit of the tug and just stand there for a moment, listening to the most terrifying silence I've ever heard.

What the hell has happened here?

There are bodies at the side of the airfield. I find myself walking towards them. These aren't people who were flying. There are a couple of faces I recognise – Meade's daughter, young Ed – and the rest, I think, are the visitors who weren't flying. They're dead. *They're all dead.*

Inside the office I find Chantelle Prentiss, our admin girl, slumped dead across the front desk. The phone is off the hook next to her upturned hand. It looks like she was in the middle of a call when it (whatever *it* was) got her. I pick up the phone and dial out but there's no answer on any number.

The world is dead.

I'm up in the plane again now, flying around and trying to find someone else who's left alive. There's no one… The whole damn world is gone, and I'm all there is left.

CARON

'So what's wrong with her?'

Caron shuffled awkwardly, doing everything she could to avoid answering her son's question. She straightened the tablecloth, then rotated the whiskey decanter on the sideboard until the engraving faced dead-centre. 'I didn't say there was anything wrong with her, Matthew, it's just that…'

'Just what?'

'Well she's older than you for a start.'

'So? You're older than dad.'

'By less than a year.'

'And Ronnie's only just over a year older than me.'

'Yes, but the gap's larger when you're younger.'

'Now you're just talking rubbish. Dad put you up to this, didn't he?'

She took a deep breath. 'Veronica's just not the kind of girl we expected you to bring home, that's all.'

'What's that supposed to mean?'

'Well, she's got…'

'She's got what?' Matthew demanded, tired of waiting for his mother to get to the point. 'Tattoos? Piercings? Stretchings?'

'Stretchings? What in heaven's name are stretchings?'

'Her ear lobes.'

'Oh, they were just *horrible*. Does she not realise those holes won't close up?'

'I think that's the point. Anyway, she likes them. *I* like them. You should stop being such a prude and try to get to know her. She's really smart, Mom. She's going to Oxford to study English next year. She has grade seven cello.'

'Yes, but—'

'—but she doesn't look like the kind of girl you want your little boy to be seen with, is that it? More to the point, Dad doesn't think she's appropriate, so he's got you doing his dirty work again. Or is it more about what you think people will say? Are you worried about the ladies in your art group?'

'That's nonsense.'

'Is it? Face it, Mom, you're a snob. Hey, look on the bright side, at least you know I'm not gay now. I know that's been playing on your mind.'

'Utter rubbish.'

'Really? I used to think about pretending to come out just to see your reaction. How would that have gone down with the neighbours? Be honest, Mom, as long as Pat Palmer's net curtains aren't twitching, you couldn't give a damn about me.'

'That's not true. And mind your language.'

'Bloody hell, Mom, will you wake up and smell the roses? You're living in a fantasy world. You rattle around this bloody house all day, knocking back the sherry, pretending everything's all right when we both know it's not.'

'I don't know what you're talking about.'

Matthew hadn't intended having this conversation with his mother now, but it was as good a time as any. 'You know exactly what I mean. Christ, everybody else can see what's going on, so I'm sure as hell you must.'

'If you're talking about your father then—'

'Of course I'm talking about Dad. He's been cheating on you for as long as I can remember, and you do nothing about it. You sit there, all prim and proper, and you pretend like it's not happening. Do you think that's going to make it go away?'

Caron started to sob. Matthew hated it when he made his mom cry, but it was happening with increasing regularity and he was beginning to see it as a necessity. How else was he going to get through to her? He hated even more how she changed the subject whenever the conversation strayed too close to the truth for her liking.

'Ever since you've been seeing her you've been different,' she said, taking a tissue from inside her sleeve and dabbing the corner of her eyes. She walked across to the mirror and checked her make-up hadn't run.

'What do you mean by different? You mean *happy*?'

'You know exactly what I mean. We've hardly seen you these last few weeks. I never know where you are or what you're doing…'

'So? I'm seventeen.'

'You're still my responsibility. *Our* responsibility. It's me the police will come looking for when things go wrong.'

'That's a bit over the top, isn't it? Nothing's going to go wrong.'

'It might. Your father said you—'

'Mom, please, just stop. I don't want to hear it. I definitely don't need to take any relationship advice from Dad. Or you, for that matter.'

'Have some respect.'

'What, like he has for you? Give me a break. Fuck's sake.'

'Matthew!' Caron leant against the corner of the table for support. 'Please stop swearing. It's come to something when you and I can't have a proper conversation without resorting to gutter language like that.'

'You've heard worse. I've heard Dad call you all kind of things before now.'

'You never used to swear, son…'

'Oh, so that's it, is it? Something else for you to blame on Ronnie? She's the best thing that's happened to me in a long time, Mom. None of this is her fault. It's not her fault you're miserable. It's not her fault Dad's been sleeping around again, is it?'

'Matthew, shut up!'

Caron slumped heavily into the nearest chair, bursting into floods of tears, her make-up now beyond repair. Her son looked down at her, feeling awkward. He couldn't stand seeing her like this, but the alternative was far worse. They'd both spent too long covering for Dad's loutish behaviour, prolonging the illusion of the perfect happy family for the sake of the neighbours. Truth was, the three people who lived behind the door of number thirty-two Wilmington Road hadn't been happy together for a long time.

'You need to stop this, Mom. You need to accept Dad for what he is and do something about it.'

'I can't change him.'

'No, but you can change *you*.' He took a deep breath. Time to lay it on the line. 'I'm sorry, Mom, but things can't go on like this. Spending time with Ronnie and her family has really opened my eyes.'

'I'm sure it has.'

'Mom, stop. I'm serious. I was round her house yesterday and her parents were there and it felt *normal*. They talked to me, made me feel welcome… Her dad showed me his music collection and we had a laugh and we watched TV and… and being there made me realise how screwed up things have got here recently.'

'Things aren't screwed up. Your dad and I just—'

'Mom, please. The only person you're fooling is yourself. Dad's been using and abusing you for years. You're scared of him, that's all. Scared you're going to lose face.'

'That's not true.'

Matthew knelt down in front of his mom. 'It *is* true. I was talking to Ronnie's mom and—'

'Not about me. Please tell me you weren't talking about me to a complete stranger…'

'Marie isn't a stranger. I've been talking to her a lot, actually. She told me she was married before. Her first husband was a total shit. He did all the kind of things Dad does. You should talk to her, Mom, you'd like her.'

'I'm sure she's very pleasant, but—'

'She said you need to do something about the situation now before it's too late, before it gets any worse.'

Caron floundered, winded by the honesty and accuracy of her son's words. 'But you don't know what it's like,' she said. 'No one does.'

Matthew put his hand on his mother's. 'I know more than you think.' He stood up and watched his mother as she finally opened up and began to cry properly, at long last beginning to acknowledge the reality she'd worked so hard to ignore. Matthew felt awkward and helpless in equal measure, not knowing what, if anything, he could do to help. His stomach churned with nerves, but he wouldn't let her see. 'I'll put the kettle on. Make you a cup of tea.'

Caron remained exactly where she was, not even looking up as he walked out to the kitchen. He was absolutely right, of course, but her problems weren't that easy to fix. It sounded simple – confront Bob when – *if* – he got home from the office tonight, then kick the bastard out. But could she really do it? Without him, she was

66

nothing. Christ, he'd told her that enough times. And all those years of marriage couldn't be undone in one day. Neither did she want them to be. There had been some good times in the very early days, back before he'd grown bored of her company and started sleeping around. She'd put up with it for a long time – what happened at the office, stayed at the office – but things had changed when he'd started working his way through her friends. That fling he'd had with the woman from the doctor's surgery had been the last straw. Everyone had known about it but her. Except it hadn't been the last straw, because she hadn't done anything about it. She'd just pretended it hadn't been happening and looked the other way. And no one said a damn thing. Yet again, everyone was talking about her, no one talking *to* her.

But Matthew was right. Veronica's mother was right too. Caron had run out of options. Bob had threatened her recently, and she knew it wouldn't be long before those threats were realised. She feared for her safety. She feared for Matthew's safety. But she couldn't see a way out.

Go upstairs right now. Pack his stuff in a suitcase and leave it outside. Dead-bolt the door tonight and don't let him back in. To hell with what the neighbours think.

Caron didn't confront her husband. She didn't bolt the door or change the locks or scatter his smalls around the front garden as she'd planned. Her sudden elation ended as quickly as it had begun because, when she went back downstairs to tell Matthew he was right and that she was finally going to do something about it, she found her son dead on the kitchen floor. His skin was white, his lips blue-tinged. Blood dribbled down his chin. She called for an ambulance, but no one answered. *No one answered…* how could that be? She went outside and screamed for help but no one came. She did everything she could to try and resuscitate her son, but he didn't respond. She banged on next door's window, even lowered herself to hammer on the door of Jeremy Phelps, the peeping tom from across the way, but no one helped. She found the lady from five doors down – the one with all the kids by different dads – dead behind the wheel of her car. Her kids were in the seat behind her, their lives abruptly ended before the school run had begun, all tangled-up with each other like they'd died trying to escape.

For the longest time she just sat there on the floor next to Matthew, holding his cold hand, her brain unable to process what had happened. None of it made any sense. Foolishly she began to try and convince herself that this was somehow her fault, that this was the price she'd had to pay for thinking those thoughts, for even daring to consider confronting Bob. It sounded ridiculous, but she couldn't think of any alternative, and no matter how bizarre her thoughts, they couldn't match the nightmare of this terrible reality. She switched on the TV for the news, but every channel was silent.

Eventually, Caron forced herself to leave the house again and look for help. She changed her clothes, fixed her make-up and hair, found a pair of sensible shoes, and walked into town. Everywhere was the same as Wilmington Avenue: everything silent, everything still.

She'd been walking for the best part of two hours when she finally heard something which gave her the faintest glimmer of hope. It wasn't much – just the muffled *thump – thump – thump* of music playing in a confined space, somewhere nearby. She kept walking, getting closer. And then she saw movement in a car up ahead: the only car with lights on and windows steamed up with condensation. The car rattled with the deafening volume of the music playing inside.

Caron yanked the door open and recoiled at the strong smell of sweat and stale fast food. There was a scrawny-looking kid in a tracksuit and baseball cap behind the wheel and he sat up fast, a guilty expression on his face like she'd caught him doing something he shouldn't. He wafted away smoke from a spliff.

'Fuck me, lady, you scared the shit out of me.'

Caron didn't wait to be invited. She sat down next to him and closed the door behind her. 'I'm sorry.'

'Do you know what happened, missus?'

'My son's dead.'

'I'm thinkin' they're all dead.'

She just stared at him, a thousand questions on the tip of her tongue. There was no point asking anything. He obviously knew as little as she did. 'What are we going to do?'

'Dunno. I'm scared.'
'Me too. Can I stay with you?'
'If you want.'
'I'm Caron.'
'They just call me Webb.'

JULIET APPLEBY

'So what time will you be home tonight?' asked Mrs Appleby, frustrated. She stared at her daughter across the breakfast table. Sometimes trying to get information out of Juliet was like trying to get blood out of a stone. She'd always been the same.

'I don't know,' she answered in a quiet, mumbling voice that her mother had to strain to hear.

'You know how your father gets if you're not back when he's expecting you.'

'I know, but I can't help it if I have to stop back after school…'

'He has to have his meal before half-six otherwise it keeps him awake all night. And you know how he likes us all to eat together. It's an important part of family life.'

'If you say so.'

'Dad says so. He likes his routine, that's all. And he likes to know where you are. He likes to know you're safe.'

'I know that, Mom, but…'

'But what, love?'

'I'm thirty-nine, for crying out loud.'

Juliet closed the front door and walked to her car. She could feel them both watching her, though they always pretended not to. She brushed her long, wind-swept hair out of her eyes and looked back. There they were, both of them hiding behind the net curtains, Mom in front and Dad standing just behind. He spent most of his life hiding behind Mom. Inside the house, he was king, and he'd make sure they both understood that in no uncertain terms. Stick him outside and force him to face the rest of the world, though, and he crumbled. The accident twelve years ago (which was still a taboo subject) had devastated his confidence and unbalanced his temperament. He struggled to interact properly with anyone outside the immediate family. Outside the house, Dad would always get angry or confrontational with some poor unsuspecting soul and it would inevitably be left to Mom or Juliet to smooth things over and sort things out.

Juliet sat down in the car and started the engine. Poor Mom, she thought, looking back at her again. She'd dedicated her life to Dad. She'd put up with years of his moaning and mood swings and tempers. In some ways, though, she was just as bad as him; as Dad relied on Mom, so Mom relied on Juliet. And who was there for her? No one. On the few occasions she'd been brave enough to start talking about leaving home and setting up on her own, it was usually Mom who came up with a list of reasons why she couldn't leave and why she had to stay, why they needed her around. It was emotional blackmail, and more fool Juliet for believing it. Her friends at the nursery told her she should just pack her bags and leave, but it was easy for them. She'd left it too late and now she was trapped in a career looking after other people's children when she should have been raising her own. Fat chance of that happening now. She hadn't ever had a 'proper' relationship. She often thought about the cruel irony of her life: there she was, a thirty-nine year old virgin, surrounded by the fruits of other people's sexual encounters.

A quick wave to Mom and Dad (even though they thought she couldn't see them) and she was off. A ten minute drive into the centre of Rowley and she'd be there.

Juliet was always the first to get to work. She arrived ages before anyone else. At this time there were only ever a couple of people around, usually just Jackson the caretaker and Ken Andrews, the head of the school to which the nursery was attached.

'Morning, Joanne,' Andrews shouted, waving to her across the playground. Bloody man, she thought. All the years she'd been working at the school and he'd never once got her name right. Occasionally she thought he did it on purpose to wind her up, other times she decided he was just plain ignorant. But the fact was he continually got her name wrong because he rarely had reason to speak to her about anything of importance, and because she'd left it too long to correct him without embarrassment. To say that Juliet melted into the background was an understatement. She preferred it when no one noticed her.

The prefabricated hut used for the nursery class had been opened up as usual. It was always cold first thing, even in summer, and this

September morning was no exception. She glanced up at the clock on the wall: half an hour until the children were due. Probably twenty-five minutes before any of the other staff would grace her with their presence. As low, depressed and dejected as she could ever remember feeling, she prepared the room for the morning's activities.

Bloody hell, what was that?

Juliet stopped what she was doing and looked up. Fifteen minutes now to the start of class and she'd just heard an almighty crash outside. It sounded like kids messing around on the concrete steps which led up to the classroom door. Juliet didn't like confrontation, even with the children, so she kept her head down and hoped that whoever it was would go away as quickly as they'd arrived. Maybe they'd just miss-kicked a football?

Suddenly another sound, this one very different to the first. It sounded like someone coughing. Juliet crept towards the window and peered outside. The playground was empty, the birds flying between the roof of the school building and the rubbish bins the only movement she could see. She was about to go back to what she'd been doing when she noticed a foot hanging over the edge of the steps. So there were kids messing around after all… She pressed her ear against the classroom door. When she couldn't hear anything outside, she very slowly pushed the it open and there, lying on the steps in front of her, was the lifeless body of Sam Peters, one of the boys who'd been in the nursery class last year. Panicking, Juliet slammed the door shut again and leant against it.

What do I do?

Shall I just pretend I didn't hear anything and let someone else find him? Will they believe me? Will they think it's got something to do with me?

Overcome with nerves, she slid down to the floor and held her head in her hands. She screwed her eyes tightly shut but she could still see Sam. She'd only been looking at him for a second or two, but there was no question he was dead. His face was contorted with pain and there were glistening dribbles of dark blood down the front of his yellow school sweatshirt.

*

No one's coming. Christ, no one's coming.

Twenty minutes later and still no one else had arrived. Where were the other children and the rest of the staff? Juliet remained where she was, frozen in position with fear. If she waited long enough, surely someone else would come and find the body? She'd just plead ignorance; pretend she hadn't heard anything.

The longer she waited, the more her conscience competed with her fear. She stood up and crept towards the window again and peered outside, immediately hiding again when she saw Sam's foot.

But she had to do *something*. She couldn't just sit here all day knowing that poor boy was out on the step.

The main school office was directly across the playground from the nursery hut. Juliet decided she'd make a run for it. She'd open the door, run down the steps, sprint to the other building then find the head or anyone else, and tell them what had happened, despite the fact she didn't know herself.

She had to do it right now.

Juliet put on her coat and, taking a deep breath, opened the classroom door and burst out into the open. Forcing herself to look anywhere but down at the body on the steps, she half-jumped, half-tripped over the boy's corpse, landing awkwardly, twisting her ankle and almost falling over. Managing to just about keep her balance she ran across the playground with the all-consuming silence ringing loud in her ears.

Ken Andrews was dead. She found him in the corner of his office, buried under a pile of papers he'd knocked off his desk in his death throes. She also found the school secretary's corpse in the short corridor which ran between the office and the staff room, and in the staff room she found three more dead teachers.

In a vacant, disorientated daze, Juliet roamed the school, struggling to function, barely even aware what she was doing. She then walked the surrounding streets for more than an hour, knocking on doors, looking for someone who could explain what had happened. But all she found were more bodies. Children and parents that she recognised, others she didn't, all of them dead.

A quarter past five.

After what had happened at school, Juliet returned home before midday and found both of her elderly parents dead. Mom was in the bathroom, sprawled across the floor with her knickers around her ankles, neck twisted, and Dad, as always, was in his armchair. She'd wept for them both of course (especially Mom), and had felt a real sense of devastation and loss, but after a while the hurt had, unexpectedly, begun to fade. In a strange, perverse kind of way, she began to enjoy the freedom that this dark day had given her. She'd never had the house to herself for any length of time like this before. She hadn't had to eat at any particular time of day (not that she felt like eating anything anyway) and she hadn't had to sit through Dad's choice of television programmes (not that the television was working). She hadn't had to explain her movements every time she got up out of her chair, or tell her parents about her day at work in excruciating detail, or listen to Mom telling her what all her friends were doing and how their kids had all flown the nest and made their own lives...

For the first time in a very long time, Juliet felt free.

Her quiet, insignificant world had been turned upside down. She'd seen hundreds of bodies and hadn't known why any of them had died. As day turned into night she tried to make contact with her few friends, her neighbours, the local police and pretty much everyone else she could think of in the local vicinity, but she hadn't reached anyone. Her telephone went unanswered. No one came to any of the doors she knocked on.

Frightened and bewildered, but also feeling strangely empowered, Juliet sat alone in her bedroom on her teddy-bear strewn single bed. She gave up trying to make sense of what had happened, and so buried herself in another trashy chick-lit novel instead.

At the end of the first day she moved Mom and Dad into the back room. When she woke up on the second day she dug two deep holes in the garden and buried them both. Dad had always said he wanted them to be buried in the same plot, but she knew Mom wouldn't have liked that. She'd loved Dad right 'til their unexpected end, but like Juliet, Mom had had enough of him too.

'What the hell do you call that?'

I looked at him for a second. Was that a trick question? 'I call it what you ordered,' I answered. 'Full English breakfast: bacon, sausage, scrambled egg, mushrooms, hash browns and baked beans.'

'Doesn't look like the picture in the menu.'

He opened the menu up, laid it out flat on the table in front of him and jabbed his finger angrily at the photograph at the top of the breakfast section.

'I know, but that's only a representation,' I tried to explain.

'Not good enough,' he interrupted. 'I appreciate there will inevitably be differences between a photograph and the actual meal, but what you've served up here bears very little resemblance to the food I ordered. The bacon's undercooked, the sausage overcooked. The mushrooms are cold, the scrambled egg is lumpy. Do I need to go on?'

'So do you want me to—?'

'That was what I ordered,' he sighed, cutting across me and tapping the photograph with his finger again, 'and that is what I expect to be served. Now you be a good girl and run along to your kitchen and try again.'

A genuine complaint I can deal with, but I have a real problem with being patronised. I was so angry I couldn't move. It was one of those second-long moments which felt like it dragged on forever. Did I try and argue with this pathetic little man, did I tell him what he could do with his bloody breakfast, or did I just swallow my pride, pick up the plate and take it back to the kitchen? Much as I wanted to take either of the first two options, common-sense and nerves got the better of me. I picked up the plate and stormed back to the kitchen.

'Bloody man,' I shouted as I pushed through the swinging door and threw the plate onto the work surface. Jamie and Keith, the so-called chefs, were playing football with a lettuce. They both just looked at me.

'Who's rattled your cage?' Jamie asked.

'Fucking idiot outside. Wants his breakfast to look exactly the same as the picture in the menu.'

'Tell him to fuck off and get a life,' Keith said as he kicked the lettuce out the back door. I stared at the pair of them, waiting for either one of them to move.

'What do you expect me to do about it?' said Jamie.

'Make another bloody breakfast,' I told him. 'You're the cook, aren't you?'

It was as if I'd asked him to prepare forty meals in four minutes. All I wanted was for him to do his job, what he was being paid for. If he'd done it right first time he wouldn't have had to do it again.

'For fuck's sake,' he said. He studied the faded photograph on a copy of the menu stuck to the wall, then took the food from the original plate, rearranged it on a clean one, added another sausage and another rasher of bacon, warmed it up in the microwave, then slid it across the work surface towards me.

'And you expect me to take this out to him?'

'Yes,' he grunted. 'Looks more like it does on the menu now, doesn't it?'

Keith started to snigger from behind a newspaper. There was no point arguing with either of the chimps I was working with, so I picked up the plate. I stood behind the doors for a couple of seconds to compose myself and looked into the restaurant through the small porthole window. I could see my nightmare customer looking at his watch and tapping his fingers on the table impatiently, and I knew that whatever I did wasn't going to be good enough. If I went back too quickly he'd accuse me of not having had time to prepare his food properly. If I kept him waiting he'd be even more annoyed… I gave it a few seconds longer, took a deep breath, then went back out.

They might have paid my wages, but customers were the bane of my life. We got all sorts of passing trade at the restaurant, and I tended to get a couple of customers like this one each week. They were usually travelling sales reps stopping in the motel just up the bypass. As a rule they were all badly dressed, loud, rude and ignorant. Maybe that was why they did the job? Perhaps their wives (if anyone was stupid enough to marry them) had kicked them out? Maybe their relationships only survived because they spent so much time apart?

I put down the plate, then waited next to his table, cringing. 'That's better,' he said, taking me by surprise. I quickly walked away.

'You're welcome, wanker,' I said under my breath.

'Just a minute, girl,' he shouted at me before I'd even reached the kitchen door. The other customers all looked up and watched me walk back to his table.

'Yes?' I answered through gritted teeth, doing my damnedest to stay calm and not empty his coffee into his lap.

'This is virtually raw,' he said, skewering his extra sausage. He sniffed it, then dropped it back onto his plate in disgust, sending little balls of dried-up scrambled egg shooting across the table.

'Is it really?' I said, and the sarcasm and mock concern in my voice was obvious.

'Yes, it is,' he shouted. 'Now you listen to me, dear. You scuttle back to your little kitchen right now and fetch me a fresh and properly cooked breakfast. And while you're there, send the manager out to see me. This really isn't good enough.'

His complaint may well have been justified, but the way he spoke to me was completely out of order. I wasn't paid enough to be patronised and belittled. It wasn't my fault.

'Are you going to stand there looking stupid all day,' he sneered, 'or are you going to go somewhere else and look stupid instead?'

That was it. The customer is always right, they say, but there are limits. Here at the Monkton View Eater, it seemed, the customer was always an asshole.

'Look, I'm sorry if the food isn't up to the standard you were expecting,' I began, somehow managing to still sound calm, even if I didn't feel it, 'I'll get that sorted out. But there's no need to be rude. I'll go and get you the—'

'Listen,' he said, his tired tone making it clear it was a real effort to have to lower himself to speak to me, 'I'm really not interested in anything more you have to say. Be a good girl and fetch me my food and the manager. You are a waitress. You are here to serve me. And if I want to be rude to you then I'll be as rude as I fucking well please. You're paid to take it.'

'No, you listen,' I pointlessly protested. 'I'm not—'

'Get the manager,' he interrupted with a tone of infuriating superiority and a dismissive wave of his hand. 'I don't need to speak to you any longer.'

It was another one of those moments which seemed to last forever. I was so full of anger that, again, I was too wound up to move. Compounding my awkwardness was the fact that all the other customers had also stopped eating and were waiting to see what I'd do next. I looked back over my shoulder and saw the Neanderthals in the kitchen peering out through the portholes, grinning like idiots.

'Well?' my shit of a customer sighed. I turned and walked, pushing through the swinging doors, knocking Jamie flying.

'Where's Trevor?'

'Fag break,' Keith replied.

I stormed out through the back door. Trevor was leaning up the rubbish bins, smoking a cigarette and reading Keith's newspaper.

'What?' he grunted, annoyed that he'd been interrupted.

'I've got a problem with a customer. He says he wants to speak to the manager.'

'Tell him you're the manager.'

'Why should I?'

He shrugged his shoulders. 'Tell him I've gone to a meeting.'

'No.'

'Tell him I've got Health and Safety coming to check the place over.'

'No.'

'For Christ's sake,' he groaned, finally looking up from the paper, 'just deal with it will you. What the hell do I pay you for? Dealing with customers is your responsibility.'

'And looking after staff is yours.'

'Oh give it a rest.'

'He swore at me! I'm not prepared to speak to a customer who's going to swear at me. Do you know how bloody insulting he was when—'

'Now you're swearing at me. You can't have it both ways, love!'

That was it. That was the straw that broke the camel's back. I ripped off the bloody stupid pinafore they made me wear and threw it at Trevor, along with my order pad and pen.

'I've had enough! Stick your bloody job!'

I couldn't afford to do what I was doing, but I couldn't take anymore abuse. It wasn't the first time something like that had happened, and I knew it wouldn't be the last. I grabbed my coat from the kitchen, then marched out through the restaurant.

'Is the manager on his way?' the odious customer shouted at the top of his voice as I stormed past. I couldn't help myself. I turned back and walked towards him. His food couldn't have been too bad because he'd managed to eat half of it.

'No, he isn't on his way,' I told him. 'The manager can't be bothered to come and speak to you, and I can't be bothered to waste my time dealing with pathetic little fuckers like you either. You can stick your meal and your attitude and your complaint up your arse, and I hope you fucking choke on your food!'

And he did.

Still chewing a mouthful of breakfast, the smug grin of superiority which had been plastered across his face slowly disappeared. He stopped eating. His eyes became wide and the veins in his neck began to bulge. He spat out his food.

'Water,' he croaked, clawing at his neck, 'get me some water…'

A noise from behind made me turn around. Two other customers in the far corner of the restaurant were choking too. A middle-aged couple were both in as bad a state as the little shit who'd caused me so much trouble. I turned back to look at him again. He looked like he was suffocating. As much as I'd wished all kinds of suffering on him a couple of minutes earlier, now I just wanted it to stop. I ran back to the kitchen to get his water.

'Call an ambulance,' I yelled to anyone listening. 'There's a customer who…'

I stopped when I saw Jamie on his knees in the corner of the kitchen, coughing up blood. Keith was on his back in the storeroom, rolling around in agony like all the others. Outside, Trevor had already lost consciousness, his fat body wedged half-in and half-out of the back door.

By the time I'd picked up the phone to call for an ambulance, everyone in the restaurant was dead.

Mom's not well.

She's suffered with her health for years and she's been practically bed-ridden since last December, but she's really taken a turn for the worst this morning. I'll have to get the doctor out to see her if she doesn't pick up soon.

I don't know what I'd do without my mom. I know I should think about it, mind, 'cause I know she's not going to be around forever. We're very close, Mom and me. Dad died when I was little and there's just been the two of us since then. I don't work because I look after her, so we don't get out much. We pretty much live out on our own here. There's our cottage and one other on either side and that's about all. The village is five minutes down the road by bike. We've never bothered with a car. Never seen the point. We can get a bus into town if we really need to, but there ain't much we need that we can't find in the village.

She's calling again. I'll make some tea and take it up with her tablets. I don't like this. This isn't like her. She always says she doesn't like making a fuss. She tells the doctor that, and the health visitor, and the District Nurse, and the priest.

It's just her way.

I need to go and get help but I can't leave the house. I can't leave Mom on her own.

Oh, God, I don't know what to do. I was up there with her when it happened. I was trying to get her onto the toilet when it started. Usually when she has one of her turns she'll let me know it's coming, but she didn't just now. This came out of the blue. It took her by surprise as much as me.

She started to choke. Mom's chest has been bad for a long time and it's been getting worse, but nothing like this. It was like she'd got something stuck in her throat, but she turned her nose up at breakfast this morning and she hadn't eaten anything else, so that was impossible. Anyway, before I knew what was happening she was coughing and retching and her whole body was shaking. I got her on the bed and tried to get her to calm down and breathe slow and not panic, but she couldn't stop. She couldn't swallow, couldn't talk. I didn't even know if she could hear me. Her eyes were bulging wide and I knew she wasn't getting any air but there wasn't anything I could do. I tried to tip her head back to open up her windpipe like the nurse showed me once but she wouldn't lie still. She kept fighting. She was thrashing her arms around and coughing and sputtering, making these horrible noises. She didn't sound like Mom anymore. It was like something out of one of them horror films. She was making this croaking, gargling noise and I thought there was phlegm or something stuck or she was choking on her tongue (the nurse told me about that once too) so I put my fingers in her mouth to make sure it was clear. When I pulled them out again they were covered in blood. Then she stopped moving. As suddenly as the fit had started, it stopped.

I knew there was nothing I could do. I sat down on the carpet next to her and held her hand until I was certain she'd gone.

I could still hear that horrible choking sound she was making in my head, long after Mom stopped fighting. I could hear it ringing in my ears when everything else went quiet.

It's been quiet like this for hours now.

Mom's dead.

I can't just sit here and do nothing. I know I can't help her, but I can't just leave her lying here either. The doctor will have to come around and check her, then someone else will come to take her away and then… and then I don't know what I'll do. I've always had my mom.

About half an hour ago I moved her. I couldn't leave her lying on the floor in the middle of the landing like that, that just wouldn't have been right. She was twice as heavy as when she was alive. I put my hands under her arms and dragged her into the bedroom, then lifted her onto the bed. I wiped the blood off her face and tried to close her eyes to make it look like she was just sleeping like they do in the films. I got one eye shut but the other one stayed open, staring at me. It was like she was still watching me, like one of those paintings of faces where the eyes follow you around the room. It was freaky, but in a way it made me feel a little better. Even though she's gone it's like she hasn't stopped looking out for me.

I tried phoning the doctor but I couldn't get an answer. Someone should have been at the surgery (it's open until late on Tuesdays) so I guessed it was our telephone that wasn't working. The lines often go down in winter because we're so isolated out here. But it isn't winter. It's early September and the weather's been fine for weeks.

I didn't want to leave her but I didn't have any choice. I shut the bedroom door, locked up the house and got my bike out of the shed. It didn't take long to get into the village. Mom never liked me riding on the road (she said it was the other people she didn't trust, not me) but it didn't matter this morning because there wasn't any traffic about. The village ain't the busiest of places, but there's usually always *something* happening. This morning it was so quiet that all I could hear was the sound of my bike. And as I went further into the village, it got much worse. So much worse that I nearly turned around and came back home, but thinking about Mom made me keep going forward.

I was cycling down past Jack Halshaw's house when I saw his front door was open. That was odd because Jack's always been careful about things like that. He used to be a friend of my dad's and I've known him all my life, so I stopped the bike because I thought I should tell him about Mom and I thought he might help me get things sorted out. I went down the path and leant into the house and shouted to him but he didn't answer. I checked to see if he was in his back garden, and that was where I found him. He was lying flat on his back and I could tell just by looking at him he was dead. There was a pool of blood all round his mouth and it looked like he'd died the same way Mom had, even though that didn't make no sense.

I didn't know what to do. I kept going until I got to the middle of the village. When I got there I just stopped the bike and stared. Whatever had happened to Mom and Jack Halshaw had happened to other people too. *All* the other people. The longer I stayed there, the more obvious it was that I was the only one it hadn't got. Inside the doctor's, Mrs Cribbins from the chip shop and Dr Grainger were both lying dead in the middle of the waiting room. Their faces were horrible – splattered with blood and all screwed up like they'd been in terrible pain when they'd died. The doctor looked like he'd been trying to scream when it had happened.

I kept going, but I wished that I hadn't. Even though it had happened early in the morning, there had been lots of people out and about. They'd all died wherever they'd been, whatever they'd been doing. And because our village is a small place I knew them all. Bill Linturn from the hardware shop was dead in his car outside the store. Vera Price, the lady who's on the till at the grocer's on Tuesday, Thursday and Fridays was lying dead on the pavement just outside the shop. She'd fallen into the middle of the fruit and veg displays they always have outside. There were potatoes, carrots and apples all over the place.

I kept looking, but there was no one left to help me. It sounds silly, but I didn't want to leave Mom alone for too long, so I got back on my bike and cycled home.

It's been almost half a day now since it happened. I can't get a picture on the telly and I still can't get anyone on the phone. I've tried listening to the radio to find out what's happening but all I can hear is silence or hissing and crackling like it's out of tune. I've been into the cottages next door on either side but both Ed and Mrs Chester are dead as well. I found Ed in his bath (the water was all pink because of the blood he'd been dribbling) and Mrs Chester was at the bottom of her stairs with her neck all twisted. I tried to move her into her living room but her legs and arms had gone all stiff and hard. She was wedged behind the door and I couldn't move her.

I think I'm just going to sit here and wait for a bit longer. Someone will come sooner or later, I'm sure they will. And anyway, I can't leave Mom here on her own. We did our weekly shop yesterday morning so I've got enough food in. Everything will be all right again in a couple of days time when the police and the government start sorting out what's happened. I'll have to phone around the rest of the family and let them know about Mom.

DAY TWO

BEGINNING TO DISINTEGRATE
Part i

Lorna watched the whole thing unfold from the bedroom window of her small rented house. Her gut reaction had been to go down and help, but she'd straightaway known there wasn't any point. One person she might have been able to save, but hundreds? Thousands? Instead she bolted the door and shut the curtains and focused on keeping herself safe. Living here had given her plenty of practice. The area itself was okay, the people definitely weren't. The estate had been built on the edge of the city in the early eighties, just that little bit too far out of town. It had become a ghetto, cut off and forgotten. Trouble was never far from her front door, but what had happened this week surpassed anything she'd seen before.

The street outside her house was quiet for once, and the silence was somehow more ominous than the usual noise. There were no kids loitering by the bus shelter today, no police officers cruising, no community support officers trying to straddle the line between the two sides, taking abuse from both directions… There was no one.

Yesterday morning, everything had just stopped, like someone had flicked a switch. The few people she could see had simply dropped where they'd been standing, and she hadn't needed to check each one of them individually to know they were all dead. The fact the Internet and TV had also become silent was all the proof she needed.

Lorna was smart. Switched on. She'd had to be. Her mom had rarely been around, and a string of waster boy and girlfriends had taught her not to rely on anyone else because the bastards *always* let her down. There was always an ulterior motive. They always wanted something from her, never the other way around. Fuck the lot of them. The only one who'd genuinely given a damn was her dad, but she'd hardly known him. He got sent off to fight in some dirty desert war when she was little and never came home.

She sat in the corner of the room, knees drawn up to her chest, and revelled in the silence. *Is there something wrong with me*, she wondered? *Am I sick in the head? The entire world dropped dead yesterday, and all I feel is relieved…*

She'd been putting it off, but she knew she was going to have to go out there, and the sooner the better. The end of the world had crept up silently and taken everyone by surprise. There hadn't been time for panic-buying (or panic-*anything*, come to that). She didn't have much in the way of food or alcohol and she needed both. She decided to go out and recce the situation this morning, to try and assess the risks. Weirdly, she hoped she didn't find anyone else alive. She was enjoying the silence.

The morning after the night before, and she was *still* screaming. Anita had found Ellie by following the noise yesterday. The only other survivor she'd so far come across, she was beginning to wish she hadn't. She understood why she was screaming, of course. She'd have probably been the same in the circumstances. Ellie lost her baby girl when everyone else had died yesterday, and since then she'd only stopped crying long enough to draw breath or snatch a few second's sleep. No matter how bad she felt for her, though, the noise was doing Anita's head in. She'd have got up and left if she hadn't been so bloody terrified herself. And where would she have gone? As far as she could tell, this miserable, wailing bitch was the only other person left alive.

'Give it a fucking rest,' she shouted across the room, but Ellie was making too much noise to hear. She just sat there on the edge of the bed, staring at the ice-cold kid in the cot. Sometimes she'd go to touch it, then pull her hand away at the last second.

Ellie hadn't wanted to be a mom. She hadn't planned it. The dad hadn't been any help. She still wasn't completely sure which one of them it was; they'd both pissed off as soon as they heard she was pregnant. Fuck, she'd cried herself to sleep for night after night when she found out she was expecting. She'd been to a clinic for an abortion, only to back out at the last minute. Thing was, she'd realised on the way there, when she was pregnant, people noticed her... talked to her... The baby gave her something to focus on, a reason to keep going. Sitting here now, looking at the little girl's tiny body which hadn't moved for over twenty-four hours, she couldn't begin to make sense of the turmoil she was feeling inside. It had hurt so much when she'd pissed on a stick from the chemist and found out she was pregnant, so how come it hurt so much more now she'd lost her?

Anita needed a break, but she couldn't go out. She went to the kitchen, lit a fag and hung her head out of the window, the next best thing. The view from the third floor up was too clear, stretching out over miles of stuff she didn't particularly want to see. And the silence… the never-ending quiet out there was harder to handle than the noise coming from the other room. Cold, pissed off and frightened, she checked the cupboards for something to eat then took some crisps and a bottle of Coke through to Ellie. Ellie didn't even look up. Anita sat down and watched her. Fuck, what she'd have given for some interaction. Someone to talk to. Something to look at on her phone. Someone to text. Something on TV. Anything…

Lorna decided against taking a car. She'd spent a long time thinking about it – several sleepless hours during the night just passed. It was the noise that put her off. With everything else so deathly quiet, did she really want to advertise the fact she was still alive? Everything on the estate was in walking distance, so the risks seemed to outweigh the potential benefits. And anyway, there was so much shit littering the roads – so many dead people and driverless vehicles – that she didn't think she'd be able to go much faster than walking speed.

A couple of hours out there maximum, she decided, then back home. Maybe try and get a little more of the local area covered every day until she'd made a full assessment of the situation. Did she even need to make an assessment of anything? She thought about all the films she'd seen before that had started like this. People in the movies were always making the mistake of trying to work out what had happened. Idiots. What did it matter? What difference would it make? Even if she found something somewhere which explained everything, how was that going to help her? All that mattered now was staying safe and staying alive. Fuck everything else.

There were a few false alarms. A cat jumping out of an open window scared the crap out of her, and The Jockey – that shit-hole of a pub you never went into unless you were already pissed and had absolutely no other option – was burning. She'd seen the smoke and heard the crackle and pop of the flames and had been transfixed. She'd stood there for a while, just staring, hypnotised by the constant light and movement and soaking up the heat. The fire was a welcome interruption in the otherwise never-ending sea of motionless grey. And then there were the birds. Picking at scraps. Squawking. Fighting. Crows and seagulls acting like vultures.

She'd lived here for years, but she still sometimes managed to get lost. All the roads looked the same, all the houses just variations on the same few red-brick themes. They were arranged in nests of roughly semi-circular crescents, branching off a few main roads. Here the side-roads were named after royalty, which always made Lorna laugh because if a fucking royal ever ended up here by mistake, they wouldn't have dared get out of their bloody car. She went the wrong way when she emerged from a convenience store where she'd been looking for food, and now she was halfway along Princess Margaret Crescent when she wanted to be on Prince Albert Way. She could double-back, or she could just keep going. Changing direction took too much effort.

When Lorna reached the junction where Prince Albert Way met the main Wildboar Road, she heard the screams. Distant. Carried on the wind. She wasn't sure if they were real or a figment of her imagination, or even if it was just the wind itself. She kept walking and then, a minute or two later, she heard them again. It was a woman, howling in pain like she was being tortured. Christ, the noise was fucking terrifying. So bad, in fact, that Lorna turned around and started walking home. *I've got enough to deal with*, she kept telling herself. *I don't need anyone else giving me more grief.*

And yet, a part of her desperately wanted to find the woman who was crying. She wanted to see her, maybe even talk to her... she just wanted to know for sure that, perhaps, she wasn't the only person left alive. Just a few minutes with her, that'd be enough. If she could get an idea how many others might be left, she'd be better placed to come up with a survival strategy. *I'm not going to help her*, Lorna tried to convince herself, *I'm going to help me. I'm just going to check things out... find out where she is, who she is. Forewarned is forearmed. And on the subject of being armed*, she thought, *I need to take precautions.* She stopped walking and swung the bag she'd been carrying off her shoulders. She took out a large kitchen knife she'd brought with her from home.

In the event, Lorna was the one who was found. Evidently, the screaming woman wasn't alone. Another girl who'd been with her came pelting down the stairs as soon as she saw Lorna approaching. Kitchen knife or no kitchen knife, she ran straight up and grabbed hold of her. 'You gotta help me,' she said. 'I can't fucking shut her up. She's doing my brain in.'

Lorna cautiously followed Anita up to Ellie's flat, exchanging names on the staircase and getting the obviously unanswerable questions out of the way quickly. 'No, I don't know what happened,' she told Anita. 'And yes, you're the only other person I've seen.'

Lorna's arrival distracted Ellie momentarily. The silence was bliss. 'Thank fuck…' Anita said under her breath.

'What's the matter with her?' Lorna asked.

'Dead kid.'

'You a doctor?' Ellie asked, the first coherent words she'd spoken in almost a day.

'Do I look like a doctor?'

Lorna took a few hesitant steps forward and peered into Ellie's baby's cot. She couldn't bear to look for anything more than a couple of seconds. The child was curled up tight, its knees drawn up to its chest, hands in tiny fists in front of its face. Its skin was mottled blue-green. Its bedding was soaked with blood and other leakage. Ellie, not listening, tried to explain.

'She just started choking. She was asleep, and she just started coughing. Hadn't fed her or nothing… I tried to help her but I couldn't get her to breathe. Didn't know what to do. And she was crying and I…'

Her words dried up. She started to sob, but not yet to scream. Lorna crouched down beside her and rested a hand on her shoulder, making eye contact and keeping it. 'You did your best. There was nothing you could do. It wasn't your fault.'

Ellie nodded and sniffed, then wiped her nose on the back of her sleeve. 'I did my best.'

'It's not just your baby, you know. It's everybody. They're all like this outside.'

She nodded again.

'What are we gonna do?' Anita asked, standing a short distance back.

'I don't know what you're going to do,' Lorna replied, standing up, 'but I'm going home.'

'You can't leave us here.'

'You'll be okay.'

'Can't you stay with us?' Ellie asked, still sobbing.

'I want to get back before it gets dark.'

'Ellie's right,' Anita said, 'we should stick together, shouldn't we?'

'Maybe, but I—'

'It'll make it easier when help comes, won't it?'

'I don't reckon there's much help coming. Christ, people used to avoid coming to this estate at the best of times, and this definitely ain't the best of times.'

She started towards the door. Anita blocked her. 'Don't go,' she said, voice low. 'Don't leave me on my own with her.'

Lorna looked back at Ellie who was now stroking her dead baby's cheek with her finger, whispering to her.

'I don't want to stay here.'

'Let us come with you then. Please. I don't know what you did, but she's calmed right down. Please... I can't take it if she starts screaming again.'

Lorna considered her options. Every possibility felt like the wrong choice. Even though she tried to deny it, the thought of going back to her empty home alone now felt less appealing than it had when she'd first set out. Maybe they should stick together? Even if it was just for a day or two... by then they'd have found more survivors, wouldn't they? Then she could just palm this pair off on someone else and not feel bad about it.

'Get your stuff together,' she told them both. 'You can come with me. Just until we work out what's going on.'

Ellie refused to leave her baby.

'For fuck's sake, she's dead,' Lorna yelled at her, all tact, decorum and sympathy out the window. 'We're not taking a dead baby.'

'I can't... leave her...' she sobbed, struggling to breathe and form sentences.

'Well stay here then. You can't bring her.'

Lorna and Anita were standing by the door, ready to go. Ellie hesitated by the crib, loyalties divided. This pointless stand-off was dragging unnecessarily. Lorna glanced outside at the increasing darkness. The street lamps had come on as usual, but every other flat and house remained dark and unlit. *Fuck me*, she thought, *is this really all that's left?*

Anita returned to her friend's side and tried to drag her away, but all that did was make matters worse. Ellie began to scream again, louder than before. The hideous sound cut right through Lorna, piercing her skull. Then Anita started shouting, more through frustration than fear.

'Wait here,' Lorna said. She didn't know if either of them heard her, but she was past caring. She slipped out of the front door and ran downstairs.

Lorna returned to the convenience store she'd visited earlier. She stepped over the body of an old guy she thought she vaguely recognised, and crossed to a narrow display unit next to the magazines and greetings cards. She found what she was looking for, grabbed it, and ran back to the flat.

'Right, we're going,' she announced when she arrived back at the flat. Ellie was still wailing, but she quietened slightly when she saw what Lorna was carrying. Lorna bit into the polythene packaging of a cheap plastic, shrink-wrapped doll and tore it open. The doll was light and hollow – a rudimentary, cut-price toy – and she passed it over to Ellie who immediately shut up. 'Get her ready, get her in her pushchair, and let's get the fuck out of here.'

'I don't fucking believe it,' Anita said. The sudden silence was beautiful.

On the way back to Lorna's place they stopped and looked out over a large swathe of countryside, buried in darkness save for lines of streetlights. 'See that?' Anita asked.

'See what?'

'Right over there… there's a house with lights on.'

Lorna's gut reaction had been to wait until morning, but she knew it would be almost impossible to find the house in daylight. The steadily increasing gloom tonight was actually helping. Though she knew roughly where they were heading, the dark was also disorientating. Distances were impossible to gauge. A walk they thought wouldn't take long actually took more than an hour. Cold, tired and scared, they eventually reached the road with the single illuminated house halfway along. Feeling increasingly unsure, and wishing she'd stuck to her original plan and stayed home alone, Lorna rang the bell. The noise cut through the unnatural silence of everything else, sounding over-amplified and out of place. The curtains twitched. She could see movement through the frosted glass and her pulse began to quicken at the thought of what might be about to greet her. As it was, it was the normality of the person who answered the door that she found most surprising: an apron-wearing, middle-aged woman. A brief and unsurprisingly awkward doorstep conversation followed. The woman introduced herself as Caron and ushered them inside, appearing genuinely relieved to see other people. The house was reassuringly ordinary, an unexpected oasis. Full of unnecessary ornaments and hideously over-decorated. Unmistakeably middle-class.

'Are you hungry?' Caron asked. 'We were just about to eat.'

'*We?*' Lorna said. 'There are more of you?'

Caron led them into the dining room. 'This is Mr Webb,' she said, introducing the scrawny-looking youth sitting at the head of the table, shovelling food into his mouth. Webb just grunted.

DAY THREE

AMY STEADMAN
Part ii

Almost fifty hours have passed since infection. Amy Steadman has been dead for just over two days.

Minutes after death, Amy's body began to decompose. A process known as autolysis has begun. This is self-digestion. Starved of oxygen, complex chemical reactions have started to occur throughout the corpse. Amy's cells have become poisoned by increased levels of carbon dioxide, changes in acidity levels and the accumulation of waste. Her body has begun the slow process of dissolving from the inside out.

There has already been a marked change in Amy's external appearance. Her skin is now discoloured; her once healthy pink hue has darkened to a dull, dirty grey. Her veins are considerably more prominent and, in places, her skin now has a greasy translucency. Amy died lying on her back, with her body arched across the feet of a metal display unit. The parts of her which are lowest to the ground – her feet, legs and backside, and her left arm – now appear swollen and bruised. Blood, no longer pumping, has pooled in these areas and coagulated.

The outward signs of the chemical reactions occurring throughout the corpse are becoming increasingly apparent. Fluid-filled blisters have begun to form on Amy's skin and, around some areas of her body, skin slippage has also occurred. Her face now appears drawn and hollowed.

To all intents and purposes, Amy Steadman is dead. As a unique and identifiable human being, she has all but ceased to exist. All that remains of her now is a decaying carcase and all traces of the personality and character she once had have disappeared. Her heart no longer beats, she no longer breathes, blood no longer circulates. The infection, however, has not completely destroyed her. Part of Amy's brain and nervous system has continued to function, albeit at a virtually undetectable level. There are several other corpses nearby in a similar condition. Until now, their function has been slight and unnoticeable. Amy has, however, finally reached the stage where her brain has become able to again exert a degree of basic control. She is only capable of rudimentary yes/no decisions. She no longer feels emotion, nor is she aware of who – *what* – she now is. She has no desires or needs: she is driven purely by instinct. The brain's control over the rest of her body is improving, but at a phenomenally slow speed.

Amy's body is beginning to move. The first outwardly visible sign of change is in her right foot which begins to twitch at the ankle. Over the next few hours this movement gradually spreads to all four limbs and across the torso until, finally, the body is able to lift itself up and stand. Amy's movements are clumsy and uncoordinated. Co-agulated blood and the gelling of the cytoplasm within individual cells (because of the increased acidity inside the body) is preventing free movement. Her eyes are open but she cannot see. She cannot hear. She cannot feel anything or react to any external stimulation. The combined effects of gravity, physical deterioration and the un-even distribution of weight across her corpse after two days of inac-tivity causes Amy to move. Initially she trips and falls on unsteady legs, like a new-born animal. Soon, however, her level of control is such that she is able to distribute her weight enough to manage a rudimentary walk. Devoid of all senses, Amy's corpse simply keeps moving forward until it reaches an obstruction and can go no fur-ther. She then shuffles around until she is able to move freely again.

Amy's body remains in this state for a further two days.

This is the best day! I can't believe it – it looks like Mom's going to be all right!

She woke me up this morning. I opened my eyes and she was standing at the end of the bed. Scared the life out of me, she did. I couldn't believe it. I mean, I was sure she was dead, but she must have been in a coma or something like that. I saw a programme about that once on telly. Anyway, she wasn't talking and she wasn't very steady on her feet but at least she was up and about. I knew Mom wouldn't leave me. She's still very ill, mind. She doesn't look well and she smells really bad, but that's nothing a good soak in the bath won't cure.

She's been really shaken up by all of this, has Mom. She's not herself at all. I've had to shut her in her room to stop her wandering off. She just keeps walking around, banging into things, and she won't sit still. I keep telling her she'll do herself an injury if she's not careful, but she won't listen. She won't sit in her chair or lie on the bed or anything. I expect she just needs to keep moving for a while after being still for so long.

I've felt so scared for the last couple of days, trying to imagine life without Mom, but now I feel much better. Everything is okay. I knew she wouldn't leave me.

I had to tie her to the bed. She just won't stay still and I'm scared she'll do herself even more harm if she keeps on like this. I know it's not right, but what else can I do? There's no one around to ask for help and I still can't get anyone on the phone. I keep telling myself that it's in Mom's best interests if I'm firm with her. If she keeps wandering off then who knows what might happen? I could find her halfway down the road or worse. What would they say in the village?

I didn't need to tie her down tight or anything like that. She's still hardly got any strength. I used the washing line from the back yard. I got Mom back into bed (I had to hold her down while I did it) then wrapped the line right the way around the bed and the bedclothes.

Since Dad died she's only ever had a single bed. That meant I could wrap the line right around a few times. I left it quite loose because I didn't want to hurt her or upset her. She can still move but not enough to get up.

I keep telling her I'm doing it for her own good but I don't know if she can hear me. She might be getting that Alzheimer's disease. She was always scared of getting that.

I went into the village again this afternoon. I didn't like it. Some of the people who got ill around the same time as Mom are getting better because they were walking around too. There were some still lying where they'd fallen, though. Poor old Bill Linturn was still in his car, dead to the world.

The people who were walking about were just like Mom. They didn't answer when I spoke to them. They scared me with their empty eyes and grey skin. I got out of the village fast and ran home and locked the door. My place was back with Mom.

More good news! I still can't get Mom to eat or drink anything, but when I went to see her just now, she turned her head and looked at me. I think she recognised my voice. She tried to get up but I told her not to. She's still trying to do more than she should. She's her own worst enemy, that one. She's wriggling and twisting on the bed all the time.

She's getting stronger by the hour. I've just had to tighten the ropes. I think she's going to be all right!

'Bewsey?'

Flynn stared in disbelief at the figure standing swaying in front of him. It was Bewsey all right, but how the hell could it be? Two days ago he'd watched the man die. It was impossible. *I'm going fucking crazy*, he thought to himself, *that didn't take long*. Over the last forty-eight hours Flynn had been forced to consider so many horrific prospects that one more didn't make any difference. He decided he was most probably hallucinating and buried his face in his grey, prison-issue pillow. He hadn't had anything to eat for more than two days, the rest of the world had dropped dead, and he'd been trapped in a ten by seven foot cell with only the corpses of his cellmates for company. A hallucination seemed likely. What was left of his mind was playing tricks on him again.

Bewsey's clumsy corpse staggered across the tiny room, tripping over Salman's dead body and crashing into the small bookcase next to the sink, sending its contents crashing to the floor. Flynn sat up fast: this was no hallucination, much as he wished it was. He backed into the shadows and watched from the relative safety of the furthest corner of his dark bottom bunk as Bewsey's body continued to awkwardly drag itself around.

For a while Flynn remained completely still, paralysed with fear and not daring take his eyes off the dead man. Bewsey's face was terrifyingly expressionless, his eyes unfocused, and he appeared to have little control over his movements. He shuffled lethargically across the floor until something stopped him moving any further forward and then, more through luck than anything else, he turned and shuffled back again. Why couldn't he be like Salman, Flynn thought? His other dead cell mate was still lying facedown in a pool of dark brown, congealed blood.

'Bewsey?' Flynn said, not sure whether or not he actually wanted to attract his attention. He was relieved when Bewsey didn't react. Still shell-shocked, he shuffled off his bunk and stood up. The corpse continued moving, completely oblivious, colliding with walls, furniture and then, eventually, with Flynn himself. Flynn grabbed hold of the dead man. 'Bewsey?' he said again. 'Can you hear me, mate? What's going on? I thought you were dead…?'

Flynn stared deep into the corpse's dull, clouded eyes. They were covered with a milky-white film, obviously unseeing. He let Bewsey go again then crawled back onto his bunk and pulled the covers tight around him.

He couldn't stand it any longer. Bewsey just never stopped, not even for a second, constantly moving around the cell, banging into things, crashing into walls. It was the noise that Flynn found hardest to handle. He couldn't take much more of it. He had to do something.

There were other bodies moving in other cells now, he could see them occasionally through the bars. He wished he was out there too, but getting out seemed an impossibility. Feeling on edge, ready to snap at any moment, he decided his only option was to try and stop Bewsey's corpse moving, to make what was left of his interminable incarceration slightly less unbearable. He didn't care why the dead man was moving anymore, he just wanted him to stop.

Unsurprisingly, there was barely anything in the cell he could use as a weapon. In fact, all he could find was the plastic water jug. If he hit him hard enough, he thought it might just be strong enough to batter Bewsey into submission. Taking a deep breath, he grabbed the dead man by the throat with one hand, raised the jug above his head with the other, and then smashed it into Bewsey's face with savage force. Although his skin was a little more bruised and bloodied than it had been, Bewsey's expression remained impassive, unemotional. Not a flicker of response. Flynn lifted the jug and brought it crashing down again and again and again…

It wasn't working. It didn't matter what he did, the dead man didn't react. Increasingly desperate, Flynn dragged his bunk bed into the middle of the cell, swinging it around so that it formed a barrier across the corner of the small room. He shoved Bewsey onto the other side, successfully confining the cadaver. Keen to separate himself from both his dead cell-mates, he did the same with Salman's lifeless bulk.

Flynn leant against the door and peered through the bars, preferring to look out than look in any longer. He could see men moving in the cells on the other side of the landing, but when he called out to them they didn't respond. He assumed they were all like Bewsey.

He heard a corpse fall down the stairs, just out of his line of vision. Then he heard slow, dragging footsteps approaching. A figure emerged from the shadows at the far end of the corridor, walking with an awkward limp as if one of its legs was inches shorter than the other. He couldn't tell who it was at first but, as it came into view, he saw that it was one of the prison officers. The dead guard lumbered towards him, his head hanging listlessly to one side.

It took Flynn several minutes to realise the importance of seeing this body: the officers had keys and, if he could reach the corpse and pull it closer, there was a slight chance he might be able to get out of this bloody cell.

Suddenly feeling more alive and alert than he had in days, Flynn watched the dead officer like a hawk. When the corpse was almost level with the cell door, he stretched out his arm between the bars as far as he could, straining every muscle to reach. The tips of his outstretched fingers brushed the corpse's sleeve, but not enough for him to get a grip. His heart sank as the body stumbled past and out of reach again.

The prison landing was largely without obstruction, and the dead guard continually staggered from one end to the other. Flynn reached out for the body whenever it came anywhere near, like he was playing some damn perverse fairground game.

Eventually, more than four and a half hours after he'd first noticed the corpse, he finally caught hold of it. He managed to grab the dead man's shirt collar and pull him back. He then grabbed the cadaver in a neck lock and, with his other hand, tied him to the bars using the belt from his trousers. Flynn tugged and yanked and pulled at the body until he'd got the keys.

Minutes later he was free.

A few weeks back, Kieran, Drew, Marc and Duncan had spent a long evening together talking about the end of the world. They sat in a dark, dank corner of the Oceana club, as far from everyone else as they could get. How they'd ended up in such a shit-hole, none of them were sure. It was Duncan's leaving do, but no one could remember whose idea it had been to come here. They all denied it. It probably had something to do with the price of booze there, or it might just have been because it was one of the only places left open at that time of night. Whatever the reason, they were determined to see Duncan off in style with the longest session any of them could remember. The chaotic noise inside the club, the bright lights and the mass of writhing, sweat-soaked, predominantly underage bodies had added to the evening's bizarrely apocalyptic vibe. It felt claustro-phobic, like being locked-down in a nuclear bunker with the cast of a bad teen-soap while the bombs exploded overhead.

Drew had been watching some film or other – so good he couldn't even remember the name of it – and that had set his mind racing. Talking about Armageddon and remembering all the films they'd seen and the books they'd read over the years proved to be a welcome distraction from their usual work, sport and sex-orientated conver-sations. In some ways it made them feel like they were kids again, escaping in their imaginations into desolate, empty worlds where they could do whatever they wanted, whenever they wanted to. No rules or restrictions. No work. No responsibilities. No deadlines. No managers constantly barking at them to get stuff done by yester-day… Unbridled freedom in a brave new world.

'Seriously?' Kieran said. 'You'd seriously do that? You'd stop at the office?'

'Why not?' Marc replied. 'It's as good a place as any. Or I'd start at work anyway, then maybe move out once things had calmed down. Think about it… you'd have everything you need there. There's the hotel, the supermarket… there's the frigging Jaguar dealership over the road for crying out loud. I tell you, mate, you'd barely need to go anywhere else.'

'What about you?' Duncan asked Kieran. 'What would you do?'

'Dunno. Depends what happened, I suppose.'

'Why?'

'If it's a war or something that's wiped everyone out, it won't matter where you go, will it? Everywhere's going to be poisoned, isn't it? There'll be radiation or germs or whatever all over the place.'

'Okay, so what if it's nothing like that. What if it's some kind of flu?'

'And I'm immune?'

'Yep. You've dosed up on Calpol like your mom told you and you're immune. You've got the whole world at your feet. No one there to tell you what to do anymore.'

Kieran thought for a moment. 'Dunno.'

'What do you mean, you don't know?' Drew protested. 'Christ, Kieran, you're the one who's always on about living for the moment. Work hard, play harder you always said.'

'What's that got to do with the end of the world?'

'You need to be ready, mate. You need to be prepared. You have to grab every opportunity with both hands.'

'I didn't say I wouldn't…'

'I know exactly what I'd do,' Drew continued, more animated than he had been all night. 'I'd find myself somewhere strong to hole-up, somewhere off the beaten track.'

'Like I said, work's as good a place as any,' Marc said.

'Hardly off the beaten track though, is it? Anyway, I'll get sorted then load up with supplies and weapons—'

'Weapons?' Kieran laughed. 'Where you going to find weapons round here? This is Cardiff, man, not the Bronx.'

Drew's enthusiasm was unabated. 'Farmers, man. There's loads of the buggers round here, and they've all got shotguns under their beds. I'd start there. Then there's the police, maybe the army even.'

'You've really thought this through, haven't you, mate?' Kieran said, swilling the dregs of his pint around the bottom of his glass, hoping someone would get up and buy another round.

'Course I have,' Drew said, sounding surprised that Kieran hadn't. 'You've got to be prepared.'

'Don't know if I'd want to survive if everyone else was gone.'

Drew looked at him in disbelief. 'You're joking, right?'

'No.'

'Bloody hell. Anyway,' he continued, 'I'll get myself tooled-up and—'

'But why do you need a gun if everyone else is dead?'

Drew sighed. 'Kieran, man, have you not seen enough films? There's always *something* needs shooting at. Jeez.'

'Well if that's the case I definitely don't want to be the only one left alive.'

'So what happens next?' Marc asked, ignoring him. 'You've got your safe place and your weapons – whether or not there's anyone else left to shoot – now what?'

'Supplies. I'd get myself a truck or a van, and I'd load it up with food and water. Biggest one I could find. Maybe even a delivery truck from Waitrose, ready stocked, something like that. I'd get as much as I could together, then stash the lot of it away.'

'You wouldn't need that much if you were on your own,' Kieran suggested.

'Have you seen how much this fat bastard eats?' Duncan laughed.

'Probably wouldn't be on my own for long,' Drew continued. 'You've really not been paying attention, have you Kieran? I might start out on my own, but there's probably going to be a busload of fucking gorgeous female survivors coming over the hill at any moment.'

'And you reckon they're going to look at you sitting there in your underpants with a farmer's rifle in your lap, shoving a bloody Waitrose pork pie down your throat, and think staying with you'll be a good move? Think again, mate, think again!'

'Power!' Drew shouted when the laughter had died down. 'Forgot about that. I'd need to get some kind of generator hooked up. Wouldn't have to be anything fancy – just a small petrol-fired generator to start with, enough to power the lights, keep me warm, and let me play Xbox.'

'Wouldn't need Xbox, mate,' Duncan said. 'You might be playing live action *Left 4 Dead* if things really get that bad.'

'That'd be cool.'

'You think? Be fucking terrifying, I reckon.'

'So what then?' Kieran asked.

'What do you mean?'

'What happens next? You're all set up, probably on your own. So what happens after that?'

'Nothing. It'd be paradise, mate. No distractions or complications. No one telling me what to do or where to be all the time. Bliss.'

'Wouldn't you get bored?'

'I'd have plenty to do.'

'You'll run out of games and films eventually.'

'Maybe after a few years.'

'But you would run out eventually.'

'And there's the loneliness,' Marc added, picking up on Kieran's point.

'I can handle it.'

'I think it'll be harder than you're making out.'

'I'll tell you what then,' Drew said, grinning, 'I'll come back here and drag in a few shop window dummies to keep me company while I drink myself stupid. I'll call them Kieran, Dunc and Marc. I'll write their names on their foreheads in black pen so I remember which one's which.'

'So then, Kieran,' Duncan said, 'I'll ask you again. What would *you* do?'

Kieran thought for a moment. 'What Drew said, I guess,' he answered, laughing as he got to his feet. 'Now, as none of you tight buggers are going to put your hands in your pockets, does anyone fancy another drink before the world ends?'

The conversation in the pub had continued for a while longer, drifting back into surreal territories on more than one occasion. The four work colleagues had talked about the various ways they thought the world might end, with conversation then turning to all the ways they'd seen it happen on film.

It was just over two weeks later when it happened for real. All the noise and bluster they'd imagined never came to pass. Only a fraction of the immediate chaos and devastation they'd envisaged actually happened. Most people simply dropped dead as if they'd just been switched off. A little noise, panic and blood first, of course, then nothing but silence. Survivors of the infection which swept around the world were few and far between. If people were looking in the wrong direction – or not looking at all – they might even have missed it. Bizarrely, that was exactly what happened to Kieran. The end of the world crept up on him and tapped him on the shoulder, and he didn't even notice.

The working day had begun like any other Tuesday. Kieran was first at the office, as usual. He'd driven in along the Pentwyn Road, enjoying the early morning sun, hoping it would last until home-time. Autumn was coming, and winter would be here soon after that. Too soon. Short days and long nights. Winter could be a bind in this job. The research and development workspaces were, by necessity, large, windowless, soulless places. Kieran hated how he'd often arrive at work in the dark on a winter morning, then not leave again until gone five when it would be pitch-black outside. Some days he didn't get to see any daylight at all. It made him feel like a bloody vampire.

But it wasn't the lack of light which was bothering him this morning, it was the heat. He couldn't understand why people did it: one cool day – not even a *cold* day, mind – and they'd crank up the heating to furnace-like levels, then go home without bothering to turn it back down. They'd all deny doing it if he asked them, of course. They weren't bothered because by the time they'd all dragged themselves into work, he'd have sorted the temperature again. Grumbling to himself, he adjusted the thermostat then sat down to check his emails.

It never ceased to amaze Kieran just how much crap ended up in his inbox overnight. The system filtered out and deleted the obvious rubbish, so there was a fair chance that every message which got through to his account might be important and had to be checked. He wanted to develop his own kind of spam filter: one which would detect and remove the things which really wasted his time… multiple invites to the same meetings from different people, countless requests for information he'd already provided, reports linked to projects he'd long since ceased to have any involvement with, inane conversations between people who didn't understand the difference between 'reply' and 'reply to all'… At this time of the morning everything annoyed him. He fired off an abrupt reply to an infuriating colleague from another department, suggesting that if he'd read his previous reply, he'd have found all the information he was asking for now. He paused just before he clicked 'send'. Too hasty. Too risky. He deleted his reply and rewrote it using far less confrontational language. A slanging match in front of the rest of the team was definitely not what he wanted this morning.

An error in a formula in an Excel spreadsheet kept Kieran occupied for far longer than it should have. He'd wasted the best part of half an hour before spotting a rogue comma in place of a period. He thought it frustrating that it had taken him so long to find, and also that such an inordinate delay could be caused by a single tiny mistake. Just one character out of place had prevented a whole stream of calculations from being completed. It was the same with everything he did, really. Attention to detail was of paramount importance, and there was no margin for error. That was one of the reasons he liked to get in before everyone else. The quiet gave him chance to get a head start before the room filled with other people and their constant chatter and noise. Well, usually it did, when he wasn't being distracted by stupid bloody schoolboy errors in simple spreadsheets.

The others were really late.

He couldn't remember anyone saying they were going to be in late today. They'd all left as normal last night, and no one had said anything about doing anything different this morning. Drew and Marc should definitely have been here by now. Maybe they'd got stuck in traffic? He'd have got up and looked out of one of the windows, had there been any. Leaving the office would have taken too much effort, so he returned his attention to his emails, chuntering angrily because although he'd replied to all the messages he'd received this morning, as yet no one had got back to him with responses to any of the questions he'd asked. *If I took as long as the rest of them*, he thought, *there'd be hell to pay*. He remembered back to his most recent trip to Japan, to the firm's head office. This simply wouldn't have been allowed to happen there. Everything felt like it was calculated down to the second in Japan. He'd hoped to bring back some of the Japanese work ethos with him, but his efforts hadn't gone down well. 'Look outside, lad,' one of the old hands on the production line had said to him.

'What do you see? This is Welsh Wales, man, not Toyko!'

Another fifteen minutes passed. Kieran was starting to get genuinely concerned now. His colleagues were no longer just slightly delayed, they were seriously late. And the fact it was *all* of them turned his concern into something resembling mild panic. *Am I the one who's in the wrong place? Am I supposed to be somewhere else? Was today the day of the offsite meeting?* He frantically checked and double-checked his diary. It wasn't like him to be this disorganised...

Nothing. A blank screen. No scheduled meetings.

He started to feel a little better when he remembered Drew having said something about running diagnostics first thing before the production line reached full capacity, but the temporary relief disappeared again quickly because the fact remained, everyone else had failed to show for work.

He fished his mobile from his pocket, checked for messages, then dialled Marc's number. It rang and rang, eventually switching to voicemail. Kieran cancelled before leaving a message, worried he'd sound like a nagging old woman. He tried Drew's number next. Same. No reply. He didn't like it when his routine was messed-up like this. He wasn't obsessive-compulsive or anything like that, but he did like logic and order to be maintained. As a software engineer, he'd learnt to think methodically and predict logical outcomes, and what was happening this morning just wasn't making sense. There was probably a simple, straightforward explanation for all of this, but he couldn't find it. Maybe there'd been an accident since he'd arrived? Any snarl up on the A48 would inevitably impact the traffic trying to get onto the business estate.

Kieran angrily shoved his chair under his desk. He headed for the door, phone still in hand. The signal strength was poor this morning. Maybe that was it? Maybe they'd been trying to call him but hadn't been able to get through? Bloody Vodafone. Sometimes he thought it would be easier to go up to the roof and shout rather than try to get through to anyone on this network. He tried a few more numbers as he walked. Mom and Dad, a couple of friends, his sister, his other half... still nothing.

Christ, it was quiet on the landing outside his office.

All the noise he'd expected to hear – the chatter from the canteen, the rumble of machinery from the production line downstairs, the hustle of people scrambling to get to their desks on time – was absent. Just the background hum of the building in its place: the low groan of the air conditioning.

Kieran soon found other people.

He walked into the canteen, then stopped in utter disbelief. *Bodies.* There were bodies everywhere. One of the canteen staff was slumped against the wall behind her till, face pressed against the plaster, blood dribbling down her chin and onto her white apron, dripping on her name badge. A little further ahead was one of the guys from the production line. It took Kieran a few seconds to recognise him, so agonised was the expression on his lifeless face. Blood pooled around his mouth which hung open in a never-ending scream. At a table nearby sat one of the HR managers, slumped forward in a chair surrounded by the corpses of several visitors. They were young and smartly dressed, probably here for interviews, he thought. The last wisps of steam still snaked up from their unfinished drinks.

And there, right on the other side of the room by the window, facedown on the carpet, was Andrew.

'Drew?' Kieran said as he stood over him. He cringed, his voice seeming to echo endlessly off the walls. He said his friend's name again... still no response. Kieran knelt down and looked around, hoping someone else would come along who could explain what the hell was going on. He reached out and rested a hand on Drew's shoulder, then shook it lightly. When he didn't move, Kieran shook him again, harder this time. Then again and again before rolling his dead friend over onto his back. He could only stand to look into Drew's pallid, blood-splattered face for the briefest of moments before staggering away, reeling with shock.

What the hell happened here? What do I do?

He looked out of the window, head spinning, barely able to focus on what was going on inside the building, never mind out there. But once he looked past the factory grounds he saw that, for as far as he could see in every direction, the rest of the world appeared to have suffered the same inexplicable fate as the people here. From the streets directly below, all the way to the centre of Cardiff in the near distance, nothing moved. Dead builders littered the housing development, construction abruptly halted. The Waitrose car park was an unruly mass of crashed cars, abandoned trolleys and dead shoppers. One of the slick sales guys from the Jaguar dealership lay sprawled in a puddle, the water ruining his expensive designer suit. Birds occasionally darted across the grey sky, and the tops of the trees shook in the wind, but other than that, nothing and no one moved.

Everyone was dead. Everyone but him.

A return to the familiar gave Kieran a meagre crumb of comfort to hold onto. He cursed himself, but he didn't know what else to do. Everyone else was dead and yet there he was, sitting in front of his computer ploughing through his work as if nothing had happened. He clung desperately to distractions, working through his daily to-do list, using the banality of the most menial tasks he could find to block out the fear. He was terrified when he thought about what was waiting for him on the other side of the office door: *What if I'm next? When am I going to die?*

It felt like hours, but only a few minutes had passed before he got up from his seat again. He'd been trying to type, but his hands were shaking. His throat was dry. He picked up a water bottle he'd brought with him from home, but he could barely hold it steady enough to drink.

I can't just sit here like this.

He had to do something. He left the office and returned to the canteen where he helped himself to a coffee from one of the vending machines. He stood on the far side of the room and stared at Drew from a distance, forcing down the hot drink so fast he scalded himself. The pain and bitter taste was welcome. It made him feel alive and helped counteract the bizarre thoughts now filling his mind: *What if it's me? What if I'm the one who's dead?* It was marginally easier to believe he'd passed away and found himself stuck in a real-life Twilight Zone episode, than to have to accept that everyone else had died just like that, without any immediately obvious reason. How could he have not noticed the world ending?

The light, open space of the canteen was reassuring. He sat at an empty table a few seats down from the dead manager and his equally lifeless guests. He tried constantly to contact the people who mattered with his mobile. When they didn't answer, he tried anyone else he could think of. He worked his way through his entire address book, then picked up Drew's phone from where it had fallen near to his corpse, and tried all his contacts too. Nothing. No one.

It was then that he remembered the drunken conversation from the club the other week. It felt perverse to now be trying to remember what was said to help him stay alive. Kieran had been trying to pluck up courage to go home, but hadn't Marc said something about the office being an ideal place to hide? He'd talked about getting food from the supermarket and maybe taking a car. All those things could wait, Kieran decided. He had enough food here in the canteen to last a while, and his own car was in the car park, visible from the canteen window. He still had a gnawing feeling in the pit of his stomach that he should try and get back, but he placated himself by constantly repeating Marc's drunken assurances that this was a good place to hide.

On autopilot, Kieran finished his drink then walked across the canteen and switched on the TV mounted on the wall. The BBC news channel was silent. He felt around the outside of the TV's housing for control buttons and changed channel. He clicked up again and again until he'd worked his way back around to the start. No one was broadcasting. Some stations showed nothing at all, others a mix of motionless studios, dead presenters and slumped audiences; real-time freeze-frames.

Face it, he told himself, *it's actually happened. You're the only one left.*

The day felt never-ending, the night even more so. All the comfort and familiarity of the office disappeared along with the light. The electricity had failed in this part of town late into the evening, but he'd remained where he was, sitting under his desk like a kid hiding under his bed, occasionally drifting off to sleep for a few seconds at a time, only to jolt back into reality and scare himself stupid over nothing. No matter how dark and unsettling it was, at least here in the office he was alone. The thought of being outside this room with *them* – his dead colleagues and friends, the unknown thousands beyond – was unbearable.

He checked his phone regularly. The signal was no better, and still no one called or sent messages. As the hours crawled by he felt increasing guilt, sitting here like a coward while his parents and his partner and everyone else he cared about was out there. But what else was he supposed to do? The probability (increasingly the *certainty*) was that they were all dead. He couldn't do anything for them. Dad would most probably be on the golf course somewhere. Mom... well she could be anywhere. Kieran pulled his knees up to his chest and sobbed himself to sleep.

It was morning but still dark when he finally left the office. He could stand being there no more. He put on his coat and filled his pockets with food from the canteen, then went outside—

—and almost immediately turned back again. Despite being surrounded by corpses inside, he'd been sheltered from the reality of the illogical nightmare. He could feel the wind and rain on his face, a constant reminder that he was no longer hiding behind walls, windows and doors. Now he felt vulnerable; naked and exposed. It was what he *couldn't* see or hear which unnerved him most of all. There was no traffic noise; no engines, horns or brakes. No people moving or talking. Everything was in the exact same place it had been yesterday. He looked back up at the canteen window, wondering whether Marc had been right and if he'd made a mistake coming out. Too late now. He couldn't go back inside... From the outside looking in, his work building now looked like a tomb.

The silence was deafening. It felt like a deadweight, pressing down on him, getting heavier by the minute. He made straight for his car: a silver Ford Fiesta Zetec. It was nothing special, but right now it felt priceless. The smell of its upholstery, the feel of the steering wheel in his hands, the noise the door made when he shut it... all reassuringly familiar. He started the engine and turned up the stereo to cancel out the quiet of the last twenty-four hours.

He pulled out of the car park and onto the road, the familiar journey home already anything but. Progress was slow. It had been the height of rush hour yesterday when it – whatever *it* had been – happened, and every stretch of road now was clogged with mile after mile of stationary traffic. From time to time he was able to use hard shoulders, bus lanes and pavements to build up a head of speed, only to suddenly have to brake again to avoid crashed cars and other obstructions. He drove around bodies with care and concentration. Even after all that had happened, the thought of wilfully causing any further damage to these poor people was abhorrent.

Home.

He finally reached the front door of his house, but paused before going in. A deep breath, one last look over his shoulder at the devastated world, then he went inside. There was no one else there: he could tell from the way the alarm had been set and from the gaps on the pegs where Mom and Dad's coats would have been hanging. The silence inside his home was as ominous as the lack of noise outside, but fractionally less intimidating. At least for now, this place still felt like it used to.

Another endless night followed; hours spent staring into space, looking for answers he was beginning to think he'd never find, imagining the fates of the people he loved and trying to block out the pain they must have felt when they'd died, trying to suppress his guilt at not going out and looking for them. The conversation from the nightclub still rattled around and around in his head. All that talk of trying to survive, of finding weapons and hoarding supplies. *Fucking idiots*, he cursed. They'd talked about the end of the world like it would be an adventure. Well, he was here to tell them it wasn't. It most definitely wasn't. It was a living hell. He was almost beginning to envy the dead. At least for them the torment was over.

But as the hours progressed, he forced himself to get a grip. The initial shock was beginning to fade – whether or not it would ever completely disappear, he wasn't sure – but he was, gradually, starting to think more clearly again. He was going to need food and, whether he liked it or not, he was going to have to think about his long-term survival. Either that, or maybe he should just end it all now. *Fuck no*, he thought. That idea didn't bear thinking about, not even for a second.

When daylight came, he got up (he'd fallen asleep fully clothed, lying on his bed), then made himself eat and drink something. His plan this morning was simple: get out, find enough food to fill the car, then get back. If it went well, he thought he'd maybe try something else tomorrow. Perhaps he'd drive a little further and start looking for other survivors, because he couldn't be the only one left alive, could he?

He drove along the roads he'd followed yesterday, knowing they were passable. His route was harder to stick to than he'd expected, because everything looked different driving in the opposite direction. A bike which had skidded out from under its dying driver had been easy to spot yesterday. Travelling the other way, however, Kieran almost didn't see it until it was too late. He slammed on his brakes and stopped just short of driving over the driver's outstretched arm.

Where to go? The Waitrose near to work was an option, but there were nearer stores. He aimed for the Sainsburys near Thornhill, thinking that if things got difficult he could always disappear into the Pendragon pub next door and drink away his fear. He took a wrong turn in the chaos, the abhorrent sights all around distracting him. There was a car flipped over onto its roof, the bodies of its dead passengers trapped inside in full view, their faces smashed up against the broken glass. Every new face he saw made him think about the people he'd loved and lost; the people who mattered who'd be out here somewhere like this. Helpless. *Dead.* The thought of Dad out on the golf course really hit him hard and he began to sob. Was he as useless and selfish as he now felt for having abandoned them all? But he kept asking himself, what could he have done…?

With his mind unfocused and tears in his eyes, he clipped the wing of another wreck then reacted too slowly and hit the kerb. He then overcompensated and lost his grip on the steering wheel. His beloved Fiesta ploughed into a low brick wall outside a house, the force of the unexpected impact throwing him forward. His face thumped against the steering wheel, and he felt his left eye immediately beginning to swell.

He tried to reverse out of the rubble, but it was no good. He'd beached the car chassis on what was left of the wall. Dazed, he got out and began to walk back home, his feet leaden, the effort almost too much.

He felt more vulnerable than ever. His head was thumping, and he could taste blood in his mouth from a split lip, and it was beginning to piss down with rain. He needed to get home – the only place left –

but he wasn't even sure where he was anymore. He'd probably driven along this road a hundred times before, but he'd never walked along it and even if he had, the devastation had rendered it unrecognisable today. As he walked, hoping he was moving in the right direction, but not completely sure, he thought back to that night in Oceana with Duncan, Marc and Drew again. He remembered their conversation, so trivial and unimportant at the time but now, in the cold light of this post-Armageddon day, he wished he'd listened closer. He wished he'd paid more attention and taken notes because, although half-drunk, his friends had clearly had enough about them to have been instinctively able to survive. But him… well he was a fucking disappointment to himself. The entire world at his feet, anything he wanted within reach, and yet here he was, soaked through and crying like a baby, limping back to hide away in his empty house. The harder he tried to survive, it seemed, the worse things got.

When Kieran got up next morning, there was a woman in the street in front of his house. He'd dragged himself out of bed feeling no better than when he'd crawled under the duvet last night, but now, suddenly and wholly unexpectedly, things had changed. He ran downstairs, pulling on his dirty clothes as he tripped down the steps, checking from every window he passed that she was still there, desperate not to let her out of his sight. He ran outside, ignoring the cold and the gravel digging into the soles of his feet. Without stopping to consider the improbability of it all, or wondering why she hadn't reacted to his noise and bluster, he grabbed the woman's arm and turned her around. Her flesh was bare, and he immediately thought she felt unnaturally cold. Her face was vacant and inexpressive, and his legs weakened with nerves. The way she looked through him but not at him, the way she almost tripped over her own feet as she turned, the way she failed to acknowledge him at all… He let go and she began to traipse away, barely lifting her feet off the ground as she shuffled down the street, now moving back in the direction from which she'd originally come. She was dead…

And then Kieran saw more of them. Many, many more of them. The nearest tripped ever-closer, its mouth hanging open as if stuck mid-scream. Temporarily paralyzed with fright, at the last second he stepped out of the way and the creature dragged itself past. Then another, coming from a different direction this time, but again seeming to be moving directly towards him. Kieran ran back to the house, not knowing what else to do. He locked the door, then ran into the front room and peered around the corner, watching that person – that *thing* – coming towards his home. It crashed into the window then fell back and collapsed in a heap on the drive before picking itself up, agonisingly slowly, and walking away. No matter how impossible it seemed, the things swarming in the street outside his house today were dead.

He sank to the floor and covered his head. He didn't know how much more of this he could take.

Kieran didn't move for hours. He didn't dare. Didn't even get up to look out of the window. He knew what was coming next. He'd seen more than enough horror films over the years. Those damn things would gravitate around his house, eventually flushing him out and ripping him apart. He'd watched countless scenes of desperate survivors fighting with each other in their inadequately fortified shelters, dead arms reaching in through the gaps between the planks they'd hurriedly nailed across windows and doors. Damn. All that talk the other week about surviving and lording it up over the rest of the world, and what had he done? Drew, Duncan and Marc had talked about mankind's imagined downfall as if it would be some incredible, liberating event, but instead of opening up the rest of the world to him, everything had become infinitely more restricted. He couldn't get those damn zombie movie survivors out of his mind... something had always bothered him before, and now it positively terrified him. Those people almost never made it to the end of the film alive. When they barricaded themselves in, it was like they were giving up; no longer running, resigning themselves to their inevitable deaths at the vicious hands of the living dead.

But something happened as he lay there, sobbing. In the quiet emptiness, he thought back over the last few days of hell, and realised how pathetic he must have looked. He was cold, scared, hungry and dirty. He'd always taken pride in his appearance, but he'd let himself go since the world had fallen apart, and he couldn't understand why.

Was it shock? Grief? Sheer fucking laziness? He thought about what his friends had said in the club that night, how they'd made excited plans for Armageddon together. And here he was, with all the chances they'd foolishly craved, ready and waiting for him. He thought about his family, and how he'd abandoned them – wherever they were – because he'd been too afraid of finding them.

Fuck it.

It's not too late.

Was he really going to allow himself to go out like this, with the most miserable of whimpers rather than a bang? He was in an incredible position – incredible yet terrifying – and there had to be more he could do than this.

Kieran cursed himself, stood up and brushed himself down. He checked himself in the mirror, wiped his eyes, sorted out his hair, then stared at his reflection.

Last chance, mate, he said to himself. *Make or break.*

The terrified survivors hiding in the ruins of Cheetham Castle ran to the gate when they heard the engine outside. The smoke from their bonfire must have worked. Shirley was too afraid to go out, but Melanie had had enough of the other woman's timidity and wittering.

'Get out of the way, you silly cow.'

'But you can't go out there. Please, Mel, please don't open the gates. They'll see us. They'll get in…'

'That's what I'm counting on.'

She shook Shirley off and pulled the heavy gate open just enough so she could slip through the gap. She ran down the track, waving her arms and screaming, desperate to be seen before the truck disappeared. Some of the dead which had gathered at the bottom of the rise now began to climb towards her, moving painfully slowly but with inexorable intent. Others moved towards the approaching truck, sniffing the air like animals, oblivious to the danger.

'Melanie!' Shirley yelled, before hiding again, terrified the bodies would see her too. Mel ignored her noise and kept running, pushing one corpse out of the way and side-stepping another. It might have been her nerves playing tricks, but they seemed a little quicker than last time she was out here, more determined.

Another burst and she was through the bulk of them. She stopped in the middle of the road and waved down the driver of the vehicle now hurtling her way at a terrifying speed. She could see its head-lamps rapidly increasing in size, could hear the roar of its engine getting louder and louder by the second. Christ, what was she doing? She hadn't intended playing a game of chicken with almost the only other living human being she'd seen since this nightmare had begun.

She could see the driver now, his face screwed up with concentration, eyes flitting from side to side, trying to anticipate the random movements of swarms of impossibly mobile corpses all around him.

'Stop you fucking idiot!' she screamed.

At the last moment she dived to one side, a trio of lethargic corpses cushioning her fall. She was faintly aware of the sound of screeching brakes somewhere behind her, but she was so focused on getting back up the hill and escaping the clumsy swipes of countless dead hands that she didn't see the truck until it thundered past her. She watched as Shirley hauled the gate fully open to let the driver through.

By the time Mel had reached the top of the climb and was safely inside the castle grounds again, the truck had stopped and the driver was out. He was a tall, relatively thin man who looked remarkably well groomed for the end of the world. He'd certainly had more chance to scrub himself up than she had.

'You could have given me a lift,' she yelled at him, furious but relieved.

'You're lucky I didn't run you down. Bloody hell, what were you thinking, standing in the middle of the road like that? You got a death wish?'

She didn't bother answering. Instead she just looked him up and down, then peered into the back of his truck which was piled high with supplies. She noticed he carried a shot gun, though she didn't like to think where he'd got it.

'So who are you?'

He put down his weapon and visibly relaxed. For a moment he seemed overcome, so much so that it was impossible for him to speak. He gazed around at his ancient, though still substantial, surroundings, and nodded approvingly. 'I'm Kieran Cope,' he said. 'I've had a fucker of a time getting here, wherever here is.'

'Where've you been until now, Kieran?' Shirley asked.

'Lost,' he answered, 'but I think I know where I'm going now. I've got my gun and my supplies, and this place looks as good as any. Don't know about you two ladies, but I plan on surviving as long as I can.'

INNOCENCE

It was fun to begin with; a game, almost an adventure. But now he's had enough. He doesn't like being on his own anymore. He's hungry, he's lonely and he's scared. He wants everything back to how it used to be.

Dean McFarlane is seven years old.

The day before yesterday, as they were walking to school, Dean's mother dropped dead.

'Dean,' Mom said, sighing, 'you've only been back at school for a couple of days, so how comes you've got yourself in trouble with the teacher already?'

'She don't like me,' he said as he followed her at speed, late for school. He'd been dragging his feet all morning. Even though she was heavily pregnant, Dean's mom marched along at twice his pace. 'She picks on me,' he whined. 'She lets Gary and them lot get away with anything. I never done nothing and she blames me when…'

'What do you mean, you never done nothing? What kind of a way to talk is that? If you never done nothing, then you must have done something…?'

Dean looked at her and screwed up his face. What was she on about now? She didn't believe him, did she? Anyway, he decided, he didn't care what she said because he knew Miss Jinks was picking on him and he knew that he was going to get Gary Saunders back at lunchtime or afternoon break because he'd got him into trouble yesterday afternoon and he'd had to see the headteacher and…

'When I tell your father what you've been up to,' Mrs McFarlane warned, 'he'll kick your backside. You know what he's like, he just won't stand for this kind of behaviour. I suggest that you…'

Mrs McFarlane stopped talking suddenly, then stopped walking. She was in the middle of the pavement, pulling that kind of puzzled, almost angry face that she pulled when she was out shopping with him and she couldn't remember what she needed, or when she didn't know which way to go, or when Dean's baby brother growing

A further two days have passed since Amy Steadman's corpse began to re-animate. It is now five days since first infection and death.

Amy has continued to move around her immediate surroundings. Until now her movements have been automatic and spontaneous and any changes in direction have occurred purely as a result of the corpse reaching a physical obstruction and being unable to keep moving forward. Amy's corpse is little more than an empty collection of bones, rotting tissue and dead flesh. At this stage she does not have any conscious control or decision making capabilities.

Although animated, Amy remains oblivious to her surroundings and to her increasing physical limitations. Her body is continuing to decay and the lack of a functioning circulatory system is beginning to cause movement problems. Gravity has steadily pulled the contents of her abdomen downwards. Blood has swollen her hands and feet and her bowels are gradually evacuating involuntarily. Her face, already tinged with the blue-green hue of decay, is otherwise drained of colour.

Until now Amy's body's nervous system has been operating at a massively reduced level. Her corpse is oblivious to changes in its surroundings such as temperature, humidity and light levels. Several hours ago her clothing became snagged and torn after becoming tangled up in the wheels of an upturned shopping trolley. Her once smart black skirt is now just a rag wrapped around her right foot. She has also lost one of her shoes which causes her already awkward gait to become even more pronounced and unsteady.

Amy does not respire, nor does she have any need to eat or drink or seek shelter or protection. Her eyes and ears operate at a massively reduced level. She can see and hear, although she can no longer interpret and understand the information she absorbs. As the rest of her body continues to deteriorate, however, the part of the brain least affected by the infection is continuing to re-establish itself, albeit at a desperately slow rate.

Less than three hundred metres away from Amy's present location, the front of another building has collapsed. Initially damaged by a truck which plunged off an elevated section of road when its driver became infected and died, the weakened structure has now given way and caved in on itself, producing huge amounts of dust and substantial vibrations and noise. Amy Steadman, although not understanding what the disturbance is, has instinctively altered direction and is beginning to move towards it.

It is just before eight o'clock in the morning and the building where Amy died has been in almost total darkness for more than twelve hours. Almost all of the visible light comes from the front of the building, and Amy is now moving towards it. She does not realise that this is an exit, but she is attracted by the brightness and also the fact that the recent noise and vibrations caused by the building collapse emanated from that general direction. Three of the four main doors are blocked, one is wedged open. Still drawn to the brightness outside, instead of turning and moving away when she reaches the glass, Amy now shuffles clumsily from side to side until she finally finds the single open door and practically falls through the gap.

Amy is ignorant to the sudden change in her surroundings. It is noticeably cooler outside and it has been raining steadily for the last two hours. A strong westerly wind is gusting across the front of the building that she has just emerged from, and the sudden strength of the wind is sufficient to knock the comparatively weak body off course. The cloud of dust which was thrown up by the collapse of the second building is steadily being washed down by the rain, covering everything in a light layer of grey dirt and mud. The noise and vibrations have faded now and there remains no noticeable indication of the previous disturbance. Without any obvious visual or auditory distractions, Amy Steadman's corpse begins to move randomly again, shuffling slowly forward until it can go no further, then changing direction and moving away again.

Several hours later, and Amy's corpse has travelled more than half a mile from the building where she died. The increased light levels outside have enabled her to see more. Previously only able to distinguish obvious movements and the stark contrast between light and dark, she is now able to make out a finer level of detail. There are other bodies nearby. Amy is now able to detect their movements from a distance of around ten metres away.

As a result of the immense devastation caused by the infection, the ground outside is littered with debris and human remains. The streets are uneven and Amy frequently loses her footing and falls, her slow reactions preventing her from taking any corrective action until it is too late. As the day has worn on, however, she has become able to move with slightly more freedom and control.

The environment through which Amy is now walking is almost completely silent. She has reached a straight section of road which leads out of town and she has now been moving in the same general direction for some time. There are numerous crashed cars and other vehicles nearby. Just ahead, straddling half of the width of the carriageway, is a family-sized estate car containing three corpses. In the back is a dead child, in the driver's seat its dead mother. The third corpse – that of an overweight male passenger in his late thirties – moves continually but is held in its seat by a safety belt. In the box-shaped boot of the car, trapped behind a protective wire-mesh grille, is a dog. It has no means of escape and is becoming increasingly angry and scared. For some time the starving animal has been quiet but the movement from the male body in the front passenger seat of the car and the close proximity of another random corpse outside has excited it again. It has begun to bark and howl and, in the empty silence, its cries can be heard from a considerable distance away.

Twenty minutes, and already three more bodies have reached the car. They crowd around it, attracted by the dog's noise, leaning against the windows and occasionally banging their fists against the glass. Their appearance and noise causes the dog to become even more agitated. Amy Steadman is now aware of the disturbance and is moving towards it. She reaches the car and joins the group of cadavers.

This section of road is relatively inaccessible by foot. Nevertheless, in the absence of any other distraction, within an hour the car has been surrounded by another seventeen corpses. By next morning Amy Steadman is just one corpse among a crowd of almost two hundred which have gravitated around the car.

BEGINNING TO DISINTEGRATE
Part ii

'Food and drink, mate, that's all we need,' Harte said to Hollis who was driving the van, trying to see a way through the bodies criss-crossing the road ahead of them. In the back, Jas did what he could to keep his motorbike steady. He wished he'd been out there riding it, but the roads today were too busy. That was a fucking joke: everyone else was dead, but the roads were too busy... He'd have probably been okay, but he'd have left the van for dust. Jas didn't want that. He didn't want to be without these two blokes. Right now they were all he had left.

'Food and drink might be all you need, Harte, but some of us want more than that,' Hollis said. 'We need to find a decent place to hole-up. Isn't that right, Jas.'

'Whatever,' he mumbled, disinterested. He gazed out of the window, looking up into the sky, not down at the dead, and counted the number of lampposts they passed. It was the best way of distracting himself he'd found so far. Counting lampposts stopped him thinking about everything he'd lost. Stopped him thinking about his family.

Two thousand, six hundred and eight... two thousand, six hundred and nine...

The van stopped unexpectedly. 'What's wrong?' Jas asked, immediately concerned, feeling his stomach knot with nerves.

'Nothing's wrong,' Harte said. 'Don't you listen? Food and drink. We're stopping here for a minute to stock up, okay?'

Jas looked around, sussing out their location. It seemed as good as place as any. They were in the car park of one of those small, metro-style supermarkets, with only a couple of corpses for company. A low fence ran around the perimeter of the car park, just tall enough to keep out most of the dead. A crashed car blocked the entrance, and Hollis had stopped the van right across the exit.

The three men got out. A corpse collided with the side of the van, startling them. Jas shoved it over the barrier and watched as it picked itself up and tried unsuccessfully to get over again.

The morning was dry but cool. A brisk wind blew in from the

inside her started to kick. Dean carried on a little further but then stopped and turned back when he realised she still wasn't moving. She was standing in the same spot, rubbing at the side of her neck. She looked in pain.

'Mom? What's the matter?'

Mrs McFarlane looked down at her son but didn't say anything. She couldn't. She tried not to let him see, but the sudden pain in her throat was rapidly worsening, taking hold. Her eyes bulged with searing agony and she dropped her shopping bag. Dean immediately began collecting up her spilled belongings, still looking anxiously into her face.

'Dean, I can't…' she said, her voice fading to a whisper. 'My throat's…'

She dropped to her knees directly in front of her son and he jumped with surprise. Her eyes now level with his, she began to retch and gag violently. The inside of her throat became swollen, and blood began trickling from lesions at the back of her mouth. She hung her head forward and dribbled a long, sticky string of bloody saliva onto the pavement, spitting up on the corner of one of Dean's shoes.

'Mom…' he whined, jumping back with panic. He looked around for help but he couldn't see anyone else nearby. If he could just find another grown-up who could help… He looked for Mrs Campbell who lived three doors down at number seventeen – she always seemed to be looking out of her living room window. Maybe she'd come out to help him and—

Clutching her stomach in agony, Mrs McFarlane let out a strangled cry of pain then rolled onto her back, her body convulsing. Now sobbing, Dean crouched down next to her and held her shoulders, trying to hold her steady and stop her throwing herself about. He wished he knew what to do, but he'd never learnt about this kind of thing at school or at cubs. He was scared she was going to hurt herself or the baby. Her eyes were wide open and she stared at him with an expression on her face which frightened him more than anything he'd ever seen before.

And then she stopped.

Dean's mom lay motionless on the ground, her eyes staring into space and her mouth hanging wide open, a trail of dark blood running down her cheek.

Dean shoved her and shook her and screamed at her but she wouldn't wake up.

I knew straightaway that she'd died because I kept shouting at her to wake up but she wouldn't move. I tried to clean up some of the blood on her face with tissues out of her handbag but that just made things worse and got her in even more of a mess. She'd got blood in her hair and in one of her ears and I couldn't get that out either.

Granddad Johnson told me once about the time he saved a man's life when he'd been an accident. He said you have to make sure the person who's hurt is breathing before you do anything else, and he showed me how to do it. He said you could feel for a thing like a little heartbeat on their wrist or their neck, or you could just listen to them breathing. I couldn't remember exactly where to hold Mom's wrist so I just listened to her instead. I put my ear right next to her mouth and listened and listened and listened but I couldn't hear anything. Everything else was quiet but I couldn't hear a sound.

I kept looking for someone to help me but there was no one, and I remembered Granddad saying you had to get the person you're looking after to a hospital quickly by phoning for an ambulance. We learnt that at school last year as well and I knew what to do. I got Mom's mobile out of her pocket and dialled 999 like I'd been shown but no one answered. That really scared me because my teacher and Granddad both said someone would always answer 999, no matter what. They've got loads of people to answer the phones there so everyone can always get through.

I was scared that Mom was going to get cold. I tried to move her closer to the house but she was too heavy. I dragged her a little way, but not that far because I didn't want to mess her clothes up or hurt the baby. I got the keys from her coat pocket and ran back to the house. It took me ages to get inside because I couldn't get the right key at first. When I got in I took one of the blankets from the drawer under Mom and Dad's bed and one of her pillows. I went back out and covered Mom up and put the pillow under her head. I was scared that something was going to happen to the baby. I put my hands under the blanket and felt Mom's tummy for ages but I couldn't feel a couple more metres, almost to the edge of their drive, but that was all. As the darkness drew in again he went back indoors. The lights weren't working when he got inside, and neither was anything else electric.

I couldn't help it. I didn't mean to do it, I got scared and it just happened. Mom's going to be mad at me.

I'd been sitting outside with her for ages but I came back in when it started to get dark. When I got inside the house it was all quiet and empty again and I got really scared. I could hear loads of noises and I knew what they all were but they still scared me. There was dripping water coming from the freezer in the kitchen and I could hear the blind at the window in Mom and Dad's room blowing in the wind, making a tapping noise. And every so often the wind made the letter box in the front door flap. Mom's been nagging at Dad for ages to get it fixed but he hasn't had time. It sounded like someone coming to the house, and the first few times it happened I ran to the door because I thought it was going to be Mom or Dad. I got really upset when there was no one there.

I didn't want to go upstairs. I wanted to hide away out of sight so I crawled under the dining room table. I only came out a couple of times, first to get some more food from the kitchen and then to try and find my torch. I got myself another packet of crisps and the last bar of chocolate from the cupboard. I wanted some bread and butter but I must have left the bread open because it had gone all hard and it tasted horrible. All of the lemonade and cans of Coke had gone. I had to drink the orange juice I don't like but I made it too strong and it made me feel a bit sick. I was really thirsty though so I kept drinking it.

It didn't feel like home anymore. Everything felt different without Mom and Dad, really strange, and it was getting colder and colder. I still didn't want to go upstairs so I put my coat back on and the dirty school jumper that I'd thrown downstairs for Mom to wash. Thinking about Mom and Dad made me upset again. I was starting to think I was never going to see Dad again. I was glad I'd missed two days of school, but I'd rather have gone and had everything back how it used to be.

I've made a real mess in here now. Mom and Dad are going to be mad at me. The dark frightens me so I tried to light the big yellow candle that Mom keeps on the sideboard. I took it under the table and used a match from the box out of the kitchen. Anyway, I lit the candle and I must have had it too close to the tablecloth because it started burning. It burned really, really quick. I got out from under the table and used the rest of the orange juice to put out the fire. I tried to pull the tablecloth off but I didn't know there were plates and things still on it and they fell on the carpet and some of them smashed. That made me upset again because the noise made me jump and because I knew that Mom would be cross that I'd broken her plates. She always got cross if I broke a plate or a dish or a cup. I didn't want to move because I was scared I might cut myself on some of the broken pieces.

I think I fell asleep. When I woke up I was all wet. I thought it was just orange juice at first but then I realised it was all over my trousers and all over the floor and I knew I'd wet myself. I haven't wet myself since I was four. It was all over the carpet and I tried to clean it up with the burnt tablecloth but all that did was make things worse. My trousers were soaked so I took them off. I put my coat over me and tried to keep warm but I couldn't stop shivering.

Exhausted, and suffering from shock and mild exposure, Dean slept intermittently for a further few hours. The morning finally arrived, bringing with it some welcome light and warmth. He went upstairs and got himself some clean clothes. He smelled from the accident he'd had in the night. He tried to wash but the water was too cold. He used some of Dad's deodorant spray to cover up the smell.

Dean was finding it harder and harder to be upstairs on his own. Dad had recently decorated the spare room as a nursery, ready for the birth of Dean's baby brother. He'd painted teddy bears and cartoon characters on the walls and there were lots of stuffed toys in there too. When Dean walked past the open nursery door he felt like the toys' eyes were moving, watching him as he crept around the house, doing things he shouldn't.

While Dean was up in his bedroom getting changed, he noticed that his mom had gone. For a second he was excited and relieved and he ran back downstairs to find her, expecting that she'd be back indoors, cleaning up the mess he'd made or just sitting on the sofa waiting for him. When he found that she wasn't there he slumped against the wall at the bottom of the stairs and began to sob. Why had she left him? Why hadn't she come back to the house? This sudden rejection hurt more than anything else. He knew he had to go and find her.

Dean grabbed his smelly coat from where he'd left it at the bottom of the banister and put on his trainers. He stepped out into the open, shut the door behind him, locked it (he was pretty sure he'd done it properly) and then put Mom's keys in his trouser pocket.

She hadn't taken her bag. Strange that she'd left it there in the middle of the street. And her phone too.

He picked up the phone and held it tightly. He picked up the bag as well but put it down again at the end of the road because it was quite big and heavy and because he didn't think there was anything that important in it. Mom always carried her purse and her money in her coat pocket because it was safer. Dean tucked the bag out of sight at the end of someone's drive, intending to take it back to the house later.

Where was she? Where had she gone?

Strange that there were other people moving around now. Strange that none of them seemed to see him, even when he got up close. Strange how all of their faces looked so cold and empty and how none of them answered when he asked them for help.

I think I know the way to Dad's work because Mom's taken me there on the bus loads of times when we've been to meet him in the school holidays. I'm going to try and walk there even though I know it's a long way. It's going to take ages.

I'm going to go and find Dad and then the two of us will go and find Mom.

DAY FIVE

north, bringing with it a succession of unpleasant smells, unwanted reminders of what had happened to the rest of the world: the stench of burning buildings mixed with the unmistakable odour of decay.

'Quiet, isn't it?' Hollis said, looking around. The approach of another body from across the way startled him, its leaden feet scuffing the tarmac.

'Too quiet,' Harte agreed. 'Don't think I'll ever get used to it. What I'd give for a bit of background noise, you know?'

Jas wasn't in the mood for standing around like this. He marched up to the supermarket door, but it didn't open. He peered in through the glass. 'Power's down here.'

'We knew it wouldn't last,' Harte said, using a crowbar to prise the two sides of the door apart. Once the gap was big enough, Jas slipped his hands inside and began to push in either direction, then used his stocky body to shove the door open further, holding it for the others. When they were all inside, he slid the gap shut again.

The windows were tinted, making everything appear darker than it actually was. Hollis went to take a step forward but Jas pulled him back. 'Wait.'

'What's the problem?' he asked, his voice low.

'Something's not right here.'

'Haven't you noticed, nothing's right anywhere anymore,' Harte whispered.

Jas ignored him. 'Where are the bodies? And why's it so clean?'

He was right. Every building they'd so far been into was in a far worse state than this one. The rest of the world had fallen apart early on a Tuesday morning, just as the school and working days were beginning. There would surely have been someone in a shop like this, even if it was only the staff. Harte held his crowbar ready and began to slowly advance. The other two watched him work his way along the first aisle, then turn and come back along the second.

'Smell the bleach?' he asked.

'What?' Hollis whispered.

'Some fucker's been cleaning up. The floor's still wet back there.'

'Then where are they?'

All the waiting around was making Jas nervous. 'Who gives a shit? I mean, come on... there are dead bodies walking the streets out there, and we're getting jumpy because someone's been mopping the floor? Fuck's sake.'

Harte was about to say something, to try and explain how he genuinely was unsettled by the idea there was someone left who still felt compelled to keep things clean, but Jas wasn't waiting to listen. He snatched the crowbar from him and marched deeper into the store, hesitating in front of the double-door marked 'staff only' by the side of the cashier's kiosk. He glanced back at the others, then kicked the door open and charged through.

There was no one there.

He found himself in the middle of a reasonably-sized storage area, stacked high with pallets and boxes. He looked around, eyes slowly adjusting to the low light level, then he heard something. It came from just behind him: a frantic scurrying. It was either a corpse or a fucking big rat and whichever it was, he needed to get rid of it fast. He spun around and when it moved again, he lunged for it.

But it wasn't a corpse, nor was it a rat.

Curled up in a ball behind a pallet of family-sized packs of toilet tissue, he found a little man cowering with his hands over his head. 'Don't kill me…' he whimpered. 'I'm not one of them…'

'Then who the fuck are you?'

He looked up, then straightened himself out. He took off his glasses and wiped tears from his eyes before answering. 'I'm Gordon.'

It took a couple of hours to calm Gordon down and get themselves properly set up in the supermarket. By then the large glass windows along the front and side of the building had been completely obscured by a mass of inquisitive dead bodies. They'd been drawn there by the noise, called from the shadows by the sounds of the four men shoring up their new base. They each knew the dangers of attracting the dead but were beyond caring. The food and drink they'd got here made those risks worth taking.

'We probably won't be able to stay here that long,' Hollis said, peering out from around the side of the storeroom door. 'This place is too exposed.'

'It's also pretty strong and full of food, though,' Harte reminded him.

'We'll spend the night,' Jas said. 'A few hours of quiet while we're asleep and most of these fuckers should have wandered off again.'

'You think?'

'I hope.'

Gordon peeked over the top of a plastic-wrapped mountain of baked bean and soup tins, looking like a cartoon kid in a scene from Scooby-Doo.

'You going to stick with us then, Gordon?' Harte asked him.

'If I can. If you don't mind.'

'Why should we mind? The more the merrier, I say.'

'There's fuck-all merry about this,' Jas grumbled to himself as he opened another beer.

'So how did you end up here, Gordon?' Hollis asked.

'What happened, happened,' he replied, 'and I didn't know where else to go. My house isn't far from here, but my wife's…' He cleared his throat and composed himself. 'My wife's dead and I didn't want to stay there with her. I used to call in here when I walked the dog. Seemed as good a place as any. Plenty to eat and drink. Warm enough…'

'You didn't try and find anyone else?'

'I thought about it. I tried on the first day, but I gave up pretty quick. And when those things started walking around… I didn't want to be stuck out there on my own, you know?'

'We know.'

'So I got rid of a couple of bodies, gave the place a quick clean, then made myself comfortable. What about you three? Where were you when it…?'

'Driving the van,' Hollis answered. 'I'd just got off the motorway, and thank Christ I had. I was on a bridge, waiting at a set of lights, and I watched everything below lose control where I'd just been. It was surreal, you know? One minute normal, the next, absolute bloody chaos.'

They looked to Jas to speak next, but he didn't. He left the room, heading towards the loading area at the back of the building. 'What's up with him?' Gordon asked.

'Family,' Hollis answered quickly. 'Doesn't like to talk about it. Got home and found his wife and kids dead.'

'Makes me glad I was young, free and single,' Harte said, almost managing a smile. 'I mean, all this shit is hard enough to deal with when you've only got yourself to worry about. Don't think I'd have been able to handle it if I'd lost kids. It was bad enough at work.'

Gordon looked confused. 'At work?'

'I'm a teacher,' Harte explained. He paused and corrected himself. 'I *was* a teacher. Golden Hill High School, you know it? Thank fuck lessons hadn't started, that's all I can say. I was trying to get to the staff room when I saw the first kid go down outside. It was Kevin Pearson. He was a little shit, but I could tell from the way he collapsed it was serious.'

'So what happened?'

'I went out to help him. I was one of the designated first aiders, and I was just thinking to myself that I hoped someone else was about, 'cause I didn't fancy giving mouth to mouth to Kevin and I didn't have a fucking clue what I was supposed to do. I was shitting myself. I got to him and saw all the blood around his mouth, and I knew it was bad. And I was thinking, why did it have to be Kevin Pearson? His dad was always up the school causing trouble, and I was panicking, thinking if I don't do the right thing the bastard will probably either sue me or batter me...' He stopped speaking, the memories too much momentarily. He wiped his eyes, grateful for the lack of light which kept his tears hidden. 'I knew straightaway there was nothing I could do for Kevin. I tried phoning for an ambulance, but it just kept ringing out and ringing out. I've got this habit of walking around whenever I'm on the phone, and I was doing that when I realised I was walking around more bodies. There's Iqbal. There's Fatima. There's Rachel from my Year Ten class. There's the head and another one of the management team... all of them dead.'

'So what did you do?' Gordon asked, not sure if he should.

'I checked every room of that bloody school. I opened every door and looked in every damn corner to try and find someone else alive. I was there for hours. Fucking hours. It got to the stage I was too scared to leave. Then I made myself go. When I realised how big and how bad this really was, I made myself walk. I only made it as far as the pub. The power was still on, so I got myself comfortable and started drinking. I'd still have been there if it hadn't been for Hollis.'

'I had the same idea,' Hollis explained, 'and I picked the same pub. When I saw the light on in the window, I figured I'd found myself a drinking partner. We drank a shit-load that night, didn't we?'

'Don't remind me,' Harte said, grimacing. 'Still makes me feel sick just thinking about it.'

'Better to be pissed than to have to face up to what was happening outside, we figured.'

'You should have seen the state of them when I turned up,' Jas said, returning to the others.

'You weren't much better yourself,' Harte said.

'Granted.'

The conversation faltered, each man looking back and wishing they hadn't. The memories were too raw. And when the pain of remembering subsided, it was replaced by the fear and uncertainty of looking ahead. As horrific as each day had been, at least they were over now. But in the morning, the nightmare would start over again.

'This is stupid,' Hollis said suddenly.

'What is?'

'Sitting around like this. We need to get ourselves sorted.'

'How?' Gordon asked. 'What's to sort?'

'There are four of us now... who knows how many more people are out there?'

'What are you suggesting?' Jas asked. 'Drive around looking for survivors?'

'Maybe we should?'

'We should get a fucking ice cream van,' Harte suggested. 'Play a fucking tune.'

'I'm serious,' Hollis said, and from the tone of his voice it was clear that he was. 'We need to stop pissing around and get ourselves sorted out. We need to find somewhere we'll be safe and where those fucking things outside won't be able to get anywhere near us. Somewhere other survivors will be able to see us.'

'So you want to hide *and* stick your arse in the air at the same time?' Jas asked.

'If that's what it takes. We're getting like animals in a zoo in this place. All I know is I don't want to end my days this way. I'm not ready to give up just yet.'

DUCK AND COVER

Councillor Ray Cox had never asked for this level of responsibility. He worked in local government purely for the social status and financial implications, not any other reason. Overpaid and underworked, he'd sat in the shadows at the back of the council chambers for years, doing all he could not to be noticed, except when it was in his interest to be seen and heard. It was a sad indictment of the apathy of his constituents that he had been elected, then re-elected, without actually having done very much for them at all. It had been different to begin with, of course. In the early days he'd tried to make an impression, to be somebody. But the novelty of office had quickly worn off. Ray's priorities changed and his prime concerns became lining his own pockets and claiming back as much food, entertainment and travel costs as he could. Serving the community had long been forgotten; never completely ignored, but usually conveniently overlooked and put to one side. In the space of a single devastating day, however, everything in Ray's world was turned on its head.

Working with the council leaders had stood Ray in good stead, both financially and on a personal level. He'd made a few very public mistakes a couple of years back, getting himself mixed up in an ill-considered and wholly inappropriate (borderline illegal) business deal. His friends in high places had seen him okay. They found him a modest little office at the far end of a particularly long corridor and gave him responsibility for the borough's tennis courts and football pitches and various other public amenities which tended on the whole to pretty much look after themselves. They had enough of their people working around him to keep him out of trouble and to ensure he made the decisions they wanted him to. All things considered, Ray Cox was pretty happy with the way things had turned out.

Full council meetings tended to be long, drawn out affairs which frequently degenerated into tedious, overblown debates about the most trivial of issues. He'd sat there for hour upon hour before now listening to arguments for and against the politically-correct renaming of school *blackboards* to *chalkboards*, whether pavements should be tarmacked or block-paved, and whether or not the threadbare chairs in the council chambers should be reupholstered with dark blue or light purple material. Ray switched off whilst these pointless debates raged, not even bothering to listen, often deciding his vote on the toss of a coin. He never contributed to the discussions and it was hard to hide his disinterest. He'd always felt the same about the Emergency Planning Committee too, although, of course, he'd pricked up his ears and listened intently when they'd briefed the councillors on what they should do in the event of an emergency. He'd even found a reason to go down and check out the bunker on more than one occasion, just to be sure he knew where he was going. The committee – or EPC as they were known – were the butt of many private jokes and whispers: a group of fairly senior council members whose role it was to plan how the Borough should be run if the unthinkable were ever to happen.

Ray had initially thought the EPC an unnecessary waste of time and money. He just couldn't see the point of it, saying 'we'll all go together when we go' whenever anyone asked him what he thought. The truth of the matter was the council did a pretty bloody poor job of running things at the best of times, so how the hell would it cope in the event of a nuclear or chemical attack or similar? And anyway, the Cold War was over, and despite the increased number of terrorist attacks around the world recently, such things never seemed likely here in Taychester. The borough was hardly of global importance. Listening to the EPC discussing the rationing of food, decontamination of the population, the disposal of mass fatalities and the like had seemed pointless and not a little surreal. If the world did come to an end, he thought, then the population would be buggered whatever happened, and no amount of council diplomacy and planning would help. Whenever he thought about the subject he couldn't help remembering an old American public information film he'd seen again recently on TV. *Duck and Cover*, it was called. In the film a cartoon turtle walked happily though a cartoon forest, whistling a tune, only to have to hide away and cower safely in its shell when a nearby cartoon atomic bomb exploded. What was the point telling school children to get under their desks in the event of a nuclear strike? As far as Ray was aware very few materials had been discovered that could withstand the pressure, heat and after-effects of a thermonuclear explosion, and he was pretty sure that if such materials did exist, the wood that school desks in Taychester were made from wasn't one of them. And even if the kids managed to survive the blast, what was the point? What would be left? Ray had always believed it would be better to be right under the first bomb. *Duck and Cover* was an absolute bloody joke as far as he was concerned, as was the Taychester Borough Council EPC and its underground bunker. If it ever did happen, he'd want to go quickly and painlessly. He didn't relish the thought of being around to pick up the pieces afterwards. There'd be one hell of a mess for the council to sort out...

Well now it had happened, and it was nothing like anyone had expected. The world had ended yesterday morning and now, sitting alone underground in the semi-darkness of the council bunker, Ray struggled to make sense of it all.

Tuesday had begun normally enough. After taking a cup of tea up to Marcia in bed, he'd left home at the usual time and had driven across town to the council house. He'd driven down the ramp into the car park below the main building and it was there his nightmare had begun. He was reversing into his usual space when he glimpsed movement behind him in his wing mirror. Thomas Jones, one of the finance directors, had collapsed at the side of his car. Ray jumped out and ran around to help him, but Jones seemed to be suffocating, choking on something. Ray shouted for help but no one came. He wasn't a designated first aider and he didn't want to risk touching Jones in case the wily bugger sued, so he ran back up the ramp to the security guard's hut, only to find another three people along the way who were all writhing in agony on the dirty concrete floor like the first man. Dan Potts, the security guard, was in a similar state also, thrashing around on the floor of his little square fibreglass cabin.

Ray started to panic. Never mind how at least five people around him had been struck down by something he couldn't see or hear, he was simply terrified he might be next. He continued out of the underground car park, running for cover, but when he reached the civic square, he stopped. His legs buckled with terror. It was happening everywhere. For as far as he could see in every direction, people were dropping to the ground, unable to breathe, grabbing and clawing desperately at their burning throats. He knew he should do something, and for a second he genuinely tried, loosening the collar of a particularly attractive woman's blouse and trying to stop her arms and legs from thrashing, but when he realised he couldn't help any of these people, the only option left was to help himself.

Ray turned and ran back underground, moving faster than he had for years. Level G, Level 1A, past his car on Level 1B and then down to Level 2. And there it was, right at the far end of Level 2: a single, inconspicuous grey metal door – the entrance to the emergency bunker. He staggered towards it, his lungs about to burst but the fear that the invisible killer might be closing in on him keeping him moving. A woman lurched out of the shadows to his right and stumbled into his path, arms outstretched, desperate for help. Without thinking he grabbed her and dragged her along with him. He smashed into the bunker door, entered the access code on a hidden keypad with a shaking index finger, then yanked it open and disappeared inside with the woman. He turned back but paused before sealing the shelter. He couldn't see anyone else. Where were the rest of the EPC? Were they already dead? He couldn't risk waiting. He had to stay alive. Ray slammed the door shut.

The woman was on the ground, convulsing. It was dark inside the bunker and the only illumination came from dusty yellow emergency lights hanging from the low ceiling. Ray crouched at her side and looked her up and down, not knowing how to help or even where to start. Before he could do anything her arms and legs went into a sudden flurry of quick spasms – some kind of seizure, he thought – then she stopped and lay ominously still. His eyes now becoming used to the low light, Ray took a torch from a rack on the wall above him and shined it into her face. Her wide, blue eyes stared desperately into space, but she didn't react. She was dead. Her pale white skin, he noticed, was speckled with spots of crimson blood. Ray wept with fear as he wiped the blood away and shook her shoulder to try and get her to respond. He'd seen her around before. A nice looking girl, he had an idea she worked in Payroll, but he'd never spoken to her. The name on her ID card was Shelly Bright. Much as he'd genuinely tried to help her, Ray now wished she wasn't there. He cursed himself for bringing her inside.

Adrenalin and fear kept Ray working uncharacteristically quickly for the next couple of hours. Like most council members he had a basic knowledge of the workings of the bunker and how the generator, lights and air conditioning and filtration systems were operated. Relatively fool-proof instructions had been provided and, to his immense relief, he was able to get the bunker fully operational in a fairly short period of time. It was a dark, depressing place which was stocked with basic supplies but nothing much of any substance. Originally designated as a regional command centre way back at the height of the Cold War, the equipment and stocks within the bunker had steadily dwindled over the last decade, and now just the basics remained. There was sufficient food and water to keep a small group alive for a couple of days, maybe as long as a week. Preoccupied as usual with thoughts of his own survival, Ray estimated that if he was careful, there would probably be enough to keep him going for the best part of a month. He didn't want to think about what might happen after that.

It was a short time later, once the initial shock of the morning's terrifying events and his sudden confinement had begun to fade, that Ray truly began to appreciate the enormity of what had happened. Shelly Bright was dead and so, he assumed, was everyone else. Of course he had no way of knowing how widespread this attack or whatever it was had been, but the fact no one else had yet tried to gain access to the bunker almost certainly meant that vast numbers of people in the immediate area had died. But surely he couldn't have been the only one who'd survived? In an unforgivably selfish moment he found himself hoping he was. Because, he realised ominously, if the other council members were dead, by default he would now be in charge of the borough of Taychester! He'd never wanted this level of responsibility. It wasn't what he'd gone into politics for.

He didn't dare move. He couldn't risk going back out there. Suddenly *Duck and Cover* seemed like sound advice. Ray sat alone in the cold, echoing emptiness of the bunker and waited.

He began to hate Shelly Bright's body. The corpse frightened him. He didn't want to look at it, but at the same time he was too scared to look away. What if she moved when he wasn't looking? What if she wasn't dead? He hated the pained expression on her face, her unblinking eyes searching for answers he couldn't give. He'd once thought her attractive (Ray found any woman under the age of forty attractive) but her smooth skin and soft, delicate features had been hardened by the pain of her sudden demise. In the wavering dull yellow light underground the shadows seemed to shift and her expression seemed to continually change. He knew she hadn't moved, but it looked like she was grinning at him now. A minute later she was sneering, then smiling, then snarling… Eventually, in a moment of uncharacteristic strength and conviction, he covered the corpse with a heavy grey fire blanket.

The day dragged unbearably. Ray couldn't switch off: his mind was filled with a thousand and one unanswerable questions and a similar number of nightmarish images, split second recollections of everything he'd seen aboveground. An inherently selfish man conditioned through years of regimented, nine-to-five working, it was only when it reached six o'clock in the evening – dinnertime – that he began to think more about his wife. Was Marcia safe? Would she be worried? Should he leave the bunker and go and find her? He already hated being underground but he knew he couldn't do that. He'd had a lucky escape this morning. If he went outside now, he'd surely be exposing himself to whatever had killed everyone else. He had no choice now but to sit and wait.

Never a man to follow procedures (usually because he didn't understand them), it wasn't until much later that Ray started to read the emergency planning guidelines which were stored in the command room. Following step-by-step instructions with the painful, awkward slowness of someone who had avoided as much contact with technology as possible over the last few years, he eventually got the radio working. He cursed the fact that he was so hopelessly inept. Forty-five minutes of fiddling and messing with the controls and all he could get was static punctuated by brief moments of silence. What he'd have given to hear another voice, someone out there who could reassure him he was going to be okay.

It felt like the morning would never come. The lack of natural light was strangely disorientating but, having slept intermittently for a few hours, Ray got up just after five o'clock. He managed to pluck up enough courage to start properly investigating his surroundings. He'd already found the stores, the plant room (where the generators and air purification equipment machinery was housed) and the bathroom, but now he also discovered two musty smelling dormitories and a hopelessly inadequate kitchen. Perhaps it was the lack of any proper illumination which made things appear worse than they actually were, but the whole place seemed to have fallen into a state of terrible disrepair. He found himself cursing those people (himself included) who'd mocked the efforts of the EPC in those endless council meetings. If only he'd listened and been better prepared…

It was only when he returned to the command room that he realised just how much the body on the ground was still playing on his mind. Even though it was covered up and was almost impossible to see clearly, he found it hard being in the same room as the corpse. What if he was stuck in there for several weeks or longer? Imagine the smell… He knew he had to do something about it. It took him an age to decide what to do, and another hour before he was actually ready to do it, but he eventually managed to shift Shelly Bright's dead bulk into one of the dormitories. The corpse was stiff and awkward to move. *Rigor mortis* had frozen her arms and legs into position and Ray had to push, pull and shove in order to get her from where she'd died, around the corner, down the corridor and into one of the dorms. Panting, sweating profusely, and scared half to death, he slammed the door shut and sobbed his way back to the command room.

If only there'd been a window in the main door or a camera so he could see what was happening outside. A paranoid part of him began to wonder whether the carnage he thought he'd witnessed aboveground was really as bad as he'd thought. It all seemed so bizarre – had it happened at all? Was this unbearable self-imposed incarceration truly necessary? Would he eventually emerge from the bunker to find everything back to normal? He'd be a laughing stock (again). If he stayed underground long enough, someone would probably have moved into his office and taken over his desk. And how would he explain the girl's body…?

The urge to open the door and take a look outside was almost impossible to resist. Just a quick look, he thought, just long enough to see what, if anything, was happening out there. Just long enough to see if there really were bodies lying around or if other people had survived.

But he knew he couldn't risk it.

In frustration, Ray leant against the door and wept. He wept for the family and friends he was sure he'd lost. He wept for the easy, comfortable life which he was certain was gone forever. First and foremost, however, he wept for himself. His retirement from office had been on the horizon and an even easier and more comfortable future had been in the offing. Now, through no fault of his own, he found himself buried underground with only a corpse for company. Even worse than that, if and when he eventually emerged from the shelter, as potentially the last council member left alive his life would inevitably become harder and more complicated unless he found a way of resigning his position. Maybe he should have stayed out there and let it get him too…?

Wait, what was that?

He could feel cold air; a slight breeze on the back of his hand. It was little more than the faintest of draughts coming from the side of the door just below its hinges. Fear gripped him and he stumbled further back into the bunker. The bloody door was supposed to be airtight. If he could feel a draught then the seal had been broken, and if the draft was coming from outside then whatever it was that had caused all the death and destruction out there had probably already seeped into the bunker. He scrambled away from the door and hid like a frightened child on the other side of the command room, waiting for it to get him.

More than an hour elapsed before Ray finally allowed himself to accept that he probably wasn't going to die, not yet, anyway. The people outside had been struck down in seconds. He'd been out there with them when it happened, and since then he'd been breathing in the same air, albeit through a filter. The fact he might have some immunity to what had killed so many seemed more improbable than the arrival of the infection itself. Ray distracted himself by eating a little food (a powdered meal he made with cold water), then fell asleep clutching a picture of Marcia which he'd found tucked amongst the crumpled bank notes, credit card receipts and out of date business cards stuffed in the back of his wallet.

He could hear something. Ray had been dozing again, but a sudden and unexpected shuffling, bumping noise had disturbed him. Something falling off a shelf? A problem with the generator or the pumps circulating the air? There it was again... He jumped up, a cold, nervous sweat prickling his brow. In the deathly quiet of the bunker the direction of the noise was clear. It was coming from the dormitory where he'd left Shelly Bright's corpse. But it couldn't have been, could it? As much as he wanted to walk the other way and cover his ears and pretend nothing was happening, Ray forced himself to walk towards the room.

Another crash. What the hell was going on in there? Was there another entrance to the bunker he wasn't aware of? Ray cleared his throat. 'Hello...' he called meekly, too scared to raise his voice any louder. 'Hello?'

He lifted his hand to open the door, then stopped. *Come on*, he thought, *this is bloody stupid*. The main entrance to the bunker was sealed and there was only one way in or out of the dorm, so how could there be anything on the other side of the door? He decided it must have been rats or some other vermin which had somehow tunnelled their way in, although how they'd managed to do that when the place was supposedly enclosed within a thick concrete skin was anyone's guess.

Another noise.

'Oh, Christ,' Ray moaned pathetically. He was completely on his own, no one to hide behind now. He knew what he had to do.

Holding his torch in his left hand (both as a source of light and a potential weapon), he opened the door. The dull yellow circle of light illuminated the back wall but little else. It must have just been—

'Bloody hell,' he yelled as Shelly Bright tripped across the room in front of him. 'What the bloody hell...?'

He shone the torch around until he found her again. There was no doubt it was her, but how could that be? She'd been dead since Tuesday morning, hadn't she? Ray remained rooted to the spot with fear. After all he'd been through, this new discovery was too much to take. He stared at the body with a mix of bemusement and sheer terror and he only moved when the dead woman turned herself around and, quite by chance, began to walk towards him. He shoved her away. She fell back, then dragged herself back up and walked away, turning again when she hit the wall at the far end of the room with a heavy, uncoordinated thud.

She was coming towards him again. Ray looked deep into her face. Her skin was unnaturally discoloured and her pupils dilated. Without waiting for her to get any closer, he slammed the door shut and held the handle tight. He felt the sudden collision as the corpse hit the back of the door, then listened carefully as she shuffled away again. He fetched a chair from the other dormitory and wedged it under the handle, preventing it from opening.

Back in the command room, Ray paced up and down, trying to block out the sound of the clumsy cadaver clattering around. He purposefully stormed over to the sealed bunker entrance, fully intending to open it and leave, but then stopped. Although no longer airtight (he could still feel the draught from outside) he still couldn't take that final step and go back out into the unknown. It might have been hellish underground, but for all he knew it might have been a thousand times worse out there. Sitting tight and doing nothing was, for the moment, the lesser of two evils. With the sounds of the body in the dormitory still ringing in his ears, Ray sank to the ground, covered his head with his hands and curled himself up into a ball.

It never stopped. The bloody thing never stopped. All day long the damn cadaver trapped in the other room barged around, smacking into the door, tripping over furniture, knocking things over… The noise, although not particularly loud, was enough to rattle Ray to the core. It was driving him mad. He had to get away from it.

It was almost seven o'clock. He'd been down in the bunker for a day and a half and he wanted out. All day he'd been sitting there in the semi-darkness, trying to decide what he should do and reaching no conclusions. Did he risk going outside or stay down there and wait? The body would have to stop moving sooner or later, wouldn't it? It couldn't just keep going indefinitely. And how the bloody hell was it managing to move at all? Nothing made any sense anymore.

Ray knew it was important to try and eat, but the limited food supplies he had tasted bloody awful. A lover of rich, fatty foods and sugary sweets, cakes and puddings, his stomach was growling angrily and he seriously wondered whether he'd be able to survive on the basic rations that had been stockpiled below ground. He was growing to detest every aspect of his grim surroundings: the stale, artificial smell of the air, the constant noise from the body in the dormitory, the lack of any decent lighting, the food… He crouched by the door in desperation, sniffing at the 'fresh' air which was seeping inside. *What's the point of sitting in here doing nothing*, he thought? He wanted out. He wanted to go home and find his wife and find out what had happened to the rest of the world. He wanted to change his clothes and eat properly and be away from that damn creature next-door. So what was stopping him? Apart from the obvious, he realised the main reason he wanted to stay underground was particularly cowardly and selfish. He didn't want the responsibility of having to do anything about the mess, and he definitely didn't want to have to take charge of what was left of Taychester. He knew he wouldn't be able to do it. But hang on a minute, why would he have to? Although in his early days at the council he'd had his fair share of appearances in the local papers, who would know who he was now and, more to the point, who would care? If he got into the car and drove away quick, no one would be any the wiser. He could get on with sorting out what was left of his own life and forget about everyone else. The longer he stayed in the bunker, the more getting out seemed like a good idea. Another muffled crash from the dead body was enough to sway him. His decision was made. Time to go. *What's left to lose*, he thought, *when it looks like I've already lost everything?*

Ray grabbed his jacket and the torch, and after overcoming a final moment of uncertainty and self-doubt, strained to re-open the heavy bunker door. He groaned with effort but it wouldn't budge and, for just a second, he panicked at the thought he might never get out. Another hefty shove and it began to shift. Relieved, he cautiously slipped outside.

It was quiet out there. And cold. And dark.

Slowly, step by nervous step, Ray moved away from the bunker entrance and began the long climb back up the twisting concrete ramp to the surface. Suddenly there was movement ahead which stopped him in his tracks: a single figure tripping through the shadows. He wanted to call out but nerves got the better of him and he couldn't bring himself to make any noise. It didn't matter anyway. It was obvious even from a distance that this person was in the same desperate condition as the body he'd left down in the shelter. It moved in the same awkward, uncoordinated way as Shelly Bright and it failed to react when he approached, even when he crossed its path and stood directly in its line of vision.

As Ray neared the surface, the number of bodies around him increased. There were numerous corpses still lying where they'd fallen, but many more were dragging themselves silently through the early evening gloom. In the strangest way he was slightly relieved because everything he'd thought he'd seen on Tuesday morning had actually happened. He hadn't imagined it. He walked past the security guard's hut and peered in through the window where what remained of Dan Potts scrambled around on the floor pathetically, trying desperately to get up but unable to cope with the confined space.

The civic square in front of the council house was a grim sight. The sun was just disappearing below the horizon, drenching the scene in warm orange light and casting long, dragging shadows. It had recently been raining and the sunlight made the ground glisten and shine. Ray counted sixteen bodies traipsing across the block-paving in various directions. Their awkwardness was vaguely comical. One of the stupid things nearest to him lost its footing and tumbled down a short stone staircase. Its clumsy, barely coordinated movements made him chuckle nervously to himself. His laughter, although quiet, sounded disproportionately loud and made him feel exposed. Now that the silence had been broken, however, he finally felt brave enough to call out.

'Hello,' he said, his wavering voice at little more than normal speaking volume. Nothing. 'Hello, is anyone there?' Still nothing. 'Hello…'

Ray took a few more hesitant steps (avoiding the crumpled remains of a foul-smelling, rain-soaked corpse), then turned back on himself to look out across the landscape of Taychester. He'd lived there all his life but he'd never seen it like this before. It was an alien and cold place, unexpectedly dark. The electricity must have failed at some point because not a single pinprick of electric light interrupted the blackness. No street lamps. No light coming from inside any of the hundreds of buildings he could see. Feeling prone, the councillor turned and walked back down to where he'd left his car.

He waited for a moment longer before setting off. Perhaps he should go back up to his office and see if there was anyone else around? Had any of his colleagues survived? He knew he couldn't risk it. He couldn't afford to get caught up in any unnecessary council business when he had so many issues of his own to sort out.

The sound of the engine was uncomfortably loud but Ray felt safe behind the wheel. He pulled out of the car park and began the drive home. He clipped the hip of a random body which lurched into his path unexpectedly. He slammed on his brakes and reversed back to try and help the bedraggled figure which had collapsed in an undignified heap at the roadside. He watched in disbelief as, without any flicker of emotion, it picked itself up off the ground and limped away, oblivious.

The house was just as he'd left it on Tuesday.

Ray pulled up on the drive. He paused before going into the house, needing to compose himself before he faced whatever was on the other side of the front door. He looked back over his shoulder around the quiet cul-de-sac where he and Marcia had lived for the last eleven years. It looked pretty much the same as it always had done, and yet everything felt uncomfortably different. This Thursday evening had the stillness and silence of early Sunday morning. No one was around. Nothing moved. Nothing, that was, apart from Malcolm Worsley, his opposite neighbour. Worsley was dead, his corpse trapped in his front garden, hemmed in by the ornate shrubs and privet hedges he'd so lovingly tended for years.

The house was deathly quiet inside. 'Marcia?' he called out hopefully. 'Marcia, are you here?'

She should have been in. She hadn't been planning to go out on Tuesday morning as far as he was aware. He walked further down the hall. He instinctively took off his coat and shoes (otherwise she'd moan at him again), then stopped himself. It was as cold inside the house as it was out on the street.

'Marcia?'

He checked the living room, dining room and kitchen and found them all empty, just as he'd left them. He then climbed the stairs, knowing his wife would most probably still have been in bed when it had happened, whatever *it* was. Christ, he hoped she was all right. But he knew she would have answered him by now. Ray prepared himself for the worst as he reached the landing. He could see into the bedroom. The duvet lay in a heap at the side of the bed, but Marcia wasn't there. The bed was empty.

The carpet was sodden. Water had seeped out under the bathroom door and had spread along virtually the entire length of the landing. It was obvious now where Marcia was. Ray walked up to the bathroom, his feet squelching, and knocked on the door.

'Marcia? Marcia, it's me, love. I'm home…'

He tried the handle, but it was locked. He pushed and shoved at it to little effect before taking five or six splashing, sliding steps back down the landing, then running back at full pelt and shoulder-charging his way into the bathroom. The lock was weak and gave way instantly with Ray's considerable weight slamming into it. He pushed the door open fully (sending a low wave of water rippling back across the tiled bathroom floor) and there, in front of him, stood what remained of his wife. Completely naked and completely unaware, she walked blindly towards him. He grabbed hold of her arms and held her wrists tight so she couldn't move. Her eyes were dark and vacant and she felt ice-cold to the touch, her skin like wet rubber. He let her go then pressed himself back against the wall and watched in heartbroken silence as she lurched past, oblivious. She staggered the length of the landing and then crashed into the door of the spare bedroom.

Ray managed to drape a dressing gown over his wife's shoulders then shut her in the third bedroom. He walked around the house methodically, locking and bolting every window and door.

Thursday night turned into Friday morning as he busied himself around his home. The flood in the bathroom (Marcia had been running a bath when she'd died) had caused massive damage both upstairs and in the kitchen directly below. The cold water made the house smell of must, or perhaps that was just the stench of his decaying wife? Ray wasn't sure. At least she'd left him with a bath full of water, he thought. That might prove useful.

Very occasionally, and only for the briefest of moments each time, Ray allowed himself to think about what had happened to the rest of the world. Had this happened everywhere? Despite his chosen vocation, thinking about other people was not something that came naturally to him and soon enough he'd concluded that his most sensible course of action was to continue to focus on his own safety, to sit tight and wait for help. Despite the fact that the electricity was off and the pressure in the taps was becoming increasingly weak, his house remained relatively comfortable and safe. There was a shop just around the corner where he could get food and drink supplies, and he still had the car if he needed to go any further afield. It made sense to stay at home. What use would he be to anyone else, anyway? One man to help hundreds, possibly even thousands? It would be far more sensible for him to concentrate on looking after himself. That was, after all, what he was best at.

A strange sense of normality gradually overcame Ray. Apart from making one hurried trip to the shop to fetch food early on Friday morning, he remained locked in his home from daybreak 'til dusk. He checked on Marcia a couple of times but there was no obvious change in her condition. He managed to get a loose dress over her head and shoulders, and eventually moved her to the garage to limit the noise her endless staggering around upstairs was making. She was constantly crashing into thing but he didn't as get annoyed as he had with Shelly Bright. Marcia couldn't help it.

With little else to do to occupy his time, Ray tried to make good the water damage to his home, but it was difficult to do anything without any power. He was actually relieved the electricity supply was off. It was safer that way. The light fitting in the kitchen was full of water from the overflowing bath. He'd drained as much of it off as he could. By the time the power comes back on, he decided, it'll probably have dried out. He'd have to get someone to come out and look at the damage later. No doubt they'd charge a fortune…

On Friday evening Ray sat at his desk in the alcove in the dining room at the front of the house. He read books by candlelight until his eyelids began to droop. It was good to keep occupied and distracted. It was a relief to have something positive to do for a while. He was finding it increasingly difficult to deal with the silence and solitude of his dead world. After searching in the attic for a while he found an ancient-looking battery powered cassette player and used it to play a tape of loud classical music to drown out the quiet.

At a quarter to two on Saturday morning, Malcolm Worsley's corpse finally escaped from his garden across the road and staggered over to Ray's house. Worsley slammed against the window next to where Ray was sitting reading. Startled, he leapt up, his heart pounding. He quickly regained his composure when he realised it was only Malcolm and he watched as his dead neighbour pressed his disfigured face against the window, leaving behind a greasy smear. As he watched, Malcolm lifted a rotting hand and slapped it down on the glass. *Strange*, thought Ray as he watched the wizened shell of his dead friend hitting the glass again and again. It didn't bother him unduly. In fact he felt quite sorry for Malcolm. The windows were double-glazed and that muffled each bang to little more than a dull thud. Tired, Ray turned up the volume on his cassette player and carried it upstairs with him to bed.

Saturday morning. Day five.

Ray had slept well. It would have been wrong to say he was happy with his situation but, all things considered, it could have been much, much worse. Regardless of what had happened to everyone else, he remained relatively safe and he was fairly warm and well protected. For a while he lay in bed and didn't move, staring up at the ceiling and thinking about how everything had changed since this time last week.

What was he going to do today? He really needed to start thinking about getting more supplies in. He'd noticed earlier in the week that decorators had been working in one of the houses down the road when all this had started last Tuesday morning, and their van was still outside. Perhaps he could borrow it and drive around to the local supermarket? If he spent a little time today filling the van with absolutely everything he'd need, it would save him having to go out again for maybe as long as a couple of weeks. By then he was sure that his situation would have improved. It couldn't get any worse, could it? In a couple of week's time, he decided, the other people who had survived like him would start to coordinate themselves and get things organised.

Ray got up, wincing at the sudden drop in temperature when he swung his legs out from under the covers. Without the central heating working the house was icy cold. He tiptoed to the toilet (stepping gingerly over the still damp landing carpet) and relieved himself in the plastic bucket he'd been having to use since the cistern had dried up. Once a day he carried it down to the bottom of the garden and emptied the contents over his roses. That felt better, he thought as he shook himself dry and walked back to the bedroom to get dressed.

He was half-dressed and halfway down the stairs when he noticed how dark it was. Feeling slightly uneasy, but not overly concerned, he continued down.

He saw them at the front door first. Visible only as shifting shapes through the frosted glass, he could see the heads and shoulders of at least four corpses, maybe more. Unusual, he thought as he continued down, zipping up his trousers and tightening his belt. As it was every morning, his next port of call was the kitchen. Still half asleep, he walked barefoot across the cold, tiled floor and fetched himself some breakfast cereal from the cupboard next to the sink. The cupboard door slammed shut (the hinges were loose and needed tightening) and the sound echoed through the empty house like a gunshot. Ray cringed, then frowned. He could hear Marcia moving around in the garage. Was it just coincidence, or had his wife just reacted to noise for the first time since she'd died? He was about to go and see her when he caught sight of something in the dining room. Like the rest of the ground floor of the house this morning, that room also seemed darker than usual. He put his head around the door, then immediately pulled it back again. Bodies… loads of them. Fighting to stay calm, he peered through the narrow gap between the door and the frame and saw that the entire width of the wide bay window at the front of the house was packed tight with dead flesh. He could see countless ghastly faces pressed up against the glass, scouring the room with their dry, clouded eyes. Why were they here? What did they want? Ray couldn't understand what was happening. None of the creatures had shown the slightest interest in him before, so why now? Were these somehow different to all the other bodies he'd so far seen? His mind wandered back to what had happened just before he'd gone to bed. Malcolm Worsley. That was it, that bugger Worsley had brought them here. He must have tipped them off that he was from the council. Did they think he'd be able to help them? Before he'd died Worsley had asked Ray to do favours for him on more than one occasion – everything from rushing through a planning application for an extension to his house to trying to get a parking fine overturned. Ray had no reason to think he would have changed his ways now just because he'd died. He peered through the gap again. There he was, the sly bugger, his dead face pressed hard against the window, letting everyone know where Ray was, wrongly assuming that he was the man who could (and would) help them.

His fragile confidence rattled, Ray felt uneasy. He ran back upstairs and peered out of the window in the spare room. Bloody hell, there were loads of them out there. A huge, ragged crowd of decomposing figures had gathered in front of his property. The nearest few corpses had been rammed up against the front of the house by the relentless pressure of countless others behind, and the whole mass had spilled out into the middle of the road. His car – his escape route – had been surrounded, swallowed up by the dead hordes.

The nervous councillor considered his suddenly limited options. Watching from behind the curtains, he saw more of the dark, shuffling shapes dragging themselves along the street towards his house. Individually they seemed weak and irrelevant and he had no reason to believe that they would do him any harm, but what could they do in these numbers? He never thought that his constituents would resort to mob rule to try and get action from the council. They'd never shown any interest before. He began to regret the day he'd stood for election.

Ray crept around to the back of the house and sat down on the edge of his bed. I'll stay here and keep out of sight for a while, he thought. Maybe they'll get tired waiting and go somewhere else.

By mid-afternoon the ever-growing crowd of bodies had filled the entire length of the street. They were hammering against the windows and door, and the sound could most probably be heard for miles around. Ray had finally plucked up enough courage to go back down and had quickly come to the conclusion that, as it looked likely he'd be staying in the house longer than he'd originally expected, his supplies were far from sufficient. He only had enough food for a few more meals. Sitting well out of sight in the kitchen with his throat dry and his stomach rumbling, he came to the crushing realisation that because of the bloody public outside, his situation was now nowhere near as comfortable or safe as he'd originally thought. Dejected, he got up, walked across the room and went out to the garage to see Marcia. Maybe her condition would have improved today? Perhaps she'd be able to offer her husband some long-overdue support at this increasingly difficult time. No such luck. His dead wife was still crashing tirelessly around the room. Her dress was torn and she was naked again. Bloody hell, she looked awful: grossly overweight, body swollen in all the wrong places, unexpectedly limp-breasted… and to top it all, her skin had turned a dirty shade of blue-green. He wished she'd just stay still. As long as she was making this much noise, the people of Taychester would know there was someone in the house and would continue to beat a slow, but very definite, path to his door. Perhaps if he went in there and found a way of keeping her quiet? Christ, what was he thinking? He'd never been able to keep Marcia quiet while she was alive, how the hell was he going to do it now?

Maybe he needed to get away and lie low for a while? But how was he going to get out and where was he supposed to go? He anxiously glanced at the clock on the wall. It was already gone two. In a few hours time the light would start to fade. He could either sit tight for another night or make his move today. He thought about the size of the crowd on the street. If there were hundreds of them out there now, how many more would there be tomorrow? Or the day after that, or the day after that? There was no way he alone could help so many people. More to the point, he didn't want to. As their council-

waiting for him indefinitely, would they?

Shelly Bright hurled herself at him yet again. There was another body almost as close now, and another… He had to move.

Ray Cox looked around at the decayed faces of the people of Taychester one last time before scurrying back into the bunker and sealing the door.

No sign of them disappearing yet. Every so often I try and open the door a little bit to see what's going on. It's been three days now and they're still all waiting for me. It looks like the whole car park is full now. How the hell am I ever going to get out? Maybe it's the noise of the generator and the air conditioning pumps that's attracting them, but I can't turn them off, can I? I'll just have to sit here and wait. They'll get bored eventually, won't they?

I try not to think too much about what's happened because I don't understand it and I don't think I ever will. All that matters now is getting through it in one piece. I don't mind spending a little more time down here on my own. I've spent years keeping a low profile. It won't be much longer. Just a few more days. A couple of weeks at the most.

Head down, duck and cover.

BEGINNING TO DISINTEGRATE
Part iii

Happy families, this most definitely was not. Caron's home had begun to resemble a hostel for troubled young adults and dysfunctional drop-outs. Lorna pulled her weight, the rest of them didn't. Ellie spent her time tending to her plastic baby's every need, whilst Anita and Webb sat out on the patio, drinking Caron's booze and smoking their way through their limited supply of cigarettes. Lorna had realised quickly that even though she never said anything, Caron was struggling. Similar to Ellie, she too had adopted a replacement child to help her come to terms with the loss of her own. Ellie's was plastic and had come from a shop, but Caron's new charge needed far more attention. Fussing over Webb seemed to be helping her cope with losing Matthew, who, Lorna had discovered, lay dead in the garage, covered with a dustsheet.

To Lorna, it seemed that whenever it felt like she was beginning to come to terms with her bizarre situation, something happened which changed everything again and kicked her back to square one. The resurrection of the dead was another such event. On the third morning, first light after they'd found Caron and Webb in Wilmington Road, many of the corpses outside had risen. It took Lorna all day to pacify her housemates. Thankfully many of the dead remained where they had fallen, and that included Matthew. Lorna didn't know how she'd have handled it if he'd picked himself up and started lumbering around the garage on unsteady feet. Caron's emotions, Webb's jealousy… it didn't bear thinking about. She'd probably have just packed up and left them all to it. They wouldn't have even noticed she'd gone until one of them wanted something or had to make a decision for themselves.

The reanimation of the dead felt like just another complication to Lorna, though she realised the implications were vast. At first she'd thought they might be able to sit out the storm in Caron's relatively comfortable three-bed semi, but with each hour that passed, that appeared to be less and less viable an option.

From studying the behaviour of the corpses, she quickly deduced that they could hear and see. They reacted whenever any noise came from thirty-two Wilmington Road, and that began to happen with increasing regularity, no matter what she told the others. If it wasn't Webb causing arguments, it was him and Anita sitting out on the patio, pissed-up on what was left of Caron's drinks cabinet, laughing at nothing like they were kids hanging around on a street corner, not the last few people left alive after a catastrophic event they could barely bring themselves to talk about, let alone understand.

One of the dead had, by chance, tripped down Caron's drive a short while earlier. It had slammed up against the front door and she'd immediately gone to answer it, conditioned through years of subservience, of pandering to the needs of her husband (who, coincidentally, she'd barely given a moment's thought to since this chaos had begun). The shape behind the frosted glass looked like any other visitor. Caron had her hand on the latch before Lorna stopped her. 'Wait. You don't know what it is.'

'It might be someone like you,' Caron whispered, indignant. The person outside – the *thing* – had continued to hammer against the door. 'I didn't leave you standing out on the doorstep, did I?'

'I know, but the dead were still dead back then, remember?'

Caron thought she knew best. She went to open the door but Lorna had managed to slide the chain across just in time. The door had opened a few inches inwards, and a greenish, blood-stained hand shot through the gap and began to swipe at the air clumsily. It stretched out, clawing at nothing. Lorna caught it and held the creature's greasy palm up close to Caron's face. Caron had stared at the discoloured flesh, a fingernail hanging off, a deep cut that didn't bleed… and the stench… it made her gag. 'Let it go. Get it away from here.'

'Thought you wanted to let it in,' Lorna had sneered. She'd shoved the corpse back out and kicked the door shut.

In the morning, the house was surrounded. Lorna had tried again to tell them it would happen, but the rest of Caron's house guests were making too much noise to listen. They were either too stupid to understand, she decided, or they simply just didn't give a shit. It wasn't until the dead had crowded Caron's dining room window to such an extent that they'd blocked out all the light, that they began to realise the implications.

'We can't stay here,' Lorna explained.

'I'm not leaving my home,' Caron protested, indignant.

'Fair enough. I am.'

'We could get rid of them,' Webb suggested.

'How?'

He didn't have an answer. Ellie turned her doll's face away from the window, shielding her. Webb walked up to the glass, and the bodies on the other side immediately began to react. The bay window was a mass of dead faces gazing into the house, pawing endlessly at the grease-stained glass with claw-like hands. Lorna pulled him back out of view.

'They're showing more interest in us by the hour. We're going to need to get out of here soon.'

'I'm not leaving,' Caron said again. The thought of leaving her home was somehow harder than trying to come to terms with everything else.

'We won't have any choice if this carries on,' Lorna said. 'I think we should get out of here now and find somewhere better to wait this out.'

'Like where?' Anita asked.

'I don't know. Somewhere stronger. Somewhere with fewer windows. A decent fence…'

'There's the community centre on Long Nuke Road,' Ellie suggested, rocking her baby.

'I thought of that, but it's too exposed. The clue's in the name. Community centres are designed to be accessible, aren't they? They're the last places you'd want to get stuck. Fuck, they were the last places I'd have gone *before* all this kicked off.'

'Where then?'

They were all looking to Lorna for an answer, but she didn't have one. 'Don't know yet. Just get ready to go is all I'm saying.'

When Webb started pissing around with Anita again, ignoring everything she'd just said, antagonising the bodies at the window and moaning at Caron because she'd run out of alcohol, Lorna turned her back on the lot of them and went upstairs. Fucking morons.

She watched the empty world from Caron's dead son's bedroom. She thought it funny that this one room had been left untouched; a shrine to the corpse in the garage. When there was so much death outside, why they all remained so respectful towards one dead teenager bemused her. Whatever the reason – and she thought it more than likely due to the fact the corpse in question was under the same roof as them – she was glad of the space. The idea of climbing out of the window, shimmying down the drainpipe and making a run for it was tempting. She might have done it too, had the prospect of a long run home to an empty house not been so unappealing. The people downstairs might all have been idiots, but at least they were idiots with a pulse.

Lorna did what she could to shut everything else out and focus. Standing in front of Matthew's window she looked out over the world, watching for any signs of life. Apart from the listless bodies in the streets, not a damn thing moved. No traffic. No lights. No noise. It felt alien, like she was the one who was out of place, like it was she who no longer belonged.

She could see a church. A strong building, standing defiant, but that was about all it had going for it. Inside it would be cold and uncomfortable, and not at all suited to their needs. A fire station? She liked the idea of cruising the streets in a fire engine – obliterating anything that got in her way – but the station building itself didn't look like it would offer much in the way of protection: large glass doors, easily accessible. A school? The idea of spending time where hundreds of kids might have died made her skin crawl. She hadn't much cared for schools at the best of times… And what about the hospital, the roof of which she could just about see? Just the thought of wards filled with the remains of dead patients made her go cold.

Maybe I'm looking in the wrong places? Maybe I need to think about the places people didn't used to go?

The problem was, she decided, she didn't know enough about this locality. She'd never been that interested in what went on outside the immediate area where she'd lived and the places she needed. Her world had been restricted to a few streets and a few faces, and that was how she'd liked it. She'd never had any aspirations to see the world or to… Her train of thought was interrupted by a flash of light. It was gone in a second and could have been caused by anything, just a brief glint of sunshine on metal. She watched for a while longer, but it didn't happen again.

This house is like a cocoon, she thought, *and that might not be a good thing*. Between Caron's double-glazing, the bodies outside and the morons downstairs, the rest of the world had effectively been blocked out.

Lorna kept watching and, just over an hour later, she saw movement again, in the same place as before. She was half-asleep, eyelids drooping, and she didn't fully realise it was there until it had gone. Sat upright, immediately wide awake, she saw a flood of slow-moving corpses following in the wake of whatever it was she'd just missed.

The next time around, watching from another window this time, she saw exactly what it was. It was hard to believe. It was its normality which made it so surreal. She walked back downstairs, not sure how to tell the others.

'What's the matter?' Caron asked, stopping in the hallway on her way to deliver a cup of tea to Webb. 'You look like you've seen a ghost.'

'Not a ghost,' she said. 'A bus.'

Almost time. The bus was due around again. She'd left Ellie upstairs watching for another couple of hours (figuring that, for some bizarre reason, whoever was driving the bus seemed to be following an established route) while the rest of them stripped Caron's house of anything of value. Lorna had pacified Caron by lying to her, telling her they'd come back later and that everything was going to be okay, when the truth was she had no intention of coming back, and she didn't know if *anything* was going to be okay anymore. The nervousness was palpable, and even though they outwardly continued to bicker and moan, they all knew this was the right thing to do. They waited by the front door, all loaded up.

'What are those?' Lorna asked, looking down at Caron's feet.

'Shoes,' she answered. Trick question?

'You're wearing heels? Bloody hell, Caron. We're about to sprint through a crowd of corpses, and you're wearing heels?'

'I've nothing else that goes with this jacket.'

Lorna just looked at her. A combination of her own nerves and a genuine affection for the stereotypically middle-class woman kept her from yelling. In a way she envied her naivety. She wished things like fashion sense still mattered. Caron grumbled to herself as Anita berated her and forced her to change into more sensible, flat shoes, even though they clashed.

Lorna checked the time on her phone. They needed to move. 'Right, once we're out there, we just run for it, understand? They're still slow enough. They won't know we're there until we've gone.'

'You're having a fucking laugh, ain't you?' Webb said, his uncertainty clear. 'There's fucking hundreds of them.'

She quickly corrected him. 'Less than eighty. I counted.'

'Where are we going, Lor?' Ellie asked, plastic baby held close.

'I already told you.'

'No you didn't. You said about the bus, that's all. You never said where we're going.'

'We want to get on a bus, so where do you think we're going? The bloody bus stop.'

Someone asked another pointless question, but she'd had enough now. They were just delaying tactics. And the thing was, if that bus continued driving the same route all day, missing it this time around would give them at least another hour to wind themselves up still further. Christ knows what state they'd be in by then.

But the bus might not come back around.

It might be one of those things behind the wheel, somehow driving on instinct.

It might go a different way this time.

It might have run out of fuel…

Too many questions. Too many ifs and buts.

Lorna shoved Caron's front door open and started running. The nearest of the dead immediately turned towards her and began to advance. She pushed the first few away, then dropped her shoulder and charged through the rest of them like a rugby player. The others followed behind her, though she gave them little thought. Caron stopped to lock the door before Webb dragged her away.

Thankfully the dead were as slow and useless as they'd appeared from the upstairs window. It was almost as if they were operating on a time delay of a few seconds. Lorna almost laughed as she ran. Down here at ground level, their lethargy was bordering on comical.

Quickly free from the bulk of the foul-smelling crowd, she allowed herself to glance back and check on the others. What she saw was what she expected: the four of them running at varying speeds, three with their heads down sprinting, Caron struggling to keep up, all arms and legs and panic. But even she was having no problem outrunning the corpses. The dead followed in an unruly, ragged mass, occasionally colliding with each other, arms outstretched as they reached for the gaps where the survivors had just been.

At the end of the street, Lorna took a right. There was a bus stop about another fifty metres ahead. There were also more bodies, too; a couple of them on this side of the road, several more crossing from the opposite pavement. One fell as it stumbled down the kerb, hitting the tarmac face-first with a nauseating wet thud.

She was at the bus stop in seconds, the others catching up within a minute or so. The nearest of the dead weren't far behind, and it was then that the obvious limitation of Lorna's plan became painfully apparent. 'So what now?' Anita demanded, panic all too evident in her voice. Lorna didn't answer, because she didn't know. Maybe try and get into another house so they could see the bus coming? Just fight off the dead until it arrived?

'Let's go back,' Caron wailed. 'This was a mistake. Let's go back to my house and I'll cook us something nice. I'll make some tea and we can think again about what we should…'

Her words trailed away as both Lorna and Webb sprang into action. Three corpses were close. Lorna grabbed the extended right arm of the first and swung the dead woman around. She offered surprisingly little resistance. Webb did the same with the corpse of a small boy, hurling the ragdoll body into another dead woman who collapsed near Caron's feet. Caron looked down at the miserable creature. 'Joan?' she said, bemused and appalled in equal measure. 'Joan Deeley, is that you?'

More of them now. Anita joined in the fight as the creatures began to swarm around them. Their miserable speed and lack of strength was laughable, but their relentless intent was truly terrifying. There seemed to be nothing else left in the world to distract these hideous things…

Except the bus.

They heard it before they saw it through the chaos, trundling steadily down the road towards them, its paintwork smeared with reds, browns and black. It was immediately obvious why: the dead were literally throwing themselves at the huge vehicle. Some simply bounced off and landed in the road, others were dragged under its wheels and crushed. Lorna hadn't noticed it before – she'd had enough to deal with – but much of the road was coated in a layer of tyre-track streaked gore.

She stopped fighting and ran out into the road and began waving her arms furiously, slipping in the foul sludge under her boots. Had the driver seen her? *Had he seen her?* The bus just kept on coming, closer and closer, the driver's view obscured by the constant stream of corpses criss-crossing in front. Lorna didn't know what else to do. She stood her ground and screamed at the driver to stop. She thought she could see two men inside the bus, their faces obscured by the wipers which smeared blood and grease across the windscreen rather than clearing it.

She screwed up her face with effort and heaved another insipid body out of the way, then screamed out loud again. 'Stop the fucking bus!'

A hiss of air brakes. Doors opening. Warm air. Strong hands dragging her inside.

'That was a bit stupid, love,' a balding, large-bellied man said as he helped her up the step. His hands lingered on her too long and she angrily batted them away.

'Four more out there,' she said, but she didn't need to explain as Caron, Ellie, Anita and Webb were already pushing past, desperate to get to safety. They buffeted Lorna further down the bus, which was filled with loose supplies and all kinds of other rubbish. She found an empty seat as far away as she could from everybody else and sat down heavily. The bus began to move, and the rough, rattling, stop-start movement was immediately familiar and reassuring. She leant her head against the glass and watched the dead world go by, not knowing where she was going, and not caring either. Outside looked like a place she used to know, but it wasn't home. Not anymore.

Webb was standing at the front between the fat man, whose name was Stokes, and the driver, offering all manner of useless advice. He was telling them how he'd looked after these four girls, kept them safe from the dead outside. Stokes seemed suckered in. He leant across and rapped on the Perspex window of the driver's cab with his knuckles. 'Told you we'd find someone else if we kept driving, didn't I?' he said. Driver didn't say anything.

PENELOPE STREET

Penelope Street is nearing the end of her life. She's very weak now and it's an effort for her just to keep her eyes open. It's easier to stay head bowed and eyes shut because she doesn't want to see what's happening around her. There's nothing she can do about any of it. Penelope wants the end to come quick, but every single second seems to take a cruel eternity to pass. She just wants it to be over now.

One hundred and thirty-three.

I've been here for one hundred and thirty-three hours now. How much longer will I last? Will I reach one hundred and thirty-four or one hundred and thirty-five? Christ, I hope not. I can't take much more of this. I wish I could make the end come faster. The frustration's worse than the fear now.

I feel so weak. I haven't got my medication and I haven't had anything to eat or drink since first thing Tuesday morning. That's more than five and a half days, surely I can't last much longer, can I? I can't do anything but sit here with my head hanging down, looking into my lap. Sometimes I look up and around but it's all too much. Everything has changed and I don't know how or why.

Arthur's body is just in front of me. I can see his feet sticking out from behind the sofa we were here to buy. He's still, but *they* move all around me, oblivious to the fact I'm here. They are the dark, decaying shadows of dead people. They are cold, empty, emotionless bodies. When I look up I see the streets outside are full of them. I can't move so they don't see me, but if I make any noise they stop. I screamed and shouted at them to begin with because I thought they'd be able to help, but now I know they can't. When they hear me they stop and bang on the glass, then even more of them come. I'm used to being stared at so I don't move. I don't react. After a couple of hours they start to drift away.

Arthur brought me here on Tuesday to choose a new sofa, not that he needed me to come. There wasn't any point in me getting involved in the decision. It was down to him to choose one and try it out and decide whether or not we were going to have it. We got here early to avoid the crowds. If there are too many people then my chair just gets in the way. We'd just got through the door when it happened. I watched it get him and everyone else. I watched them all die and I wish it had taken me too. I kept waiting for it to come, hoping and praying it would, hoping and praying this impossible life would soon be over. I can't stand being alone like this. It makes me feel more helpless and vulnerable than ever.

I'm so hungry. Thirsty too. My mouth's dry and I'm so dehydrated that it feels like my tongue's swollen to ten times its normal size. I can't talk properly now, not that there's anyone left to talk to. There must have been a fire near here, and people must have been trapped inside. I smelled the smoke first, then the burning bodies. It was like sitting in the middle of a damn barbecue, the whole world stinking of roast meat. Every so often I can still smell it and even though I know what's burning, it still makes the hunger pains worse.

The very worst part of all of this is not having any control. I've not had much control for a long time, but now I don't have *any*. I can't do a bloody thing about the situation I'm in. I can't do anything to help myself or to bring the end any closer. Help might be just around the corner, but I can't even get myself out of this damn building, never mind anywhere else. An inch might as well be a hundred bloody miles for all the good it'll do me now.

Just trying to look up takes so much energy. There are more bodies outside now, gazing in at me with their cold, vacant eyes. I feel like a bloody shop window dummy, but then I have done since the accident. People always stared at me since then. Perhaps I should have got used to it, but I've never been able to handle the sideways glances and the way they avoid me. They either used to patronise me or ignore me altogether and talk to Arthur instead. Either way, they made me feel like a freak. People always saw the wheelchair before they saw me sitting in it. I'm paralysed from the neck down, not up. I can't move my body, but that was the only difference between me and everyone else. My arms and legs might be frozen, but I've always been able to feel hurt and to get scared and feel panic like everyone else. Christ knows I'm scared now.

I would have been all right if it hadn't been for him, that stupid bloody husband of mine. If he'd left me there after the fall instead of trying to be a hero I would have been okay. It would have taken time to get well again, but I would have been okay eventually. But no, Arthur knew best, didn't he. It was him trying to move me that did the real damage to my neck. He blamed himself and so did I. And now here I am, trapped in this cold, dark, empty place, starving to death with just his corpse for company. I can't move an inch. What did I do to deserve this?

Come on death, hurry up. The joke's over. I want this to finish now. I'm sick and tired of sitting in this bloody chair just waiting…

Emily lived her life on the Internet. It connected her world, made her feel less alone. She thought it strange that the people closest to her were usually thousands of miles away, while the people she was physically nearest might as well have been in another universe. The Internet put Emily in contact with the people who knew her better than the rest of them. It made fantasy worlds feel real. And in those make-believe places filled with virtual versions of people, it made her feel like she belonged. Even now, even after everything that's happened to the physical world, she's still doing all she can to cling onto her virtual reality.

Without the Internet, Emily is just Emily. She lives with her nan in just another house on just another street. By looking at the faded blue front door, you'd never know that the girl upstairs in her bedroom is a fucking awesome killer, or that she races so fucking hard and so fucking fast that last month she ranked seventeen on a league table of several hundred thousand racers.

Nan says to Emily, *you should get out more, find yourself a nice boy*. Nan says she doesn't spend enough time mixing with other people, even though Emily tells her she spends *all* her time with other people. How can she expect her to understand? Nan can't even set up a programme to record on the bloody satellite TV box. She still checks the listings in the paper then sits there waiting for programmes to start instead of time-shifting and catching-up on demand like everybody else.

Or, at least, she did.

Nan doesn't do anything anymore. Like the rest of the world, it seems, Nan's dead. She went out to the shops last Tuesday morning, and never came home. There's a part of Emily that thinks she should have gone out looking for her, but what's the point? They're all dead out there. As far as she can tell, she's the only one left.

It happened in the online world too. One minute she was up to her neck in the middle of a grudge match with that little bitch Oko575 from Hiroshima, the next she was alone. She could still see

Oko575 on the screen, of course, but she was frozen in space like a screen-cap. It was the same everywhere Emily looked, every game.

She tried to follow the progress of events via all her usual online social outlets, but it wasn't the updates and tweets she tracked, it was the silence. One minute there was the usual chaos of activity coming from all directions, then there was nothing. A wave of quiet had spread out across the world. Nothing trending. Nothing happening. No one else left online.

Emily was comfortable with the real-world isolation. She was used to it. She didn't need anyone else. She actually liked being alone like this. Okay, so she wasn't so keen on the number of corpses she could see from her bedroom window, but that was something she knew she'd get used to eventually. The online quiet, however, was a different matter altogether. Wherever she went, whatever game she tried, she was alone. It was unnerving. It was unnatural. Online, she'd always had company available on demand.

It was several days in, long after the dead had begun to rise outside, that she finally found someone. An eight year old kid in Texas, by all accounts, as scared as she herself was beginning to feel. Emily found him by chance as she wandered the desolate streets of a virtual town once full of orcs, wizards and warriors. It was unsettlingly quiet there now, just a handful of frozen characters in view almost all the time. Those avatars she could still see, she decided, were the poor buggers who'd died playing.

Emily turned the music up to full in her bedroom to try and counteract the lack of noise everywhere else, then kept herself busy building an empire unchallenged, stripping virtual corpses of anything of value after one-sided battles, hoarding worthless treasures. She'd caught a glimpse of unexpected movement in the corner of her screen, and in the stillness of everything else it was as startling as if someone had sneaked up behind her in the real world and yelled in her ear. She chased the avatar through the streets, desperate not to lose sight of it. It didn't feel like a game now. It felt like it mattered, that there was far more riding on this than achievements, experience points and upgrades. She was too fucking good for the kid in Texas. She knew this virtual place like the back of her hand and she soon had him cornered. They had a desperate conversation by text:

181

Don't log off. You okay?
Ok. Scared
Me too
U know what happened?
Don't know. Everybody dead here
Same here
Except me
And me
Must have happened all over
That's what I figured. What we gonna do?

Emily paused. Then she typed. The obvious answer was the only answer.

Play

And they did. For hours. Every game they both had that they could still get onto. Time difference be damned – they spent every minute they could online together, clinging onto each other, in touching distance yet thousands of miles apart.

Until this morning.

This morning, just before eleven-thirty UK time, the kid in Texas disappeared. Emily cried – she actually *cried* – when she realised her buddy had gone. She had no way of finding out what had happened to him, but her mind went into overtime just the same. Had he been killed by a crowd of increasingly vicious corpses the size of the crowd of increasingly vicious corpses now gathered outside Nan's house? Or was the kid okay and it was just the computers that had failed them? Had the servers gone down? Had the Internet given up and finally stopped working? Emily knew there'd been a chance that would happen eventually, but she'd hoped it would have lasted a while longer yet. Surely there would have been systems in place to keep everything up and running? She wished there was something she could do, but there wasn't. She could get her computer to do plenty, but she didn't know how it worked under the hood. She'd been proud to call herself a nerd, but there were painfully obvious limits to her geekiness.

And now the power had died too. It was so bloody unfair.

Emily's computer was useless. Just a plastic and metal box now. Completely bloody lifeless. As lifeless as the several hundred corpses outside, scrabbling at the windows to get in. Her constant music had attracted them, that much was clear, but even though it had been silenced with the power, they weren't going anywhere. They seemed to know she was here.

But what hurt Emily most of all was the fact that if the kid in Texas did manage to get back online, she had no way of connecting with him. She had her phone, but it wasn't the same. No signal. Battery half-dead. She didn't have any means of calling or updating anyone, but she still clung onto the white glow of the phone screen regardless.

She knew she should conserve the power, but she didn't. She *couldn't*. She wanted to stay online, wanted to preserve her last connection with the digital world. She held onto the phone until the battery drained to nothing, playing crappy games, flicking through old photos, messages, emails… anything. And when the last dregs of power disappeared, Emily felt a gut-churning emptiness the likes of which she'd never known before. She knew she was finally, completely, hopelessly alone. All bridges to her virtual world now burned, no way of accessing anything, no more updates or notifications, her digital self now as good as dead. Nothing but reality left.

She sat in Nan's kitchen and sobbed, conscious that the noise she was making was having an ever-increasing effect on the ever-increasing hordes, but unable to stop. A little after midnight, the front door gave way under the pressure of the crowd, and the house quickly filled with cold flesh. Emily tried to get away and to fight but there were too many of them. She couldn't move. Couldn't breathe. Couldn't escape.

The dead smothered her, suffocated her, cut off all her options. But it didn't matter anymore. She'd preferred her virtual reality to this. *Not online*, she thought, *not worth living*.

DAY SEVEN

It is now several days since Amy Steadman's corpse took its first unsteady steps. It is a week since infection.

Her body continues to move at a lethargic pace, her mobility still limited. She has, however, been moving constantly and has now covered a considerable distance since leaving the crowd on the motorway. The dog trapped in the car – the cause of the disturbance which originally drew the large mass of cadavers to the scene – became quiet after several hours. Many of the dead, Amy's corpse included, gradually drifted away. By pure chance Amy's body continued to follow the route of the road forward. Although she has subsequently come across numerous blockages and occasional distractions, she has kept moving in the same general direction and has covered several miles.

As time has progressed so she has continued to regain further control over her movements. She now walks with slightly more fluidity and speed, although her muscles and nerves are continuing to decay. Her limbs – previously stiff, awkward and largely inflexible – are now able to bend and flex to an extent, although her overall range of motion is still severely limited. She can draw her hands into fists and can move her fingers independently. There has been a substantial increase in the number of voluntary head movements she makes, suggesting Amy is aware of the direction of sound.

The long and wide motorway, straight for a considerable distance, slowly curved around to the right as it merged with another major road which skirted the centre of the city of Rowley. Amy's body, however, did not change course. Instead, she continued to move in a relatively straight line, leaving the tarmac then tumbling down a grassy embankment. After managing to get up again, she crossed the width of a field, stumbled through an open gate, then found herself following a narrow gravel path which ran alongside an isolated bungalow. After walking the length of the gravel path, she reached another road. The steep banks on either side of the road have channelled Amy's corpse and prevented her from going in any other direction but forward.

The process of decay, combined with the physical toll of the distance travelled, has caused the condition of her body to deteriorate considerably. Amy's skin is now extremely discoloured. The chemical reactions continuing to occur throughout her body have manifested themselves as numerous weeping sores and lesions. In the fall down the embankment, her corpse sustained a number of lacerations to the right hand and arm, her upper torso and also her face. Thick, congealed blood has slowly seeped, rather than poured, from these cuts. Her circulatory and respiratory systems are no longer operational; blood is no longer being pumped around her body.

Amy's self-awareness has increased. Although still at an extremely rudimentary level, she is now aware of her own general shape and size and compensates for her mass whilst moving. She can now use her hands (but not yet her fingers) to move obstructions with limited success. Her balance has also improved although she is still occasionally unsteady on her feet and has difficulty on uneven ground.

A sudden heavy downpour of rain has drenched Amy's body and she's struggling to cope with the steep gradient of a road down a hillside. A canopy of trees hangs overhead which, coupled with the increased cloud cover, has substantially reduced the amount of available light. The loud, echoing sound of the rain hitting the leaves overhead is confusing Amy. She is surrounded by noise. She moves her head constantly, trying to identify the source of the directionless sound.

Both of Amy's feet are bare and the exposed flesh is wearing away. She leaves a bloody residue on the ground with virtually every footstep. Already there are insects feeding off her and the many other corpses scattered around the countryside. Amy's body has just passed another corpse, this one trapped in the wreckage of a car. Over the course of the last seven days it has been ravaged by scavenging animals. The sheer amount of dead meat which is now available will inevitably prove an unexpected benefit to many millions of predators and parasites. It is likely that, over the coming months, the population of these creatures will increase massively. The lack of any form of pest control will further allow their numbers to multiply unchecked. It is still very early days, but it is already clear the removal of almost all of the human population is having an unprecedented effect on the ecosystem.

A brief burst of sunlight bathes everything in unexpected brightness and warmth. Although unable to detect or understand the change in temperature, Amy notices the increased light levels. Her eyesight is still poor – she sees shapes and detects movement but has so far been unable to make out any finer level of detail. Her ability to absorb and interpret what she sees is improving, but at the same time her physical condition continues to deteriorate. Her eyeballs and the associated nerves and muscles are rotting.

Amy's body has reached a junction where the road she has been following joins a more major route. Here a crowd of bodies has gathered around a young survivor. Caught out in the open looking for food, a ten year old girl has become lost and has found herself dangerously exposed. With nowhere else to hide, she has shut herself in a telephone box. She is on the ground with her back pressed up against the door to prevent it from opening. There are already seven bodies surrounding the girl with a further three approaching. Amy Steadman's corpse is also close. Whilst the young survivor is aware that by keeping quiet she can evade detection by the corpses, she is trapped and is struggling to contain her emotions. She is sobbing uncontrollably, and the bodies on the other side of the glass are reacting to every sound. Although they don't understand why, they are driven to try and get closer to her. One of them begins to bang on the glass. Others copy, and this new sound attracts the attention of even more of the dead.

Amy's corpse has now reached the telephone box. Although she doesn't understand what she is doing, she has an instinctive, insatiable desire to reach the source of the noise at all costs. She grabs hold of the nearest corpse and attempts to take its place. Less decayed than some of the other cadavers, Amy viciously rips at them, pulling and pushing them out of the way. Their flesh is weak and is literally torn from the bone. Amy keeps moving until she is standing directly in front of the telephone box. She leans forward and presses her decaying face against the glass, staring down at the girl with dry, unblinking eyes.

As long as the girl continues to move and make noise, the bodies remain.

JACKSON

You can learn a lot about them by watching. Sometimes it pays to be slow like them. Bide your time. Take it easy. Don't panic and you should be okay.

I'm not a biologist or a doctor. I don't know what's happened to them or why it hasn't happened to me and to be honest, I don't care. I don't know if I'm immune or whether I'm just riding my luck and it'll get me eventually. I might only have a day left, but I might last another twenty years. I know hardly anything about this strange new world, but I'm learning how to survive.

I never had any training for this kind of thing. I did a couple of years in the Boy Scouts but that's all. I could have done with a stretch in the forces, but it wasn't for me. I couldn't stand the shouting and the discipline. I've never been able to handle being told what to do. Unless I'm the one doing the ordering, then I work better on my own and I always have done. I used to get on with other people well enough but, given the choice, I prefer my own company every time. Especially now. I wouldn't be able to trust anyone else to stay quiet or still enough when the bodies are about. The rest of the world is dead and everything I do is exaggerated by the stillness. I can't take any risks.

If I move they'll see me. If I make a sound they'll hear me. They have numbers on their side and I know that if I give them half a chance, they'll kill me.

So what have I learnt about them? They're pretty simple creatures now, easy to read. There doesn't seem to be a lot of conscious thought going on in their festering brains, but I have noticed them beginning to follow certain behaviours. And those behaviours are changing almost by the day.

It's a week now since it happened. I checked enough of them at the start to be sure they were dead, but something inside them has survived and it's growing stronger. It began when they picked themselves up and started to move again, then they were able to hear and see. Over the last twenty-four hours I've seen them become even more animated. They're beginning to show rudimentary emotions: anger, although that could just be a physical manifestation of frustration, and either fear or pain, I can't tell which.

Enough of this. I'm wasting time. Daydreaming is dangerous. Hypothesizing pointlessly about what might or might not be happening to them won't help. All I can do is respond to the changes day by day and try to stay one step ahead of the game. My comparative strength and my intelligence should see me through. I have to keep control and hold my nerve. Start to get jumpy or twitchy and I'll make mistakes. Make mistakes and I'm dead. No second chances.

These things don't communicate with each other, but they're developing a strange tendency to move together in large groups. It's almost like they're herding. Something happens to attract one or two of them, then more and more follow the first until there's a huge crowd of the fuckers. I can use that behaviour to my advantage, but there are dangers too. The advantages? When they're together it's easy to pick them off in bulk. I haven't yet, but I can imagine being able to take out hundreds of them at a time if I have to. And the dangers? If I'm the one causing the disturbance that's attracting them, I'm fucked.

Attacking a group of them can be unexpectedly useful. Starting fires also helps. A little heat and light is enough to draw them out from a wide surrounding area. The stupid things can't help themselves, and they stumble towards the flames without giving me a second glance. I can walk right past them and they won't notice if there's something more interesting happening nearby. Their senses are dull and basic. Give them something obvious to focus on and they lose sight of everything else. I've been collecting fireworks. Feels strange to be rooting through toy shops now, wrong almost, but if I'm cornered all I have to do is set off a rocket and wait for them to react. I got the idea from a Romero movie, back when this kind of thing was just fiction.

Darkness is my best friend.

The creatures are still clumsy and slow. Take away their sight and the advantage I have over them is massively increased. That's why I now travel almost exclusively after nightfall.

So what's the plan? You have to have a plan, don't you? I'm heading for the coast. I've a hell of a distance to cover still and it's not going to be easy travelling on foot, but I can't think of any other option. I tried using a car, but the noise caused more trouble than time saved, and if there's one thing I've got plenty of, it's time. And why the coast? Seems as good a place as any. Nowhere will be completely safe anymore. The coast strikes me as being rough and inhospitable, and with the ocean on one side I'll have less land to have to watch. Maybe I'll find myself a lighthouse, somewhere strong and remote like that. Somewhere they can't get to.

I'll be all right on my own. Maybe I'll get lonely, maybe I won't. Whatever happens, I'm just glad I survived. In a strange way I'm almost looking forward to whatever the future brings. The only thing that's guaranteed is it'll be free of the countless bullshit trappings of my previous daily life. A future without the drudgery of trying to hold down a job and pay bills. A future without politics, crap TV, religion and who knows what else. I know I sound naïve, because for every problem the infection has solved, it's created hundreds more, but you have to be positive, don't you?

I often wonder how many people like me are left out here? Am I the only one, or are there hundreds of us creeping quietly through the shadows, avoiding the bodies and, by default, avoiding each other too.

Doesn't matter.

Everything will be all right in the end.

More to the point, I'll be okay.

OFFICE POLITICS

It's over a week since billions of people died. In that time, millions of them have risen up and are now walking the streets, their bodies rotting. Everything has changed. Almost nothing is as it was. *Almost* nothing.

There are thirty-seven houses on Marshwood Road. Only one of them has a freshly cut back lawn. Only one has had its dustbins emptied and the rubbish placed neatly in black plastic sacks at the end of the drive, ready for collection. Only one has had its curtains drawn each night and opened again each morning since the infection killed more than ninety-nine per cent of the population.

Different people deal with stress, loss and other emotional pressures in a wide range of ways. Some implode, some explode. Some shrivel up and hide in the quietest, darkest corner they can find, others make as much noise as possible. Some accept what was happened, others deny everything.

Simon Walters is handling the end of the world particularly badly. The arrival of the infection and the subsequent after-shocks have felt like trivial irritations, further complicating his already over-complicated life. One of life's perennial victims, in his eyes no one has problems big enough to match his. Simon has failed to cope with what has happened, and as a last ditch defence mechanism, he has shut out all other suffering to concentrate fully on his own.

The sudden clattering of the battery-powered alarm clock shattered the early morning quiet. Simon groaned, rolled over and switched it off. It sounded louder than ever this morning. How he hated that damn grinding, whining noise. No, he didn't just hate it, he absolutely loathed it. Especially today. When that unholy clanging began he knew it was time to get up and start another bloody day. The noise was marginally more bearable on Thursdays and Fridays as the weekend neared, but today was Monday, the beginning of yet another week, and the noise was worse than ever.

'Morning, love,' he yawned as he rolled over onto his back and looked up at the ceiling. June, his wife, didn't move. Lazy cow. Okay, so she only had to drop the kids off at school and work and none of them needed to be there until around nine, but she could at least make an effort once in a while and get up with him. She'd been the same all weekend, hadn't got out of bed once. Perhaps when he came home from work tonight he'd sit her down and force her to talk, try and get to the bottom of what was on her mind. God knows something needed to be said. Her personal hygiene standards were slipping. Her once-silky, chestnut brown hair was greasy and lifeless and she was starting to smell. He wondered whether she'd even been bothering to wash? He'd tried to say something to her about it yesterday afternoon but it was a delicate subject and he found it difficult to find the right words. He'd tried his hardest to be tactful but he'd obviously screwed it up and upset her because she'd not said a word. She'd just stared into space and ignored him. She hadn't even had the decency to look at him. Late last night he'd brought her up a glass of wine and a slice of cake as a peace offering but she hadn't touched them.

Simon rubbed his eyes and looked at the clock again. Five past seven. There was no avoiding it, he had to get up. He wanted just to curl up and pretend the day wasn't happening, but he couldn't. He had responsibilities. He kicked off the covers then yawned and stretched and stumbled into the bathroom.

This country is going to hell in a hand-basket, he decided as he stared at himself in the mirror. No water again. The taps had been dry for almost two days now. There really was no excuse. He paid his bills and he expected better than this. The bloody water company hadn't even had the decency to answer the phone when he'd called the emergency number.

God, he thought, *I look awful*. He was bloody tired: tired of his job, tired of his family and their attitude, tired of being taken for granted, and tired of himself. Forty-seven years of age and stuck in a rut with no obvious way of getting out. The only way he could see himself getting back in his family's good books would be to pander to them, and the only way he could afford to do that would be to get promoted at work or find himself a better job. Bloody hell, how he hated his job. He'd worked for the bank for thirty years and in that time he'd seen huge changes. It was no longer the same job he'd walked into after leaving school at age sixteen. Back then it had been a career to be proud of, and working for a bank had given him some kind of status and standing in the community. These days his association with the financial industry made him a social leper. People had once looked up to him but now it was as if he was personally being blamed for all the grief the banks had caused. In reality he was little more than a glorified salesman, left at the counter all day to sell loans, accounts and insurance policies to people who either already had enough loans, accounts and policies or who had only come into the branch to pay a bill. Maybe it was his own fault, he wondered as he began shaving with his old electric razor. He'd seen plenty of people join the bank after him, only to overtake him and be promoted up through the ranks at speed. In fact, he'd trained three of the last five managers he'd worked for, teaching them how to cashier when they'd first joined the company.

The bank needs people like me, Simon told himself as he tugged and pulled at a weekend's worth of stubble with his razor. If it wasn't for the folk at the bottom, the high-flyers and the people at the top wouldn't be able to do their jobs and make their massive profits. Some of his colleagues laughed at him because he'd been in charge of the stationery cupboard at his branch for longer than most of them had been in the bank, but they'd be laughing on the other side of their faces if he didn't put in a stationery order, wouldn't they? How could they sell their loans and their accounts and their insurance policies without the right brochures and forms? And how could they fill them out without any pens? He did more for his branch and the company overall than any of them ever gave him credit for.

The batteries in his razor ran out mid-shave. The left side of his face was mostly clean shaven, the right still covered with stubble. Bloody typical.

They were going to have to go shopping. The kitchen cupboards were practically empty. He should have gone to the supermarket at the weekend. More to the point, June should have. Why was everything left to him all of a sudden? As he sat munching dry cereal, Simon scribbled out a grocery list. He'd leave it on the table for June. Hopefully she'd get the message and go out later and get everything they needed so he could eat properly tonight.

Simon shook his head dejectedly. He wished he understood what was going on. He'd never known anything like it. He was struggling to get on with his family, the house was in a state, and the water, gas and electricity supplies had all failed or become intermittent. To lose one would have been bad enough, but all three at the same time? How could these utility companies be allowed to operate so shoddily? *Imagine the grief if I didn't do my job properly*, he thought. *There'd be hell to pay.*

As ready for work as he was ever going to be, Simon got up and packed his lunch away into his briefcase. It wasn't really very much of a lunch, just a few dry crackers, some biscuits, a packet of crisps he'd found at the back of the cupboard, and a rubbery apple. He jammed his food in amongst the hundreds of old circulars, leaflets, handwritten notes and photocopied procedures that he carried to and from work every day. He never looked at any of it (most of it was probably out of date) but he felt safe when he carried a case full of papers to the office. It was a security blanket, something to hide behind.

'Are any of you out of bed yet?' he called up from the bottom of the stairs. Was he really the only one who could be bothered anymore? Agitated and nervous (he always felt that way before work) Simon left his briefcase at the foot of the stairs and stormed back up to try and motivate his lazy family. He could hear something happening in Jamie's bedroom. At least he was making an effort.

'Ready for school, Jim?'

What was left of Jamie was on the other side of the door, trying to claw his way out, reacting to his father's voice. Simon shoved the door open and sent his son's wasted body tripping backwards. 'Sorry about that,' he said, watching the corpse regain its footing and lurch forward again. The dead boy crashed into him. 'Steady on,' Simon laughed, 'take it easy!' Jamie grabbed at him with barely coordinated hands. 'I haven't got time to muck about now,' Simon said. 'I've got to get to work. I'll see you tonight, okay?'

Still laughing, Simon picked up his son's emaciated body, carried him across the room and dumped him on the bed. Jamie immediately rolled off again and staggered back towards the door.

'Make sure you change your sweatshirt before you go to school, okay?' Simon pointed a disapproving finger at the dribbles of blood and other emissions which had seeped down the front of his dead son's crusty beige jumper. He left the room and shut the door behind him, holding onto the handle for a moment as the remains of his child clattered against the other side.

He knocked on the next door, then went inside. *She's just like her mother*, Simon thought as he peeled back the bedclothes to reveal his daughter Hannah's decaying face. She'd just turned seventeen when she'd died last week. He shook her shoulder, trying to wake her. She'd been working in a hairdresser's salon for just over a month and he didn't want her being late. Jobs were hard enough to come by as it was. She needed to make a good impression. Her dead eyes stared through him unblinking.

'Make sure you're not late,' he told her. No response. Simon leant down and kissed his daughter's discoloured, room-temperature cheek. There was a spider crawling in her hair, spinning a web between her ear lobe and her skull. He flicked it across the room. 'I'll see you tonight, love. Have a good day.'

Having checked the children, Simon took a deep breath before going back into the bedroom he shared with June. 'I'm off to work now, love,' he said quietly. 'I'll see you tonight. Maybe we could talk later? I'd like to know what it is I'm supposed to have done to upset you.'

For a second longer he stood and stared sadly at the body in the bed. June didn't move. Eighteen years of marriage (a few of them had been pretty good years too) and yet she couldn't even bring herself to look at him. How had everything gone so wrong, so quickly?

Simon pushed through the growing crowd of rotting bodies at his front gate and began the short walk to work. He didn't know what these people wanted, but they'd been loitering here for days now. Didn't they have homes to go to? More to the point, didn't they have jobs? Was he solely responsible for keeping the country running? It was beginning to feel that way. There wasn't a single car out on the roads again and he couldn't see any of the usual faces he used to see heading off to work or taking the children to school or walking the

197

dog. All he could see today were more of these dirty, ragged people. Some of them tried to grab at him and pull his clothes, and he couldn't understand why. What did they want from him? What had he done to them? He ran to the end of the road, hoping they'd be gone by the time he got back tonight.

His first port of call (as it was every morning) was the newsagents on the corner of Marshwood Road and Hampton Street. The shop was quiet. Simon picked up his paper (last Tuesday's again – bloody annoying – he'd bought the same paper seven times now) and dug deep in his pocket for change. There was no one about to serve him, and in temper he slammed the coins down on the counter (next to the coins he'd left there on Friday) and stormed out of the shop, cursing.

More bodies up ahead. He asked them to move but they ignored him. Sick of being treated like a second class citizen, he pushed them out of the way and marched on towards the high street, a man on a mission.

Simon hated his job. He felt his guts churn and his bowels loosen as he neared the bank. A traditional and imposing, late-nineteenth century building, its architectural beauty had been compromised by the ever-expanding array of Perspex signs hung above and around its solid wooden doors, and the gaudy advertising hoardings plastered across the inside of its large, arched windows. An ATM had been crow-barred into what had once been a street-level window. Ignoring the unwanted attentions of yet another rancid, dribbling man who came at him repeatedly, he checked the screen of the machine. Bloody thing was down again, and no doubt he'd get the blame. Nothing short of 99.85% uptime was good enough for the bank. Another target missed, and he hadn't even made it through the front door yet.

The staff door at the side of the building was already open, completely against policy. Which idiot had left it like that? Didn't they know there was a strict security procedure to be followed each morning before anyone could go inside? He entered the building and slammed and bolted the door shut behind him. He'd let himself out last thing on Friday evening and he'd assumed that one of the others would have locked up after him. Christ, could the bank have been left open all weekend?

By quarter past nine only three other members of staff had arrived for work. The branch manager (Brian Statham, ten years Simon's junior) had already been in his office when Simon had arrived. Statham obviously wasn't happy. He was pacing about the room furiously, slamming into the door and occasionally banging against the glass, making a heck of a din. Two clerks – Janice Phelps and Tom Compton – were dead at their desks. Janice was slumped over her computer whilst Tom had fallen off his chair and lay spread-eagled on the carpet. Simon was appalled by the lack of work being done in the branch. He knocked on Statham's door to voice his concerns but his manager wasn't interested. He was only marginally more responsive than the others and Simon took it upon himself to address the situation because there was no way the branch could run with a skeleton staff like this. He dug out the telephone numbers of some of the missing staff from their personnel files and tried to call them to find out where they were, but none of the phones were working. The damn lines were *still* down.

Let's just get on with it, Simon decided. It was half-past nine, time to open to the public, and it was all down to him. He walked the length of the banking hall, unlocked the heavy wooden doors and pulled them open.

Nothing happened. A few random figures in the street stopped and turned to see what the noise was but, other than that, nothing. Simon remembered a time when the banking hall would have been filled with an endless queue of customers all day every Monday, and how that queue would have been hanging out of the door first thing. How things had changed.

He wandered back behind the security screen and took up his position behind his till.

Simon didn't mind hard work. He could cope with an in-tray piled high with papers and a huge queue of customers. None of that bothered him just as long as everyone was pulling his or her weight. He'd happily work until midnight if everyone else worked that late too, but today that just wasn't happening. He was already annoyed by the number of staff who hadn't shown for work, but what really irked him was he was the only one actually doing anything.

It was almost midday. The bank had been slowly filling with customers for the last half-hour. After waiting until almost eleven o'clock before the first customer of the day had appeared, a scruffy bunch of punters had now dragged themselves up the concrete wheelchair access ramp and through the swinging doors. Unsavoury looking types, they hadn't actually seemed to want anything, and had just wandered up and down on the other side of the glass panel which separated the back-office from the public area. Simon had shouted for them to come to his till. They'd crowded around his position when they heard his voice and had slammed their hands and faces against the glass, but he still didn't know what it was they actually wanted.

Behind the counter, absolutely nothing was happening. Simon glanced back over his shoulder occasionally and shook his head with despair. What a bunch of lazy bastards. There he was, trying his best to deal with the public, while they all just sat there and did nothing. Janice hadn't moved from her computer and Tom was still on the floor. Statham – inexperienced, overpaid and bloody useless in Simon's opinion – was still pacing up and down in his office. None of them had lifted a damn finger to help him all morning.

Usually he could take it. Usually he would just stand at his till and stew in silence or find a reason to disappear off to the stationery room and hide there for as long as he could, but today was different. Today it wasn't that the others were doing very little, they were doing absolutely *nothing*. Simon wasn't going to let them take advantage of him any longer. He'd had enough. Maybe it was the way his family had been treating him which pushed him over the edge? Or the deteriorating state of the country? Or was it the fact that even the customers in the banking hall (and there were many more of them now) were ignoring him too? He couldn't go on like this: no heat or light, no computers or telephone, and not even any money in his bloody till. The balance had been tipped and it was time to do something about the situation, once and for all. For the first time in as long as he could remember he was ready to stand up for himself and speak his mind.

'Staff meeting,' he announced. The bodies in the banking hall responded to his voice and pushed themselves against the glass, desperately inquisitive. A short distance away, Brian Statham's body also threw itself against the door of its office. Unperturbed, Simon slid his 'till closed' sign into position and locked his drawers. 'I want a staff meeting right now,' he demanded. 'I've had enough of this.'

Simon flung the door of the manager's office open and Statham's body lurched towards him. 'We need to talk, Brian,' he said as he shoved the decaying bank manager back into the room and blocked the way out with a desk. 'Things just can't go on like this. I'll get the others.'

Feeling strangely empowered, Simon went back out into the main office. He grabbed Janice Phelps' shoulder and peeled her off her computer, then tipped her back on her swivel chair and wheeled her through to the manager's room. Tom Compton was a little more awkward. He put his arms under the dead man's shoulders, dragged him along the floor, and dumped him into one of the padded customer chairs on the other side of the office. He was bloody heavy. Simon had to use all his strength to get him in and sit him down.

With Statham trapped behind his desk and the other two now in position, Simon took the floor. 'You all know me pretty well,' he began, trembling with nerves and hoping the others couldn't tell. 'I'm a reasonable man and I'll do whatever's expected of me.' He paused and looked at the lifeless faces surrounding him. The ignorant bastards weren't even listening. He continued regardless. 'We've all got a role to play here. Now in the past you might have thought you were better than me and that your jobs were more important than mine, but I want to put things straight. We're all small cogs in a much bigger machine.' He paused again, pleased with the cliché he'd just used. 'Without me none of you would be able to do your jobs properly. Without me this branch wouldn't function.'

Simon stopped to let the enormity of his words sink in. Almost on cue Tom's body slid off its chair, its head thudding against the wall on the way down. Simon, thrown off his stride momentarily, seethed with anger. He picked up the corpse and shoved it back onto its seat. 'You see,' he yelled, finding it hard to keep his temper in check, 'that's exactly the kind of thing I'm talking about. You all think it's funny, don't you? You think you can all have a good laugh at my expense. Well you can't, not anymore. I've had enough. I've had enough of being the butt of all your stupid bloody jokes and having to do all the donkey work. It's not fair, and it's going to stop.'

Statham's corpse became increasingly animated as Simon raised his voice. The others failed to respond. Their lack of reaction incensed him.

'How dare you?' he screamed. 'How dare you treat me like this? Show some respect, will you? I've been working flat out all morning while you've been sat on your backsides doing nothing. If I stopped working, this place would grind to a halt. Well, things are going to change round here. I'm not going to carry you anymore, do you hear me? From now on you're on your own.'

Still nothing.

Simon grabbed Janice Phelps by the scruff of her neck and screamed into her green-tinged face. 'Are you even listening to me?'

Janice wasn't, but the other bodies in the banking hall clearly were. The dead hordes began to beat their rotting fists against the walls, driven wild by the desperate man's voice. Simon ignored them as best he could. 'There's not a lot that any of us can do today, not until the power comes back on,' he continued, now fractionally calmer. 'I'm going to shut the branch and I suggest we all go home. We'll come back tomorrow morning and try again, okay?'

He looked around the room but no one said anything. The hammering on the wall behind him continued unabated.

Simon remained standing in the middle of the manager's office for a moment, surrounded by his dead colleagues, and he realised he actually felt a little better. The others hadn't agreed with him but, unusually, they hadn't banded together and turned against him either. More importantly, he'd just taken a managerial decision and no one had argued. Could it be that he was about to be shown some respect? Had the rest of them finally realised just how important he was to this branch and to the company? Bloody hell, he thought, maybe he should try the same approach when he got back home tonight? Maybe he could make his family listen too?

'I'm going to lock up,' he said, his voice cocksure and uncharacteristically strong.

Simon still had the key in his pocket from when he'd opened up hours earlier. Brimming with unexpected confidence he stepped over the outstretched feet of Tom's body (he'd slid off the chair again) and left the manager's room. He walked through the back-office to the security door which separated the staff area from the customers. Security conscious and procedure-driven as always, he peered through the fish-eye lens viewing hole before going through.

Bloody hell, the banking hall was full of customers now. Now this was how it should be on a Monday. With no computers working and no cash in his till he couldn't serve any of them of course, so he'd just have to go out and make an announcement. He'd tell the customers what was going to happen in exactly the same way he'd just told the staff. He was getting pretty damn good at taking charge.

A deep breath and he opened the door. A huge mass of rotting flesh immediately surged towards him. Oblivious to the danger, Simon pushed deeper into the crowd, wading through, fighting to keep moving forward as the dead pushed against him.

'If I could have your attention for a second please, ladies and gentlemen,' he shouted, struggling to stay upright. Another wave of decaying corpses came at him from the general direction of the main entrance and knocked him off-balance. He was being pushed further back into the building and he reached out to try and steady himself. The movement of the bodies backed him up against the wooden counter. He climbed up onto the other side of his till position and stood tall above the crowd. Before trying to speak again he brushed himself down. He was covered in stains from the customers. He picked bits of them off his shirt and tie.

'Now look,' he shouted, 'I'm sorry but we've got some problems here today. Our computer systems are down and staff shortages mean that we've not been able to get into the safe. I apologise for any inconvenience, but I'm going to have to ask you all to leave. If you'd like to come back tomorrow morning I'm sure we'll be able to…'

Another forward surge from the crowd distracted him. The sound of his voice seemed to be generating plenty of interest and the bank was filling up now instead of emptying. More and more customers were trying to get inside. The situation was getting out of hand.

'Please listen. I realise this is unusual and I understand you've all been inconvenienced, but I do need your cooperation. There really is nothing more I can do for you today. Come back tomorrow when I'll be more than happy to help…'

But they still weren't listening. Even more people were coming into the building. Simon couldn't stand it when people didn't listen to him. 'Let's have some respect here,' he yelled, shouting at the top of his voice again to make sure even the people still struggling to get inside could hear him. 'A little common-sense, please…'

Simon had gradually edged further and further along the counter. He now found himself at the far end of the banking hall, opposite the doors he'd originally come out here to close. Between him and the other end of the long, narrow space was a mass of at least a hundred furious customers. He looked down into the faces of the nearest few. Christ, they looked riled. If he wasn't careful this situation might turn nasty. He banged on the wall behind him, hoping one of the others in the manager's room would come and help, none of them did. The staff meeting which *he'd* called seemed now to be continuing in his absence.

'Could I have a hand out here please,' he shouted, watching anxiously as another wave of bodies attempted to cram themselves into the already tightly-packed building. 'Tom, Brian… could one of you come and—'

His words were abruptly cut short when several of the corpses, with nowhere else to go, reached up for him. One of them managed to catch hold of his grubby bank uniform trousers. He tried to pull away but lost his footing and slipped down from the counter, falling into the bodies like a bizarre middle-aged crowd surfer at a concert. Fearing for his safety, he covered his head with his hands and curled up into a ball. Then, crawling on his hands and knees across the heavily stained terracotta carpet, he began to move, weaving between the decomposing feet which surrounded him. For a fraction of a second he wondered if he should try to help get the others out, but he knew he couldn't go back. It was too late. The momentary flickering flame of defiance which had burned briefly today had been extinguished just as quickly as it had been lit. Terrified, he closed his eyes and kept pushing forward, working his way around the bodies. He accidentally knocked a handful of them down and they fell into each other like dominos, only to be trampled by others. He kept on moving, forcing himself forward inch by painfully slow inch until he was level with the front door of the bank. Should he try and stand up to close and lock it? Hating himself for being so weak, Simon instead kept on crawling until he was out of the building, and had made it down the ramp and onto the street. The crowd slightly thinner there, he picked himself up and started to run, glancing back at the overrun bank before sprinting home.

Ten o'clock. A half-eaten can of cold baked beans and three-quarters of a bottle of whiskey later.

The house was silent, save for the occasional thump from Jamie, who really should have been in bed by now. Simon sat alone in darkness at the kitchen table, his head in his hands. He couldn't stop thinking about the events of the day now ending. It was bad enough that he'd left the bank wide open and abandoned his colleagues, but that wasn't the worst of it. For a moment back there, he'd actually felt like somebody. It had felt good. It had felt *damn good*. But he'd been brought back down to earth with a bang. He was still a nobody. A forty-seven year old stationery clerk and cashier with no prospects, a family that had virtually disowned him, and an increasingly uncertain future. Maybe he should accept the hand that had been dealt him and just get on with it? *Stick with what you know*, that had always been one of his late father's favourite sayings. *Don't take risks and don't take chances. We're not all made for great things. The world will always need the little men too. Stick with what you know.*

Simon got up and walked out into the hallway, dragging his feet. He paused to look out at the crowd of bodies at the end of his drive before climbing the stairs to bed, a final generous tumbler of whiskey in hand. He undressed, put his dirty shirt in the washing basket with all the others, then put on his pyjamas. He could still hear Jamie banging around in his bedroom. Bloody teenagers. He should be resting or studying. One day my son, he thought, all these problems will be yours. If only he knew what *he* had to put up with every day. His attitude would soon change if he was the one who had to face the daily indignities and humiliations of office politics. Christ, he hoped Jamie didn't make the same mistakes he had. If he'd worked harder at school and not just taken the first job he'd been offered after leaving, maybe things would have been different. Then again, maybe not.

No point dwelling on all that now, he thought as he climbed into bed beside June. She had her back to him, still in the same position as he'd left her this morning. She hadn't done the washing or the shopping. In fact, it looked like she'd spent another day in bed. Bloody hell, she didn't know how easy she had it.

He wrapped his arm around his wife's rapidly putrefying torso and pulled her close. He wished she'd talk to him. He didn't want to go to sleep yet. He wanted someone to listen to his problems and tell him he was doing his best, that it was the rest of them who'd got it wrong. But June wasn't interested, and the silence was deafening.

Simon felt humiliated and let down by everyone, even those closest to him. He'd tried so hard today but, ultimately, all he'd done was make matters worse. Christ, how was he going to face them all at work tomorrow?

BEGINNING TO DISINTEGRATE
Part iv

'You've got to be fucking kidding me,' Jas said, leaning over the front seats of the van. Hollis was behind the wheel, Harte and Gordon beside him. Jas was in the back with his bike and as much food and drink as they'd been able to load up from the supermarket before the swollen crowds of bodies around the building had forced them out.

'I'm serious,' Gordon said. 'I know this isn't the nicest of spots, but it's got everything you said we were looking for.'

'They were in the middle of knocking the bloody place down. Doesn't that tell you something?'

They'd stopped on a stretch of road overlooking a huge and particularly ugly-looking block of flats. More accurately, the one remaining huge and particularly ugly-looking block. Next to it, an enormous pile of rubble and a half-demolished neighbour. Further down the hill, a masonry-strewn space where, until recently, a third block had obviously stood.

'They *were* knocking it down,' Hollis said, 'but *they're* dead. It looks strong enough to me. For the record, I think you might be onto something here, Gordon. It might not be The Ritz, but it does have its advantages.'

'Like what?'

'Safety, security, difficult to access… do I need to go on?'

'Yes,' Jas said, still not convinced.

Hollis sighed and flicked on the wipers to clear the glass and get a better view. A lone corpse buzzed around the outside of the van.

'Much as I hate to admit this, Gord,' Harte said, 'I think you might be right. This place is good. There's gonna be plenty of space in there, and it's only a stop-gap, isn't it? Once things settle down again we can move on.'

Hollis chuckled to himself. 'Once things settle down again! Bloody idiot. You make me laugh, Harte. Ever the bloody optimist.'

'And it's on a hill,' Gordon said.

'So?'

'Two things. First, I know we don't know a lot about what's going on right now, but one thing we do know is the dead still obey the laws of physics, don't they?'

'What are you on about?' Jas grumbled.

'Think about it… the bodies will have no trouble falling, but they'll have real problems trying to get back up.'

'He's got a point,' Hollis said, sounding more surprised than he should have.

'I said I'd got two points, actually,' Gordon continued, indignant. 'Being up on a hill like this means it'll be easy for other people to see us too, doesn't it? If we get some lights in the windows, that kind of thing, anyone else will see us for miles around.'

It pained him to admit it, but Jas knew he was right. More than that, he also knew he was outnumbered. 'So if we are going to stay here, we're going to need to make sure it's completely clear, right?'

'Right,' Harte said.

'What are you thinking?' Hollis asked.

Jas leant forward again and pointed to the area around the base of the apartment block. 'We need to get that space cleared and barricade it as soon as we're done. Make a fucking noise, draw out the dead, then kick 'em down to the bottom of the hill and block ourselves in.'

'And how are you planning on doing that?'

'I'll use the bike. You watch me, mate. I'll be like the fucking Pied Piper out there.'

Jas had always loved the noise his bike made. It was such a loud, ugly, brash, fuck off to everything. Now they were having to stay increasingly quiet to survive, and riding the bike allowed him to vent his frustrations. He felt like screaming most of the time, and this was just about the only way he still could.

Hollis, Harte and Gordon were where he'd left them, parked up overlooking the flats, engine off. They watched from a distance as he cruised the maze of narrow streets behind the grotesque building. It was a bizarre sight, strangely surreal. Often he would disappear, only to emerge again a few seconds later with a slowly marching crowd of bodies in his wake. Once he'd got enough of them following, he'd drive down the steep hill and the dead would trickle after him. And Gordon had been right: once they were down at the bottom, they struggled to get back up.

'We'll keep pushing them back,' Hollis said, feeling increasingly confident and positive. 'It's perfect. All that space at the foot of the hill... we'll build some kind of barrier. There are diggers down there from the demolition, and more cars than we're ever going to need. We'll clear this bloody place and make it our own. Stop those fucking things getting anywhere near us.'

Neither Harte nor Gordon said anything. They both agreed, but the idea of all that work didn't appeal. For now they were happy to sit back and watch the bizarre, almost comical sight unfolding in front of them. The trickle of bodies had become a veritable torrent now, a river of death slowly flooding down the hill, pooling at the bottom.

Several hours later.

With the vast majority of the local corpses now forming a single vile decaying mass at the bottom of the hill, Hollis risked driving the van around to the flats. He parked in the shadows. Gordon opened the door to go inside the building and, almost immediately, the foetid remains of a demolition worker, still wearing his high-vis jacket and safety helmet, lunged at him from out of nowhere. Gordon fell back, the corpse on top of him. 'You're fucking useless, Gord,' Jas said as he ripped off the dead man's helmet then swung at his head with his crowbar, splitting his skull and sending him flying.

'We're going to have to check this whole place out,' Hollis said. 'Every room. Shouldn't take long.'

Gordon held back, keen to let the others go first. They each armed themselves with makeshift weapons, then grouped at the main entrance. 'We should split up,' Jas suggested.

'You never seen a horror film before?' Harte joked. Jas remained stony-faced.

'You come with me,' he told him. 'Hollis, you get Gordon.'

The building reminded Hollis of a three-cornered hat. He and Gordon went left while the other two went right.

Gordon's initial nervousness seemed to reduce with each door they opened and every empty apartment they found. 'We're lucky to have come across this place,' he said, chattering anxiously. Hollis shoved another door open and they quickly checked out the few rooms within the flat: an open-plan living area and kitchen, a dingy bathroom and two bedrooms. The decoration was old and tired, the entire place stripped bare save for a couple of piles of rubbish left by the former occupants.

'Lucky?' Hollis said when they were done. 'How do you work that out?'

'Because this place is in such a good position and it's already been vacated. Imagine if it had still been full of families.'

'Then we wouldn't have given it a second glance,' he answered, working hard and becoming increasingly annoyed that Gordon wasn't. 'We'd have just kept going. Maybe we should have anyway. Jas said he was working security at a mall that hadn't been opened, imagine that. Still, I guess this'll do for now.'

Gordon followed Hollis as he finished checking the flat then moved onto the next. Hollis opened the door, then paused. Not empty. Something here… He'd only taken two steps in when it came at him – another demolition worker corpse, staggering like a dead weight. Gordon squealed like a baby and ran for cover but Hollis wasn't fazed. He grabbed the dead man by the lapels of his donkey jacket and swung him around, then forced him out of the door and out to the balcony. The body couldn't match his speed or coordination, its dead feet scrambling on the ground for purchase. Too late. With a heave of effort, Hollis upended it. Gordon looked down, then looked away again. On the ground below, the dead thing's head popped open like an overripe watermelon; a star-shaped puddle of bright red in all the dusty grey.

'Don't know how I'd cope without you here to help,' Hollis said sarcastically, wiping his hands clean on the back of his jeans as he walked towards the neighbouring flat.

The next door along was blocked. Hollis waited for Gordon to show some initiative, but he wasn't showing any. 'Your turn,' he said. 'Come on, Gord, break a sweat.'

Gordon pushed the door but it wouldn't open. He looked to Hollis for help, but Hollis just looked back at the door. This one was his. Gordon took a step back, then shoulder-charged. The door flew open, and he flew through. Hollis was about to follow him inside when he came flying back out the other way, a girl holding him by the neck. She slammed him up against the wall opposite, almost tipping him over the balcony like Hollis had the body from the previous apartment, and he whimpered. Hollis tried to pull her off him. He hadn't seen a corpse as vicious as this one before.

'Fuck off!' she screamed. She let Gordon go and he slid to the ground. Hollis just looked at her, shocked. The last thing he'd expected to find in this ruin was another survivor.

'I thought you were one of them.'

'I though *you* were one of them,' she replied, breathless.

'What, a corpse that knocks the door?'

'Piss off,' she said.

'You on your own here?'

She shook her head and gestured for them to follow. They did. Hollis stopped in the doorway and looked around, amazed. There were more faces looking back at him than he'd seen since this nightmare had begun. A girl cradling a doll, another smoking a fag, a kid drinking from a can of lager, a prim and proper housewife sitting in a moth-eaten armchair, dabbing at her eyes with a handkerchief, a guy with a straggly beard in a bus driver's uniform, and a balding, overweight bloke who came marching over to him, hand outstretched. 'The cavalry's here then?' he said, hopefully. 'Got any idea—?'

'What's happened? No. You?'

'Bloody hell,' Gordon said, peering cautiously around the door.

'That guy on the bike, he with you?' the fat man asked.

'Yep. You saw him?' Hollis replied.

'We saw what he did. Smart move.'

'But you didn't think to let us know you were here? Maybe come out and help?'

'Sorry... didn't want to get in the way.'

'Are there more of you?'

'This is us, unfortunately,' the girl who'd attacked Gordon said, regaining her composure.

'You picked a good place for a hideout,' Hollis told her. 'That's why we're here. We're planning on fortifying the place.'

'Be our guest,' she said. 'Welcome to the party.'

THE HUMAN CONDITION
Part i – GOING UP

Barry Bushell sat at the dressing table in his wide, palatial executive hotel suite and fixed his make-up. He wondered whether this was just a fad, just a phase he was going through, or if he'd spend the rest of his life dressing as a woman. He wasn't gay and he wasn't transsexual. This wasn't something he'd always wanted to do. He wasn't a drag queen or lady-boy in training. Barry Bushell was just a typical, red-blooded, heterosexual man who happened to have recently discovered that he felt comfortable wearing women's clothes. And when the rest of the world lay dead and decaying in the streets a couple of hundred feet below him, why the hell shouldn't he wear whatever he damn well wanted?

The last seven days had been the strangest of Barry's life so far. Every aspect of his world had been irrevocably changed. If he was honest, his problems had started long before last Tuesday. A few months ago he'd been happy and settled and had a long-term plan. He'd moved into his girlfriend Tina's flat with her and, for a while, life had been good. Better than good, in fact. But their relationship had abruptly ended on what had, until recently, been the worst day of his life. Out of the blue Barry lost his job when the company he worked for went into administration and its CEO went to jail. Penniless and distraught, Barry had returned home unexpectedly early to find his brother Dennis in bed with Tina. She'd proceeded to tell him that Dennis was better in bed than he was and that their relationship was over. By three o'clock that afternoon he'd lost his lover, his brother, his job and his home. That nightmare day had, of course, seemed like the best Christmas ever in comparison with last Tuesday when Barry had helplessly watched the entire population of the city (and, he later presumed, the world) drop dead. After the cruel and unexpected blows that life had dealt him recently, there was a part of him that found some solace in the sudden isolation and quiet. His anger with the rest of the world somehow made the pain easier to deal with. He blamed the inexplicable chaos for his sudden 'gender-realignment' (as he had labelled his drastic change in appearance). And now here he was, alone. As far as he could tell, the last man on Earth. Almost certainly the last man on Earth wearing a dress, anyway.

Five days ago, many of the bodies in the streets had risen. At first Barry had gone back down to ground level to try and find out what was happening, only to quickly return to his comfortable hide-out as soon as he realised that things had worsened, not improved. The people down there were dead. Although they were moving, there wasn't the slightest spark of life left within them. Their sudden reanimation was as impossible to explain as their equally sudden demise days earlier. Barry climbed all the way back up to the top floor of the twenty-eight storey, five star, city-centre hotel and barricaded himself in the Presidential Suite. It was the best place he could find to hide. Within the hotel's three hundred or so bedrooms, its many kitchens, function rooms, dining rooms, bars, restaurants and sports facilities, he'd been able to find pretty much everything he needed to survive, and a vast wardrobe of women's clothing, make-up and accessories to boot. He'd even found a pair of size eleven stiletto shoes.

Barry stood up, smoothed the creases out of his dark blue dress, and looked himself up and down in the full-length mirror to his right. *God I look good*, he thought, pretty damn convincing save for the slight trace of a five o'clock shadow. His first experiments with make-up last week had been over-the-top, leaving him looking like a drag queen, but now he was definitely getting the hang of it. He wore a long straight blonde wig which he'd taken from a shop-window dummy, but he hoped in time his own hair would grow to a sufficient length for him to be able to style it. He'd started painting his fingernails and he was finally getting the hang of walking in heels. That had been the hardest part of all but it had been worth the effort. The knee-high leather boots he'd found in a bedroom on the seventh floor went perfectly with this outfit.

Am I just confused, Barry wondered in a frequent moment of self-doubt, *or have I gone completely fucking insane?* Whatever the answer, he was relatively happy, all things considered. He could do whatever he wanted now. He was in charge. If he wanted to wear a dress then he'd wear a dress. If he wanted to walk around naked, then he could do that too.

It was starting to get late. This was the part of day he really didn't like, when he found it hardest being alone and when he started to think about everything that had happened and all he'd lost. His sudden change of outfit had been deliberately timed to give him a much needed confidence boost to help him get through the dark and lonely hours until morning. As much as he was comfortable in his own company, there were times when he wished this eternal isolation would end. He lit lamps in all the windows of the suite, praying that someone out there would see them, but at the same time also hoping no one would. He had to let the world know where he was, but in doing so he left himself feeling exposed. But he had to do it, he continually told himself. He would be safer with other people.

Barry walked around the perimeter of the vast suite (which covered almost the entire top floor of the building) lighting candles, lamps and torches in every available window. He kept himself busy. So busy, in fact, that he was unaware of a sudden flurry of movement and confusion outside. For the first time in a week, other survivors had entered this part of the city.

'You're a fucking idiot, Nick,' Elizabeth Ferry screamed. 'I said keep out of the city, not drive right through the bloody city centre. Fancy a little late night shopping did you?'

'Shut up,' Nick Wilcox yelled back. 'If it hadn't been for the fucking noise you two make with your constant bloody arguing, I wouldn't have taken the wrong turn in the first place.'

'Don't bring me into this,' Doreen Phillips said, listening in as usual. 'It's got nothing to do with me.'

'Oh, it's never got anything to do with you, has it?' Ted Hamilton said from the seat directly behind her. 'Of course it's your fault, Doreen. You're a bloody troublemaker.'

Doreen turned around and glared at Ted who was, as usual, filling his face with food. 'And you're a greedy fat bastard who should—'

'For crying out loud,' Elizabeth said, interrupting her. 'Just give it a rest.'

Doreen stopped talking, folded her arms and slumped into her seat like a scolded child.

'Just keep going, Nick,' John Proctor said from three seats back. His voice remained comparatively calm. 'We're here now and shouting at each other isn't going to help. Just keep driving.'

Nick took one hand off the steering wheel for a second, just long enough to wipe his face and rub his eyes. He'd been driving for hours and he was struggling but he wasn't about to let the others know. They annoyed him beyond belief. He'd only found five other survivors since all of this began. Why did it have to be this five? This small, volatile, and dysfunctional group had been together for just three days, discovering each other by chance as they'd each individually wandered through the ruins of the world. Elizabeth and John Proctor had met first, Elizabeth having walked into the church where he used to preach, just as he was tearing off his dog-collar and walking out. A cleric of some thirty years standing, his already wavering faith had been shattered by the unstoppable infection which had raged across the surface of the planet and killed millions. If this God of ours is so all-powerful, loving and forgiving, he'd asked Elizabeth, then how could the fucker have let this happen? John's sudden loss of faith had been as powerful and life-changing as his initial discovery of the church in his early days at college. Elizabeth had, in all seriousness, suggested that the plague might be some kind of divine retribution – a great flood for our times. Did she think he was a 21st century Noah? He told her in no uncertain terms that she was out of her fucking mind if she believed any of that crap.

Ted Hamilton, a plumber, part-time football coach and full-time compulsive comfort eater, had been on the roof of an office block working on a corroded pipe when the infection struck. He'd had an incredible view of the destruction from up there, but that was where he'd stayed, too afraid to come down. He'd sat on the roof for hours until he saw Doreen Phillips walking down the high street, shopping bags in hand, stepping gingerly over and around the mass of tangled bodies which covered the ground. Together they'd wandered aimlessly in search of help which never came. Their constant shouting and noise had, however, eventually attracted the attention of Paul Jones, a sullen and quiet man who preferred to keep himself to himself but who had recognised the importance of sticking together, no matter who these people were or how stupid they appeared.

Paul had suggested establishing a base from which they could explore the dead land around them and, perhaps, find more survivors. As obvious and sensible as his plan had been, it also proved to be unnecessary because as they struggled to establish themselves in a guest house on the edge of a small town, more survivors had found them. Three days ago the eerie silence of the first post-infection Friday morning had been shattered by the unexpected arrival of a fifty-three-seater coach driven by Nick Wilcox. Nick – who had previously driven coaches for a living, usually taking bus loads of pensioners around various parts of the south coast – had ploughed through the town with a nervous disregard for anything and everything, destroying any corpses that got in his way. Paul and Ted ran out into the road and flagged him down and it was only Elizabeth's quick reactions (fortunately Nick had picked her and John up a day earlier) which stopped him from gleefully running them both down.

The motley collection of survivors made the coach their temporary travelling home. It was relatively strong and comfortable with room inside for them, their belongings, and enough supplies to last for a couple of weeks. And the coach had a huge advantage over everywhere else they'd previously tried to shelter because it moved. When things got ugly or there were too many bodies around for comfort, they just started the engine and drove somewhere else.

'Keep going, Nick,' John said again, his calm and deceptively relaxed tone helping diffuse the tension. 'Get us onto a major road, then follow it back out of the city.'

'Problem is I can't see the bloody road, never mind follow it.' Even with the headlights on full-beam, Nick could see very little. The streets were teeming with movement, the dead continually swarming around the vehicle.

'Does anyone know where we are?' Elizabeth asked hopefully. 'Anyone been here before?'

No one answered.

'We could just stop,' Ted eventually suggested, his mouth still full of food. 'We've done it before. Sit still and shut up and they'll leave us alone after a while.'

'Come on, Ted,' Elizabeth said, 'there's got to be a better way. They'll take hours to go, you know that as well as I do, and there are hundreds of them around here. We've never seen them in these kinds of numbers.'

'I'm not sleeping on the floor again,' Doreen protested, her voice high-pitched and grating. 'It's bad for my back. It's all right for you lot, you don't have to—'

'Doreen,' Ted interrupted, 'with all due respect, love, would you shut your fucking mouth. You couldn't keep quiet if you tried so there's no point talking about it.'

Nick managed half a smile as he steered the bus around a sharp bend in the road and powered into another pack of corpses. He knew as well as the rest of them that many hours of total silence would be necessary if they wanted to try and fool the dead into leaving them alone. With Doreen on board five minutes of silence was impossible, never mind anything longer.

'Bloody hell,' Ted said suddenly, swallowing his last mouthful of food and wiping his greasy mouth on his sleeve. 'Look at that.'

'What?' Paul asked, quickly moving along the length of the bus towards the others, surprising them with his sudden involvement. Ted pressed his face against the window and pointed up.

'Up there.'

'What is it?' Elizabeth anxiously demanded.

'Lights,' he answered, not quite believing himself. 'Up there, look.'

Visible fleetingly amongst the shadows of numerous tall, dark buildings, the light – although relatively dull – burned bright in the total blackness of everything else.

High above the disease-ridden streets, Barry's quiet and solitary life was filling with contradictions. He wanted to be surrounded by light, but the brightness left him feeling vulnerable and exposed. Likewise, the darkness sometimes made him feel safe, but it was also unsettling; he was scared of the shadows that filled the hotel at night. He wanted some noise to end the eerie silence but, at the same time, he wanted the quiet to remain so he could hear everything that was happening elsewhere. He wanted to sit out of sight in the comfort of his suite, but he also felt compelled to constantly check the windows. He knew he was alone in the building and that it was secure (he'd checked every room and had got rid of every dead body over the last week), but his nervous paranoia left him feeling convinced there were bodies climbing the staircases and walking the halls, moving ever closer. He felt sure that rotting hands would reach out of the shadows for him whenever he opened a door. Whatever he was doing he felt uncomfortable and unsafe, and it was far worse at night. Each successive evening he found the darkness harder to cope with, and that led to the cruellest paradox of all: Barry's fear kept him awake night after night. Only when the morning (and the light) finally came was he able to relax enough to sleep. Invariably he would drift and doze through the morning and early afternoon and miss almost all of each precious day.

He wandered listlessly along the long west wall of the suite, the heels of his boots click-clacking on the marble floor. Where was this all going to end, he wondered? Was he destined to stay here at the top of the hotel indefinitely? It wasn't a bad option, in fact he struggled to think of anywhere else that would be safer or more comfortable. The height of the building meant it was unlikely the corpses down below would ever see or hear him. The only problem would come when his supplies ran out. Okay, so he appeared to have the entire city at his disposal, but even if he managed to find everything he needed, there remained the problem of dragging it up literally hundreds of steps to his new home. Maybe he could set up some kind of winch or pulley system? Perhaps he could use the window-cleaner's cradle he'd seen hanging halfway down the side of the building?

His mind full of questions and half-considered answers, Barry reached the corner of the room and stopped walking. He turned around and was about to retrace his steps when he happened to glance down into the dark streets hundreds of feet below. In disbelief he watched the bizarre sight of a coach ploughing through the rotting crowds, sending whole and dismembered bodies flying in all directions, hurtling at speed towards the hotel. He waited for a fraction of a second – just long enough to convince himself that what he was seeing was real – before throwing off his boots and sprinting out to the staircase barefoot.

'Next left,' Paul ordered. He'd moved up to the front of the bus and was now standing next to Nick, doing his best to guide their driver through the mayhem and towards the light. 'No, wait, not this one. Take the next one.'

Nick yanked the steering wheel back around, making the whole coach lean over to one side. Their breakneck journey had become so turbulent that even Doreen Phillips was uncharacteristically quiet and subdued.

'Can you see where it's coming from?' Nick asked, glancing up for a second and glimpsing the light again.

'Not sure,' Paul admitted. 'It's bloody high up, though.'

Nick braced himself as he forced the bus over a low mound of rubble and mangled metal at the side of the road. The passengers behind him – not expecting the sudden jolt – bounced up in their seats as the huge vehicle clattered up and then back down onto the road.

'Take it easy,' Ted protested.

'Next left,' Paul said for the second time, his voice more definite than before.

'You sure?'

'Positive. I can see it. We're almost directly under the light now.'

Nick slammed on the brakes and swung the bus around the corner into another street which was as difficult to navigate as the last. Huge crowds of lumbering bodies dragged themselves towards the approaching vehicle from all directions. Nick kept his foot down, knowing the quicker they moved, the more chance they had of cutting through the rancid crowds. Scores of corpses were wiped out by the flat-faced frontage of the coach, thumping into it with a relentless *bang, bang, bang* like hail on a tin roof.

'How far now?' Nick asked.

Paul crouched down low and looked up to his right. 'Almost there.'

John got up and scurried down to the front of the coach, holding onto the seat-backs and struggling to keep his balance. 'It's a hotel,' he said. 'Look, there's a name on the side of the building.'

'So where do I go?' Nick asked, unable to see anything in the relentless gloom.

'There must be a car park or something?' John suggested. 'Maybe around the back or underground?'

'Get as close to the main entrance as you can,' Paul said. 'We need to minimise the distance we have to cover on foot.'

'And how am I supposed to do that? I can't see a fucking thing.'

'Here!' Paul shouted. 'Sharp right! Now!'

With no time to properly consider his actions, Nick turned the wheel as instructed. The dark silhouette of the hotel loomed large in front of him. 'Where?' he screamed, desperate for help and guidance.

'Just keep moving,' Paul yelled back. 'Keep going forward until—'

He didn't get to finish his sentence. The low light and constant criss-crossing movement of hundreds of bodies made the distance between the front of the coach and the front of the hotel impossible to accurately gauge. His foot still down hard on the accelerator, Nick sent the coach over a kerb, then crashed through the glass doors at the front of the building. Their velocity was such that the coach kept moving forward until the twisted metal and rubble dragged under its wheels eventually acted as a brake. Three-quarters inside the building, with its back end jutting out into the street, the bus came to a sudden, undignified halt in the hotel's imposing, marble-floored reception. The front wheels were wedged over the lip of an ornate and long-since dried up decorative fountain.

No one moved.

'My back...' Doreen moaned from somewhere on the floor under a pile of carrier bags full of clothes and other belongings.

'Is everyone all right?' John asked. No one answered. 'Is *anyone* all right?' he asked again, slightly revising his original question.

Paul shook his head clear and got back to his feet. He glanced over at Nick who was trying to stem the flow of blood from a gash just above his right eye. 'Nice driving,' he sneered.

'Fuck off,' Nick spat back at him.

'Shit,' Elizabeth said from somewhere in the darkness behind them both. 'We've got to get out of here.' There was sudden fear in her voice which they all picked up on. Without pausing for explanation the survivors grabbed as many of their bags of belongings as they could carry, and ran for the door at the front of the coach which Paul had already opened. He glanced down the side of the long vehicle and immediately saw what Elizabeth had seen. A large part of the hotel entrance had collapsed. Although still partially blocked by the bus, there was now a gaping hole where the main doors had been, and hundreds of bodies were already swarming into the building.

'Over here,' a voice yelled at them from the darkness. Barry Bushell stood at the bottom of the main hotel staircase at the other end of the vast, dust-filled lobby, waving a torch and gesturing for them to follow him. The light inside the building was minimal and they struggled to make him out at first. Nick was the first to locate him. He ran across the rubble-strewn room, closely followed by Doreen, Elizabeth and Paul.

'Come on, Ted,' John pleaded. 'Leave your stuff, we have to move.'

Ted was busy collecting his belongings. Loaded up with bags and boxes he tripped, falling into the dried-up fountain.

'Keep going,' he wheezed, already out of breath. 'I'll catch up.'

John could see he was struggling. 'Just leave that stuff. We'll manage without it.'

'*I* need it,' Ted said, groaning with effort.

'But they're coming! Drop the bags and get your backside over here!'

Ted was oblivious to the number of approaching bodies which were now dangerously close. They seemed to move as one, like a thick liquid slowly seeping out over the ground floor of the hotel, a slow-motion flood. Most of the coach had already been surrounded. John looked around to see that the rest of his group had all but disappeared. Just Elizabeth remained, standing at the bottom of the staircase, waiting for him.

'Move, Ted! Don't be a bloody idiot!' John screamed. Ted, now on his feet again, tried to speed up but, if anything, he was slowing down. He was desperately unfit and overloaded with food. He glanced back and, seeing how close the nearest bodies were, he tried unsuccessfully to increase his speed. But he couldn't make his short, pudgy legs move any faster. It was hopeless. 'Move!' John yelled at him again, nervously backing away towards Elizabeth.

Most people would have dug deep and done everything possible to cover the remaining distance to get to safety, but Ted did the opposite. He'd had enough. He was already exhausted and the staircase ahead of him seemed to stretch up into the darkness forever. He knew he'd never make it. An eternal pessimist, he'd already decided his number was up. He made one last pathetic attempt to move a little quicker but it was nowhere near enough and the distance still seemed impossible. Ted stopped and John watched helplessly as the mass of bodies engulfed him.

Elizabeth was already on her way up the stairs. John turned and ran after her. He couldn't see where he was going, but as long as he kept going up, he thought he'd be okay. He could soon hear voices up ahead.

'So what the fucking hell have you come as?' Nick asked the stocky, six foot tall transvestite who'd saved them. They'd briefly stopped to regroup on a landing a few flights up. Barry used his torch to check who was with him. It was the first time any of them had seen him clearly, and he could see the puzzled expressions on their faces. Suddenly self-conscious, he didn't know what to say. He hadn't needed to explain his bizarre dress-code to anyone else yet, and in the chaos of the last few minutes, he'd forgotten what he was wearing. For a moment he felt foolish before remembering how good these clothes made him feel. What he was wearing was of absolutely no consequence to anyone else. He'd saved their lives. Fuck 'em.

'I'm Barry,' he answered. 'Barry Bushell.'

'So why are you wearing a dress?'

'Because I want to.'

'Well I think you look lovely, dear,' Doreen said as she passed him on the landing. In dire need of a cigarette, she patted him on the shoulder and pointed upwards. 'This way, is it?'

'Just keep going,' he replied. 'Top floor.'

Doreen nodded and kept climbing, her nerves negating her tiredness. Nick waited on the landing for John to catch up. 'Where's Ted?' he asked. John shook his head.

'Didn't make it,' he said, panting with effort. 'Silly bugger got caught.'

'Shit,' Nick mumbled, genuinely saddened for a moment. Then he shook his head and carried on up the stairs.

The climb up to the top floor seemed to take forever. Even though their appreciation of material possessions and the value of property had been massively reduced by the events of the last seven days, the opulence and scale of the vast penthouse apartment Barry had claimed as his own still impressed all of them.

'Nice place she's got here,' Nick said as he looked around the low-lit rooms. Some of the group were sitting around a rectangular dining table, others were sprawled on a nearby sofa.

'Shh…' Elizabeth scowled. 'Leave him alone. He's obviously got problems.'

'We've all got problems, but we don't all feel the need to cross-dress, do we?'

'Lovely place, though,' Doreen agreed. 'Just think of all the famous people who must have stayed here. Royalty? Film stars?'

'Why?' Paul said. Doreen looked puzzled. How could he not be excited by the prospect of sleeping in a hotel room that might have been used by millionaires and mega-stars?

'Just imagine who might have sat around this table…' she continued.

'Why waste your time thinking about empty people like that? The people who could afford to stay here had too much money and not enough sense. You shouldn't look up to them. The only difference between you and them was the size of their bank accounts compared to yours. Anyway, they're all dead now. You're not.'

'It was more than that,' Elizabeth continued, siding with Doreen for once. 'It's about glamour and watching them do the things that you always dreamed about doing and…'

'So did you two used to read all the celebrity gossip and buy all the glossy magazines?'

'Absolutely,' Elizabeth said quickly.

'And I bet you used to watch soap operas and reality TV shows?'

'Never missed my soaps,' Doreen told him with something resembling a bizarre sense of pride in her voice.

'Pathetic,' Paul said. 'Bloody pathetic. It's got nothing to do with glamour or anything like that. You both used to swallow all that crap because your own lives were pointless and empty.'

'Thanks a lot,' Elizabeth said angrily. 'Let us know when it's our turn to tear you to pieces.'

'Where are all your celebrities now?'

'Dead, probably,' Nick interjected. 'Face down in the fucking gutter.'

'You know what I think?' Paul continued, even though he knew neither of them cared. 'I think that if by some strange twist of fate

223

one of your precious celebrities had survived and was sat here now instead of one of us, you'd still be treating them like some kind of fucking god.'

'As long as it was you they were here instead of, I wouldn't care,' Elizabeth said. 'Sometimes you're so far up your own backside that—'

'I've got more food than this,' Barry said, dropping a tray onto the table, deliberately interrupting the conversation. 'I'm just trying to make it last. I'm trying to avoid going outside.'

'I'd be trying to avoid going outside if I looked like that,' Nick said, smirking.

'Leave it, Nick,' John sighed. 'Christ, what's the matter with you lot? We've just lost our transport and poor old Ted, and all you can do is argue and mock each other.'

'Honestly,' Nick continued, not listening to a word John had said, 'we wait all this time to find someone else alive, and they turn out to be a fucking faggot!'

Barry grabbed Nick by the throat, dragged him off his chair and slammed him down onto the floor. He tightened his grip, painted nails digging into his skin.

'Let's just get this over and done with, shall we?' He paused for an answer which Nick was in no position to give. 'Listen, mate, I might be wearing a dress, but I'm not a fucking faggot, and it wouldn't matter if I was. I'm not surprised you've got a problem with what I'm wearing. Fact is, I like it. I don't know why, but dressing like this is helping me come to terms with the fact that all my friends and family and probably everyone else I've ever known is dead. I'm not a pervert, I'm just a normal bloke who's decided to try wearing dresses for a while, okay?'

Barry let Nick go. Subdued, he slowly got up. 'Okay, okay… Keep your hair on.'

Barry let the obvious reference to his shoulder-length wig go. 'It doesn't matter what any of us is wearing, does it? It's not going to make any difference. Same as the colour of our eyes won't make any difference either, or whether we're right or left handed. Fact is we're all in this mess together and we'll need to work with each other to get ourselves sorted.'

'Well said,' John agreed.

'So tell me,' Barry continued, his voice louder and more confident, 'who exactly have we got here and what the hell are we going to do about the fucking big hole you've made in the front of my hotel?'

Introductions and pointless discussions about what had happened to the rest of the world took the group through the final hours of day seven and well into day eight. Spirits were temporarily high: Barry had the company he'd craved and the others had found a safer, far more comfortable hideout than the back of Nick's coach.

John pulled up a chair and sat in front of the widest window in the suite for hours, watching the night melt away and be overtaken by the first light of day. As the sun began to climb, more and more of the shattered world was revealed. Down at street level it had been difficult to fully appreciate the enormity of what had happened. From twenty-eight floors up, however, the extent of the devastation was clear.

'You okay, John?' Elizabeth asked, disturbing him.

'I'm fine,' he replied, almost managing a smile. 'I was just looking out there. Look at it, Liz. The whole bloody world's in ruins.'

Elizabeth leant against the window. He was right. For as far as she could see the world was dead, drained of all colour and life. Apart from the bodies in the streets, nothing moved. From this height they could see for miles into the distance, and the scale of what had happened around them was humbling. It was soul-destroying.

'Much happening out there?' Nick asked as he joined them. He'd been sitting on his own but preferred the company of others.

'Not a lot,' John answered.

'I wouldn't be too sure about that,' Elizabeth said, her face still pressed hard against the glass. She'd diverted her attention away from the horizon to the more immediate area directly below. 'Have you seen what we've done?'

Nick peered down. The largest crowd of bodies that any of them had yet seen had gathered around the entrance to the building and were pushing their way in through the huge hole the survivors had made with the bus last night. 'Bloody hell,' he said.

Concerned, John stood up and looked down. The sight of the massive gathering made his legs weaken. His mouth suddenly dry, he swallowed hard and looked around for Barry.

'What's the problem?' Barry asked, walking over to the others. John pointed and Barry looked down. 'Christ almighty.'

'They can't get up here, can they?' Nick asked.

'Of course not,' Elizabeth said quickly. Barry was less confident.

'I can't see why not,' he said. 'If enough of them keep pushing forward from behind, my guess is the furthest forward will start climbing eventually.'

'But they won't get up here. We struggled to get up, so surely they won't be able to…'

'This place has one main staircase right in the middle of the building,' he explained, still staring deep into the vast crowd below. 'There are a couple of fire escapes, but they're blocked off as far as I know. To be honest, I didn't look into security too deeply when I got here. There didn't seem to be any need when the place still had a front door.'

'So what are you saying?' Elizabeth pressed.

'I'm saying that if there's enough of them and they keep coming, who knows what they'll be able to do. Give them enough time and there's every chance they'll manage to get up here.'

'But we can get out if we need to?'

'Well, I think we'll be able to get down no problem,' Barry said, 'but what we do once we're down there is anyone's guess. Thanks to you lot the building's surrounded and I can't see an obvious way out.'

'Let's all keep calm and try and get things into perspective,' John said quietly, doing his best to prevent panic from spreading. 'The chances of them getting to us are slim and we're so high up here that they'll probably disappear long before they even get close.'

'You reckon?' Nick said. 'There doesn't seem to be much else going on in town this morning, does there? Looks like we're the main attraction.'

Barry, Elizabeth, Nick and John stood side by side at the window and stared down. The streets below were filled with grey, staggering bodies and in the absence of any other distraction, the whole damn rotting mass seemed to be converging on the hotel. There were already thousands of them down there, and thousands more were dangerously close.

DAY NINE

THE GARDEN SHED

Lester Prescott thrives on order and uniformity. His pristine home is situated in a relatively well-to-do residential area. He is well respected socially and is the most accurate and productive accountant ever to have been employed by Ashcroft, Jenkins and Harman. Lester Prescott thinks in black and white. Show a child a cardboard box and they'll turn it into a spaceship, a plane, a car, a robot suit or whatever else their uninhibited imaginations can create. As far as Lester Prescott is concerned, however, a cardboard box is, was and only ever could be a cardboard box.

Lester often finds it difficult to connect with people. Although he tries hard, over the years he has proved himself to be a boring and dull husband, an unimaginative lover and, perhaps worst of all, a disappointment as a father. People's emotions and reactions cannot be governed by procedures, and that frustrates him. Their lives are never as clear cut and predictable as the columns of figures he can interpret with ease. He struggles with spontaneity.

Lester and his long-suffering wife, Janice, have been married for twenty-seven years. For twenty-five of those years they've lived in the same semi-detached house a third of the way down Baker Road West. Twenty-three years ago next month their daughter Madeline was born. An only child, Maddy left home at the age of eighteen to study. She loves her parents dearly but only sees them when she absolutely has to. She recently qualified as a nurse and now works in a large hospital on the other side of town.

Last Tuesday morning, Janice, Maddy and more than six billion other people were struck down by the most virulent virus ever to blight the face of the planet. Most unexpectedly, Lester Prescott survived.

Day eight ends and day nine begins. What will this day bring? This last week has been harder than I could ever have imagined. None of it makes any sense. I've started coming here at night to Maddy's room to try and understand. I sit on the end of her bed and remember how things used to be. The room is just as she left it when she went to university. Mother and I didn't see any point changing anything until she'd got herself married and settled down in her own home. It'll never happen now, of course. Our home is a little oasis of normality in a world gone completely mad.

The chain of events which began last Tuesday are as inexplicable today as when they first happened. It began like any other Tuesday at the offices of AJH. I arrived at work at ten to eight, got my desk ready and then started on my figures. Bill Ashcroft, the senior partner, was the first person I saw die. He was talking to his secretary Allison when it took him, and I then watched it work its way through the entire office, killing everyone, and I just sat there in the middle of it all, helpless and too afraid to move, waiting for my turn. I still don't understand why I escaped, but before I knew it I was the only one left alive.

I left the office as quickly as I could, stopping only to put my papers away, lock my desk, pack my briefcase and fetch my newspaper and coat from the cloakroom.

The journey home was harrowing and painfully slow. Outside it was as if someone had simply flicked a switch: everyone seemed to have died at almost exactly the same moment. I saw hundreds of bodies, thousands even. It seemed to take forever to work my way back home through the chaos.

I had been thinking about Janice and Maddy constantly since leaving the office, and I'd hoped to return home to find Janice sitting there waiting for me. After all, I had survived, so why shouldn't she have too? But it wasn't to be. I found her in the kitchen, lying on her back on the floor in an inch of water. The tap had been left running and the room was awash. Dear Janice was soaked through. I set to work sorting things out straight away. I dried her off as best I could, then wrapped her in a blanket and covered her with black plastic refuse sacks which I taped up. It wasn't an easy or pleasant task but I managed to get it done. It seemed a little undignified at the time, but I was acting in accordance with the instructions from the government anti-terror information booklet we received last summer. Janice often used to mock me because, by nature, I am occasionally pedantic and perhaps a little obsessive. She used to say that my attention to detail was infuriating, but thank goodness I am that way is all I can say. As a result of the filing system I use in my study I was able to find the booklet immediately and deal with my wife's body quickly, humanely and hygienically, just as instructed.

As I worked to move Janice's body and clean up the mess in the kitchen, I kept a constant eye out for Maddy. I felt sure she'd be home before long and I wanted to make sure that Mother had been properly dealt with before she arrived. My mood darkened with every minute. As if losing my closest companion wasn't enough, with each second that passed it appeared increasingly likely that my only child was gone too. Eventually, at half-past one that afternoon, I decided I couldn't sit and wait any longer and so I set out to find her. I took my pedal bike from the garage, but once again my progress was frustratingly slow. I arrived at the hospital after an hour and ten minutes hard cycling, and immediately started to look for her. According to her timetable she should have been on duty but I couldn't find her there. I had an awful time searching through the bodies on the ward for Maddy. So many poor, innocent people had lost their lives so suddenly and without explanation…

When I couldn't find her in any of the areas I knew she covered, I worked my way back from the hospital to the house she shared with her friends Jenny and Suzanne. It was there that I found our little girl in her front yard, lying face down in the grass. Such a cruel, undignified end to such a beautiful young life. It broke my heart to see her like that. I packed her things, then used her car to bring her back home so I could deal with her body as I had Mother's.

I read through the government booklet again that afternoon. It said that the bodies of the deceased should be buried away from the house. I dragged them both the length of the garden to the small area of lawn between the garden shed and Maddy's old swing. We gave her that swing on her sixth birthday but Mother and I decided we'd keep it even after she'd grown up and stopped using it. It was always there to remind us of her. She used to have so much fun playing on it with her friends. Even now whenever I look at it I see young Maddy swinging in the summer sunshine. We'd hoped we'd have grandchildren to use it one day.

I unlocked the shed and went inside.

The garden shed has always been my escape. As well as being a very practical and convenient storage space, it was also a quiet little haven where I could sit and work or read my paper or listen to sport on the radio without interruption. Maddy and her mother liked their television and their soap operas but I couldn't abide the constant noise. Quite often – almost daily in the summer months, certainly most weekends – I would shut myself away in the shed and relax in my own company with a cup of tea or a wee glass of something stronger.

Before I picked up my tools I sat down in my chair in the corner of the shed and tried to take stock of all that had happened. Sitting there it was hard to comprehend the enormity and finality of events and I could scarcely believe that my wife and daughter's bodies lay just inches away. With tears in my eyes I looked around the little wooden hut and remembered all I had lost. On the wall opposite I stored the summer things that Maddy and her mother used to use; plastic patio furniture, sun-loungers and deck chairs, garden games and the like. In a small wooden box tucked away in one corner I found a collection of brightly coloured buckets and spades which I had again kept for those grandchildren we'd now never have. They reminded me of summer holidays long gone where Maddy, Mother and I would play on the beach in the blistering sun. Distant memories now…

With a heavy heart I stood, picked up my spade and the garden edging tool, and set to work. I took a rough measurement of the length and width of Maddy's body (she was slightly taller and thicker set than her mother) and marked out the shape of the two graves in the turf close together. I carefully lifted the turf and then spent the next two hours digging before placing them both in their plots. Although we used to go to church most Sundays I wasn't quite sure what I should say before I buried their bodies. It was difficult to think of the right words. I loved them both very much but I've always found it hard to properly express my feelings. Being gushing, emotional and romantic is something I've always struggled with, much to Janice's chagrin. In any event I thanked God for their lives as I thought I should, and I asked that they would now find peace. I was confident they would, but I was less sure about what the future held in store for me.

I'm not the kind of man to sit there feeling sorry for himself. I wouldn't have been doing anyone any favours if I'd done nothing. I spent a lot of time during the first two days of the crisis trying to understand what had happened, but I soon realised it was impossible. I read through the government booklet again but it was of little use. It kept talking about how the authorities would help and how I should wait for further instructions. I was ready to wait, but I was pretty certain that no instructions would ever be forthcoming. As far as I could tell (and I didn't do anything to verify the validity of my supposition) I was the only man left alive.

I started to plan. It's in my nature. I had plenty of food in the house, but I knew I needed more. I needed to be ready to fend for myself for a long, long time. With that in mind I took the car around to the shops and started to collect supplies: food, cleaning materials, clothing, bedding, medicines… even books, paper and pens. I had already realised how important it would be to keep myself occupied, both physically and mentally. I had written a comprehensive list of things I needed, several pages long, and I managed to get just about everything on it. It didn't feel right taking goods without paying, but I had no means of making payment and no one to make payment to. I made a duplicate list – a ledger if you like – of what I'd taken and noted the cost of each individual item. When some semblance of normality finally returned, I decided, I would go back and settle my debts. The proprietors of the various shops I visited, if any had survived, would undoubtedly understand.

The third morning was as disorientating as the previous two. Just when I was beginning to get used to my situation, it changed again. On the third morning many of the bodies suddenly got back up onto their feet again. When I saw the first of them I hoped that was the end of it, that this was the first indication of an impending return to normality. It quickly became clear that was not going to be the case. The bodies which moved were uniformly unresponsive and slow. I stood out in the middle of the road in front of the house and stopped Judith Springer from number nineteen as she staggered past the end of the drive. I had known both Judith and her husband Roy for many years. She looked the same as always (save for a few unpleasant signs of deterioration) but she failed to react as a normal human being should. For goodness sake, she wasn't even breathing!

I shut my door on the rest of the world again and went through to the back of the house. What about Maddy and her mother? Had their condition changed also? I found myself faced with the bizarre and repulsive, yet still very real possibility, that the wife and daughter I had buried two days earlier might now be trying to escape from their graves, digging their way back out through the dirt I'd shovelled over them. I crouched down next to the two slightly raised humps in the turf. There had been no change as far as I could see. I didn't know what to do for the best. I lay there and put my ear to the ground and listened but I couldn't hear anything and I couldn't feel any movement. I reassured myself that not all of the bodies outside had moved. Had I just buried Maddy and her mother too deep for them to get out? In the terror of the moment I seriously contemplated exhuming their bodies, but what would that have achieved? What difference would it have made if they could move? Judith Springer was most certainly dead, despite the fact that she was somehow mobile again. I decided it was kinder both to Maddy and her mother to leave them both where they were and preserve what remained of their dignity.

I sat out in the garden shed again that afternoon and read a book and occasionally dozed. My sleep was punctuated with desperate dreams; twisted nightmares about my dead daughter and wife. It was almost dark when I woke and went back inside. The low light increased my unease. I regretted having slept and I tossed and turned all night in bed.

As the situation outside continued to change, I made a conscious effort to try and keep myself positive and motivated. I had left the car parked on the drive and had stored the provisions I'd collected at the far end of the garage. In fact, I had amassed such an impressive mountain of supplies that it filled almost the entire length of the cold, rectangular room. On the morning of the fourth day I sat at my desk in the study and made a list of my daily dietary requirements. I used reference books, our family medical dictionary and an encyclopaedia to calculate the minimum I would need to eat each day to survive. I then spent the entire day in the garage, dividing the tins, boxes and bags of food into equal-sized daily allowances, making sure there were sufficient levels of the various vitamins, proteins and whatever other chemicals I needed for each day. I also allowed myself a daily luxury – a can of beer or a packet of sweets for example. It quickly became apparent that I wouldn't be able to get quite everything I needed from my provisions. I decided I would have to look at fetching vitamin and mineral supplements when I next went out, if they proved necessary. During the day it also occurred to me that none of the food I had was fresh. Perhaps, I thought to myself, I could start trying to grow my own vegetables if my situation remained unchanged for any length of time. Janice and I had always maintained a small vegetable plot, but I would probably need to expand the operation over the coming year. Sitting there on the garage floor surrounded by packages of food rations, I found the idea of having to fend for myself on such a basic level strangely exciting.

I worked long and hard that day, and by eight o'clock when the light had begun to fade, I was finished. On the garage floor lay forty-three separate food parcels, one for each of the next forty-three days. I tried not to think of them as rations but that, in effect, was what they were. Talk of rationing made it sound like wartime, but it most certainly wasn't. For me to have been at war I needed an enemy, and at that moment in time I was very definitely alone and unchallenged, despite the ghoulish creatures drifting along the streets outside in ever increasing numbers. I locked the side garage door, and let myself back into the house.

Things changed again on the morning of day five.

When I threw back the curtains I found myself looking down upon a street scene very different to the previous evening. Outside my house a vast crowd of people had gathered. Initially elated, I dressed and readied myself to go out and see what they wanted. These people – although similar in appearance to the empty souls I'd seen previously – behaved differently. They were definitely gravitating around my home with a purpose, not just drifting by. I stood outside, separated from the crowd by the metal gate across the end of the drive, and for what felt like an eternity nothing happened. I didn't know what to say. The faces of the people were vacant, and they seemed to look through me as if I wasn't there. The nearest few figures were being continually jostled and pushed against the gate by those immediately behind, and yet they didn't protest or stand their ground. I tried to speak to them but they didn't acknowledge my words. Every time I opened my mouth there was a ripple of sudden movement (bordering on muted excitement) throughout the crowd, but not one of them seemed capable of responding properly. I lost my temper. Perhaps it was just my frustration getting the better of me? Whatever the reason, I ended up shouting and screaming at them like a madman, desperate for someone to answer or even just acknowledge me. It was an embarrassing show of uncontrolled emotion which I immediately regretted.

I returned to the house and stood at the bedroom window and continued to watch. Although the behaviour of the bodies outside had changed somewhat, it occurred to me that my overall situation had not. Ultimately, what the sick people on the other side of the gate did or didn't do had no bearing on my survival. There had been no substantial change in either my situation or my priorities: I had to continue to fend for myself. As the government booklet said, I needed to sit and wait for help to arrive.

I could see more and more of the bodies approaching from various directions, perhaps drawn to the house as a result of my undignified rant in the street earlier. Whatever the reason, with little else happening in the neighbourhood it seemed that my home was rapidly becoming the centre of attention. It dawned on me that with everything else dead and silent around me, there was nothing else to distract them, and more and more of them would undoubtedly keep coming. I decided that I had few options: I could lock the doors, close the curtains and sit and wait until they disappeared again, or I could pack up now and run. After having worked so long and so hard for everything I owned I knew there was no way I could bring myself to leave home, especially not now that my beloved family were buried in the back garden. I was going to stay.

Although accountancy was my chosen vocation, I have always had a talent for working with my hands and am immensely proud of some of the improvements I have made around the house over the years. I made furniture for Maddy's room, I decorated throughout (several times), I re-glazed a few windows and I laid the patio and built a low brick wall around it. On top of that I devised and constructed practical storage solutions in the attic, the garage, the study, the utility room and the shed. There was much that could be done to make my property more secure.

I approached the strengthening of the house with real relish and planned it meticulously. If nothing else, the project would keep me occupied for a few days at least and being occupied would help the dragging hours pass more quickly.

I needed to go out to the hardware store and get materials – timber, fixings, tools and various other bits and pieces – but I couldn't get the car off the drive. The crowd around the front of the house was more than fifty bodies deep in places now. Even if I had been able to get the car onto the road, in doing so I would inevitably have allowed the crowd to get closer to my property. I didn't relish the prospect of trying to herd the uncooperative throng back onto the street.

When we first moved into Baker Road West there had been a large expanse of grassland beyond the fence at the bottom of our garden. Five and a half years ago the council sold the land to a housing developer who built more than double the sensible number of houses there they should have. I certainly would never have considered buying a plot there. They were packed together and the gardens were virtually non-existent. I had an acquaintance who lived there and I dropped him back home after golf on a couple of occasions. The estate was like a rabbit warren, a twisting maze of cul-de-sacs, groves and crescents which all looked the same. To squeeze more homes in, many of the later phases were built with garages at the bottom of their gardens with access from a communal road leading across the back of several properties. By chance, one of the roads led across the back of my property also. Although I hadn't yet solved the problem of getting to the hardware store, this provided me with a convenient means of getting everything back to the house when I returned.

I decided to walk. As potentially dangerous as it might have sounded, it also seemed the most sensible option. I climbed over the back fence, crept down the road, then quietly made my way down to the hardware centre at the bottom of the hill. The store catered for trade as well as the general public. There were trucks and vans which could be hired to help transport bulky loads (I'd hired one previously when I built the patio) and I decided I would use one again to move the equipment and materials.

In a little under two hours I was done. My trip passed with little incident, save for a few uncomfortable moments in the hardware store car park when another crowd of dishevelled people gathered around the front of the building after I had gone inside. I took my time and moved around quietly, hoping they wouldn't notice me. I used the trade entrance at the rear of the building to load up a small flat-bed truck, and was done before any of them saw me. Once home I parked the truck on the other side of the back fence and heaved everything over. I left the truck just in case I needed to use it again.

The people in the streets had become increasingly inquisitive. I couldn't do anything without huge swathes of lethargically shuffling individuals following my every move. They appeared washed out and empty, and although they were individually easy to brush away, their incessant, unwanted attention made me uncomfortable. If they continued to come, I thought to myself, the house might be surrounded by incalculable numbers and I might end up using the hardware store truck as a means of escape. I couldn't imagine leaving, and I decided it was more important than ever to make my property as strong and secure as possible.

I began at the front of the house. My place is already separated from the road by a knee-high brick wall topped with iron railings and a strong iron gate. It seemed sensible to increase the height of the barrier, to completely block the house and myself from view as far as was possible. I sank a row of six-foot concrete posts into the flower bed directly behind the wall, then placed fence panels between them. I then used nylon rope and chains to secure a split panel onto the gate, which I locked with chains and a hefty padlock I had taken from the store. The front of the house was the hardest place to work. The relentless interest of the people on the street was unsettling. On more than one occasion I had to push them back to get them out of the way. I asked them to move but the bloody things seemed incapable of any positive response and in the end I had to manhandle them off the drive.

I did a beautiful job on the ground floor doors. In a moment of inspiration I decided to build a second timber frame around each entrance and fitted new doors on top of the existing ones. Solid wooden fire doors, separately hinged and able to open independently. Perfect. I did something similar with the windows, making wooden shutters which completely blocked out the light. I couldn't help but make a terrific amount of noise as I fitted them. I had no option but to drill into the masonry around the windows and doors. I could see over the newly raised fence from the top of the ladder whilst at the front of the house, and the effect the noise was having on the people in the street was dramatic. Some of them began to bang angrily on my new gate. At times the noise they made threatened to drown out the sound of my drill. I was almost relieved when the battery pack ran out.

It took the best part of two days to make the house as secure as I wanted it. By the time I'd finished I was exhausted. I worked whenever it was light, knowing I would have plenty of time to stop and rest once the job was complete. At six-thirty on Tuesday evening – more than a week since the nightmare started – I sat out on the lawn next to Maddy and her mother and looked back at the house with pride. They would have been impressed with what I'd achieved. If nothing else they would have been proud of the fact I had survived when so many others had fallen. Perhaps Janice wouldn't have been too keen on the aesthetic side of the alterations, but she'd have surely appreciated their practicality. I sat between the graves of my wife and my daughter with a can of beer and the remainder of my daily rations and finally allowed myself to relax. The food and drink tasted better than ever. I had a normal appetite for the first time in days. Rationed food wasn't so bad after all, I decided. I had a fairly wide selection of tastes and flavours in each day's supply. I fully appreciated that my choices might become more limited as time progressed but, for now, it was more than sufficient.

I slept well last night.

This morning I discovered that the situation outside has deteriorated again. Things have suddenly become much less certain, and I feel increasingly unsure. Although the house remains secure, today the enormity of what has happened to the world has again become painfully apparent.

I lay lazily in bed for a while, resting after the efforts of the last two days. When I finally got up I went to the front of the house and opened several of the new wooden window shutters. I immediately saw that the crowd outside had more than doubled in size. It now stretched from one end of the street to the other – completely filling the entire length of Baker Road West – and initially I couldn't understand why. Surely once I had finished work on the house and was out of sight the people outside should have drifted away, shouldn't they? The bathroom window was open slightly and I listened. Although not one of them spoke, there was a constant and very definite noise coming from the unwanted masses. The sounds of shuffling feet, of bodies tripping and falling, of things being knocked over in the street and smashed, of tired hands being slammed against my fence… individually they were insignificant but when added together they became uncomfortably loud. I realised this was no longer a crowd which would simply drift away again. I could see still more people arriving and joining the fringes of the huge gathering.

I ran to the back of the house, thinking that if I did have to leave quickly I could use the hardware store truck which I'd left parked on the road behind the fence at the end of the garden, but it was no good. Standing on my stepladder, I looked over the fence and saw the truck was surrounded. Those bloody things had somehow found the entrance to the road and had filled it for as far as I could see in both directions. There were bloody hundreds of them out there, wedged in so tight they could hardly move.

The front of the house was cut off, as was the back. Increasingly concerned, I fetched my binoculars from the study and tried to make a full assessment of the situation. The news wasn't good. My house – number forty-seven – is two-thirds of the way down Baker Road West which is a fairly straight road. To the left of my property, approximately two hundred and fifty yards (ten houses) away, is a large pub, The Highway. To my horror, I saw from the bedroom window that the pub car park was full of even more people. The crowd was immense, dwarfing the numbers at the front and back of my house. And, worst of all, all that separated them from my garden and my house was eleven wooden fences. The fences around my property are all in relatively good repair, but the same couldn't be said of those belonging to some of my neighbours. I would frequently see their fences wobbling in strong winds and I doubted whether they'd be able to withstand much force. I had an uneasy feeling in the pit of my stomach that the mass of bodies in the car park would probably be able to exert more than enough collective pressure to bring them down.

At the other end of the road, almost out of sight from where I was watching, was another crowd of similar proportions to the one outside the house. What had I done? What an idiot I had been. I realised I was responsible for bringing all these people here. In my haste and enthusiasm to protect the house and make it secure, the noise I had made had inadvertently revealed my location to untold thousands of the damn things.

Did I sit and wait this out or take my chances and run? My two original choices seemed suddenly to have been slashed to one as I realised I had no obvious way of getting out.

I read through the government booklet again and again, hoping I'd find a page I'd somehow missed previously that might give me some idea of how to deal with a situation like this, but no matter how hard I stared at the pages, there was nothing. There was information on dealing with bomb threats, hostage situations, flu epidemics and terrorist attacks, basic first aid advice and a list of emergency telephone numbers (useless as the phone had been dead most of the week) but nothing to help me with the sudden and very real threat I was now facing. Apart from me the entire population had died, and now most of them had returned from the grave and were gravitating around my house. What the hell was I supposed to do?

During the course of the day now ending I have watched the crowds draw ever closer. Just before one this afternoon, the fence around the pub car park finally gave way under the collective weight of hundreds of bodies pushing against it. With the barrier down the people then pushed, shoved and surged to get into the first garden, only to then stop when they slammed into the next fence. It began to wobble and shake precariously but it remained intact for a time, finally falling about an hour and a half later when it could no longer withstand the pressure being exerted from behind. The strength of the crowd was incredible. As each fence collapsed it was as if a dam had burst its banks, and the people poured through like an unstoppable wave.

Bill Peters, who lived at number fifty-five, had a good, sturdy fence with concrete posts and a strong base which held up their progress for a while, but even Bill's fence wasn't good enough. They finally broke through at a quarter past four, leaving them just three gardens away from my home.

Day eight ends and day nine begins.

It's a little before one in the morning, and I'm sitting alone in Maddy's room watching them. I can see them from the end of the bed: hundreds, probably thousands of shifting, bobbing heads moving in the cold moonlight. The recent nights have been overcast and dark but tonight the sky is clear and the moon is full and I can see everything. I wish it would disappear back behind the clouds. I'd rather be blind to this.

Over the days I have done all I can to secure my small plot of land. This is my home, and everything I've ever worked for is here. This place is my world, and I'll continue to defend it for as long as I'm able. But just now, sitting here alone, the emptiness of the place has struck me. Behind the double-strength doors and the window shutters and high fences, there's nothing anymore. It's just a shell. The house feels like a tomb.

I miss Janice and Maddy. I miss their conversation and their noise. I miss their soap operas and gossip.

I feel relatively calm. I'm nervous and I don't want to face what's I know is coming, but I will keep a level head. I have maintained my dignity and pride since this catastrophe began and I will continue to do so. There will be no kicking and screaming and no shame.

Oh, Christ… The splinter and crack of wood shatters the silence and another fence goes down. I can see that the crowd is closer than ever now, surging awkwardly across Pauline and Geoff Smart's lawn and slamming against the fence on the other side of their garden. They are now just two properties away. It won't be long.

Three-fifteen.

The penultimate fence is down and a few thin wooden slats are all that separates the crowd from my home. I'm standing at the window now, looking directly at them. There doesn't seem to be any point keeping out of sight anymore; it won't make any difference. Their progress is unstoppable. They're coming here whatever.

This doesn't feel right, hiding up here alone. I shouldn't be cowering like this, just watching them, waiting for them to invade. I should be down there. I should be alongside Maddy and her mother when it happens. For goodness sake, it's not the house I should be defending, it's my family. All that effort making our home secure, when all along I should have been out there, protecting my girls.

Lester Prescott left his daughter's room and shuffled across the landing to the bedroom he and Janice had shared for the last twenty-five years. Tired, and with a heavy heart, he opened the wardrobe and took out his favourite jumper. Threadbare and tattered, it was the jumper he always used to wear when he was out working in the garden at weekends. He pulled it on over his head and then sat down on the edge of the bed to tighten his shoe laces and pull up his socks.

He took one last long look around his home and then went outside, taking with him a few cans of beer from his supplies. He walked the length of the garden with pride, even now stopping to pick a weed from between the slabs on the patio and to tidy the edge of a flower bed where the uncut grass had begun to encroach on Janice's prized plants. He stopped when he reached the garden shed and looked down at the two uneven mounds in the lawn where he'd buried his wife and only child.

Seems a shame it all has to finish like this, he thought as he disappeared into the shed and fetched a spade and garden fork with which he could defend himself when the fence came down. He then squeezed his backside onto the seat of Maddy's swing and looked back at the house. *All that work*, he thought. *All those years of relentless number-crunching, day after day, week after week.* Maybe he should have taken more time off? Perhaps he should have spent more time at home. And when he'd been at home, should he have spent more time sitting doing nothing with his family instead of working on his projects or hiding himself away in the garden shed? Lester opened his first beer and drank half of it in a series of quick, gassy gulps.

He'd never been much of a drinker and it made him feel slightly sick. He belched and wiped his mouth and looked at the fence which was now rocking and shaking with the force of untold numbers of bodies on the other side. *Hope the drink takes the edge off this fear*, he thought, shaking his half-full can and stifling another belch.

Bloody hell, Lester said sadly to himself, *this is like waiting to see the dentist. Let's just get it over with*.

Lester was on his final can when it happened. For the briefest of moments he'd actually become distracted with pointless, random thoughts about nothing in particular and he'd almost forgotten what was coming. The sudden sharp crack of splintering wood brought him crashing back to reality in an instant. He jumped to his feet and grabbed the garden fork, holding it out in front of him like a four-pronged bayonet.

The fence had given way at the other end of the garden, nearer to the house. It was difficult to see much from his present position, but he was vaguely aware of dark, swarming movement close to the garage door, frighteningly indistinct. The top of the fence, already weakened closer to the house, now began to dip and bow halfway up the garden. Lester watched as it drooped further and further down, finally falling so low that he could see the heads and shoulders of the advancing bodies on the other side. Their ultimate intent, although to a large degree still random and uncoordinated, was obvious and inevitable.

As the first few bodies began their stilted, awkward walk towards him, Lester took up position in front of the graves of his family. His heart began to race. What would they do to him? Were they capable of an attack or would they just trample him down? He couldn't look away, his fear making it impossible to do anything but stare directly at the advancing shadowy shapes. He wanted to stop them. He didn't care what they did to him, but he wanted to stop them from trampling the graves of his wife and daughter. *I might not have been very good at telling you how I felt about you when you were alive*, he thought, picturing Maddy and Janice in his head, *but I can show you now...*

As the closest bodies lifted their emaciated arms out for him, Lester lunged forward with the garden fork. He smashed into the chest cavity of the nearest cadaver, skewering it and sending it crashing to the ground. He wrenched the fork back out and swung it around at other sinewy figures, catching one of them on the side of the head, practically decapitating it. Fuelled by adrenalin and fear he attacked again, diving deeper into the crowd, desperate to defend his family's honour. The final section of fence that was still standing now came down with a tremendous groan and crack and a heavy thump and hundreds more bodies poured into Lester's garden. He wanted to keep fighting but he didn't have room to move. They were surrounding him on all sides now, reaching out for him, grabbing at him tirelessly. Disorientated by the chaos, out of the corner of his eye he spied the dark silhouette of the garden shed and he ran towards it, pushing and kicking more bodies out of the way. He reached out for the door handle, knowing that the end of his life was close, running to delay the inevitable. He flung the door open and crashed inside. The door flapped shut in the wind behind him, the sudden noise leaving the mass of bodies in no doubt as to where he was hiding. Now sobbing uncontrollably, Lester collapsed into his deckchair in the corner and waited.

So many memories.

The garden shed – the coldest, weakest and most exposed part of his property – suddenly felt as reassuringly strong and warm as anywhere else. In the half-light he looked around and saw nothing but memories: the tools with which he and Janice had lovingly tended their small plot of land, the battered wooden tea-chest on which he used to leave his paper or his book and his drink when he dozed in the shed on long, relaxing Saturday afternoons, the plastic table and chairs which had been dragged out onto the patio each summer when they'd entertained family and friends... And finally the box of garden games and the buckets and spades and all those memories of being with Janice and Maddy. All about to be lost forever now. Most of it already gone. Lester knew he didn't have long.

More through luck than judgement, a single skeletal hand managed to wedge itself between the flapping door and the frame and pulled it open. The creature dragged itself into the shed, followed by an apparently endless queue of others. *Do I know you?* Lester got up and stared at the rotting shadow which lurched towards him. *Were you once a friend? Someone I used to work with? Have I passed you on the street? Did I work on your accounts?* The creature's face, repellent in the cold moonlight and shadow, was vacant and unrecognisable. *What gives you the right?*

Lester tried to push the bodies away but their numbers were too great. One of the corpses trying to get inside tripped and fell, pushing those in front of it forward with unexpected force. Like dominoes they crashed into Lester and knocked him back. He slammed against the back wall of the shed unexpectedly, feeling a sudden stinging pain between his shoulders as the ten steel prongs of his garden rake punctured his skin. Anaesthetized by fear, it was more a disorientating discomfort than pain as such. Lester lifted his arms and shielded his face from the rotting bodies which continued to advance, pushing into him and forcing the spikes deeper into his back.

Warm, he thought to himself as blood from the puncture wounds seeped down his back, *I feel warm*. The relative heat of his blood was strangely comforting. Lester's legs buckled and he crashed to the ground, taking several bodies with him. The rake dislodged itself in the fall, and he was able to roll over onto his back in amongst all the spindly legs. He closed his eyes and screwed up his face as an incalculable number of rotting feet trampled him.

Lying near to the bodies of Maddy and her mother outside, Lester looked up at the roof of the garden shed for as long as he could keep his eyes open. *How much easier it would have been*, he thought, *to have just laid down with you two from the beginning*.

KATE JAMES

It's days since Michael, Carl and Emma left here. I'm not exactly sure how long. I've lost all track of time. I've lost track of everything.

Things changed as soon as they went. I know now that I should have gone too. I wish I'd had the strength to do it. I wanted to at the time, but I just couldn't bring myself to take that first step out the door. My head was telling me they were right to go, but when it came down to it, nerves got the better of me. When it came to the crunch I couldn't move. Like everyone else here, I was too scared. I was born in Northwich and I've lived here all my life. Might as well finish it here too. Might as well stay here now and end my days near the places which used to mean something.

Come on, Kate. Get a grip. You've got to stop thinking like this.

The rest of the people here are as frightened as I am. I can sense it coming off them. You can almost taste the fear in the stale air now. No one looks into anyone else's face anymore. People just stare at the ground because if you start trying to communicate, you know you're going to end up talking about the mess we're in, and then you realise just how bad things really are. We all know this is never going to get any better, but when you talk to other people you start remembering everything you've lost.

The community centre has become silent like a morgue. It's been like this for days.

This morning four of them went out to get supplies. They went not through choice, but because we've got nothing left. Absolutely nothing. No food, no water, no fresh clothes, no medicine... nothing. They went out in one of the cars that had been left in the car park. The noise of the engine sounded so loud and the rest of us just sat there in fear because it made us feel more vulnerable and exposed than ever. The sudden noise made me realise just how quiet this dead world has become.

I could still hear the car in the distance even after they'd been gone a while. I couldn't tell if they were getting closer or still moving away. The engine noise eventually faded to nothing but then returned about an hour later. I stood at the little window by the main door and waited for them. The world was still save for the bodies and the dead leaves blowing across the ground. After what felt like forever there was a sudden burst of frantic, frightened activity as the car sped around the corner. I opened the door and started to help them get the things they'd collected inside.

The four men who'd been out were subdued. They looked even more desperate (if that was possible) than they had before they'd left. I knew something was wrong but I didn't want to know what. At that moment my ignorance was my only defence, and a pretty bloody poor defence it was too.

It was as we unloaded the car that I noticed the bodies approaching. Three or four of them at first, but their numbers increased dramatically. They were as slow and clumsy as any we'd seen before, but they were dragging themselves towards the community centre with real intent. It was almost as if they'd followed the car, but that wasn't possible, was it?

One of the men looked back over his shoulder and saw them closing in. 'Come on,' he said, his voice filled with fear, 'get inside.'

They barged past me, throwing bags and boxes into the community centre. The last man in – I think it was Stuart Jeffries – pushed me away and slammed the door shut behind us, locking it quickly then leaning against it.

Jag Dhandra, one of those who'd been out, was sitting on the floor next to me, slumped against the wall. His face was pale, his brown eyes wide with shock. Tears were rolling down his cheeks. 'They can see us,' he said when he saw I was watching him.

'What?'

'They can fucking see us! Those bloody things out there can see us and hear us and…' He stopped talking and tried to compose himself. 'We were getting the stuff. We were busy with what we were doing and we didn't notice them at first. When we looked up and tried to get out there were hundreds of them all around the building. They were just stood there, waiting for us.'

'But why? How could they…?'

'They can hear us!' he said again, his voice louder, more desperate. 'It's like the bloody things are coming back to life!'

The rest of the people in the community centre were all listening to Jag's terrified rant. When he stopped, I became aware of another noise behind me – an intermittent dull thumping coming from outside. I walked back towards the door and I could feel it moving as the bodies outside tried to get to us. Although weak, they were hitting the side of the building with controlled force. I looked out through the window and saw there was already a crowd of more than twenty of them gathered around the front of the building.

Christ, we didn't realise how lucky we'd been until then. Out on the edge of the town we'd somehow managed to stay relatively isolated and safe. Maybe it was because of our location, fenced-off and tucked out of sight in the shadow of a once busy main road, or perhaps it was just because we'd hardly dared make a sound for days that we'd managed to escape their attention for so long. Whatever the reason, the trip out for supplies had blown our cover.

This afternoon the group has disintegrated. Already on the very brink, the people here seem now to have lost the last little bit of control they'd each managed to hold onto. And once a few people began to crack today, most of the others quickly followed.

The food and supplies the men brought back with them didn't last long. Like a pack of starving dogs we (me included) pounced, desperate to eat. I couldn't help myself. I felt ashamed as I scrambled around on the dirty floor on my hands and knees, degraded, ripping open bags and boxes, desperate to find anything that might give me a little nourishment. Had it not been for the fear distracting me, the hunger pains that have ripped at my gut for days now would have driven me out of my mind.

A couple of minutes ago, two men and a woman began to fight. I don't know what caused it. It started in another room and I didn't know it was happening until the woman ran from her attackers and tripped and fell on top of me. My face got smashed into the floor and I tasted blood in my mouth. The shock stopped me from feeling any pain at first, but I can feel my split lip stinging now. The woman got up, but then both men grabbed her and dragged her back, trying to stop her screaming. One of them threw her against the wall, and the force of impact seemed to make the entire building shake. I was scared. Bloody terrified. As they hauled her away I grabbed hold of all the bags and boxes I could lay my hands on and crawled into the shadows.

The fighting's continuing. Getting worse. It's spilled out into the hall again. The supplies have disappeared but people are still hungry and want more. Almost everyone is involved, battling over the last few scraps like dogs. I'm sitting in virtual darkness in the quietest corner of the building I've been able to find, hoarding the odds and ends I managed to grab. I don't dare make a sound for fear of them turning on me and trying to take my things. I've got a tin of cat food, a bottle of milk drink which has gone sour, a box of headache tablets and a tube of toothpaste. I've started to eat the toothpaste. I can't bring myself to eat the cat food yet, but I know I'll have to eventually.

The noise in here is frightening and confusing. It's late, and in the low gloom it's difficult to see what's happening. Every so often there's a lull in the frantic noises and scuffles around me and in those random moments of quiet I can hear other noises coming from outside the building. The dead are surrounding us.

Ralph (who thought he was in charge to begin with but who's hardly said a word for days) has suddenly become more vocal and animated again. He's on his feet and now he's climbed up onto a chair to look out of one of the small rectangular windows which run along the length of the main hall. Has he heard them too? His face is pressed against the glass and he's trying to look down at the ground. He's looking around the hall again now, trying to get people's attention. 'They're trying to get in,' he yells, his voice too loud. 'The bloody things are trying to get inside!'

For a second, the entire group is silent. The arguments and the fights stop. And in the silence they can all hear it now: a constant barrage of bangs, thumps and crashes coming from all sides. The noise the men in the car made earlier was enough to attract a few of the corpses, but the shouts and cries and screams coming constantly from this place since then must have attracted many, many more.

After the brief moment of stunned silence, panic again tears through the building.

Ralph jumps down from the chair and loses his footing. He's fallen onto another man – Simon Peters, I think – who grabs him by the scruff of his neck to try and calm him down. Ralph is kicking and screaming and I'm trying to push myself further and further back into the shadows because I know that the trouble in the middle of the hall is about to boil over into something far more serious.

Ralph's on the ground now. Didn't see what happened, but he's lying there, panting and struggling to get back up, his face pressed against the filthy floor. He's looking over at me and I can see absolute terror in his face. Like a man possessed, he gets back up again and now he's gone for Simon, knocking him out of the way. Pumped full of adrenalin and fear, he's punching and kicking Simon and now their positions have been reversed and Ralph's the one who's attacking. Ralph picks up a chair and holds it above his head. Simon's trying to crawl away but it's too late and… and I can't bear to look, but I can hear him hitting Simon again and again and again.

Quiet again.

Simon's lying in the middle of the room in a crumpled heap, twitching. Ralph's standing over him, chair held high, ready to strike again if anyone moves.

Someone – I couldn't see who – just ran at Ralph and tried to grab the chair from him. He's swung it at them, catching them on the side of the head. Now Jag Dhandra has sprinted the length of the hall and tripped over Simon's motionless body. He's picked himself up again and is running towards the main entrance.

I know what he's doing.

Jesus Christ, he's going to open the door.

Oh, God, he's completely lost it. People are trying to stop him but it's too late and the door's open. I can already feel the cold air blowing into the building from outside. People are screaming, and the more noise they make, the quicker those things outside will react. I can see them rushing to grab their belongings and move deeper into the community centre and—

—and now I can see them.

Bodies.

There's an endless stream of grey, featureless bodies filling the room. I have to get out of here. Jesus, I need to find a way out, but there's no way back through the hall. Now there are other people around me, all moving in the same direction, all trying to get away from the sea of dead flesh which continues to flood in through the open door. I'm trying to stand up but it's difficult to move. The main hall is almost half full of corpses now. Ralph is still in the middle of the room, swinging the chair around like a madman again, knocking several of the bodies off their feet. Their flesh is decaying and each blow from the chair seems to tear them apart. Now Ralph has lost his footing and has gone down in the bloody mire. I can see him struggling on the floor. He's trying to get up but he's being trampled by the dead.

I'm being carried deeper into the building by a stream of panicking people, and all I can do is go with them. I can't stop and I can't fight. Somehow I've managed to keep hold of the cat food and tablets and I'm grabbing them as tight as I can as the crowd surges through the semi-darkness. One of the women to my right has climbed up onto a chair and is getting out through a small skylight in the ceiling of one of the store rooms. Others are following her. I don't have any choice, and I follow too. I have to keep moving.

I manage to get up and squeeze my head and shoulders through the skylight but the gap's too narrow. I don't think I'm going to make it. I try to turn back, but there are people pushing me from below, all trying to get out too. I can feel the window frame digging into my skin, cutting me, and I kick and push and scream…

Then somehow I'm out. I pick myself up, and now I'm standing on a small square area of flat roof. There are already too many of us up here. A couple of people have either jumped or fallen. It's not very high and I'm sure I'll survive the drop if I have to, but I don't want to go down there. I'm at the very edge of the building now and there's a vast crowd of dark, shuffling bodies below me. I try to get over to the other side but I can't. The constant stream of people fighting to get out of the community centre pushes me back towards the edge and I try to stop myself but I know I can't and they—

Kate landed in the middle of the crowd of cadavers, their empty bodies breaking her fall. Winded, she scrambled to her feet and began to run, disappearing into the municipal park behind the community centre. Around her, other people scattered in all directions. The autumn evening was cold and a patchy fog added to her disorientation. She kept running, moving away from the community centre, heading deeper and deeper into the darkness, but she couldn't keep going for long. Kate was undernourished, out of shape, and terrified. For a while she slowed to walking pace before finally giving into her exhaustion and stopping completely. She found a children's playground which had been hidden by the mist and sat on a swing and held her head in her hands. In the near distance she could hear the dying screams of the people she'd left behind.

Alone.

Terrified.

Too tired to move.

Kate James spent her final day in Northwich. She cowered under a slide until morning when the daylight left her hopelessly exposed. Her every movement attracted the attention of hordes of obnoxious bodies. She made it as far as a nearby house, but when she closed the door she realised she'd only succeeded in buying herself a little time. There were already crowds outside. The end result would inevitably be the same. This house would eventually go the way of the community centre.

At nine o'clock in the evening, sitting in complete darkness in the attic of the nondescript semi-detached house, halfway down a similarly indistinct street, Kate gave up. It was too much. She took the headache tablets she still carried and every other packet of pills and bottle of medicine she could find in the silent house, and swallowed enough to be sure she wouldn't wake up again.

OH NO, NOT YOU AGAIN

Somehow I survived when everyone else died. Don't know how that happened. It's not like I did anything special. It's not like I *am* anything special. I'm just *different*. That's what they used to say, anyway.

On that Tuesday morning I watched the rest of the world fall around me and there was nothing I could do. Looking back, I keep asking myself if I should have tried harder – or maybe tried at all – but I don't think it would have made the slightest bit of difference. One or two folks I might have been able to help, but hell, *millions* died. At the time I was terrified, not thinking straight. I kept telling myself, *any second now and I'll be gone too…* It didn't make any sense that they'd all been infected and I hadn't. Mind you, it's been a long time since anything's made much sense in my life.

So I went back to the flat and shut myself away. The chaos outside quickly turned to silence, then back to chaos again when the dead began to walk. It was like a bad movie. I'd stare from the window and laugh at them for a while, watching them tripping over and walking into things, then I'd remember, this was *real*.

The phones worked for a few days, but they were useless anyway. No point trying to make calls when there was no one left to answer. I tried every number I could think of just in case: my parents, my sister, friends, work colleagues, Cassie. It hurt hardest when she didn't answer. We're still on good terms, even though we're not together anymore.

I got ill after Cassie and I split up, really ill. I was out of circulation for the best part of six months. I'm totally over it now, but it still hurts when I look back. It's funny; I can look outside at the dead bodies walking, literally falling apart in front of my eyes, and I don't give them a second's thought. But when I think about that night… our last night… it still creases me up with pain.

I guess what hurts the most is knowing she was right to leave me. I was never going to be the man she wanted. She and Martin were always better suited, even though it still pains me to admit it. I really should have seen it coming, though. More to the point, I should have tried harder. Christ's sake, I introduced them to each other, even though I knew they'd get on. What a bloody fool! And then he started coming to the flat more often, then *too* often, then turning up when I wasn't there and making lame excuses. I think I'd worked it out pretty early, I just didn't want to do anything about it, you know? I kept thinking, if I don't ask and she doesn't tell me, I can't get hurt.

Bloody moron.

There was this thing I learnt during a session on my back-to-work rehabilitation course after my illness. They called it *Path of the Heart*, or some-such new-age rubbish. Basically, the idea was this: sometimes in life you're inevitably going to come up against things you don't want to deal with, generally huge, make-or-break decisions like splitting up with Cassie, that kind of thing. So when one of those moments presents itself, you've usually got a few choices. You can either deal with it head-on, or avoid it and take the easier option. But the thing is, if you avoid really important decisions like that, they inevitably come back around and bite you on the backside at some point further down the line. You just keep going around in circles, never moving forward, until you finally man up and do what you have to do. You have to follow the path of your heart. I know it sounds corny as hell, but I'm beginning to believe it also happens to be true. If I'd confronted Martin way back when, maybe Cassie and I would have still been together.

I took the easy option, trying to show Cassie how great I was instead of telling Martin how good he *wasn't*. I did try... I made more of an effort around the house, tried to cook a few meals, that kind of thing, but I can see now it was never going to be enough because I was avoiding the real issues. To their credit, they both sat me down to tell me straight. She was lovely about it, saying she'd been trying to tell me things weren't working out for a long time, but I didn't buy that. And Martin? He was a man about it, but he made me look and feel like a bloody fool. I should have punched him in the face or showed some emotion, but I didn't. Idiot. As it was, I just let Cassie go. I didn't fight. Didn't think it would help. Didn't know if I could. I just stood at the window and watched them loading up the car. I even helped carry some of her stuff out.

Back to reality. *Reality*. That's a bloody joke. I'm on my own, watching the dead population of Smithfield drag themselves around in circles outside. I've been shut in here for over a week now, and I've not set foot outside the building. I've survived so far by looting the other flats in the development: shutting dead neighbours in their bathrooms and bedrooms while I ransack their kitchens for food. I know I'm going to have to go out there eventually, but I'll probably be okay for a while longer.

But there's something I need to do.

It's been eating at me for ages; a niggling, nagging pain, burrowing deeper and deeper. You see, I've been able to accept that they're all dead out there, except for Cassie. I'm not naïve, I know she's almost certainly gone the same way as everyone else, but I need to be sure. There's a part of me wondering if she might somehow have survived like I have? And if she has, then what the hell am I doing sitting here when she might be alone and afraid over there? I keep putting it off, but I know I'm going to have to go over to Martin's house eventually and see for myself. I won't be able to rest until I know for sure. I can keep avoiding it, keep telling myself it's too dangerous and that the chances of her having survived are too slim, but I know those are just empty excuses. One way or another, I need to find out. I need to man up. It sounds so clichéd I could genuinely vomit, but I need to start following the path of my heart.

Day nine. Finally going to do it. I'm on my bike, and I think it's going to be the best way to travel – quick and easy to control. I'll be quiet, and I'll be able to ride through and around the dead, silently slipping through the narrowest of gaps. I've packed a few things and I'm ready to leave. I'll be back here later, unless by some miracle I find her alive. Who knows where we might go…

The journey is as frightening as expected but, thankfully, it's also passing quickly. I need to cover these few miles fast and with the minimum of fuss. Thank Christ for the speed advantage I have over the dead. They're often so slow that they've barely even registered the fact I'm approaching before I've gone again.

There's been little incident so far, save for when I was riding around the outskirts of Maryvale. I had to avoid an immense crowd of them, gathered around a factory building. I couldn't work out why there were so many of them in one place, then it dawned on me it had to be other survivors – someone else like me. I didn't hang around to find out if I was right. I'd rather be alone. I think I work better by myself. The only exception to the rule is Cassie. We made a good team, Cassie and me.

When the streets get too busy nearer the centre of town, I change my route. I'll follow the canal for the last couple of miles. I wish I'd thought of it sooner. It's far quieter down here on the towpath than it was up there. The only bodies I've seen have been in the canal. Some of them are swollen like fleshy balloons, full of dirty water. Others don't look like they've been in as long. The one I can see now, being dragged along by the current, is still moving, flapping its arms like it's waving at me. When it sees me on the side it starts to struggle, trying to get out of the murk like it doesn't even realise it's wet. It's hard to believe how useless and stupid these things have become. A couple of weeks ago they were individual people with personalities and free will and dreams and aspirations. Now look at them. Bloody useless. They don't even know *what* they are anymore, let alone *who*.

Dumb as they may be, they still scare the hell out of me.

Damn. There's another one up ahead now, and this one's not in the water, he's on the towpath, blocking my way through. Shit. There's a strip of grass verge along the canal-side, so there's little chance of this one loosing his footing and falling in. I stop pedalling and weigh up my limited options as I wait for him to get closer. Maybe I should turn around and go back? Try and get back up to street level and take my chances with the crowds up there? Or do I just keep going and deal with the foul thing that's slowly dragging itself towards me? And it occurs to me, we're back to the bloody path of the heart again, aren't we? I've got a problem to sort, and I can either face it head-on now or avoid it and soon end up having to deal with something much worse.

I reverse back, then stop again. Deep breath. Then I start pedalling, trying to build up as much speed as I can in the short gap between me and the dead man. My tyres churn the gravel and I grip the handlebars tight. I ride straight into him, head down, then brake hard and steer away from the water immediately after impact. I hear a colossal splash and look up in time to see the hideous corpse being carried away with the flow, dead arms flailing. Job done.

The path ahead now is clear.

There's movement in Cassie and Martin's house, and my heart's thumping so hard I can hear it. I try not to get my hopes up, because I know it might not be her. If a door's been left open, anyone or anything could have gotten inside. It's most likely one of the dead, trapped.

This is it. This is what I came here for.

Just for a second longer I stay hiding in the porch of the house across the way, trying to clear my mind and focus on what I'm about to do. I feel like turning tail and heading back home, but I know I can't. I have to do this. I have to see it through, otherwise I'll never be able to move on. I'll always be thinking, *what if...?* I have this memory of a beautiful summer's day I once spent with Cass. We were out in the middle of nowhere, just the two of us, walking hand in hand through the sunshine without a damn care, talking about nothing of any significance. It was a perfect day. We couldn't recreate it. Though I tried many times, it was never the same. The last time she got scared. There was a bloody huge thunderstorm and she started crying, telling me she just wanted to go home. *He* came around that evening. I knew something was wrong even then, I just didn't know how to make it right again. It felt like the harder I tried, the less she wanted to be with me.

The street's almost empty. I take advantage of the space to run over to the house. I lift my fist to hammer on the door, but before I can make any noise it opens inward and I fall through the gap. I'm facedown on the carpet in the hallway, and I hear the door slam shut and lock behind me. I know for certain that someone else alive is here with me now. Is it Cassie?

'Eddie? Eddie, is that you?'

My heart sinks. Shit, it's not her, it's *him*, and somehow that feels like the cruellest trick. I pick myself up and turn around, clinging onto the vain hope she's here too, even though I know she's not.

'Martin? Is Cassie...?'

'She's dead,' he sobs, his face crumbling. He reaches out and grabs hold of me and I'm stuck in an awkward embrace with a man I despise. And then I break down too, because I know now that she's gone forever.

I couldn't have picked anyone I'd rather be stuck at the end of the world with less, but there's no denying, the company is welcome. I hadn't realised how much I'd missed it. Everything has changed, I guess. We're no longer in competition. We've both lost Cassie. He talks about her a lot, and I actually enjoy listening. In a weird way, it makes it feel like she's still here.

'We were at her sister's the weekend before it happened,' he tells me.

'Really?'

'Yep. Hard going, that was. I never liked Ruth.'

'Me neither.'

'Too stuck up for her own good. Judgemental.'

'And Nigel's an arsehole.'

'Tell me about it! Supercilious shyster. Always talking down to you, you know? Like it was an effort to have to have anything to do with you.'

'I thought it was just me.'

'Cass said he was like that with everyone.'

'What about her dad? What did you think of Ken?'

'Ah, Ken was a good man. We got on well. I'd only been speaking to him on the phone the other day before it happened... We'd been making plans for him to come down and stay with us for a while.'

I can't respond to that. I didn't like Ken, and I don't think he liked me. Martin opens another can of beer and slides one over. I'm not drinking. Can't risk getting drunk, not here, not now. 'Cheers,' I say, then I tuck it down at the side of the chair with the others.

Martin raises his can towards a picture of Cassie on the mantelpiece. 'She was bloody beautiful...'

'She was,' I agree. And then it occurs to me, there are important questions I haven't asked yet. 'Martin, what happened?'

'What, to the rest of the world?'

'No, to Cassie. I need to know. That's why I came here.'

He pauses, drinks more beer, then readies himself to answer. 'I was at work when all this kicked off. Obviously Cass was all I could think about. I mean, there were people dying in the office all around me – friends, people I knew well – but all I could see was Cass. I tried calling home on my mobile, but she didn't answer. And I was thinking there might be a problem with the phones or she might not have hers with her… but all along I think I already knew she was dead.

'It took hours to get back here. It's less than twenty miles to the office, but I'm sure you saw it yourself – the chaos, the utter carnage on the streets. I drove as far as I could, then walked the rest. I waited outside on the doorstep for a bloody age. Couldn't bring myself to take that final step, couldn't come inside because I didn't want to see her. As long as I stayed out there, I could believe she was still alive…'

It hurts to ask, but I have to know more. 'Where was she?'

'In the back garden. She must have been out there reading when it happened.'

Each question gets harder. 'And did she…?'

'Did she what?'

'Get up again? Start walking around?'

He sobs and holds his head in his hands. 'I couldn't believe it when I looked outside and saw her moving. It sounds crazy, but I thought she was okay, you know? I hadn't seen any others at that point, so I thought I was wrong and maybe she hadn't died, that she'd just been in some kind of coma. And then I felt terrible because I'd left her out there for days and it had been raining and…'

'And what?'

His voice changes. The emotion is clear. It's an effort for him to tell me this. 'I went out and called to her, but she didn't respond. I mean, she was looking straight at me, but it was like she couldn't see anything. She was staring into space, looking at nothing. I went to her and I grabbed her hand and… and Jesus, she was so cold. Her skin felt unnatural and her eyes were vacant. I knew she was dead, but I still couldn't accept what I was seeing.'

'Where is she now, Martin?'

He gets up and walks to the window. A couple of corpses immediately notice him at the glass and start moving this way. He doesn't react. He's traumatized. We both are.

'I didn't want to leave her out there like that, so I tried to get her indoors. I wanted to make her comfortable. Sounds stupid, but I wanted to make her well. I couldn't bear to see her suffering like that.'

'Is she in the house?'

For a split-second I'm hopeful of seeing Cass again, but Martin shatters that. He turns around to face me, shaking his head. 'I tried…'

Anger has replaced fear now. 'What did you do?'

'I couldn't get her in. Couldn't even get her up the steps and onto the patio. It was pouring with rain and she was soaked through and… and I just wanted her not to hurt anymore, you know? I wanted the torment to end.'

'Her torment, or yours?'

'*Hers*. You have to believe me, Ed, she was in such a state. She wasn't Cassie anymore. I stood out there and looked right into her face and she couldn't see me. More to the point, I couldn't see *her*. She looked like Cass, but it was obvious she'd gone. She was just a shell, just an empty shell…'

'Where is she?'

He doesn't answer. His reluctance is unnerving. What has he done? Finally, he speaks. 'I had to stop her, you understand? I couldn't leave her out in the garden, walking round and around like that. It wasn't right. It wasn't right…'

'What did you do?'

'I had to do it.'

'*What did you do?*'

'I cut off her head.'

And he drops to the floor and howls with pain.

Martin's confession appeared to do him good. He'd been racked with guilt, filled with remorse. We didn't talk for several hours, spent the time in different rooms. I went upstairs and looked through Cassie's things, the things I remembered from when they were a part of my life and my home. I'm sitting on the end of the bed, smelling one of her dresses, when he comes upstairs.

'She's at peace now,' he says.

'I know.'

'I did what I had to.'

'I know that too.'

'I couldn't just leave her out there, exposed to the elements like that.'

'I understand.'

There's a long silence, neither of us knowing what to say to the other. What else is left to say? We've both lost the only person who mattered to us, though I lost her long before he did.

'So what happens now?' he asks.

'I don't know. I suppose I'll just go home.'

'Shouldn't we stick together?'

'Should we?'

'I think so. It makes sense. You're the only other living person I've seen since this all started. To be honest, Eddie, I don't want to be on my own anymore.'

'You get used to it,' I tell him, feeling empty again.

'I don't want to.'

'I didn't have any choice. You saw to that.'

'I know,' he says, crying again. 'I'm sorry. You're a decent bloke. I wish there'd been another way…'

'Dress it up how you like, Martin, but there is no other way. You did what you did. You killed me that day.'

He drinks from a bottle of vodka. More Dutch courage. 'So why did you come here?'

'To see if Cassie was still alive, why d'you think?'

'But you must have known…?'

'I suspected. *Expected*, even. But I couldn't stand not knowing for sure. I couldn't sit at home, thinking about what might have been.'

'She still mattered that much to you?'

'She did. More than you'll ever know.'

'She'd have been touched.'

'Whatever.'

'No, seriously. I'm full of admiration for you, friend. She always said you were a decent bloke at heart. I've just been sitting here, feeling sorry for myself, crying into my booze, but you've actually done something about it. I'm lost without her, Ed. Don't want to go on without her, if I'm honest. Don't know if I can.'

First light. I've had hours of listening to Martin drone on, and I'm tired of it now. What does he want from me? Sympathy? The man who stole Cassie from me, the man who screwed up my life and my health, wants *me* to feel sorry for *him*? After what he did? After what he did to her?

The sun starts to come up, filling the garden at the back of the house with orange light and long shadows. There's a patch of disturbed earth at the side of the lawn. Its shape is simple, yet distinctive. There's a cross at the head of the grave: two sticks, lashed together with cord.

All night I've listened to him grizzle and whine, not knowing what to do but sit and soak it all in. But just now, things have started to make a little more sense. 'I learnt an important lesson when you took Cassie from me,' I tell him.

He sounds surprised. 'You did? What was that?'

'To follow the path of the heart.'

'The path of the heart? Sounds a bit wanky and pretentious, if you ask me.'

'It is, and I didn't.'

'So what is it?'

'A way of thinking, I guess. A philosophy.'

'Explain.'

So I do. 'I think it's the real reason I came here, actually. Way I see it is this: we go through life, and from time to time we come across big issues, hurdles that we need to sort out before we can move any further forward. And if we don't deal with them, we just end up going around in circles until we do. We keep coming back to the same point. We get faced with the same decision, the same situation, time and time again until we do something about it.'

'Cassie used to say you had a problem moving forward. She said you went around in circles a lot of the time. Couldn't let go of things.'

'Did she?'

'She said you struggled with decisions. Wanted everything to stay the same.'

'She was probably right. Thing is, I've learnt from my mistakes.'

'And what have you learnt?'

'Have you not been listening? To follow the path of the heart. To stop avoiding problems and start dealing with them. Like I said, that's why I'm here.'

'You came to see if Cassie was alive, and she's not.'

'I know. You're here, though.'

'So? You're starting to sound like a crank, my friend.'

'I'm not a crank, and I'm not your friend.'

'Calm down,' he laughs. 'Don't take it all so serious. The whole world's fucked beyond repair. I reckon you're way off the path of your bloody heart. I reckon we all are.'

'I'm not so sure. It's starting to make sense again now. I'm ready to do the things I should have done a long time ago.'

'And what's that?' he asks, setting things up beautifully. I don't say anything, I just kill the cunt.

ROBERT WOOLGRAVE

I'm starting to think I might have got this all wrong. Really fucking wrong. I've gone about it all the wrong way. I thought I was so bloody clever to start with, thought I knew what I was doing. I was too quick off the mark. Think I might have fucked everything up.

Fuck the lot of them – that was the attitude I had from the start. Didn't see any point doing anything else. I had to be selfish, didn't I? When you're the only one left, how could it be anything other than every man for himself?

But hindsight is a fucking wonderful thing. If I'm honest, though, I wouldn't do anything different if I had the time over again. I did what I think pretty much everyone else would have done in the same situation. After it happened I spent some time looking for other survivors, but it was pretty bloody obvious pretty bloody quickly that I was the only one left. I took one of the cars from work and drove around town. I stopped in loads of different places and shouted out, but no one came. I drove right into the middle of the pedestrian area, stopped the car right outside the shopping centre among the corpses and yelled my bloody lungs out, but still no one came. There didn't seem any point trying after that. If there were other people left alive, surely I'd have found them there.

When the bodies rose again I decided enough was enough. Scariest fucking thing I'd ever seen that was, watching them pick themselves up and start moving around. Worse than watching everyone dying around me last week. Worse than anything I remember from the movies. Completely fucking terrifying.

I didn't know where to start. I made the office my base. It was a choice between the office and my flat. The other flats in the block were filled with corpses, so it was a no-brainer. I got some of my stuff together, then collected as much food as I could carry in the back of the car. I dumped it all in the office and set about trying to fortify the place, to make it better protected. I work at CarLand, which is a bloody stupid name for what is – what *was* – one of the biggest and busiest second-hand car lots in the country. Now it's just a bloody big and bloody quiet car park.

The office was built a couple of years back to replace the wooden shack which used to be here. It's a two-storey concrete and glass building right in the middle of the lot; a showroom on the ground floor, offices upstairs. I spent time clearing out all the desks and computers and other crap from the first floor and started trying to make myself comfortable. And that was where I made my first mistake. It was too easy to concentrate on comfort at the expense of everything else. I should have stopped to think.

I took a van and fetched myself some stuff from the furniture store on the other side of the business park: a sofa bed, a couple of easy chairs, a table and some other odds and ends. Nearly crippled myself getting that bloody lot up the stairs. Then I started to get greedy. By the fourth day it was looking more and more likely I was in for the long haul so I made another trip out for food and drink. I stopped at the electrical superstore on the way back and took as much as I could carry, planning to keep myself occupied with phones, movies, music and games. I didn't feel bad taking the stuff. Anyone would have done the same.

For a couple of days I was comfortable and I felt safe. Thought I was living a life of bloody luxury, I did. Space, quiet, comfort and nothing to do except eat, drink, listen, watch and play. After a while I stopped watching films. It didn't feel right. They left me feeling empty and they reminded me of how everything used to be. I tried watching porn but I couldn't get turned on looking at women I knew were dead. And music… I stopped listening to music too. I didn't like wearing headphones, didn't like not being able to hear what was going on around me even though there was nothing. Playing games, on the other hand, seemed to help. I couldn't concentrate on anything too taxing, but I got a bigger kick than ever out of fighting games. Taking out my frustrations on the screen really seemed to help.

Things started to go wrong last Saturday morning. I didn't think I'd been making much noise, but I obviously had and it was having an effect on the bodies outside the office. The bloody things wouldn't leave me alone. They hadn't seemed interested in me at first, but that changed. Christ, they only had to see me moving in the window and they'd turn and start walking towards the building. Bloody things. They were slow moving and weak and it didn't take much effort to get rid of them, but there were more and more of them coming all the time. It didn't matter what I did or didn't do, once they knew I was there they just kept on coming. I had to do something about them. I couldn't stand them being so close.

I spent all day Monday trying to make the office even more secure. I went outside with as many sets of keys as I could find and I started moving cars closer to the building. I took my time and planned it right. I parked as many cars as I could right around the outside of the building, then moved another layer up and parked them close to the first, then another layer after that. It took me from ten in the morning until late afternoon to get the job done but it felt worth it to make the place secure. I left myself a way to get in and out if I need it and I also left a couple of cars ready just in case I have to get away quick. Bottom line is, though, none of those fuckers are going to get me while I'm in here.

Something happened when I was moving the cars on Monday that really bothered me. I had to start getting aggressive with some of the bodies. It worked both ways, because those fucking things started getting aggressive with me first. I couldn't believe it – one of the fuckers just went for me. No provocation or anything. If it had been any stronger then I'd have been in real trouble, but as it was I just threw it to the ground and carried on. When I was in the cars they were less of a problem. When I was on foot, though, things got a little nastier. By the end of the day I had to start getting violent to keep them under control and I didn't enjoy that at all. I had to do things I really wasn't comfortable with. I mean, I had kids and old ladies coming at me for Christ's sake. Fucking hell, at one point I was battering a little kid around the head with a jack from the boot of one of the cars and I thought, *what the fuck am I doing?* I had to do it, though. I had no choice. It was get them before they get me – kill them or be killed by them. After a while I gave up trying to manhandle them and I started wiping them out with the cars. I feel bad about it now, but there was a part of me that actually enjoyed it at the time. Fucking hell, by the end of the day I was chasing the fucking things round the car lot, running them down and giving myself points for killing them with style or at speed, better than any game. Crazy really. It was only when I got up next morning and saw what I'd done that I realised how dumb I'd been. I must have killed more than fifty of the damn things. There was blood, guts and bits of bodies everywhere.

But there were still more coming.

I don't feel so good today. I'm scared. It's late on Wednesday night and there are hundreds of them outside again. You'd think they'd have seen what happened here and given up. There's no way they can get to me, but they're just relentless. They stand outside, edging ever closer, watching and waiting for me to come out. I've tried blocking up the windows, but it doesn't make any difference because I know they're still there, and they know I'm here. I've started thinking some bloody crazy thoughts too. Are they here for revenge?

Christ I feel sick.

Don't know whether it's something I've eaten or just nerves, but my guts are bad. I've lived on crap since this started – mostly chocolate, crisps, biscuits and other snacks because that's easiest. I haven't had bread or anything fresh for days. It's probably nothing, just adrenalin, but it's made me think. I stuck my head out of the door for a second this afternoon and all I could hear was thousands of flies buzzing and I started thinking about the germs and diseases that are out there. I've probably been breathing them in for days now. For Christ's sake, the whole fucking car lot is packed with human remains.

This building is starting to smell. It's starting to smell worse than outside. I can't stand it any longer. I've had diarrhoea since yesterday morning and I can't flush any of the toilets now. They're all backed-up with shit and I don't know what to do about it. I don't have any spare water or bleach. I should have been better prepared.

It's dark now, and there's nothing to do but sit here and wait for morning. I'm scared. I don't want to play games anymore. I don't want to be distracted. I want to know what's happening around me so that I'm ready for anything but, at the same time, I don't want to look. I don't want to see the dead outside. I can't sleep. I can't even bring myself to shut my eyes now, and even if I could, the pain in my guts would keep me awake.

Those fucking things just won't go. They're waiting for me. They try to climb over the cars to get closer to me but they can't do it. They don't have the coordination or the strength today, but tomorrow they might.

I'll stay here for as long as I can but I know I'll have to try and find some medicine and proper food soon. Maybe I'll try and get away in the morning. Maybe I'll wait another couple of days. Maybe I'll never get out.

I've gone and built myself a fucking prison.

DAY FOURTEEN

BREAKING POINT

The farmhouse was lost, and with it all security, comfort and certainty. The two of them sat together in the back of the Land Rover, locked in a desperate embrace, afraid to let go because all they had left now was each other.

Why are we even bothering when the odds are stacked so high against us? What's the point? When everything's gone, why are we still trying to survive? They both asked the same questions individually, but kept their answers private, maintaining the pretence, refusing to dwell on the hopelessness of their situation for the sake of the other. Both Michael and Emma knew their situation was dire.

Their desperate flight from Penn Farm, overrun with dead flesh, had been unplanned, unexpected and terrifying. It had all happened so quickly: a long, drawn out wait and then, finally, *suddenly*, they'd reached breaking point. The number of bodies converging on their isolated hideout had reached unmanageable levels, and then Carl had… well, Carl had reached breaking point too. In many ways the final loss of the farmhouse had come about as a direct result of his actions, and yet neither Michael or Emma felt any anger towards him. The fragility of his state of mind was wholly understandable in the circumstances. Michael wondered if he too might go the same way before long. He even wondered if that might be for the best. Could insanity possibly be any worse than this reality? Might it even make things easier?

They'd waited in this desolate, windswept car park on the edge of one side of a steep valley for as long as they'd been able. Times past, people had come to this isolated place to admire its beauty. Today all that Emma and Michael were interested in was its remoteness. From their high vantage point they looked down over a landscape which felt eternally empty now, and their microscopic size amidst the vastness of this place was humbling. The world should have been theirs for the taking. Christ, as far as they knew, they were the only ones left alive, surely they should have inherited everything by default? And yet here they were with nothing.

That was because *they* were here too. The relentless, tireless dead. Millions of slowly decaying bodies which hounded them incessantly, never stopping, and never giving up.

As it was, they'd only seen one body since they'd been up here. Who had it once been? How had the dead man managed to get this far on foot? Surely he couldn't have followed them all this way, so how had he ended up out here in the middle of nowhere at the same time as Michael and Emma? They couldn't help asking these and other unanswerable, irrelevant questions when the hideous creature first lumbered into view. The gnarled corpse had been horrific: all grubby skin and bone, the gusting wind blowing its ragged, flapping clothing against its skeletal frame, highlighting its brutal emaciation. Its grotesque face, deformed by decay, had appeared both expressionless and impossibly furious at the same time.

The two of them had remained perfectly still, waiting for the monstrosity to disappear again, too afraid to go out and confront it, despite knowing full well that either of them working alone could have taken it down in seconds. They chose instead to wait, sitting motionless in the back of the Land Rover until the dead man had gone. It seemed to take forever for him to disappear, but neither of them moved even a muscle until he was completely out of sight, both fearing there might be more of the dead nearby. The damn things followed the herd. If they'd attracted the attention of just this one, countless more might soon follow.

'We need food,' Emma said after they'd been sitting in their wind-beaten, blood-splattered Land Rover for what felt like weeks, continually watching the road ahead and behind should other corpses appear. Michael didn't answer. She was right, of course, but why bother? 'We can't just sit here indefinitely, can we?'

'Why not? You got any better ideas?'

She looked across at him. He stared out through the rain-lashed window, doing all he could to avoid making eye contact.

'I can't take this anymore. I'm hungry,' she said, and she scrambled over into the front and sat down behind the wheel. She started the engine, and the sudden noise and movement forced Michael into life.

'What the hell are you doing?' he protested as she pulled out onto the road. He climbed over into the front and collapsed into the seat next to her.

'What does it look like I'm doing? I can't stand this.'

He wanted to argue and make her turn back but he knew he couldn't. He had no counter.

Another unplanned drive through the heavy-skied gloom of a cold late-September afternoon came to a sudden end outside a lone house, as far away from everything else as Penn Farm had initially seemed. Michael silently thanked Emma for forcing his hand. For a while he'd begun to genuinely believe they might die up on that rocky outcrop, too scared to ever move.

'So what do you reckon?' she asked. Michael looked around. The house stood alone at the roadside, no other buildings in sight. He could see a solitary corpse in the distance, too far away to be of any real concern.

'I'll go in and check it out,' he replied, and before she could say anything else he was gone. He checked the front door – locked – then walked around the side of the building. He peered around each corner, checking the garden was empty, before trying the back door. It was open, and he slipped through into a small, square kitchen where a rustic-looking table and chairs filled almost the entire floor. He stared at the never-finished remains of someone's last breakfast until a sudden noise behind disturbed him and he spun around to see Emma standing in the doorway. She hadn't wanted to wait outside alone.

'Well?'

'Don't know yet,' he said. 'Haven't got any further than here.'

He walked around the edge of the table and down a short hallway towards the front door. Something grabbed at his leg and he recoiled, jumping back with shock and tripping over the corner of a rug. He was flat on his backside before he knew what was happening, face to face with a woman's corpse lying on its belly. He scrambled back away from the hideous thing, unable to take his eyes off its repulsive, disease-ravaged face. One of its legs was badly broken: horrifically swollen in all the wrong places. A sharp point of broken bone had torn through the skin and was now scraping along the wooden floorboards as the creature tried to move closer to him. It reached out but its grasping fingers fell short every time. It tried to grip the rug and pull itself closer, but its weight was too much for its weakened muscles to shift.

Emma was standing in the kitchen doorway, unable to move. Michael was still sitting on the ground. He drew his feet up closer, keeping out of range of the dead woman's thrashing arms, moving back as she inched forward.

'Get rid of it,' Emma said, but Michael couldn't. This was the first of the dead he'd been this close to since their escape from the farm house, and it terrified him with its undeniable, vicious intent. And yet, physically, he knew it was nothing. It appeared so pathetically weak that he couldn't understand why he, Carl and Emma hadn't been able to defend their home in the woods from these pathetic things. Their flesh was weak. They were rotting. Hollow. This one had been an elderly woman – no match for him in life, let alone death – and yet he still couldn't bring himself to fight. He pictured himself booting her face, caving it in until just a bloody mess remained, but he couldn't do it. Patchy white hair. Dribbles of decay staining her cardigan and her floral print dress. Slippers.

For fuck's sake…

Forcing himself to get a grip and move, Michael stood up, grabbed the corpse by the scruff of the neck, and half-dragged, half-threw it back into the room it had been slowly crawling out of. He pulled the door shut, safe in the knowledge it couldn't reach the handle from the floor, and that even if it did, it would probably only be able to push, not pull.

And again he thought, *if this is our enemy, how the hell did we lose the farmhouse?*

The rest of the small house was clear. The dead woman in the lounge banged the door repeatedly, doing little more than filling the building with unwanted noise.

Michael and Emma sat in the kitchen together and ate. What they didn't eat now, they'd take. Despite their hunger, their nervousness had stolen their appetites and each mouthful was an effort to swallow. Emma didn't think she'd be able to keep much down. Her stomach turned over every time the dead woman hit the door.

'We can't stay here,' she said.

'I know.'

'That noise... it'll bring more of them.'

'I know.'

'So where are we going to go?'

Michael didn't answer. He *couldn't* answer. He got up and walked to the front of the house. Emma followed. There was another body outside now. They watched from the safety of the shadows as a creature which used to be a paramedic awkwardly lumbered past in its loose and badly soiled jumpsuit uniform. It looked like it was going to keep walking, but an inconvenient *thump* from the corpse in the lounge attracted its attention. It pivoted around awkwardly on leaden feet, then came towards the house, crashing into the window through which Michael and Emma had been watching, pawing at the glass.

Another noise from the woman in the lounge, louder this time, perhaps in response.

'We could shut her up,' Emma suggested.

'What, tie her hands behind her back?'

'You know what I mean.'

Michael knew exactly what she meant, but just the thought of having to face that foul old hag again made his legs weaken. He'd never been particularly good at handling confrontation, and the longer this nightmare continued, the less-equipped he felt to be able to deal with the dead. They were weak and yet so driven to attack: so relentlessly hostile and so bloody unpredictable. He couldn't face it, not yet.

'Let's go,' he said, and the dead paramedic began beating on the glass in response to his voice and movement. It was just a matter of time before more corpses arrived here.

Between them they carried a small supply of food and other supplies out to the Land Rover, carefully creeping around the back of the paramedic and avoiding yet another corpse which was tripping unsteadily down the road towards the house now.

Michael started the engine and watched as both of the creatures turned and moved towards the Land Rover with renewed interest and speed. 'Which way?' he asked.

'Any way,' Emma replied. 'It doesn't matter. Just go.'

No maps. No satnav. No real idea where they were or where they were going...

As the afternoon disappeared into the evening and the light began to fade, Michael and Emma found themselves skirting around the edge of a small town. Their nerves increased as their surroundings became more urban and less open. There seemed to be movement around them constantly now. The road immediately ahead was blocked by a crash which neither of them saw coming until they were almost upon it: during the final rush hour, two buses travelling in opposite directions had collided with each other at speed. One was still standing upright, the other over on its side. Michael swung the Land Rover around, bumping up over a low central reservation, then accelerated back the way they'd come. The road they'd just driven along, virtually empty a few minutes earlier, was filling with teeming movement now as hordes of the dead gravitated towards the Land Rover's noise. A group of them that had been trapped in a building – some kind of coach station, it appeared – managed to get free and spilled out onto the carriageway like a slick. Michael swerved, then steered hard the other way to avoid ploughing into another group emerging from a side street like a gang. Maybe the dark made things look worse than they actually were, but there seemed to be hundreds of bodies up ahead of them now, *fucking hundreds*.

'Get off the road,' Emma said, sounding calmer than she felt.

'And go where?' Michael demanded, more than a hint of desperation in his voice. 'We can't risk going any deeper into the town.'

She grabbed his arm and pointed towards the entrance to a multi-storey car park on the far side of a traffic island they were fast approaching. 'Head up. Just get up off the street.'

Michael grunted something unintelligible then steered up the exit ramp, crashing through a barrier. He drove up floor by floor, using whatever gaps in the stationary traffic he could find to keep climbing, having to fight against his instincts and ignore the road markings. He was turning and turning the car now like they were riding a helter-skelter in reverse, half-expecting to still come across other drivers coming back down the other way.

They finally stopped when they reached the top floor of the car park and there was nowhere else to go. A sudden sharp shower of rain hammered down and wind whipped across the rooftop, but the conditions didn't stop Michael from getting out, running over to the edge of the building, and looking down. He held onto a metal railing as another gust of wind buffeted him.

'See much?' Emma asked when he returned.

'Not a lot. The dumb fuckers haven't worked out we're up here.'

'Not yet,' she said under her breath as she climbed over the seats and bedded down in the back. 'Just give it time.'

Several days passed. It was now dawn on the third day since they'd reached the car park. Each hour seemed to drag on forever. The meagre, barely sufficient supplies they'd gathered from the house were supplemented by bags of shopping they'd found in other cars nearby. Emma and Michael sat in the Land Rover together through the light and the dark and the wind and rain. Conversation was infrequent and difficult, the atmosphere unremittingly grim. Their situation, whilst by no means completely hopeless, was unclear at best.

Several times Emma tried asking the questions Michael was doing his best to avoid. 'So what *are* we going to do? And please answer me this time, Michael. Don't just ignore me again...'

But that was exactly what he did. Rather than answer or argue, Michael got out and walked to the edge of the roof again and looked down, as he'd done countless times since they'd got here. This time Emma followed.

'This is crazy. We have to do something.'

'Like what?' he demanded, his voice unexpectedly loud. Emma took a step back with surprise at the strength of his response. He sounded desperate, close to tears. 'You keep asking me the same thing again and again, but I can't give you any answers. Just look down there, Em. It's fucking hopeless.'

He pointed down and Emma leant over to see. The crowd of bodies around the car park had been growing steadily since they'd first arrived. Now a huge mass of them filled the street directly below. She didn't know why they kept coming. Was the rest of the world really so quiet that they could hear even the slight noises she and Michael made up here? Had this crowd grown from the remnants of the dead attracted here by the noise of their arrival? But why so many?

'They know,' Michael said, his voice a little calmer now. 'It's the only explanation. They know we're up here – some of them, anyway – and that's enough. And I think they'll keep trying to climb up until either they get to us or we have to go back down.'

He stared down into the silent, constantly shifting mass of dead flesh so far below. He couldn't tell whether their movements were controlled or involuntary, but he was sure he saw several of them lift their heads and look up. He tried to block the thought from his mind, but suddenly all he could think about was this car park steadily filling up with the dead, floor by floor, until he and Emma were trapped and surrounded again, until the point of no return had been reached. Breaking point.

Another endless day slowly turned to night. Emma busied herself by looting from the few cars on the top floor of the car park they still hadn't touched, occasionally creeping down to the floor immediately below. She'd found scraps of food in one car, the odd bottle of water in another, some warmer clothes for both of them in a third. Michael, spurred into doing something because Emma suddenly seemed so busy, filled the tank of the Land Rover with fuel siphoned from other vehicles, then built a bonfire in an empty space and lit it, desperate for warmth. Emma came running over as soon as she saw the flames.

'What the hell are you doing?'

'Keeping warm.'

'But you can't… What if they see it?'

'Who, the bodies?'

'Yes!'

'They won't.'

'How do you know?'

'Because we're on the top floor of a fucking car park, Emma. We're fifty fucking feet off the ground!'

'But what if they *do* see it?' she screamed at him. 'What if it brings more of them here?'

'For Christ's sake, think about what you're saying. How can they possibly see it from down there?'

'How do you know they can't? There are other buildings this tall. What if there are bodies up there too? They'll see it.'

'And how are they going to get here? Get a bloody grip.'

'Don't talk to me like that—'

'Then don't talk to me at all! Anyway, if this fire doesn't bring them up here, your bloody screaming will.'

'I'm not screaming.'

'You fucking are!' he yelled at her.

They both shut up, aware that they were being as loud as each other. Michael's last words echoed off the walls of empty buildings.

'We should just go,' she said, quieter now, calmer. 'Take our chances and get out of here.'

'There are still too many of them down there. We can't. We're trapped. I don't want to go anywhere near any of those fucking things, do you? We'll keep waiting. They have to go eventually, don't they?'

'You reckon?'

Michael turned his back and walked away. He didn't know how much more of this he could take.

Michael had been sitting in the front of the Land Rover, staring out into the darkness for what felt like forever, when he thought he saw movement out of the corner of his eye. It was almost dawn – yet *another* dawn – and he glanced back over his shoulder to check on Emma. She was still asleep behind him, her head buried under blankets to block out the rest of the world. He peered deeper into the gloom around the ramp which led up onto the rooftop, desperately hoping not to see anything. Had it, as he now prayed, just been a trick of the low light? A scavenging bird landing and taking off again, feeding off the scraps like he and Emma did? Ash being blown from the remains of last night's fire? But then he saw it again, and this time he knew exactly what it was. He could tell from the slow, stilted movements, from the unsteady awkwardness and listless gait, that it was one of the dead. How it had managed to drag itself all the way up here, he had no idea. It must have heard them looting and arguing and reacted to their noise. And now, hours later, the total lack of other interruptions had combined with the bizarre, dogged persistence the dead now displayed to allow this one to finally reach the top floor.

Was this corpse alone, or was this the first of thousands? Was this the beginning of the deluge he feared?

What do I do?

Michael sat perfectly still and watched the creature as it approached. He moved only his eyes and tried to work out what his next move should be. Maybe if he just ignored it, it might go away like the lone body they'd seen out on the hills? But this one couldn't get away – there was nowhere left for it to go. Perhaps he should wait for it to reach the edge of the roof and hope it would take a final step too far and fall off. As the corpse staggered closer, the first shards of morning sunlight allowed Michael to make out all the details he didn't want to see. It was a pathetic, miserable sight. Barely able to support its own emaciated weight, it dragged its feet along and its leaden arms swung with every step as if it was half-heartedly attempting to march. It had dark greasy hair covering most of its face and its clothing glistened with damp decay where the light struck. Bizarrely, something about its lethargy – its apparent ignorance, apathy almost – annoyed Michael. The corpse reminded him of a useless teenager, like one of the kids in the school classroom where he'd been delivering a talk when this nightmare had begun. It looked pathetic, and he asked himself, *why am I afraid of you?*

Michael looked back at Emma again when she stirred in her sleep, and his sudden movement was enough to make the corpse react. It started towards the car and, as it approached, he thought about the cruel irony of their situation. He was still alive. He was still strong. He could still think and eat and sleep and laugh and cry and do all the other things he'd always been able to do, and yet he and Emma were the ones who'd become prisoners of the dead, trapped on this car park roof. The body continued to come closer and Michael watched it intently. Its face was hollow and vacant, infuriatingly expressionless. It barely looked capable of moving much further forward, let alone causing either of them any harm. And yet he still couldn't bring himself to do anything about it. He thought back to the farmhouse

282

again, to the life he'd almost had there with Emma before things had fallen apart. They should have done so much better. Had that really been their last chance as they'd feared, or could they try again? Was he really going to allow what was left of his time to be ruled by these foul, decaying creatures, this one in particular? Or was he going to do something about it?

Michael got out of the car, waking Emma in the process, and marched towards the corpse. His sudden surge of determination waned just as quickly as it had begun. He slowed, then stopped and stood his ground. The body continued its desperately slow approach. *It's just you and me*, he thought, looking deep into the foul aberration's distorted face and doing all he could to ignore the bilious feeling at the back of his throat. It suddenly felt as if everything boiled down to what happened next; that these few minutes would somehow shape every single day he and Emma still had left. So was it sink or swim? Fight or flight? Win or lose?

The corpse took another lurching step forward, and Michael flinched.

'Get back in the Land Rover,' Emma said from somewhere behind him. 'Quick!'

He looked at the dead body as it reacted to her voice. Then he turned to Emma and said: 'No.'

Before she could stop him, Michael lunged forward and grabbed the corpse. The smell up close was foul, and the soggy noises the pitiful cadaver made as it squirmed in his grip made him want to vomit. Its flesh was cold and pliable under his fingers. It tried to push his arms away but its comparative lack of strength meant it didn't stand a chance. Michael straightened his arms and surprised himself by lifting the creature's entire soggy body several inches off the ground. It continued to try and fight, but it was miserably weak. He lifted the corpse higher before running to the edge of the rooftop and hurling it over. He watched as it tumbled down like a shop window dummy, stiff arms and legs sprawling, then crashed into the crowd below, hitting the deck with a sickening crunch which Michael could clearly hear over the silence of everything else. Down at ground level, the dead immediately surged again, tripping and sliding inquisitively over what was left of their fallen brethren.

Breathless, and feeling strangely exhilarated, Michael returned to the Land Rover.

'We're going,' he said.

'Where?'

'I don't care.' He wiped his hands clean on a towel then threw it out of the window. 'Anywhere but here. I'm not going to be a prisoner.'

He started the engine, and another corpse dragged itself up onto the rooftop, seemingly in response to the noise.

'Are you sure about this? You were the one who—'

'I know what I said,' he interrupted, 'and I was wrong. And no, I'm not sure about this, but if we do something and fuck it up, at least we'll have *tried*. You were right, we can't just sit up here and either starve to death or wait for them to get us. I'm taking back control, Em.'

She was about to speak again, but it was too late. Michael put his foot down and the Land Rover juddered across the wet asphalt. He swerved around a tight corner, smacking into the lone approaching body and sending it flying, then ploughed down the steep, stomach-churning incline into the darkness. Emma held on to her seat, her safety belt, the door... anything she could grab hold of as the Land Rover hurtled further and further down. With each level they descended, the amount of dead flesh around them increased, but it was never enough to stop them. On one floor Michael clipped the wing of another car, and his response was simply to accelerate harder and get out of this gloomy, germ-filled concrete maze as fast as he could. Eventually he smashed through another barrier alongside the one they'd broken through when they'd first arrived here, then raced out onto the street. He gripped the steering wheel tight and thundered through the mass of rotting flesh, no longer bothering to try and avoid hitting them, just doing whatever he had to do to get away.

They stopped at a cut-price supermarket on the way back out of town. Emma had spotted it in a side road: ignored and overlooked by the bulk of the dead. Michael slammed on the brakes and reversed up to the doors. They'd done this before.

'We should fill the car up,' Emma said as she climbed out and ran into the store, 'then just get away again.'

Michael didn't answer. He was already inside, dragging a pile of plastic shopping baskets over towards the nearest aisle. He looked around anxiously and began to fill them. Fortunately there were no corpses inside that he could see, but a handful had already appeared at the floor-to-ceiling windows which ran the length of the shop floor. They slammed their hands and slid their decaying faces against the glass, moving from side to side, slowly matching the movements of the two looters inside.

By the time the first four baskets had been filled at speed and carried back over to the Land Rover, there were eight corpses at the windows. By the time they'd filled ten baskets, there were twenty of them. By the time they'd collected enough, it had become impossible to gauge how many of the damn things there were. The full expanse of glass had become a solid mass of greasy grey flesh, and a crowd had formed around the front of the Land Rover too. Neither Michael nor Emma said anything until they were loaded up and ready to leave. They stood a short distance back and surveyed the chaos outside together.

'Are we in trouble now?' Emma asked.

'Only if we wait around here much longer. We need to move.'

'Just drive through them?'

'Exactly. Before they reach critical mass.'

'Critical mass? What the hell are you talking about?'

'Critical mass, breaking point... it's all the same thing. We're safe until we let them get to a certain level. When there's too many of them, the balance of power shifts and we're screwed. Until then, we just about stay in control. We just have to keep moving.'

'Breaking point... is that what happened to you on the car park roof?'

'Something like that, I guess. You ready?'

Emma nodded, and the two of them ran for the back of the Land Rover and scrambled over the supplies they'd collected. Michael dropped into the driver's seat, started the engine, put his foot down, and careened away. Emma held on tight behind him.

'So what's the plan now?' she shouted over the noise of the engine and the relentless thump of the stream of unsteady bodies they ploughed into and through. At first Michael didn't answer, concentrating instead on mounting the pavement to weave around the back of a truck, then avoiding another clutch of corpses to get back onto the road.

'No plan,' he told her.

'Great.'

'Plenty of food, though.'

She couldn't really argue, but she did. 'We need to be better organised that this, Mike. We can't just keep stopping and starting.'

'Why not? I'm beginning to think that's exactly how we need to be. The same thing's going to happen wherever we go, isn't it? Wherever we are, whatever we do, we're going to have about ten minutes grace before we're surrounded. Fact is, we're massively outnumbered, Em. We just have to deal with it.'

'So is this it then? Just drive, loot, drive, sleep, drive, fight...? We're going to end up spending the rest of our lives stuck in this bloody car.'

'If you can think of a better solution, I'm all ears.' He gripped the wheel and swerved to avoid a child's corpse which walked down the white line towards them, arms outstretched in a classic ghoul-like pose. 'We need to drive out into the middle of nowhere, find somewhere practically inaccessible, then hope there's a building or something we can use nearby.'

'There's a café on the top of Snowdon,' Emma offered.

'That's not as dumb as it sounds.'

'It wasn't dumb at all,' she said, offended. 'I was being serious.'

'But it's impractical. Too extreme. There are probably loads of places like that, but less remote. It's just a question of finding them.'

'Let's stop and get a map or something. Plan things properly instead of just lurching from crisis to crisis.'

'We're not lurching from crisis to crisis. It's all the same bloody crisis, in case you hadn't noticed. We just need to find somewhere as isolated as the top of Snowdon, then only a handful of them will ever be able to reach us. Christ, it'll be hard enough for us to get there.'

'Déjà vu. Haven't we been down this road before? Wasn't that the big selling point of the farmhouse? Look where that got us.'

'It *almost* worked,' he replied, wincing as the Land Rover powered into another corpse.

'Yes, but *almost* is the same as *didn't*. It's not that simple. There are too many of them.'

Michael braked as he reached a cross-roads. The Land Rover skidded to an abrupt halt. The dead poured towards them from every conceivable direction.

'This is bloody crazy,' Emma said under her breath. She ducked instinctively as another corpse lunged for the Land Rover. It tripped in the road and fell forward, its skull cracking against her window with a sickening thump.

Michael struggled to keep control of both the Land Rover and his temper. 'I'll keep driving until we find a bloody light house or something like that, shall I?'

Emma didn't bite. She gripped the sides of her seat as he accelerated again. And then she saw it.

'Stop!'

Michael instinctively reacted, bringing the Land Rover to another juddering stop and wiping out four more straggling cadavers in the process. 'What?'

'Over there,' she said, pointing ahead and way over to their left. 'Look!'

Michael saw it immediately and sped up again. 'You're a bloody genius,' he told her as he steered them towards an industrial estate. Through the chain-link fence he could see a vast expanse of tarmac covered with caravans and motorhomes of varying shapes and sizes. She'd found a temporary solution to their problems: a way of getting as far as they could from the towns and the cities and the dead without having to resort to living out of the back of this bloody Land Rover any longer.

'That one,' Emma said as they approached, pointing out the largest, most luxurious, and strongest-looking motorhome she could see.

DAY SEVENTEEN

AMY STEADMAN
Part v

Amy Steadman's remarkable physical transformation has continued unabated. It is now more than two weeks since her death. As her body has festered, however, the low level of muted brain activity has continued to increase. Defying all previous understanding of the changes undergone within the human body after death, as Amy's flesh and bone has deteriorated she has, paradoxically, regained a remarkable degree of self-awareness. The increasing physical limitations of her decomposing body result in much of this mental improvement remaining undetectable.

Time has taken its toll on the millions of cadavers now walking the streets. They are steadily disintegrating; countless internal and external chemical reactions affecting the composition and strength of their flesh. Amy's corpse is no different. Her skin has darkened and dried out in places as fluids have drained away. Her body has become a breeding ground for huge numbers of insects. Amy's corpse is infested. She is riddled with maggots.

Operating on a basic level, the bodies are driven by an instinctive desire to continue to exist. Self-preservation is each corpse's only concern. Because of their worsening physical state, however, their ability to defend and protect themselves is severely limited. As a result their reactions now appear clumsy and overly aggressive. The bodies will fight to protect themselves at all costs even if, perversely, this results in them sustaining physical damage. It's not uncommon to see a body attack another corpse in self-defence, and sustain substantial damage in the process. This is the norm with those bodies that are particularly badly decayed. Where the process has been slowed – as with Amy Steadman who died indoors, shielded from the elements for several days – the actions of the dead are slightly more reserved and controlled.

It is now early on Thursday morning and a light, misty rain has been falling since dawn. Amy's body is shuffling along the side of a warehoused-sized furniture store. There are a large number of corpses nearby, although the reason for their swollen numbers is not immediately apparent. It may be that there has previously been an incident here which initially attracted their attention, and that this is simply the residue of that crowd gradually disappearing. The fact that many of these bodies seem to be moving in the same overall direction, however, indicates that this could be the beginning of such an incident, not the end.

Amy's corpse continues to drag itself around the building and the surrounding streets until a single noise in the near distance attracts its attention. It is the sound of a survivor preparing to leave his shelter to search for essential supplies. Amy, along with all the other corpses in the immediate vicinity, immediately begins to gravitate towards the source of the sound.

The young male survivor is based in an office building in the centre of a sprawling car lot. Over the last few days he has attempted to fortify and strengthen his hideout with limited success, but as the behaviour of the bodies has changed, so he has been forced to change his priorities. Failing dismally to prepare for the potential long-term problems caused by the infection, he is struggling to stay sane and stay alive. The survivor failed to anticipate the herding behaviour of the dead, nor did he consider the potential duration of his incarceration. Initially naïvely believing that he could continue to enjoy something resembling a pre-infection standard of living, he is now dangerously ill-equipped, having focused his early efforts on comfort rather than practical necessities.

His health is deteriorating. As a result both of the increased number of bodies in the locality and the fortifications he made to his shelter, he is unable to easily venture out for supplies. He has been trapped for days without access to clean water, sanitation, medicine, and food of any real nutritional value. He is dehydrated and malnourished. After an aborted attempt to fetch supplies three days ago, his mental state has also deteriorated. At this point in time the differences between this survivor and the corpses which surround him are remarkably slim. Because of their vast numbers and their emotionless state, the bodies now have a clear advantage.

The survivor has now emerged from the office building in the middle of the car lot where he has hidden for the last two weeks. He moves slowly in a futile attempt to avoid detection. Because of his poor physical condition, his movements are uncharacteristically clumsy. He plans to take a car and drive to a supermarket and he is confident that once he is in the car he will be relatively safe. His activity, however, has not gone unnoticed. His pained, awkward movements and rasping breathing have already attracted the attention of several of the nearest cadavers. An inevitable chain reaction is spreading throughout the crowd as more bodies gravitate towards him.

Amy Steadman's body is close. She has crossed the main road between the furniture store and the car lot and is heading towards the office building, focussing on the increased levels of movement all around it. The dead are closing in from every direction.

Some of the bodies are distracted by the movement of other corpses around them. Amy, however, is able to differentiate between the dead and other distractions. She will not hesitate to attack anything that threatens her, but she no longer wantonly attacks other bodies. She concentrates on moving towards the source of the disruption, although she does not fully understand why. She likely assumes it represents a threat.

The lone survivor is weak and, after a long period of frightened inactivity, he finds the sudden effort of moving at speed unexpectedly difficult. Just leaving the building has left him breathless and light-headed. Overcome with nerves, he has stopped in the shadows at the side of the building and is trying to summon up the strength to make a run for the car he previously left ready for an occasion such as this.

Amy's corpse – along with more than fifty others – is less than ten metres away from the front of the office building. The survivor is now aware of the sudden movement all around him, but he is being dangerously indecisive. He knows he can either retreat (as he did a week ago) or continue with this attempt to fetch supplies. He knows that either option is equally dangerous: if he turns back he will starve and his sickness will worsen, yet if he leaves he risks attack from the advancing hordes. He also knows that he will have to leave eventually and that going back inside will only delay the inevitable. He decides to run for the car.

Indecision has ultimately proved to be this survivor's undoing. The brief but unnecessary delay has given sufficient numbers of bodies enough time to drag themselves into the narrow space between him and the car. He attempts to run towards the vehicle, managing to avoid the first few corpses which attack. Within another few metres, however, there are too many of them. He tries to double-back, but once the first of the dead has caught hold of him he is trapped. He easily releases the first corpse's grip, but wastes precious seconds fighting it. By the time he's free and the first body is down, another eight are on him.

Amy Steadman's corpse is at the front of the crowd which swallows up and kills this survivor.

Half an hour later and the scene has changed again. With the survivor now dead and the area silent, the bulk of the crowd of bodies has begun drifting away. Amy Steadman's body limps alone through the early mist along a wide road strewn with death.

DO YOU REMEMBER THE FIRST TIME?

In the seventeen days since it happened, Maxwell has rarely needed to leave his home. In the last fourteen days, in fact, he hasn't had to go outside at all. He's what people used to call a 'Prepper': someone who planned for the worst, because they knew it was going to happen someday. And Maxwell was right. All the effort he put into stockpiling and planning his survival before the event has definitely paid off now. The fact he's alive was all down to chance at the end of the day, though he doesn't know that. Or if he does, he doesn't care. Maxwell is convinced the reason he's still here after millions of others were wiped out is because he knows what he's doing. In a world where all reason appears to have gone out of the window, it's hard to argue with his logic.

Flood, fire, flu epidemic, alien invasion, terrorism, war... he'd got all bases covered. When you take things down to base level, the requirements for survival are largely the same whatever the shade of shit being hurled at the fan. Food, water, medicinal supplies... all generic entries on any self-respecting Prepper's standard tick-list.

People who didn't know Maxwell called him a loner. Some avoided him, thought he was a bit strange. Very few understood him. *She* did. They hadn't been together for long, but she'd seemed to instinctively understand what he was doing and where he was at. Sometimes, when he's lying in bed at night, listening to the silence, he can still hear her voice and feel her lips on his. Kathryn was special. Everything his first time should have been and so much more besides. He can't get her face out of his head.

Who's laughing now? When he thinks about all his detractors, he can't help but feel a little smug. There's a part of him wishes they could see him. Maybe they can? Maybe some of the corpses outside remember more than he's given them credit for? Maybe they're looking at him, thinking *we're sorry, Max, you were right... we shouldn't have taken the piss...*

He knows that none of this matters now, because he's won. If this was a film and he was the star, they'd call it *King of the Dead*.

Externally, Maxwell's modest house is indistinguishable from pretty much every other house on the street. It's all part of the plan. A small, run-of-the-mill terraced house with a door at the front, one at the back, and a side-passage giving access to a small, walled backyard. A small backyard that's full of equipment and supplies. He had most of it already, but in the two day's grace between the fall and the resurrection of the rest of the population, he went into town and scavenged everything he was missing and more besides. Maxwell has so much stuff in his home now that he's struggling for living space. He could have set-up somewhere else, but the familiarity was important. Loading up and clearing out would have taken too much effort and risk. He knows there'll be plenty of time for all that. When this is over, he tells himself regularly, he'll get out of town and find himself somewhere perfect. It'll be like all the best post-apocalyptic dreams he ever had. Bloody hell, he hadn't realised how much he'd been looking forward to these days. The only downside is the loneliness, but he'll cope. The freedom is more than enough of a trade-off. The dead world is his oyster...

But he really does miss her.

Maxwell spends his days checking and rechecking his provisions, then checking them again. The undeniable buzz of all this preparation is still enough of a distraction from the monotony of keeping his head down and staying quiet. He knows that's what it's going to take to stay alive.

He's a smart kid. He watched from the window and worked out the rules of the dead quickly enough, figured out how they were becoming increasingly self-aware and, therefore, increasingly dangerous. He also knows that the danger will continue to increase for as long as the dead remain mobile. Their decaying bodies will inevitably fail them in time. It'll be another six months, he reckons, something like that. He knows he can hold out that long.

Maxwell has always felt different to everyone else, but now that difference is stark. When he's watching the dead, he can't make up his mind whether they've undergone a radical transformation or if they've barely changed at all? They look completely different, of course, but they still hang around in packs and follow the herd, fitting in and trying not to be noticed, just like they used to.

Maxwell never tried to fit in, never subscribed to the same bland shite as everyone else. The mainstream was too mediocre for his liking, constantly exploiting the mundane for profit and gain. Shit, it had come to something when even geeks and nerds had become cool. Didn't anyone understand how wrong that was? When a minority is accepted and swallowed up by the mainstream, he'd told Kathryn that night, it gets diluted and sanitized until it eventually becomes the majority. When they saw some of the clothes he wore and learnt about the things he enjoyed, people thought he was being ironic. But he wasn't. He was just being Maxwell.

He's distracted watching a pack of them now. They're regressing, he thinks, becoming more animal-like. Their humanity is being stripped away in layers, and now what he's seeing is base-level instinct. Guttural. Clumsy. Unrefined. Brutal. He studies them with a confident superiority, predicting their movements. One of them – a man in his early fifties when he died, perhaps, judging from his clothing and shabby appearance – has lost his balance. He trips down the kerb and clatters into the side of a parked car. The dead man is an awkward mass of barely-controlled flesh now, struggling with his own substantial weight. The impact with the car is enough to set off the vehicle's alarm, and the sudden noise and flashing headlights disturb the eerie stillness of everything else. The sound is ugly. It makes Maxwell feel nervous and he wants it to stop. These days, silence is his friend.

Maxwell predicts the alarm will draw hundreds of those things closer from miles around. He makes a mental note to remember how effective it is, because it might be useful. Already there are more than twenty corpses lumbering towards the car. He covers his mouth with his hand when he laughs involuntarily. They're so bloody dumb and predictable. As soon as the noise stops, they start moving away, spreading out like ink across blotting paper. But the alarm's not finished yet. It's silent for about thirty seconds, then it goes off again, and every last one of the dead bodies which has started moving away immediately swivels around and pointlessly trudges back again.

And it goes on and on and on.

For hours.

Stupid fucking creatures.

Shit. Maxwell has a problem.

Something's got into the back yard overnight. A fox or a starving dog must have got over the wall somehow. Thankfully almost all of the perishable stuff is in the house, but the damn vermin has had a go at some of the medical supplies Max left off the ground on a pallet outside because he didn't have room indoors. He doesn't think too much damage has been done, but this stuff will need replacing. He can't afford to take risks and leave himself open to infection. Christ alone knows the air's going to be full of all kinds of germs from here on in. What's happened this morning isn't the end of the world (he smiles to himself when he thinks that – that's been and gone already) but he does need to do something about it. He'll probably be okay, but probably isn't good enough anymore. And the thing is, from what he's seen, he's sure that in the short to mid-term, things are going to get far worse out there before they get any better. He needs to sort this out fast. The sooner he gets it done, the less risky it should be.

Maxwell spends the rest of the day reorganising his stuff and bringing everything inside but he knows there's no escaping the fact he's going to have to go out in the morning.

Maxwell gets up early, just before first light. He knows the dead have no concept of night and day – he's seen them milling about at all hours – so going out at this time is purely for his benefit. The shadows will help. It's light enough so that he can see what he's doing, but still dark enough to remain hidden. On a less practical level, he knows it's better to get this done now than to spend the whole day thinking too hard about leaving the house and getting worked up unnecessarily.

He has a specific set of clothing he's prepared for occasions such as this. He wears a wetsuit as a base-layer. He doesn't think the dead things outside bite like they did in the movies, but he's not taking any chances. He reminds himself that this time last month he didn't think the dead could walk, either. The wetsuit provides protection, yet it enables him to remain mobile too. Over it he wears several warm, loose-fitting layers. He also wears a utility belt – more DIY-expert than Batman-like in its design, but it does the same job. From it he hangs his tools: screwdrivers, pliers, a hammer, a crowbar… they can all double-up as weapons if push comes to shove.

He moves quietly through the shadows, passing so close to some of the corpses that he can hardly believe they don't notice him. Their senses have clearly been severely dulled by what happened, and that's no surprise. The surprise is that they're still managing to function at all.

For the first ten minutes, Maxwell intentionally walks in the wrong direction. When he's a safe distance from his home, well away from his intended destination, he uses the trick he picked up earlier this week and smashes a car window to set off the alarm. He waits out of sight until the noise has done its work and all the dead nearby have been drawn out of hiding.

This morning, Maxwell is going to the hospital. Although he might be able to get what he needs from a supermarket (and there are several of those between the hospital and home), he's steering clear of such public places. Let's face it, if anyone else has survived, that's where they'll be heading. Maxwell's not interested in any other survivors (except one). Other people will present more problems than solutions. It's a pretty safe bet they'll be nowhere near as prepared or as able as he is. The last thing he needs – the last thing he *wants* – in these circumstances is to saddle himself with freeloaders. His provisions have been sourced on the basis of catering for one, and his home/hideout has just enough space for him alone to live comfortably. Harsh as it sounds, anyone else who's made it this far can go to hell. And anyway, if they've lasted 'til today, they obviously don't need him.

He waits in the open garage of another house and daydreams, wishing Kathryn could see him now. Imagine if she'd survived, that it was just the two of them… She thought some of the things he did were strange, but he knew all along he was right. The apocalypse has justified his odd behaviours.

It doesn't take long to get to the hospital. Obviously the wards and other public spaces are no-go areas full of corpses, but he'd never planned on going there anyway. There are kitchens and supply areas where he can get everything he needs, both today and in the future. He knows his way around the hospital campus. He's never been here as anything other than a visitor and an A&E patient on a couple of occasions, but he's spent long enough poring over the plans and Google Earth to know where he's going.

Avoid main entrances and obvious doors. Find other ways to get where you need to go. Think about what other survivors would do – less prepared survivors – and do the opposite.

He talks to himself constantly, reassures himself he's doing the right thing, focuses on getting the job done and getting back home. This isn't as easy as he thought it would be. Being away from the house has added an additional layer of realism to the situation he wasn't expecting. He wasn't prepared for the unending scale of the devastation this morning, nor how everything has deteriorated in the two weeks or so since he last ventured out. How things feel, how things smell… Everywhere he looks he sees something worse than before. The corpse of a child in the backseat of a car, pawing the glass constantly with tiny, brittle fingers; imprisoned bodies prowling the rooms of their mausoleum homes, unable to escape; half a woman dragging herself along the middle of the road, tattered stumps where her feet used to be…

Maxwell stops and presses himself flat against a wall when a cadaver approaches. He stands completely still and studies its decay as it moves past him, oblivious. It has sustained appalling injuries, as if its unprotected face has been smashed into something at force. Its bottom lip is split down to the chin, and there are yellowed teeth protruding from its broken jaw at unnatural angles. Its swollen brown tongue moves constantly around the inside of its mouth. No spit. Too dry to lick. Maxwell stays exactly where he is for a moment longer, feeling faint. It'll pass, he knows it will. It's just shock.

The smells begin to affect him more than the sights. There's an ever-present fug of death hanging in the air here, a noxious stench which seems to coat everything. He's wearing a basic facemask as a precaution, but even that's not enough. Maybe, if the opportunity presents itself, he'll be able to find something more substantial in the hospital stores for next time. Christ knows he's probably going to need it. The longer this goes on, the more the bodies will decay. He's already outnumbered by insects, several million to one. It's only going to get worse.

Am I really the only one left alive?

He wishes Kathryn had given him her address after the party. He could go and check. One way or another, he thinks he'd just prefer to know.

He's distracted. He forces himself to find focus. Get a grip. *Concentrate.*

Maxwell pushes himself away from the wall and steps on the outstretched hand of a girl who dropped dead and never got up again. The horrible sound of bones breaking under his boot, fingers crunching, threatens to make the nausea return. He takes his time, looks up into the swirling clouds overhead and waits for the sickness to pass. He almost turns and goes back home, but stops himself before his nerves give out. *Do this right*, he thinks, *and I won't have to leave the house again for a long time. Fuck it up, and I could be back here before the month's out.*

He imagines her watching him from afar. Waiting for him. He imagines doing this for her.

Up ahead is the large storage building he's been aiming for. According to the information he accessed online before the Internet died, this is the largest such facility on the campus. There's a loading bay around the back, and a smaller entrance on the side which he manages to pry open with his crowbar. One last look around, then he disappears inside.

The building is surprisingly light. Clear Perspex panels in the roof let in a decent amount of early morning illumination. He stands still, waiting for the sound of his forced entry to fade. And when it does, he becomes aware of more noise coming from deeper inside the vast space. There are several corpses in here, and he has to assume they're all aware of him now. No matter. He thinks he can work around them. They're not people anymore, just... *things.*

There's a small office up ahead. He goes inside and shuts the door behind him, grateful of the space. A dead woman is slumped face-down over a desk. She's holding a mobile phone, which he wrenches from her death-grip. Even after all this time it still has a little battery remaining. He spends a few seconds looking through her digital life and remembering his own. Maybe he should spend this time trying to get online? Should he check the major news sites to see if they're responding or if they've been updated? What's the point? What does it matter if anyone else is left alive out there? If he discovers the whole of the rest of Europe has survived this, so what? What difference will it make? He is where he is. Strange thing is, he thinks he'd actually be disappointed now if he found there were other people still alive. He couldn't face having to go back to living in the old world. Not now. Not after the taste of freedom that Armageddon has given him.

The dead woman's name is Amelia. She partied hard. He flicks casually through her photographs – most taken in various pubs and bars, others taken at home as she relaxed with her boyfriend and parents. There's a video of her playing with a dog. He watches it over and over, transfixed by the little black and white dog catching the same thrown ball again and again.

And then the battery gives up the ghost.

The screen dims and the pictures disappear and no matter how many times he tries to get the phone to come back to life, it doesn't. All those images are still trapped in there somewhere, but he has no way of accessing them. Digital Amelia has ceased to exist. All that's left of her now is this rapidly decaying mass of flesh and bone. He knows Kathryn's like this somewhere, or worse. But he consoles himself with the fact that he's still thinking about her, and surely that's keeping her alive in some way?

He looks at Amelia's body, and remembers his time with Kathryn. He'd liked her a lot, but she'd barely looked at him before the office party. They'd both got drunk and ended up having a quick, fumbled fuck in the toilets. His first time. His only time. He's daydreaming again now, imagining what life would have been like if she'd survived too. Christ, she'd have been blown away by what he'd achieved… But he has to accept she's gone. Truth be told, she was gone long before all this madness started. She was gone by the time the hangovers had cleared.

He struggled with people. Things, Maxwell could always deal with: plans, preparations, contingencies, supplies, whatever it took. It was people he had trouble with. Couldn't handle their unpredictability. Didn't like the fact he was never in complete control when other people were involved.

There's a noise.

Something close behind him, just outside the office door.

Maxwell holds his breath and stands perfectly still, cursing himself for being a dumb fucking idiot and getting distracted. And then he sees it. Another one of *them*. He knows he needs to get moving, that every second he spends here now is a second too long. He waits until the corpse has gone, then lets himself back out and starts looking for the stuff he needs. He finds it quickly enough – the store is well-organised and labelled – and loads up his rucksack.

And now one of them has seen him. It's at the end of this aisle, and there's no other way out. Shit, he's cornered. Maxwell's going to have to get past it to get home.

He hasn't had to kill any of them yet, but how difficult can this be, right? He's seen enough films, read enough books… and it's not even like this is going to be a fair fight. These creatures are already dead.

Nervous. Mouth dry.

He gets his crowbar ready, passes it from hand to hand. It's his weapon of choice, though he's not yet had to use it. Quick, quiet and effective.

The corpse is getting closer. He tries to visualise what he knows he has to do. These things still have some degree of control, and the only place that control can emanate from is the brain. So it's the old horror movie cliché, isn't it? He's going to have to aim for the head. He visualises again, tries to prepare himself for the crunch of breaking bone, the blood splattering, the softness of decayed brain… If he gets this right, one strike should do it. Get the angle right, get the amount of force right, and he'll be okay. He knows he can do this…

Another deep breath. Pulse racing.

Crowbar held high, he walks closer to the creature. It's directly ahead of him, and it has locked onto him with clouded, unfocused eyes.

And now Maxwell can't move.

She's a little shorter than he is. In the half-light she still looks quite pretty, a little like Kathryn, in fact, though he knows that's just his mind playing tricks. Her hair is white-blonde. Her body, though distended by decay, is still clearly feminine. Her blouse is tight across her chest. She's wearing glasses. That takes him by surprise... *after all she's been through*, he thinks, *how can she still be wearing glasses?* The dark, narrow frames suited her face, he can tell. What would she have been like before she'd died? Would she have liked him? Would she have wanted to talk to him? Listened to him? He's transfixed both by what she is now and the thought of what she used to be.

And Maxwell can't do it.

It's not like the movies. This is *real*. So far he's done whatever he's needed to do to survive, but this feels like a step too far. What has she done to him? What's she done to deserve this or, in fact, to deserve any of what's happened to her since the world ended? It's not fair. It's not right.

And she moves ever closer. Does she want him to help her?

He lowers the crowbar.

'Please...' he says, not sure what he's trying to say or why he's even bothering. 'Just go. Leave me alone. I don't want to hurt you...'

But she won't listen. She keeps walking towards him. Unsteady. One leg weaker than the other, almost a cripple's gait. One shoe on and one shoe off. She's too close now and he reaches out to stop her. Holds her. Looks into her face. The touch of a woman. It's been a long time. Three years since that night with Kathryn. He pushes her away and, as his grip tightens, he feels her decaying flesh give way under the pressure of his fingers. It's sobering. Like wet putty. Reminds him what he's dealing with. He pushes her back and she comes at him again. And again. And again. And she won't stop and all he wants is for her to go and for him to be out of here and he wishes he'd never left the house because this is harder than he imagined and he curses himself for leaving that stuff out in the yard at home and... and another corpse is close now, also blocking his way out. This one is much larger, wearing gore-streaked overalls. It lumbers awkwardly into an overloaded shelf, sending supplies scattering in all directions and filling this cavernous room with noise. And when the noise of the crashing supplies fades to nothing, Maxwell realises he can hear other sounds now too. More of the dead. Awakened. Closing in on him.

The dead woman lunges again. Maxwell shoves her back and looks into her face. He wants to see an enemy, something he can hate, but all he sees is *her*.

More bodies visible through the racking, heading for this aisle.

It felt like a game before. He never thought it would be like this. All that Prepper training... that was all about practicalities, not realities, and definitely not emotions.

It all boils down to this moment, he realises. I have to do it.

She comes at him once more, dead arms flailing.

Fight or flight.

Maxwell raises the crowbar, screws his eyes shut, and does it.

The first cut's the deepest.

Once she's down, he does what he has to do to get rid of the others. There are five in total. It gets easier with each one he cuts down, but it's not as painless as it looked in the movies.

Maxwell's made it home. All supplies replaced. Everything as it should be.

Things feel different tonight. Tonight he's not feeling so self-assured. His confidence has taken a knock. Things have changed. He realises now there's more to survival than bottles of water and ration-packs. He realises tonight that there's stuff you need to know to survive that you can't read in books or pick up online.

And when Maxwell lies in bed and tries to sleep tonight, it's a different girl's face he can't get out of his head.

THE HUMAN CONDITION
Part ii – GOING DOWN

John Proctor slumped against the wall, his head in his hands, and watched the others through the gaps between his fingers. Christ, how he'd grown to despise these people over the last week and a half. *Ten days*, he thought. *Ten fucking days. That's how long we've been here now. That's how long we've been sitting here doing nothing but shout, argue and fight with each other. This can't go on much longer.*

In every aspect of his life before this disaster, John had been taught (and had taught others) to always look for the good in people. But trapped up here on the top floor of this hotel, waiting to either starve to death or be flushed out by an army of dead bodies, he couldn't help but concentrate on the irritating personality traits which made the five other survivors trapped here with him the worst cell-mates imaginable.

Barry Bushell. Now there was an interesting character. John still wasn't sure what the dress-wearing man was about. Barry had been understandably annoyed when the other survivors had arrived and compromised the safety of his precious hotel hideout. Even now he continued to maintain a distance from the others, spending much of his time alone in the master bedroom. John had initially admired his confidence in wearing women's clothing in public, but he still couldn't understand why he did it. There must have been some underlying sexual confusion, he thought. Whatever the reason, he'd been equally surprised when, a couple of days ago, Barry had reverted to wearing 'normal' clothes. He'd asked him why he'd made the change, and Barry had explained it was just to shut the others up. He'd said he'd had enough of the constant jibes from Nick and Elizabeth, and the endless pointless questions and sideways glances from that bloody woman Doreen. Why couldn't they just leave him alone, he'd asked? What difference did it make to any of them what he was wearing? That said, John found it far easier to relate to Barry when he was wearing jeans and a T-shirt rather than full drag. It really shouldn't have made any difference, but it did. Barry now sat on his own in the doorway of his bedroom, quietly reading a book he'd already finished once this week.

Elizabeth and Nick had a strange relationship. One minute they were fighting, the next laughing. They were of a similar age and background, and maybe that was the connection? John sensed that the decision to fight or laugh was usually down to Elizabeth. She used her femininity to twist Nick around her little finger, dangling him on a string. Then again, maybe he was doing her a disservice? Perhaps he was jealous?

Now Doreen Phillips he couldn't stand. There were no ifs, buts or maybes when it came to Doreen, he simply couldn't abide the woman. He hated her grating voice and her witch's cackle of a laugh. He hated her smell and the cloud of cigarette smoke which followed her around the room. He hated her wizened, wrinkled skin and her yellow teeth. Most of all he hated the fact she moaned constantly about everything to anyone who'd listen. She had more aches, pains and problems each day than the rest of them combined. No matter how low or desperate you might be feeling, Doreen always had it worse. John tried to avoid all contact with her, which wasn't easy being trapped together in such a confined space.

It was interesting how little everyone seemed to have to do with Paul Jones. Nick in particular hardly spoke to him. Perhaps there was an element of competition, both of them considering themselves the all important alpha male? Whatever the reason they kept their distance from each other, although Paul tended to keep his distance from everyone. He both infuriated and fascinated John. Such an isolated and solitary person and yet, when he could be persuaded, he brought so much to the group. He was obviously intelligent, but his distance from the rest of them came across as an unpleasant arrogance. Maybe he just wasn't very good at relating to other people? Or did he think he was better than the rest of them?

Funny, John thought, *that we should easily overlook the good and find so many faults with each other*. There they were, all living through the same nightmare, and yet they couldn't put aside their differences and work together for love nor money. They focused on trivialities rather than trying to work together for the common good. It spoke volumes about the human condition.

Doreen and Nick were at the dining table playing cards, their poker faces emotionless. Close by, Elizabeth dozed on a couch. Like Barry, Paul also had also marked out a small area as his own: sitting on a chair, looking out of the wide floor-to-ceiling windows at the front of the hotel. From there he could see the rear-end of the bus sticking out of the gaping hole where the main entrance to the building had been. Ten days on and the dead were still fighting through the rubble to get inside.

Boredom and curiosity caused John to get up and wander over to Paul. Paul didn't react, hoping he'd go away again. He didn't.

'Any change?'

'Yeah, they've all gone. What do you think?'

'Still more of them coming?'

'Obviously.'

'You'd think they'd have given up by now, wouldn't you?'

'Fuck all else left to distract them, isn't there? Just the noise up here.'

John knew he was annoying Paul, but he couldn't help incessantly asking questions. It was a coping mechanism, he'd long-since decided. 'You think they'll ever stop?'

'What, stop moving or stop trying to get in here?'

'Both. Either.'

'Yes.'

'Yes what?'

'Yes they'll eventually stop moving and yes, they'll eventually stop trying to get in here.'

'When?'

'Quarter past six tomorrow night. Christ, how the hell should I know?'

'Sorry.'

'They'll stop moving when they've rotted so much they just can't do it anymore, and they'll stop trying to get in here when there's so many of them crammed into this fucking building that there's no more room. And please don't ask me which is going to happen first because I don't have a fucking clue.'

John took that as his cue to go. A sudden tirade like that from Paul usually meant you should go before he told you to. Dejected, he ambled slowly back into the middle of the huge penthouse apartment. It had been an impressive sight when they'd first arrived there, palatial and immense. Now the Presidential Suite looked as dilapidated and rundown as the rest of the world; a millionaire's home taken over by squatters.

John wandered into the kitchen area to look for scraps of food he knew he wouldn't find. They were rapidly running out of everything, but he kept looking regardless. Maybe he'd find something in the rubbish that one of the others had missed…

As he waded through the discarded boxes, bags, wrappers and other litter that covered the floor, he thought about what Paul had just said. He was absolutely right, the bodies would keep trying to force their way into the building until there was no more room. That was a terrifying prospect which had generated a lot of very animated discussion but little action over the last ten days. If things kept progressing as they had (and there was no reason to suggest they wouldn't) then a time would inevitably come when the building in which they were sheltering would be filled to capacity with dead flesh, leaving them stranded and starving. But what could they do? They'd talked and talked about it without reaching any conclusions or workable solutions. There had always been enough food in the kitchen and enough space between them and the dead to enable them to put off making difficult decisions until tomorrow, and then the day after that, and the day after that. John sensed that very soon, one way or another, they'd have no choice but to act.

He had, for his part, tried to do something constructive. Granted it wasn't much, but (as he frequently reminded them), it was more than anyone else had done. A keen photographer, five days ago he'd found a camera and batteries lying around the suite which Barry had brought back with him from an early trip into town. In a moment of inspiration he'd crept out onto the landing, attached the camera to the end of a fire-hose, and lowered it down the middle of the staircase. Through trial and error he'd managed to work out what length of hose was necessary to lower the camera between floors and, at the same time, he set the timer to take a single picture once the required level had been reached. With a surprising degree of accuracy he had soon developed a means of taking photographs of each level down as far as the hose would reach. He had, therefore, found a way of measuring the progress of the dead when they finally appeared. Their incalculably vast numbers meant that those bodies at the front of the crowd were continually being pushed forwards, inevitably beginning to climb the stairs. With corpses continuing to pour through the bus-shaped hole in the hotel's outside wall, once the ground floor reception had been completely filled there was nowhere else for them to go but up. Moving almost as one huge dripping mass, the enormous crowd was slowly being funnelled deeper and deeper into the building, climbing higher and higher.

Each time John hauled the camera back up to the top floor, the group crowded around to check the progress of the slowly advancing cadavers. There had been no sign of them initially, but John continued to take his photographs every morning regardless. And then, yesterday, the dead had been photographed on the twenty-second floor. It was a simple enough calculation to make – they'd covered twenty-two floors in about nine days, so they were climbing at the rate of just over two floors a day. The second simple calculation made was altogether more disturbing. It was Thursday today. If their rate of climb continued at the same speed (and there seemed no immediate reason why it shouldn't) then the bodies would reach the twenty-eighth floor sometime on Saturday, Sunday morning at the very latest.

Bizarrely, John enjoyed his role of chief cameraman and body-watcher. It gave him a purpose. Perhaps even more importantly, it became something he could hide behind and use as an excuse for not doing anything else.

Three forty-five. The afternoon sun was dropping down towards the horizon, filling the Presidential Suite with orange light and long, dragging shadows. Rather than spreading themselves around the edges of the apartment, on this rare occasion the six survivors sat together around the dining table. They needed to talk. No food, very little time.

'So exactly how much stuff have we got left?' Doreen asked.

'Enough for a day,' Barry replied, 'maybe two at the very most. After that there's nothing.'

'We must have something?'

'No,' he said again, shaking his head. 'Nothing.'

'It can't have all gone, can it?'

Nick had reached breaking point. How were they supposed to get through to this bloody woman? 'Listen, Doreen, the cupboards are empty. We're down to our last crumbs. There isn't an extra little stash of food tucked away for emergencies. After this we'll have absolutely nothing. Zip. Fuck all.'

Doreen slumped back in her chair. 'So what are we going to do?' More sighs came from around the table.

'That's what we're trying to work out, you stupid cow,' Nick said, sitting on his hands so he didn't throttle her. 'Bloody hell, are you on the same planet as the rest of us?'

'Wish I wasn't.'

'So we've got two problems,' John summarised, trying his best to control the conversation. 'We need to try and get out and get supplies but—'

'—but this building is full of bodies,' said Barry, before adding, 'thanks to the hole you lot made in the front door.'

'So what do we do?' Doreen asked again.

'Is there any way of getting out of here and back up again?' Elizabeth wondered.

'Don't think so,' Barry answered quickly. 'Getting down's no problem, we can use the fire escape.' He nodded over at an inconspicuous looking door in the far corner of the room. 'The problem is what to do once you're down there. Open the fire escape door on the ground floor, and you'll find yourself right in the middle of a few thousand bodies. And if you manage to get outside, you're not going to get back in again afterwards. It'd be impossible empty-handed, no chance if you're carrying supplies.'

'But there must be a way?'

'Get a sheet, hold it like a parachute, climb up to the roof and jump off,' Nick suggested.

'You think that'll work?' Doreen said, her bewilderingly stupid response meeting with groans of disbelief.

'Try it and let us know, Doreen,' he said.

'But how would I get back up again?'

'Flap your arms,' Nick said. 'You know what I think? I think we should just get out of here. This place is fucked. We should go downstairs and torch the place on our way out. Set light to the building and watch the whole fucking place go up in flames.'

'What good's that going to do?' Barry said.

'Well it would distract them for a start. Christ, the heat and light this place burning would generate would be more than enough of a distraction to let us get away. They're not going to be interested in a handful of people sneaking out the back door with all that going on, are they?'

Nick's suggestion was met with an awkward, muted silence. They each thought long and hard about it, but none of them were sure. It wasn't the wanton destruction that put them off, rather it was the thought of being out on the run again, searching for places to hide...

'What about the cradle?' John said. 'We've talked about it before, haven't we? Barry said there's a window-cleaner's cradle half way up the side of the building. We could use that to get us down, couldn't we? We might even be able to use it to get back up as well...'

'What about power?' Paul said. 'How do you think you winch it? You think the window-cleaners used to pull themselves up thirty floors by hand? No power, no cradle.'

Another idea quashed.

'Seems to me that if we can get out of here in one piece, then maybe that's what we should do,' Elizabeth said dejectedly.

Barry shook his head. 'I don't want to leave here. I can't see any point running.'

'Of course there's a point,' Doreen said.

'Is there?'

'Yes,' she answered, sounding far from convinced. 'There must be...'

'Well let me know when you find it.'

'So what are we actually saying?' Nick asked. He pointed at Barry. 'Does she just want to sit here and starve? Good plan, well done!'

Barry was unfazed. 'But why run?'

'Because I don't want to die.'

'Good answer. Why don't you want to die?'

'Stupid question. No one wants to die, do they?'

'But is it the end of your life you're worried about, or is it death

312

itself that scares you?' Barry said.

'What? You're just talking bollocks now.'

'No, I'm not. Are you worried that you're not going to achieve everything you've always wanted to achieve, or is it the prospect of being torn apart by hundreds of bodies that bothers you most?'

'What point are you making, Barry?' John wondered.

'Sorry, I'm just thinking out loud. I'm not trying to wind anyone up. I think what I'm saying is that I genuinely can't see an easy way out of this. If we run we'll find somewhere else to hide for a while, then something will happen and before you know it we'll be moving on again, then again, and again, and again…'

'Not necessarily,' Elizabeth said.

'No, but that's *probably* what will happen, and we have to accept that. We're not in control here. Christ, I thought I'd hit the jackpot finding this place until someone drove a bloody bus into the building.'

'But running's got to be better than just rolling over and waiting to die, hasn't it?'

'I'm not so sure,' Barry said. 'That's what I used to believe, but I just don't know anymore. Every morning when I wake up, it's getting clearer and clearer that my life is just about over. We're massively outnumbered and society is finished. Christ, we're sitting here talking about risking our necks just to get food. What kind of a life are any of us going to have if getting the basics like food and shelter are so difficult?'

His words were greeted by almost total silence. 'Still don't understand you,' Doreen said. 'What were you saying about death and dying?'

Barry rubbed his tired eyes and explained further. 'I don't want to keep struggling and fighting forever,' he said sadly, 'and I don't think any of you do either. If I'm completely honest, I just want to relax and let things happen naturally. We're in the minority now, and I don't think we were supposed to survive. So, while I don't relish the idea of letting those things out there tear me limb from limb, I guess I'm not bothered if I die.'

'But that's—' John started to say.

'Not normal? I accept that. It's not what any of you were expecting me to say, I know. We've been pre-programmed all of our lives to keep fighting and keep struggling. All I'm saying is I've realised there's no point anymore. Just sit back and relax. Let nature take its course.'

More silence.

'No,' Nick said. 'There's no fucking way I'm just going to sit here and wait to die. Absolutely no way…'

'I'm with you,' Paul said, similarly unimpressed. John looked up in surprise. He couldn't remember when the two men had last agreed on anything. Strange how their dislike of each other could be put to one side when their backs were against the wall.

'So what do we do?' asked Elizabeth.

That was the million dollar question which no one could answer. The ominous silence continued for several minutes until Paul spoke again. 'Exactly how full of bodies is this place?'

'They're almost up to the twenty-fourth floor,' John said. 'I told you that a few minutes ago. You don't listen to a word I say.'

'No, you told us how far up the staircase they'd managed to get, you didn't tell us how full of bodies the building is.'

John struggled to see the difference and he wasn't alone in his confusion. 'What do you mean?' Elizabeth asked.

Paul shook his head. Christ, these people were infuriating. More to the point he was annoyed with himself. Why hadn't he thought of this before? 'A couple of minutes ago we were talking about getting out of here, weren't we?'

'Yes.'

'So how were we going to get out?'

'Do you always answer questions with questions?' she snapped.

'Do you?' he replied, before re-phrasing and asking his previous question again. 'There's another way out of here, isn't there?'

'The fire escape,' Barry answered.

'Which is still clear, correct?'

'As far as we know. Why, what are you thinking?'

'Is the fire escape anywhere near the main staircase?'

'Of course not,' John interjected. 'What would be the point of that? The fire escape needs to be on the other side of the building.'

'My point exactly. The fire escape gives us a way of moving around

314

the building that's well away from the main staircase where we think all the bodies are.'

'And there's a good chance the bodies are still only on the staircase,' Nick added, finally understanding where Paul was coming from. 'Which means that if we're careful we could still go out onto the landings and into the rooms.'

'What's the layout of a typical floor?' Paul asked.

'Just one U-shaped corridor,' Barry answered. 'Staircase in the middle, fire escape at either end I think.'

'And when you first set yourself up here, did you clear the place out?'

'I checked all the rooms for bodies and I took what I needed but—'

'Did you take everything?'

'No, I didn't need to.'

'So there's your answer,' Paul said, rocking back on his chair, almost looking down his nose at the others. 'We go back down as far as we need to and grab what we can. Should keep us from starving to death for a few days longer. Delay the inevitable.'

'But that's all you're going to do,' Barry reminded him. 'You'll just be delaying what you know is going to happen anyway.'

'He's right, isn't he?' Doreen said. 'It's not going to change the fact that those bloody things will be up here with us in the next couple of days, is it? It's not going to help us get away.'

'No,' Paul agreed, 'it won't. But it will give us a little time and space.'

'To do what?'

'To decide how we're getting out of here and where we're going to go.'

Eight thirty-five. Pitch black. Paul, Nick and Elizabeth crept down the fire escape staircase towards the lower floors of the hotel. Hunger, claustrophobia and fear had combined to deadly effect to kick-start their hastily considered, semi-improvised plan. The risks seemed to increase with every step of the descent. Paul had suggested they go all the way down then work their way back up, but they'd only made it as far as the seventeenth floor when he stopped.

'What's the matter?' Elizabeth asked, immediately concerned.

'I want to have a look.'

'What for?'

'What do you think?'

'But you said…'

'I know what I said. We know those things are on the stairs, but we don't know for sure where else they are, do we?'

Paul moved to the door and gently pushed it open a fraction. He shone his torch out onto the landing.

'Anything?'

'Can't see any movement,' he replied, his voice little more than a whisper. 'I'm going to have a look around.'

Without waiting for either of the others, Paul slipped out onto the landing. He switched off his torch, concerned that the light might attract unwanted attention, and then slowly moved down the hallway to the first corner. The layout, as far as he could see in the gloom, was pretty much as Barry had described: a long corridor with a right-angled right turn towards the central part of the building where, he presumed, he'd find the staircase and tens of thousands of rotting bodies. He moved closer and peered around the corner, holding his breath for fear of making any sound which might tip the balance and alert the dead to his presence. He couldn't see anything. It was too dark.

Paul felt his way further along the wall and paused at the door to one of the hotel's many bedrooms. Did he go inside? It would be worth having a quick look around the room before he going back to the other two waiting on the fire escape. He wanted to see the layout of a typical room so he could get a feel for what they were dealing with. How quickly would they be able to thoroughly check a room for food? What were they likely to find? Would there be a mini-bar or similar? Christ, he needed a drink, and his stomach started to growl at the thought of eating again.

Paul tried the handle. Damn thing was locked and it needed a swipe card. No surprise really. Barry had a few master cards which he'd taken from the bodies of cleaners and other staff. Elizabeth had one with her. He shoved the door again, hoping it would open. It didn't matter. He'd go back to Elizabeth and…

Wait.

What was that?

He sensed movement up ahead. He felt something brush against his arm and he froze. He lifted his torch and switched it on. Ahead of him the whole corridor was packed with bodies, all of them oblivious to his presence until he'd started messing with the door.

'Fucking hell,' he mumbled as he tripped back away from the dead. Illuminated now and then by the unsteady light from his shaking torch, he saw that the corridor was filled with constantly shifting corpses which had spilled out from the staircase. Almost as one they began to move towards him. He ran back to the fire escape and hammered on the door. Elizabeth opened it slowly and he barged through, shoving her out of the way.

'Move!' he yelled, slamming the door shut behind him.

'Bodies?' she asked, already beginning to climb back up.

'Fucking hundreds of them,' he answered breathlessly. 'It's worse than we thought.'

He looked around for Nick but he'd already gone. He was way ahead of them both, on his way back to the top floor. Cowardly bastard. Paul made a mental note never to put himself in a position where he needed to rely on Nick for anything.

They pounded up the stairs, no longer concerned about the volume of noise they made, just desperate to get back to the Presidential Suite.

'Wait a minute,' Paul said, stopping Elizabeth in her tracks. Breathless, he shone his torch at the nearest fire door. Floor twenty-six. It was worth taking a chance to see if this floor was the same as the one ten floors below.

'What are you doing?' Elizabeth asked, almost too afraid to know.

'According to John they haven't reached this floor yet. We thought they were just filling the stairs, but there's so bloody many of them they're filling the entire building. We should check this level for food before we go back. We won't have another chance.'

They slipped out through the fire door, leaving it propped open with a fire extinguisher, then moved slowly along the corridor to the first corner. Paul put his head around and shone the torch down its length.

'Clear,' he said, the relief in his voice obvious. 'Stick to this end of the corridor and stay away from the stairs.'

The layout of floor twenty-six was different to floor seventeen. Here there were several large suites instead of many smaller rooms. They went into the nearest.

'So what are we looking for?' Elizabeth asked.

'Anything. Just make sure you split what you find into two piles. Keep one for us, then we'll share the rest with the others.'

'But that's—'

'—that's completely fair. How many of those fuckers are here helping? If they want more they can come and get it themselves.'

He began to ransack the room.

A little under an hour later Elizabeth and Paul returned to the Presidential Suite, carrying with them almost the entire contents of the minibars of the suites on the floor immediately below. They'd found little in the way of any substantial food, but that didn't matter. The others gratefully took what they were given and ate and drank quickly as Paul broke the bad news about what they'd seen on the lower levels.

'Feels like a last supper, doesn't it?' Barry said quietly to no one in particular. He couldn't see who was where. No one had lit any lamps this evening.

'So what do we do next?' John asked, sitting on his own a little way behind Barry. 'We never decided. Do we just sit here and wait for them, or do we run?'

'Nick will run,' Paul said, remembering how he'd left them on the fire escape. 'You're good at running, aren't you Nick?'

'Shut your fucking mouth,' Nick said angrily, glad of the dark because he didn't know how to react.

'So what do we do?' John asked again, desperate for someone to answer and give him something to cling onto.

'Let's just think about it logically, shall we,' Barry suggested. 'They're still coming in through the front door, and they're climbing the stairs because of the growing pressure of other corpses behind them. So what's going to happen when they reach the top? They're not going to turn back around and start heading for the ground floor

318

again, are they?'

'They're going to keep coming,' Paul said ominously. 'They'll spread out onto the landings like we saw downstairs.'

'And even when there's no more room on the landing up here,' Barry continued, 'they'll still keep coming. Before we know it they'll be up against our door and then, when the pressure gets too great, it'll give and this place will be flooded.'

'Lovely,' Doreen mumbled.

'So you don't think we've got any chance?' asked Elizabeth.

'It's like I said earlier,' Barry replied, 'what's coming is coming. I think we're all going to die, and the only choice left is how it happens. Now I don't personally intend on being torn apart, but I also don't like the idea of running either.'

'So what are you going to do?'

'Not sure yet. I haven't decided.'

'You don't have long.'

'I know.'

'I'm running,' Nick said.

'You would,' Paul said quickly. 'But fair play, I'll probably run too.'

'What about you, Doreen?' Elizabeth asked.

'Too tired to run, too scared not to. We'll just have to wait and see what tomorrow brings, won't we?'

Next morning. First light. John picked up his camera and walked across the landing to carry out his self-imposed daily duty and measure the progress of the dead. He walked out to the staircase and leant over the banister, then immediately pulled himself back again, no longer any need for cameras. They still had several flights of stairs left to climb, but he could now see the first few bodies. He ran back to tell the others.

'How far?' Elizabeth asked as he burst back into the room.

'Not far.'

'How long?'

'Not long.'

'More specific?'

'Couple of hours.'

Doreen began to sob.

'Shut up you silly cow,' Nick barked at her with his usual lack of compassion. 'All you're going to do is bring them up here quicker with your stupid whining.'

'So we just sit and wait?' John asked.

'That's what I'm doing,' a voice said from behind him, 'but I'm not ready to die just yet.' Barry emerged from his bedroom wearing a skirt and blouse, a blond wig, full make-up and his favourite high-heeled boots. He stormed into the main part of the suite with rediscovered confidence, completely at odds with the others who sat around dejectedly, each contemplating the dark decisions they would soon have to make. 'I did a lot of thinking last night,' he explained.

'We can see that,' Nick said.

'And…?' Paul pressed.

'I wanted to know if I was wrong. I didn't know if I'd been looking at everything the wrong way.'

'And?' Paul pressed again.

'And, unfortunately, I think I'm right,' he admitted. 'In fact the more I think about it, the more I've come to realise our situation really is hopeless. I can't see any obvious way out, and I'm not just talking about the hotel here, I'm talking about what's left of our lives in general. Whatever we do, wherever we go, we're fucked.'

'Nice. Thanks for that.'

'Seriously, just stop and think about it. I'm not being defeatist here, I'm just being honest. Whatever we decide to do, it's going to be a struggle. We're going to have to fight for absolutely everything, and that's bloody stupid when you think there's probably only a few people left. The world's our oyster, but I don't think we can have any of it. What does that say to you?'

Blank, confused looks. Silence.

'It's like you said,' Elizabeth eventually mumbled. 'We're fucked.'

'Exactly. There's nothing any of us can do about it. We're massively outnumbered and nowhere is safe. The only thing we have any control over now is what we do with the time we have left.'

'But we don't know how long that is,' John protested.

'We never have done,' Barry argued. 'Seems to me we can either spend our last few days and weeks hiding in the shadows out there, starving to death, running from place to place and freaking out every time someone farts…'

'Or?'

'Or we can stop trying so hard to survive and just let things happen naturally. Go out with a little dignity.'

'You're talking crap,' Nick said.

'Am I? Do you really think you're supposed to survive all of this? There are some things that are bigger than us.'

'Please don't start talking about God and divine retribution and all that shite,' John sighed. 'I've given all of that up.'

Barry smiled and brushed away a stray wisp of long, blond hair. 'That's not what I'm talking about at all. What I'm saying is that whatever happened here was the twenty-first century equivalent of the asteroid that wiped out the dinosaurs.'

'Now you've really lost me,' Paul said.

'This is our ice-age. This is our apocalypse. This is the end. We should just accept it and let nature take its course.' Barry's comments were met with silence. 'Our problem is we've all fallen foul of the programme. We think we're so bloody superior and we think the planet can't go on without us. It's part and parcel of the human condition. Truth is the world's going to thrive without us here to keep screwing it up.'

'The human condition?' Nick said. 'What the hell are you on about?'

'I can't think of a better way to put it. I was looking out of the window last night, watching birds flying from building to building…'

'Fucking hell,' Paul said, 'he's really lost it. I've long had my doubts about him but I think he's finally lost it.'

'I was watching the birds,' Barry continued, ignoring him, 'and I started thinking about the difference between us and the animals. Seems to me there's one huge difference that doesn't often get talked about.' He paused to give the others opportunity to make a cheap joke or to hit him with another insult but, unusually, they didn't. 'The difference is that we know we're eventually going to die and they don't. Animals strut about the place thinking they're going to go on forever, we spend our lives worrying about how they're going to end. That's what I mean when I talk about the human condition. We're too busy thinking about death to enjoy life.'

There followed an unusually long moment of quiet contemplation and reflection which was only disturbed when John remembered the bodies on the stairs. 'That's all well and good,' he said anxiously, 'but what are you going to do now? Are you going to wait for the bodies to get in here, or are you going to kill yourself and get it over with?'

'Neither.'

'What then?'

'I'm going to sit in here and relax, and what will be will be. I'm going to try and slow the bodies down, then let nature take its course.'

'Are you high? How are you going to slow them down?'

'Well we've already established that they'll keep moving forward until they can't go any further, so instead of letting them stop here on this floor where we are, let's help them keep going.'

'What are you suggesting?'

'Channel them up onto the roof.'

'And?'

'And that's it. What they do up there is their business. If they stay true to form they'll follow each other up, one after another, until there's no room left. Then they'll either come back down, which I doubt, or they'll end up pushing each other over the edge.'

'Brilliant,' Paul said, grinning with genuine enthusiasm. 'That's absolutely fucking brilliant!'

He couldn't believe what he was hearing. A man in a dress was suggesting they spend their last few days on Earth sitting in a luxury hotel suite watching three week old corpses falling off the roof.

'It's got to be worth a go, hasn't it?' Barry said.

'Okay,' Paul agreed, surprising even himself. 'Let's do it.'

The roof of the building was accessed via a final narrow flight of steps. With the bodies continuing to make unsteady progress towards them, Paul and Barry crept up towards the door that would lead them outside.

'It's locked,' Barry grunted.

'Don't you have the key? You've got keys to everywhere else.'

'Sorry.'

'Smash it open then.'

'What about the noise?' he instinctively asked. Paul looked down the staircase behind them, back into the heart of the building. Even from here he could see the constant movement of the dead.

'Bit late to worry about that.'

With limited space to manoeuvre his coiffured bulk, Barry held onto a handrail, swung back, then crashed his shoulder against the door. It rattled in its frame but didn't open. Another couple of attempts were equally unsuccessful.

'Let me,' Paul said, pushing Barry to one side. 'You're not wearing the right shoes for breaking and entering.'

He launched a barrage of well aimed kicks at the lock. The wood began to splinter and crack. Another few heavy blows and it flew open, allowing the two men to scramble out onto the roof. A phenomenal wind threatened to knock them off their feet.

'Jesus,' Paul said, having to shout to make himself heard, almost enjoying the volume of his voice. 'Bit blustery.'

Barry didn't answer. He was busy trying to wedge the door open. For the bodies to be able to keep moving forward, the way out onto the roof would need to remain unobstructed. Paul picked up a strip of metal lying on the asphalt and used it as a prop.

'That'll do,' Barry said. 'Let's get back inside.'

The two men clattered back down the staircase towards the Presidential Suite. Paul stopped and stared at the bodies still coming towards them. Was it his imagination, or were they moving slightly faster now? He tried to think logically as the distance between the living and the dead rapidly evaporated. Previously the bodies had been driven forward by the pressure of others pushing them from behind, but now those corpses furthest up the stairs knew there were survivors above them. Rather than wait to be pushed forward, those at the front were now moving under their own steam.

'They're getting faster,' Paul said quietly. 'I think we should—' He stopped speaking instantly when one of the bodies looked up at him. Was he imagining it? No, now Barry had seen it too. The foul creatures were actually looking at them…

'Move,' Barry said, and Paul didn't argue.

'Done it?' John asked as they burst back through the main doors together.

'Sort of,' Barry said.

'What's that supposed to mean?'

'We might have a problem…'

'What's the matter?' Doreen asked, concerned.

Paul was still by the open doors, looking back down the corridor. The first bodies appeared on the landing. Elizabeth covered her mouth in horror and stifled a scream. John scrambled away from the open door as Paul slammed it shut.

'Fuck me,' said Nick.

'They saw us,' Paul said, sounding almost embarrassed. 'They know we're here now.'

'Did you open the door to the roof?' Doreen asked.

'Yes, but…' Barry began to say.

'You pair of bloody idiots,' she screamed at them both.

'Be quiet, Doreen,' John pleaded from behind the sofa. 'Please, Doreen, don't let them hear you.'

'Bit late for that,' she said. She looked around and saw she was the only one still out in the open. 'So is that it? All that noise and effort and that's it? That's all you're going to do?'

Barry tried to respond but he couldn't coordinate his brain and mouth enough to make it happen.

'What else can we do?' Paul shouted. 'We're completely screwed.'

'Pathetic,' Doreen said. 'Absolutely bloody pathetic. If you think I'm going to sit here and wait for those damn things to have their way with me, then you're very much mistaken. I'm a woman with standards. I've still got my pride.'

More interested in the relentless approach of the dead than the prattling of a nervous old woman, no one paid her any attention. Infuriated by their lack of response, Doreen took it upon herself to take action.

'You're bloody useless, the lot of you,' she said. 'Wish I'd never got mixed up with your little gang. Enjoy your little party or whatever it is you're planning…'

She was tired and she'd really had enough. Wiser and more shrewd than any of them gave her credit for, she'd listened to everything that Barry had said and she'd found herself agreeing with him. Death was inevitable, and she didn't have the energy or the desire to go on running. She opened the door again, stepped outside, then slammed it shut. With a total lack of nerves she walked into the bodies and pushed her way through them. Although their numbers were imposing, they were individually weak and even with her bad back and countless other ailments, getting through them was easy. They swung their rotting fists at her and tried to grab at her with gnarled, talon-like hands but she was as wiry and thin as they were and she slipped past, weaving between them with the sudden grace and subtlety of a woman whose various disorders and complaints were ten per cent physical and ninety per cent attention seeking bullshit. She pushed deeper into the throng until she reached the foot of the final staircase. She then gave a loud whistle and threw herself up the last few steps and out onto the roof. Distracted by Doreen's sudden speed, noise and movement, many of the bodies turned away from the door to the Presidential Suite and began to follow her.

Bloody hell, it was cold outside. Doreen wrapped her cardigan tight around her willowy body and braced herself against the wind. Now what did she do? She hadn't quite thought this through. She knew what she was doing, but now that she was standing unprotected out on the roof, the consequences of her actions really began to hit home. This was it. No more running or hiding or sleeping on the floor. No more fear or confusion or disorientation. No more arguments or fights. It was finally time for a long overdue rest. It felt good, actually.

Doreen walked to the edge of the roof and peered down.

Bloody hell, it's higher than I thought. That was probably a good thing, she decided. Although she was only a few feet higher up here than she'd been in the suite just below, the difference was stark. Perhaps it was because the protection of glass and concrete had gone. Perhaps it was because now there was nothing left between her and the rest of the world.

She looked back as the first few bodies staggered out onto the roof.

This is it then, time to do it.

She'd been toying with the idea of suicide for a few days – a few weeks if she was completely honest – but she'd always clung onto the slim hope that things would somehow get better. Like Barry had said, she just kept trying to survive. Suicide had always seemed to be the coward's way out before today, but after listening to him earlier she'd come to realise that this was far from a cowardly act. Her fate was sealed whatever she did, but by ending her life this way she'd hold onto some dignity and control. This choice was all she had left. And she might even help those miserable bastards in the Presidential Suite in the process.

She climbed up onto the low concrete wall which ran around the perimeter of the building. The wind seemed to blow even stronger as she gingerly stood upright. She held out her arms like a tightrope walker, struggling to keep her balance.

Bloody hell, I can't do this. I can't go through with it.

She looked down to the street many hundreds of feet below. Save for the occasional body staggering by, the pavement on this side of the hotel was relatively clear. Her mind began to fill with stupid questions: was it going to hurt? Would it definitely kill her or might she survive and end up lying helpless on the ground with her arms and legs broken as the dead swarmed over and around her? She thought about the old adage she'd heard countless times before – it's not the jump off the top of the building that kills you, it's hitting the ground that does it – and she managed half a smile. Would she feel anything? What would the fall be like? Would she know when she'd hit the ground or would it all be over before then…?

Doreen looked around and watched more bodies piling out onto the roof. They hadn't noticed her yet. They wandered around aimlessly like the empty, soulless vessels they were. She turned her back on them again and looked forward across the town, knowing there was no going back now. Even if she changed her mind, she couldn't get back inside.

Do I do it now or wait for them to get closer to me? Do I wait until the last possible second? Is it worth clinging onto a few more seconds of life? What good will it do? Do I want to stand here, freezing cold and terrified, trying to keep my balance and not think about those bloody things behind me, or do I just let it happen? Think about finally being able to stop and rest. Think about not having to run and hide…

Doreen closed her eyes, tipped forward and let gravity take over.

*

'Well?' Elizabeth asked, sobbing. Barry peered out onto the landing through the spy-hole in the door.

'Not good. There are too many of them. They know we're in here now.'

Elizabeth began to cry uncontrollably. John tried to put his arms around her, but she pushed him away.

'So what do we do now?' Nick asked, sounding nothing like the confident, cocksure man who'd first arrived at the hotel.

'Can't see that anything's changed,' Barry answered, his face still pressed against the hole in the door. 'We're still in here, they're still out there. If you were thinking about running, now's your last chance.'

'I'm going,' Paul said, already edging closer to the fire escape door. 'I'm not sitting here waiting for them to get in. Fuck that. I'm getting out of here…'

'And me,' Nick said.

Barry looked across at John and Elizabeth. They both began to edge closer to the two men waiting by the fire escape. 'Come on, Barry,' she said, almost pleading with him. 'Don't stay here. It's suicide.'

'You don't have to keep fighting, you know. That's the difference between us in here and those things out there. You can stop and switch off if you want to. They'll just keep going until there's nothing left of them.'

'Come on, Barry,' John said.

'Nah,' he replied, smoothing a wrinkle in his skirt. 'I think I've had enough.'

The four remaining survivors disappeared through the fire escape door and began their dark descent down towards the ground floor.

The hotel suite was suddenly quiet, save for the thumping coming from the mass of decomposing bodies on the other side of the main door. More importantly, Barry's space was his again. His and his alone. Just how he'd wanted it.

He knew he didn't have long. He tearfully walked around the vast suite, collecting together his things. He salvaged everything he could from the little that was left and packed it all against the wall of the master bedroom. Another noise from outside distracted him, and he peered through the spy-hole and saw that the corridor was now a solid mass of flesh. It wouldn't be long before they broke through.

He wiped a tear away from the corner of his eye, taking care not to smudge his make-up, then took one long, final look around the suite which had been his home for the last few weeks of his life. He took a moment to walk around and look out of each of the windows in turn, staring at the remains of the city where he'd lived and remembering... The memories were harder to deal with than the thought of what was to come. It surprised him how much it still hurt to think about all he'd lost. The little he had left to lose didn't seem to matter so much now.

With the door rattling and shaking in its frame as more and more of the damn things threw themselves against it, Barry slipped quietly into the master bedroom. Once inside he shoved the bed across the entrance to the room and wedged it into position with other furniture and belongings. If he'd had a hammer and nails, he thought, he would have nailed it shut. It really didn't matter. That door wouldn't be opening again.

Barry Bushell, tears streaming down his cheeks, selected another outfit from his wardrobe and changed. Finally feeling presentable, he lay down on the bed and picked up a book. With his hands shaking so badly that he could hardly read, he lay there and waited.

'Keep moving,' Elizabeth yelled, slamming her hands into the middle of Nick's back, sending him tripping down the last few stairs to the ground floor. He grabbed hold of the handrail to stop himself falling.

'What now?' John asked, still a little further back. They'd finally reached the bottom. It was another of his pointless questions, pointless this time because they didn't have any choice. Nick teased the door open then quickly closed it again.

'Well?' Elizabeth asked hopefully.

'Not as bad as I thought,' he replied. 'There are hundreds of the fuckers, but I was expecting more. We'll probably make it through if we're fast and we keep moving.'

Paul shoved Nick out of the way and peered around the side of the door. He pulled his head back in and composed himself.

'This is it then. Time to say goodbye. I'd like to say I'd had fun, but I'd be lying.'

'Goodbye?' Elizabeth said, surprised.

'We'll stand more of a chance if we split up.'

'You reckon?'

Paul shrugged his shoulders. 'Who knows. Anyway, see you. Good luck.' He took a deep breath, opened the door again, then slipped out into what was left of the hotel reception.

It was surprisingly bright after the enclosed gloom of the fire escape and the air, although still heavy with the stench of death and decay, was somehow fresher. Several of the nearest bodies noticed his sudden appearance and immediately turned towards him. Paul, terrified, but pumped full of adrenalin, ran, pausing only to stare in utter disbelief at the main staircase of the hotel which was a solid column of still climbing flesh, almost like a single grotesque organism.

He skipped and weaved through the lifeless corpses which even now fought to get into the rubble-strewn hotel ruin, then he burst out onto the street. The dead were fewer in number out here, but he knew they'd be upon him soon. Not knowing where he was going or why, he just ran.

'Bastard,' Nick sobbed as bodies began to slam against the other side of the fire escape door. 'That bloody bastard, he's let them know exactly where we are.'

'Don't think it matters now,' John said as he descended the final few steps. The three remaining survivors stood together at the foot of the staircase. Elizabeth thought about Barry, twenty-eight floors above them, and the sense of his actions became painfully clear. It was no longer about surviving, it was about choosing where and how to die. Still tearful, and without saying anything to either of the others, she opened the door and barged past the rancid corpses clawing against the other side. In a blind panic, John ran out after her.

But Nick froze. He couldn't do it.

As the fire door had swung shut again, one of the bodies had become trapped, leaving it wedged open. More of the sickly cadavers immediately began to gravitate towards the opening, clambering over the first trapped corpse. Nick watched in horror as the first of them lunged at him. What did he do? Still breathless from the sudden descent, he began to climb back up again.

He realised what he was doing was pointless, but he couldn't stop.

His legs burned with effort, but he couldn't slow down either. He looked around and saw that, for now, he'd left those fucking things at the bottom of the stairs for dust.

It took him more than half an hour to get back to the twenty-eighth floor. He burst through the fire escape door, keen to find Barry and apologise for everything he'd said and—

—and the Presidential Suite was full of bodies. The dead reacted to his unexpected appearance *en masse*. They surged towards him like a tidal wave of green-grey gore and knocked him clean off his feet. As their sharp, bony fingers dug into his flesh he lay on the ground and looked across at the open fire escape door through which he'd just emerged. If he really tried, he thought, he might be able to crawl through it and give himself a little more time. Maybe get back down to another floor and wait there…

For a second or two longer he fought, then he stopped. What was the point? Barry was right. Just give up, lie back, endure the pain, and wait for it to all be over.

Elizabeth didn't know that John had followed her out until she heard him shouting at her to slow down. She glanced back over her shoulder and saw him running after her but she wasn't interested. She didn't want to be with anyone else now, certainly not him. She kept moving, increasing her speed. Not knowing the city particularly well, she didn't have a clue where she was going. She'd wanted to head out of the centre but had inadvertently found herself running deeper into the main shopping area instead. The bodies there were still relatively dense in number but she moved with enough speed and control to be able to barge through them.

She needed to rest and so took a left into a dark alleyway. Momentarily free of the dead, she stopped running and rested with her hands on her knees, sucking in as much precious oxygen as she could. There was a door halfway down the passageway. She looked through a small, dusty window, and when she couldn't immediately see any movement inside, she pulled the door open and slipped through, too tired to care.

Bloody hell, she thought as she climbed a wide, white marble staircase. Of all the doors in all the alleyways, she'd found the staff entrance to Laceys department store. She'd never been able to afford to shop here although she'd always wanted to. It was one of those places that made you feel unworthy if you walked in without a purse full of gold and platinum credit cards. Today, of course, it was a grim shadow of its former self just like everywhere else, but what the hell, she thought, it was still Laceys.

Barry Bushell's words continued to play heavily on her mind as she climbed further up the stairs and deeper into the store. How right he'd been. She couldn't think of anywhere she'd be completely safe anymore, and even if she could, she had no way of getting there now. She continued to climb, stopping when she reached the jewellery department on the third floor. There were no bodies around that she could see. Always a sucker for gold and pretty stones, she found herself drawn to the cobweb-covered display cabinets. They were still filled with beautiful pieces that would have been worth a fortune a month ago. Today they were worth nothing. But hell, she could still dream, couldn't she? Dreaming was just about all she had left...

Elizabeth enjoyed her long-overdue shopping trip around Laceys. She worked her way through the building floor by floor, hiding from the occasional lurching corpse and staring in wonder at all the things she used to want but had never been able to afford. When she reached the ladies clothing department she changed out of her dirty clothes and dressed in the most expensive outfit she could find. She climbed to the very top floor and sat on a plush leather sofa where, draped in jewellery, she drank wine, ate chocolate, and took enough headache tablets to kill an elephant.

Paul Jones stopped running and hid in a newsagent's until the after-effects of his sudden appearance and disappearance had faded away and the bodies had lost interest again. Fortunately Elizabeth and the others – whatever they had decided to do – seemed to be causing enough of a commotion to take the pressure off him for a while. He lay on the floor of the shop behind the counter and read the last ever editions of half a dozen newspapers and lads' mags until the sun disappeared and the light faded away. All the headlines on the newspapers that had once seemed so important and relevant now seemed puerile and trite. All the glamorous girls and handsome men in the magazines were dead.

Walking slowly through the gloom of early evening without fear or concern, Paul eventually reached a construction site. With a rucksack full of booze on his back, he climbed to the cab at the very top of a huge crane which towered over the foundations of a never-to-be-finished office block. Protected by the height and enjoying a view which was even more impressive than the one from the hotel, he drank and slept.

In the morning, when the sun finally came up, he looked back across town at the hotel he'd left behind and watched the occasional stupid body fall from the roof. Many hours had passed, but even now the dumb fuckers were still dropping like stones. He laughed out loud without fear of retribution.

Paul Jones had decided to take his own life, but not yet. He'd do it when there really were no other options left.

Once John had lost sight of Elizabeth he'd stopped running too. He slowed his pace to match that of the dead and, for a time, had been able to walk among them undetected. *I can do this*, he thought, *I can outwit them. I can move around them and between them and I can do this. Barry was wrong. They were all wrong. I don't have to run and I don't have to give up. It's not over yet...*

For almost a day he managed to survive, but his foolish confidence proved to be his undoing. It took only a glance into the sun and a single sneeze to blow his cover. One sneeze in the middle of a vast crowd of bodies and his position was revealed. And John, being a cowardly man, tried to run. Instead of standing his ground and continuing to mimic the actions of the bodies all around him, maybe blaming the sneeze on the corpse next-door, the stupid man tried to get away. Deep in the middle of a mass of several hundred rancid, rotting, dripping cadavers, he didn't stand a chance. They ripped him to pieces before he had chance to scream for help.

Wouldn't have mattered. No one would have come.

Barry Bushell lasted for several more days. The hotel suite was overrun with bodies but, as far as he could tell, they didn't know he was in the bedroom. He remained quiet and still. Without food or water, however, he soon became weak.

Barry died a relatively happy man. He'd rather not have died, of course, but he'd managed somehow to retain the control he'd so desperately craved – the control that the infection had stripped from the millions of bodies condemned to walk tirelessly along the streets outside until they were no longer physically able.

Dressed in a silk negligee and lying in a comfortable (if slightly soiled) bed, he died peacefully in his sleep halfway through a really good book.

DAY TWENTY-THREE

AMY STEADMAN
Part vi

It is now more than three weeks since infection, and Amy Steadman's body has been moving away from the site of its death for most of that time. Amy bears little resemblance now to the woman she used to be. Her face, once fresh and clear, is now skeletal and heavily decayed. Her skin is discoloured and waxy. Her once bright eyes are dull, dark and dry. Because of her physical deterioration, Amy moves slowly and forcefully. Movements which had previously appeared random and uncoordinated, however, are beginning to possess an ominous purpose and determination.

This putrefying cadaver has no need to respire, eat, drink or rest and yet Amy continues to struggle across the dead and increasingly grim landscape. As her condition has continued to worsen, she has become increasingly aware of the extent of her decay. She now understands that she is vulnerable. Every unexpected movement or sound she detects is automatically assumed to be a threat and she reacts accordingly.

Now and then, the thing which used to be Amy experiences the faintest flicker of recollection, flashes of memory. She has no concept now of who she used to be, but it is vaguely aware of *what* she once was. Earlier today she fell in the rubble of a shop-window display blown out into the street by a gas explosion. She inadvertently grabbed a handful of rubbish which included a cup. She held the cup by its handle momentarily and tried to drink before dropping it again and walking on. Yesterday, when she found herself by a car, she attempted to reach for the handle and get in.

There are considerably more bodies around here than in most other places. Throughout this silent, empty world the slightest distraction continues to attract the unwanted attention of disproportionate numbers of these grotesque creatures and here, on the outskirts of the city of Rowley, something is drawing untold numbers of them ever closer.

Amy's corpse has left the street she'd been staggering along. Whilst making her way across a barren field, she has reached an unexpected blockage. Eleven bodies are pushing forward, trying to force their way through a wooden gate. The gate has a sprung hinge which constantly pushes back against them. Even when moving together they struggle to make progress. Occasionally one or two of them manage to stumble through the gap, but an ever-growing crowd remains stuck. Aware of the movement of the dark shapes around her, as she approaches the gate, Amy's corpse lifts her hands and begins to grab at the nearest bodies. With twisted, bony fingers she slashes at the other cadavers. Her corpse is stronger and more determined than most. She moves with more purpose. The other bodies are unable to react with anything more than slow, shuffling movements. They do not have the speed or strength to defend themselves.

Amy knows that she must continue to move forward, although she does not understand why. She negotiates the gate (her relative speed and strength forcing it open) and continues towards the disturbance up ahead, unsure whether it's something that might help her, or a threat she must eliminate. Whatever the reason, whatever it is, the putrefying collection of withered flesh and brittle bone which Amy Steadman has become is driven to move relentlessly towards it.

Amy stumbles through more fields, moving further away from the remains of the city she once called home. Like all of the bodies, every single aspect of her life has now been erased. Virtually every trace of race, gender, social class, wealth and intellect has been wiped from all the dead. Amy's corpse, like the many hundreds of similarly faceless cadavers around her, is now almost completely featureless and indistinct. Her clothes are ripped, ragged and stained. Her face is emotionless. Only the level of their individual decay distinguishes the bodies from each other. Some – the most severely rotted – stumble around aimlessly, helpless and virtually blind. Those which are deteriorating more slowly, however, are those which present the greatest danger.

Amy has become aware of a dark mass on the horizon. It is a crowd of many thousands of corpses. Oblivious to the implications, she continues to stagger towards the immense gathering. Before long she reaches the edge of the diseased throng. When the massive numbers of cadavers ahead stop her from moving any further forward, she again reacts violently, ripping and tearing at the dead flesh on all sides until her path through is clear.

Deeper into the crowd, the bodies are even more tightly packed. Still more of them continually arrive at the scene, crawling slothfully towards this place from every direction, blocking the way back and preventing the corpses already there from doing anything other than trying to move further forward still. A chain-link fence stops them progressing.

It takes several days for Amy's body to fight through far enough to finally reach the fence. She is pushed hard against the wire by the advancing crowds behind, and from there she simply watches. On the other side of the fence is a swathe of clear land. Most of the time it is quiet, but occasionally there are deafening noises which whip the diseased hordes into a riotous frenzy. The bodies are surrounding what is possibly the last operational airfield in the country.

Amy's corpse is just one of a crowd now more than a hundred thousand strong. And thousands more are still approaching.

Kilgore sat alone at a metal table in the furthest, darkest corner of the bunker mess hall, trying not to be noticed. The wide, low-ceilinged room was largely empty. Only the occasional noise from the kitchen and the constant electrical hum of the strip lights and air-con disturbed the silence.

Spence ambled into the hall and fetched himself a tray of food. With only a couple of other people eating, none of whom he knew well, he walked over towards Kilgore. 'Mind if I sit here?'

Kilgore jumped with surprise. He looked up at Spence with tired eyes and shook his head. 'Go for it,' he said, then he quickly looked down again. He played with his fork, stirring the lukewarm, piss-weak stew, pushing lumps of meat-substitute around and making tracks in the watery gravy, but not actually eating anything. Spence sat on the bench directly opposite.

He'd encountered Kilgore on a number of occasions before they'd been ordered underground. He'd always had a reputation for being a moaner: the kind of person who instinctively complained and whinged pointlessly about everything he was ordered to do. The kind of person who made the simplest of routine tasks sound like some impossible undertaking. An incessant talker and compulsive liar, he wound the officers up and he wound his fellow soldiers up. Kilgore wound everyone up.

He was crying.

Spence shuffled in his seat and started to eat, wishing that he'd chosen another table. Kilgore's show of emotion made him uneasy. He hated it when he heard people crying down here. It reminded him of the emptiness he felt. The three hundred or so people he'd been buried underground with were, on the whole, professional and well-trained, battle-hardened soldiers; men and women who'd been conditioned to suppress their emotions and just get on with doing whatever it was they'd been ordered to do. But that was getting in-creasingly difficult with every passing day, almost every hour. The fact some of them were showing emotion at all indicated just how uncertain their situation had become. And the longer they spent down here, the worse it got. No one seemed to know what they were doing or why. No one knew what had happened or what was going to happen next. By now they'd all heard rumours about the dire state of the infected world aboveground from the few advance parties which had ventured outside, and that only served to make their time buried underground even more difficult. What did the future hold for the millions of people left on the surface, scarred by plague? More importantly, Spence thought, what did the future hold for him and the rest of them underground?

The tap, tap, tap of metal on plastic disturbed his train of thought. He looked at Kilgore again. His hand was shaking. He could hardly hold his fork still.

'You okay, mate?'

Kilgore shook his head. More tears. He wiped them away on the back of his sleeve. 'No,' he said quietly.

'Want to talk about it?'

'What's there to talk about? What good's it gonna do? We're stuck down here, you know. There's no fucking way we're getting out.'

'Why d'you say that?'

Kilgore dropped his fork and took a swig from his mug of cold coffee. He leant back in his chair and ran his fingers through his wiry hair. For the briefest of moments he made eye contact with Spence, but he looked away quick. Eventually he cleared his throat and tried to talk.

'You been up there yet?' he asked, looking up.

'Not yet.'

'It was my first time out today,' Kilgore explained. 'I was shitting myself. I've never seen anything like it. I tell you, man, you can't even begin to imagine what's going on up there until you see it…' He stopped, took another deep breath and tried again. 'Fucking hell, I can't even…'

'Take your time,' Spence said quietly, figuring he needed to know. Kilgore tried to compose himself.

'Sarge says we're going aboveground. He tells us we're going on a walkabout looking for survivors in Ansall. You know Ansall? Little town just outside Hemmington? Anyway, we're ready and outside in minutes, before we've even had chance to think about it. I put the mask on and I'm standing there in the suit and that's when it hits me. I'm standing there thinking about what I've heard it's like and I start thinking Christ, get a fucking hole in this suit while we're outside and I'm a dead man. I'm thinking, catch the suit on a nail or a door handle or whatever and I've fucking had it. We're all feeling it. No one says a bloody word. Then Sarge gives the nod. We get into the transport and he gives the order to open the doors.

'Those bloody doors slide open and Christ, for a minute it looks fucking beautiful out there. You don't realise how much you miss daylight until you see it again. I tell you, the world never looked so good as it did this afternoon. It's about one o'clock and it's properly gorgeous. The sky's blue, the sun's burning down and there's not a fucking cloud in the sky. We roll up to the top of the ramp and for a few seconds everything's all right. For a couple of seconds it feels good and you start to think everything's going to be okay. It feels good just to be getting out of this fucking place for a while. Even though we've all got our masks on it feels good to see trees and grass and hills instead of fucking concrete walls and metal doors.

'I had Smith sitting next to me. You know Smith? The big guy with the crooked nose? Anyway, we start moving away from the base and he suddenly sits up and starts staring out of the window. He's cursing and pointing and we all crowd around to look at whatever it is he's seen. And that's when we see them. People. I was thinking we should stop and try and help them but then I remembered what I'd heard from the others who'd already been out there. Sarge stops the transport for a second and we watch as they keep coming towards us, all slow and awkward like their legs are stiff. I could only see a couple of them at first, but they kept coming and then there was more and more of them. They're coming out of the trees and from around the side of the entrance door and I counted at least thirty before we started moving again. I could see even more in the fields around us. From a distance they looked normal, just slow moving, but when they got close you could see they were sick. Fucking hell, they looked like they were rotting. Their skin was all discoloured – grey and green – and it looked like it was hanging off their bones like it was a few sizes too big. Some looked like bloody skeletons, all shrivelled up and dry.

Jesus, you've never seen anything like it. Sarge screams at the driver to ignore them and keep moving and she puts her foot down. She drives into a couple of them – there was nothing she could do, they just walked out in front of us. I watched one of them go down. We hit it so hard it virtually snapped in half. Its legs were all fucked up. But then I look behind and watch as it tries to get up again. Fucking thing's lying there with both its legs smashed to fuck and it's trying to get up again…

'So we just sit there in silence for a fucking age. No one says anything. No one knows what to fucking say, you know? Anyway, we follow the track away from here and we see more and more of them everywhere. Christ alone knows how they know where to go, but it's like they're all moving towards the base. They stop and turn around when they see us, then start following. I mean, we've got to be doing about thirty or forty miles an hour and these things are following us like they think they're gonna catch up. We get onto the main road and start heading for Ansall and I'm thinking about what we're gonna find there. I'm thinking fuck, if there are this many people out here in the middle of nowhere, what the hell are we gonna find in town?'

Kilgore paused to finish his drink. Spence said nothing. He just stared into the other soldier's face. He didn't want to hear anything else, but at the same time he had to know.

'The roads were an absolute fucking nightmare,' Kilgore continued. 'It was like someone had flicked a switch and everything just stopped. I tell you man, everywhere you looked all you could see were bodies and crashed cars. Christ, I saw some fucking horrible sights out there. Anyway, because we're on the road now the driver puts her foot down and speeds up. Our truck's heavy enough to just smash through most of the wreckage. I started getting freaked out by it all, and I could see it was getting to the others too. It's the sheer bloody scale of it. Everything's been wiped out up there, you know, there's nothing that ain't been touched. I thought I was gonna have a fucking freak-out. It was so bloody hot in the suit, and the truck was like a fucking sun-trap, and all I could think about was the taste of fresh air and all I wanted to do was take off the mask and feel the sun and the wind on my face and… and then it occurs to me that none of us are ever going to feel that ever again. And then I start getting really fucking frightened thinking about whatever's in the air that's done all this. I'm thinking again about my suit getting ripped and not knowing until it's too late. I can see Fraser's face opposite me. His eyes are darting all round the place like a bloody mad man.

'So we get to Ansall, and I don't mind telling you I was scared shitless. I've never been so fucking frightened. I mean, you're like me, mate, you've seen plenty of service, but I tell you, you ain't seen nothing like what's up there. Remember last winter when we were stuck in that school in the middle of that fucking gunfight that went on for days? Well this was worse. At least back then we knew who the enemy was and we could shoot back at them.

'It was still bright, but between the buildings the streets were dark and it was bloody cold. Coming into the shadow from the sun made it hard to see what was happening. We stopped on the edge of this little market and Sarge tells us to get out and start having a look around. We were supposed to be looking for survivors but all I could see was people in the same state as those we'd seen around here. The first one I saw up close was this little old lady. She's half-dressed and her tits were hanging out and they're all cut up but not bleeding, and I'm just stood there thinking this is probably someone's mom and that my mom could be like this somewhere, and the rest of my family and probably yours too. And when you start thinking about home you get this urge to just get in a car and try and get back there to find out what's happened to your folks and your girl and... and then you think, there's no fucking point.

'Fraser calls out for help and I look around for him. He's holding his weapon out in front of him and he's moving towards this build-ing. It looks like an office or something and I can see there are people trapped inside. They're stood there banging on the glass, and it looks like it's a real effort for them to move because they're so sick. The door's been blocked by a crashed motorbike, so me and Fraser shift it out the way. He throws the door of the building open and straight-away the people start pouring out. I only have to look at them for a second and I know they're just like all the other poor bastards we've already seen. One of them walks straight into me and I look right into its face. There's nothing there. I swear, not a single bloody flicker of emotion. Not a fucking sign of life. It's not even breathing. And I realise, these bloody things are dead but they're still fucking moving.

'Sarge gets on the loudhailer. He's shouting the usual crap at them about how we'll help them if they cooperate and he's trying to get them out of the buildings and into the market square. I turn around to look back at the others and fucking hell, there must have been a couple of hundred of the bloody things getting close to us already. They're crowding round and they start reaching out and trying to grab hold of us when they get close enough. I'm thinking about my bloody suit again and I keep pushing them away but they keep coming back for more. Sarge fires a few warning shots into the air but it doesn't make any difference. Next to me Fraser starts hitting one of them and the fucking thing doesn't even notice. Every time he hits it he's doing more and more damage but the damn thing just keeps coming. Its fucking face is falling to pieces but it just keeps on coming.

'Every way I turn now I can see more and more of them. We're looking at Sarge for some frigging inspiration and he's just looking back at us, scared as we are. I lose sight of him when a couple of them rush me. I lose my footing and before I know it I'm on the ground with them on top of me. There's no weight to them. All I keep thinking is be careful of the fucking suit, make sure you don't get cut. I'm punching and kicking out but the bloody things just don't give up. I manage to get back up and I can see we're surrounded. And there are more of them coming out of the shadows all the bloody time. I see Wheeler heading back to the transport and I can see the driver's already back in her seat getting ready to leave, and I'm thinking fuck orders, I've gotta get out of here, and I start fighting my way through the crowd.

'Fraser's the last one back in. He tries to shut the door behind him but gets caught by one of them that manages to grab his leg as he climbs up. I'm watching and I can't look away and I'm thinking this can't be happening. It's a kid, probably not even fifteen, and its body is so light and empty that it's hanging off him and Fraser's just dragging it along. It's got hold of his boot somehow and he's using the butt of the rifle to smash its hand away. He pushes it off and tries to get it back out the door. Wheeler leans out and pulls the door shut but the bloody thing hasn't gone. Its head and shoulders are wedged in and Wheeler's banging and pulling at the door, trying to get rid of it. The kid's got one arm inside the transport and it's still trying to get at Fraser and he's just standing there. He lifts up his rifle and blows a fucking hole in the middle of its face, then kicks what's left of the body out onto the street.'

Kilgore rubbed his eyes and looked up into the light, then let his head fall. 'And that, mate,' he said, struggling to light a cigarette with shaking hands, 'is just about all that you, me and everyone else who's stuck in this fucking hole has got to look forward to. We either spend the rest of our time buried here, or we end up stuck out in that bloody mess up top, shrink-wrapped in our fucking plastic suits until whatever it is that's done all this finally catches up with us.'

HOME

Steninger is less than two hours from home. He hasn't been this close for almost a month. He hasn't been this close since it happened. Twenty-three days ago millions of people died as the world fell apart around him.

I've been here hundreds of times before but it's never looked like this. Georgie and I used to drive up here at weekends to walk the dog over the hills. We'd let him off the lead and then walk and talk and watch him play for hours. That was long before the events which have since kept us apart. It all feels like a lifetime ago now. Today the green, rolling landscape I remember is washed out and grey and everything is lifeless and dead. The world is decaying around me. It's early in the morning, perhaps an hour before sunrise, and there's a layer of light mist clinging to the ground. I'm alone, but I'm surrounded. I can see them moving all around. They're everywhere. Shuffling. Staggering. Hundreds of the damn things.

One last push and I'll be home. I'm starting to get nervous now. For days I've struggled to get here but, now I'm this close, I don't know if I can go through with it. Seeing what's left of Georgie and our home will hurt. It's been so long and so much has happened since we were last together. I don't know if I'll have the strength to walk through the front door. I don't know if I'll be able to stand the pain of remembering everything that's gone and all that I've lost.

I'm as scared now as I was when this nightmare began. I remember it as if it was only minutes ago, not weeks. I was in a breakfast meeting with my lawyer and one of his staff when it started. Jarvis was explaining some legal jargon to me when he stopped talking mid-sentence. I asked him what was wrong but he couldn't answer. His breathing became shallow and short and he started to splutter. He was choking but I couldn't see why and I was concentrating so hard on what was happening to him that I didn't notice it had got the other man too. As Jarvis' face paled and he began to scratch and claw at his throat his colleague lurched forward and tried to grab hold of me. Eyes bulging, he retched and showered me with blood and spittle. I recoiled and pushed my chair back away from the table, then stood with my back pressed against the wall and watched the two men choke to death. Seconds later, the room was silent.

When I eventually plucked up the courage to get out and look for help I found the receptionist who had greeted me less than an hour earlier lying in a pool of red-brown blood. The security man on the door was dead too, as was everyone else I could see. It was the same when I finally dared step out into the open – an endless layer of twisted human remains covered the ground in every direction I looked. What had happened was inexplicable and its scale incomprehensible. In the space of just a few minutes something – a germ, virus or biological attack perhaps – had destroyed my world. Nothing moved. The silence was deafening.

At first I'd instinctively wanted stay where I was, to keep my head down and wait for something – anything – to happen. I walked back to the hotel as it was the only nearby place I knew well, picking my way through the bodies, staring at each of them in turn, looking deep into their grotesque, twisted faces. Each of them bore an expression of sudden, searing agony.

When I got back, the hotel was as silent as everywhere else. I locked myself in my room and waited there for hours until the unending solitude became too much to stand. I needed explanations but there was no one left alive to ask. The television was useless, as was the radio, and the telephone went unanswered. Even the Internet seemed to have died, frozen in time. Increasingly desperate, I packed my few belongings and made a break for home. But I soon found that the hushed roads were impassable, blocked by the tangled wreckage of incalculable numbers of crashed vehicles and the mangled, bloody remains of their dead drivers and passengers. With my wife and my home still more than eighty miles away I stopped the car and gave up.

It was early on the first Thursday, the third day, when the situation deteriorated again to the point where I began to question my sanity. I had been resting in the front bedroom of an empty terraced house when I looked out of the window and saw the first one of them staggering down the road. All the fear and nervousness I had previously felt was immediately forgotten as I watched the lone figure walk awkwardly down the street. It was another survivor, I thought, it had to be. Someone who, at last, might be able to tell me what had happened and who could answer some of the thousands of impossible questions I desperately needed to ask. I yelled out and banged on the window but the person outside didn't respond. I sprinted out of the house and ran down the road, then grabbed hold of their arm and turned them around. As unbelievable as it seemed at the time, I knew instantly that the thing in front of me was dead. Its eyes were clouded, covered with a milky-white film, and its skin was pock-marked and bloodied. And it was cold to the touch... I held its left wrist in my hand and felt for a pulse but found nothing. The creature's skin felt unnaturally clammy and leathery and I let it go in disgust. The moment I released my grip the damn thing shuffled slowly away like it didn't even know I was there.

Out of the corner of my eye I became aware of more movement. I turned and saw another body, then another and then another. I walked to the end of the street and stared in disbelief at what was happening all around me. The dead were rising. Many were already moving around on clumsy, unsteady feet, whilst still more were slowly dragging themselves back up from where they'd fallen and died days earlier.

A frantic search for food and water and somewhere safe to shelter led me back deeper into town. Avoiding the mannequin-like bodies, I barricaded myself in a large pub on a corner where two once busy roads met. I cleared eight corpses out of the building (I herded them all into the bar before forcing them out the front door) and then locked myself in an upstairs function room where I started to drink. Although it didn't make me drunk like it used to, the alcohol took the very slightest edge off my fear.

I thought constantly about Georgie and home but I was too afraid to move. I knew I should try to get to her but for days I just sat there, hiding like a coward. Every morning I tried to make myself leave but the thought of going back out into what remained of the world was unbearable. Instead I sat in booze-fueled isolation and watched the world decay.

As the days passed, the bodies themselves changed. Initially stiff and staccato, their movements gradually became more purposeful and controlled. After four days I observed that their senses were beginning to return. They were starting to respond to what was happening around them. Late one afternoon in a moment of frightened frustration, I hurled an empty beer bottle across the room. I missed the wall and smashed a window. Out of curiosity I looked down into the street below and saw that huge numbers of the corpses were now walking towards the pub. Attracted by the noise (which seemed louder than it actually was in the otherwise all-consuming silence) they moved relentlessly closer and closer. During the hours which followed I tried to keep quiet and out of sight but my every movement seemed to make more of them aware of my presence. From every direction they came and all I could do was watch as a crowd of hundreds of the damn things surrounded me. They followed each other like herding animals and soon their lumbering, decomposing shapes filled the streets outside for as far as I could see.

A week went by, and the ferocity of the creatures increased. They began to fight with each other and they fought to get to me. They clawed and banged at the doors but didn't yet have the strength to get inside. My options were hopelessly limited but I knew I had to do something. I could stay where I was and drink enough so that I didn't care when the bodies eventually broke through, or I could make a break for freedom and take my chances outside. I had nothing to lose. I thought about home and I thought about Georgie and I knew that I had to try and get back to her.

It wasn't much of a plan but it was all I had. I packed the meagre supplies and provisions I found lying around the pub into a rucksack and got myself ready to leave. I made crates of crude bombs from the liquor bottles behind the bar and those in the cellar and storeroom. As the light began to fade at the end of the tenth day I hung out of the broken window at the front of the building, lit the booze-soaked rag fuses which I had stuffed down the necks of the bottles, and then began to hurl them down into the rotting crowds below. In minutes I'd created more chaotic devastation than I imagined possible. There had been little rain for days. Tinder dry and packed tight together, the repugnant bodies caught light almost instantly. Oblivious to the flames which steadily consumed them, the damn things continued to move about for as long as they were physically able, their every staggering step spreading the fire still further and destroying more and more of them. And the dancing orange light and the crackling and popping of burning flesh drew even more of the desperate cadavers closer to the scene.

I crept downstairs and waited by the back door. The building itself was soon alight. Doubled-up with hunger pains (the world outside had unexpectedly filled with the smell of roast meat like a summer hog roast) I crouched in the shadows and waited until the rising temperature in the building was too much to stand. When the flames began to lick at the door to the room I hid in, I pushed my way out into the night and ran through the bodies. Their reactions were dull and slow and my relative speed and strength and the surprise of my sudden appearance meant they offered virtually no resistance. In the silent, monochrome world, the confusion that I'd generated provided enough of a distraction to camouflage my movements and render me temporarily invisible.

Since I've been on the move I've learnt to live like a shadow. My difficult journey home has been painfully long and slow. I move only at night under cover of darkness. If the bodies see or hear me they will come for me and, as I've found to my cost on more than one occasion, once one of them has my scent then countless others will follow. I have avoided them as much as possible but their numbers are vast and some contact has been inevitable. I'm getting better at dealing with them. The initial disgust and trepidation I felt has now given way to hate and anger. Through necessity I have become a cold and effective killer, although I'm not sure whether that's an accurate description of my new found skill. I have to keep reminding myself that these bloody aberrations are already dead.

Apart from the mass of bodies I managed to obliterate during my escape from the pub, the first corpse I intentionally disposed of had once been a priest. I came across the emaciated creature when I took shelter at dawn one morning in a small village church. It had appeared empty at first until I pushed my way into a narrow storeroom at the far end of the grey-stone building. I was immediately aware of shuffling movement ahead of me. A small window high on the wall to my left let a limited amount of light spill into the storeroom and allowed me to see the outline of the body of the priest as it came at me. The cadaver was weak, barely coordinated, and I instinctively grabbed hold of it by the neck then threw it back across the room. It smashed into a bookshelf and was buried by falling prayer books. Constantly thrashing its leaden arms and legs, it eventually pulled itself back up onto its dead feet. I stared into its vacant, hollowed face as it dragged itself back into the light. The first body I had seen up close for several days, it was a damn mess. Just a shadow of the man it had once been, the creature's skin appeared taut and translucent and it had an unnatural green-grey hue. Its cheeks and eye sockets were sunken and its mouth and chin speckled with dribbles of dried blood. Its black shirt and dog-collar hung loose around its scrawny neck.

For a moment I was distracted by the thing's sickening appearance and it caught me by surprise when it charged at me again. I was knocked off-balance but I managed to grab hold of it by the throat. I straightened my arm to keep it at a safe distance, then used my free hand to feel around for something to use as a weapon. My outstretched fingers found the stem of an ornate candleholder behind me and to my right. I gripped it tight, then lifted it high above my head and brought the base of it crashing down on the dead priest's skull. Stunned but undeterred, the body tripped back, then came at me again. I lifted the candleholder and smashed it down again and again until the head of the corpse was little more than a pulp of blood, brain and bone. I stood over the cleric's twitching remains until it finally lay still.

I hid in the bell tower of the church and waited for the night to come.

It didn't take long to work out the rules.

Although they have become increasingly violent as time has gone on, the creatures remain predictable. I think that they are driven purely by instinct. What remains of their brains seem to operate on a basic, primitive level and each one is little more than a fading memory of what it used to be. I quickly learnt that this reality is nothing like the trash horror movies I used to watch or the books I used to

352

read. These things don't want to kill me so that they can feast on my flesh. In fact I don't actually think they have any physical needs or desires – they don't eat, drink, sleep or even breathe as far as I can see. So why do they attack? It's a paradox but the longer I think about it, the more convinced I am that they see me as a threat. I'm different and I'm stronger and I think they know that I could easily destroy them. I think they try to attack me before I have chance to attack them.

Over the last few days and weeks I have watched them steadily disintegrate and decay. And therein lies another bizarre irony: as their bodies have continued to weaken and become more fragile, so their mental control seems to have returned. They have an innate sense of self-preservation and will respond violently to any perceived threat. Sometimes they fight amongst themselves and I have hidden in the darkness and watched them set about each other until almost all of their rotten flesh has been stripped from their bones and they can barely stand.

I know beyond doubt now that the brain remains the centre of control. My second, third and fourth kills confirmed that. I had broken into an isolated house in search of food and fresh clothes, when I found myself face to face with the rotting remains of what appeared to have once been a fairly typical family. I quickly disposed of the father with a short wooden fence post I had been carrying as a makeshift weapon. I smacked the repulsive creature around the side of the head again and again until it had almost been decapitated. The next body – the dead man's dead wife, I presumed – had proved to be more troublesome. I entered a large, square dining room and the body of the woman came at me with unexpected speed. I held the picket out in front of me and skewered the damn thing through the chest. Its withered torso and parchment skin offered next to no resistance and the wood plunged deep into its abdomen and straight out the other side. I retched and struggled to keep control of my stomach as the remains of its putrefied organs slid out of the hole I had made in its back and slopped down onto the cream-coloured carpet in a slimy crimson heap. I pushed the body away, expecting it to collapse like the last one had, but it didn't. Instead it staggered after me, still impaled and struggling to move as I had clearly caused a massive amount of damage to its spine with the fence picket. I panicked. I ran to the kitchen and grabbed the largest knife I could find before returning to the body. It had managed to take a few more steps forward but stopped immediately when I plunged the blade through its right eye into the core of what remained of its brain. It was as if someone had flicked a switch. The dead woman slumped down and slid off the knife and dropped at my feet like a bloodied rag-doll. In the silence which followed I could hear the third body thumping around upstairs. To prove my theory I ran up the stairs and disposed of a dead teenager in the same way as its mother with a single stab to the head.

It's an unsettling admission, but I have to admit that I've grown to enjoy the kill. The reality is that it's the only pleasure which remains to me. It's the only time I have complete control. I haven't ever gone looking for sport, but I haven't avoided it either. I've kept a tally of kills along the way and I've begun to pride myself on finding quicker, quieter and more effective ways of destroying the dead. I took a gun from a police station a week or so ago but quickly got rid of it again. A shot to the head will immediately take out a single body, but I've found to my cost that the resultant noise invariably makes thousands more of the damn things aware of my location. Weapons now need to be silent and swift. I've tried clubs and axes and whilst they've often been effective, real sustained effort is needed to get results. Fire is too visible and unpredictable and so blades have become my weapons of choice. I now carry seventeen in all – buck knifes, sheath knifes, Bowie knifes, scalpels and even pen knifes. I carry two butcher's meat cleavers holstered like pistols and I hold a machete drawn and ready at all times.

I've made steady progress today. I know this stretch of footpath well. It twists and turns and it's not the most direct route home but it's my best option this morning. Dawn is breaking. The light is increasing and I'm beginning to feel uncomfortably exposed. I've not been out in daylight for weeks now. I've gotten used to the dark and the protection it affords me.

This short stretch of path runs alongside a golf course. There seem to be an unusually high number of bodies around here. I think this was the seventh hole – a short but tough hole with a raised tee and an undulating fairway from what I remember. Many of the corpses have become trapped in the natural dip of the land here and the once well-tended grass has been churned to mud beneath their tireless feet. They can't get away. Stupid things are stuck. Sometimes I almost feel privileged to have the opportunity to rid the world of a few of these pointless creatures. All that separates me from them now is a wooden fence and a stretch of tangled, patchy hedgerow. I keep quiet and take each step with care for fear of making any unnecessary noise. I could deal with them, but it will be much easier if I don't have to.

The path climbs and curves away to the left. There are two bodies up ahead and I know I have no choice but to dispose of them. The second seems to be following the first and I wonder whether there are more behind? However many there are, I know I have to deal with them quickly. It will take too long to go around them and any sudden movement will alert any others that might be moving through the undergrowth. The safest option – the only option – is to go straight at them and cut them both down.

Here's the first. It's seen me. It makes a sudden, lurching change in direction which reveals its intent. With its dull, misted eyes fixed on me, it comes my way. Bloody hell, it's badly decayed – one of the worst I've seen. I can't even tell whether it used to be male or female. Most of its face has been eaten away and its mottled, pock-marked skull is dotted with clumps of long, lank, grey-blonde hair. It's dragging one foot behind. In fact, now that it's closer I can see that it only has one foot! Its right ankle ends unexpectedly with a dirty stump which it drags through the mud. The rags wrapped around the corpse look like they might once have been a uniform of sorts. Was this a police officer? A traffic warden? A soldier? Whatever it used to be, its time is up.

I've developed a two-cut technique. It's safer than running headlong at them swinging a blade through the air like a madman. A little bit of control makes all the difference. The bodies are usually already unsteady (this one certainly is) so I use the first cut to stop them moving or at least slow them down. The body is close enough now. I crouch down and swing the machete from right to left, severing both of its legs at knee level with a single swipe. With the corpse now flat on its stomach I reverse the movement and, backhanded, slam the blade down through its neck before it can move. Easy. Kill number one hundred and thirty-eight. Number one hundred and thirty-nine proves slightly harder. I slip and bury the blade in the creature's pelvis when I was aiming lower. No problem – with the corpse on its knees I lift the machete again and bring it down on the top of its head. The skull splits open like an egg. It's harder pulling the blade out than it was getting it in.

I never think of the bodies as people anymore. There's no point. Whatever caused all of this has wiped out every trace of individuality and character from the rotting masses. Generally they look and act the same now – age, race, sex, class, religion and all other previously notable social differences are gone. There are no distinctions, there are only the dead; a single massive decaying population. Kill number twenty-six brought that home to me. Obviously the body of a very young child, it had attacked me with as much force and intent as the countless other 'adult' creatures I had come across. I had hesitated for a split-second before the kill, but then I did it just the same. I knew that what it used to be was of no importance now, that it was just dead flesh which had to be destroyed. I took its head clean off its shoulders with a hand-axe and hardly gave it another thought.

Distances which should take minutes to cover now take hours. I'm working my way along a wide footpath which leads down into the heart of Stonemorton, and I can see bodies everywhere I look. The earlier mist has lifted and I can see their slow, stumbling shapes moving between houses and along otherwise empty streets. My already slow speed has reduced still further now that it's getting light. Maybe I'm consciously slowing down? The closer I get to home, the more nervous and unsure I feel. I try to concentrate and focus my thoughts on reaching Georgie. All I want is to be with her again, what's happened to the rest of the world is of no interest. I'm realistic about what I'm going to find – I haven't seen another living soul for weeks and I don't think for a second I'll find her alive, but I've survived, so there must still be some slight hope. My worst fear is that the house will be empty, because then I'll have to keep looking. I won't rest until we're together again.

Damn. Suddenly there are bodies right ahead of me. I can't be completely sure how many are here as their awkward, gangly shapes seem to merge and disappear into the background of gnarled, twisted trees. I'm pretty confident dealing with anything up to ten at a time. All I have to do is take my time, keep calm and try not to make more noise than I have to. The last thing I want is to let more of them know where I am.

The nearest body has locked onto me and is lining itself up to be kill number one hundred and forty. Bloody hell, this is the tallest corpse I've seen. Even though its back is twisted into an uncomfortable stoop it's still taller than me. I need to lower it to get a good shot at the brain. I swing the machete up between its legs and practically split it in two. It slumps forward and I take its head clean off its shoulders before it's even hit the ground.

One hundred and forty-one. This one is more lively than most. I've come across a few like this from time to time. For some reason bodies like this one are not as badly decayed as the majority of the dead and for a split second I start to wonder whether this might actually be a survivor. When it lunges at me, vicious but unsteady, I know immediately that it is already dead. I lift up my blade and put it in the way of the creature's face. Still moving forward, it pierces its right eye and then falls limp as the machete slices into the centre of its rotting brain.

My weapon is stuck, wedged tight in the skull of this monstrosity, and I can't pull it free. The next body is close now. As I tug at the machete with my right hand I yank one of the meat cleavers out of its holster with my left and swing it wildly at the shape which is stumbling towards me. I make some contact but it's not enough. I've sliced diagonally across the width of its torso but it doesn't even seem to notice the damage. I let go of the machete (I'll go back for it when I'm done) and, using both cleavers now, I attack the third body again. The blow I strike with my left hand wedges the first blade deep into its shoulder, cutting through the collar bone and forcing the body down. I aim the second cut at the base of the neck and smash through the spinal cord. I push the cadaver down into the gravel and stamp on its expressionless face until my boot does enough damage to permanently stop the bloody thing moving.

With the first cleaver still buried in the shoulder of the previous body, I'm now two weapons down with potential kill number one hundred and forty-three less than two metres away. This one is slower and it's got less fight in it than the last few. Breathing hard, I clench my fist and punch it square in the face. It wobbles for a second, then drops to the ground. I enjoy kills like that. My hand stings and is covered in all kinds of foul-smelling mess, but the sudden feeling of satisfaction, strength and superiority I have is immense.

I retrieve my blades, clean them on a patch of grass, then carry on my way.

In the distance I can see the first few houses on the edge of the estate. I'm almost home now and I'm beginning to wish I wasn't. I've spent days on the move trying to get here – long, dark, lonely days filled with uncertainty and fear. Now that I'm here there's a part of me that wants to turn around and go back, but I know there's nowhere else to go and I know I have to do this. I have to see it through.

Here at street level, I'm more exposed than ever. Christ, everything looks so different to how I remember. It's been less than a month since I was last here but in that time the world has gone to ruin along with the dead population. The smell of death is everywhere, choking, smothering and suffocating everything. The once clear pavements are sprouting with weeds. Everything is crumbling around me. The world is changing, and yet it's still recognizable. I know this place. It's not the decay, it's the memories and familiarity which makes everything so hard to handle.

This is Huntingden Street. I used to drive this way to work. Almost all of this side of the road has been burnt to the ground and where there used to be a long, meandering row of between thirty and forty houses, now there's just a line of empty, wasted shells. The destruction has altered the entire landscape and from where I'm standing I now have a clear view all the way over to the red-brick wall which runs along the edge of the estate where Georgie and I used to live. It's so close now. I've been rehearsing this part of the journey in my mind for days. I'm going to work my way back home by cutting through the back gardens of the houses along the way. I'm thinking that the back of each house should be more secure and enclosed and

I'll be able to take my time. There will be bodies along the way, but they should be fewer in number than those roaming the main roads.

I'm crouching down behind a low wall in front of one of the burnt out houses. I need to get across the road and into the garden of one of the houses opposite. The easiest way will be to go straight through – in through the front door and out through the back. Everything looks clear. I can't see any bodies. Apart from my knives I'll leave everything here. I won't need any of it now. I'm almost home.

Slow going. Getting into the first garden was simple enough, but it's not going to be as easy as I thought trying to move between properties. I'm having to climb over fences that are nowhere near strong enough to support my weight. I could just break them down but I'll make too much noise and I don't want to start taking unnecessary risks now.

Garden number three. I can see the dead owner of this house trapped inside its property, wearing a heavily stained dressing gown. It's leaning against the patio window and it starts hammering against the glass when it sees me. From my position mid-way down the lawn the figure at the window looks painfully thin, skeletal almost. I can see another body in the shadows behind it.

Garden number four. Damn, the owner of this house is outside. It's moving towards me before I've even made it over the fence and the expression on what's left of its face is terrifying. My heart's beating like it's going to explode as I jump down and ready myself. A few seconds wait that feels like forever, then a single flash of the blade and it's done. The residual speed of the cadaver keeps it moving further down the lawn until it falls flat. Its severed head lies at my feet, face down on the dew-soaked grass like a piece of rotten fruit. One hundred and forty-four.

Garden number five is clear, as is number six. I've now made it as far as the penultimate house. I sprint across the grass, scale the fence, and then jump down and run across the final strip of lawn until I reach another brick wall. On the other side of this wall is Partridge Road. The turning into my estate is another hundred metres or so down to my right.

I throw myself over the top of the wall and land heavily on the pavement below. Sudden searing pains shoot up my legs and I fall into the road. There are bodies here. A quick look up and down the road and I can see seven or eight of them already. They've all seen me. This isn't good. No time for technique now, I simply have to get rid of them as quickly as possible. I take the first two out almost instantly with the machete. I start to run towards the road into the estate and I decapitate the third corpse at speed as I pass it. I push another one out of the way (no time to go back and finish it off), then chop violently at the next which staggers into my path. I manage a single, brutal cut just above its waist which is deep enough to hack through the spinal cord. It falls to the ground behind me, still moving but going nowhere. I count it as a kill anyway. One hundred and forty-eight.

I can clearly see the entrance to the estate now. The wrecks of two crashed cars have almost completely blocked the mouth of the road like an improvised gate. Good. The blockage here means there should be fewer bodies on the other side. Damn, there are still more coming for me here, though. Christ, there are loads of the bloody things. Where the hell are they coming from? I look up and down the road again and all I can see is a mass of stumbling corpses coming at me from every direction. My arrival here has created more of a disturbance than I thought. There are too many of them for me to risk trying to deal with. Some are quicker than others and the first few are already close. Too close. I sprint towards the crashed cars as fast as I can. I drop my shoulder and barge several cadavers out of the way, my speed and weight easily knocking them to the ground. I jump onto the crumpled bonnet of the first car and then climb up onto its roof. I'm still only a few feet away from the hordes of rabid dead but I'm safer here. They haven't got the strength or coordination to be able to climb up after me, and even if they could, I'd just kick the bloody things back down again. I stand still for a few seconds to catch my breath, staring down into the growing sea of decomposing faces below me. Their facial muscles are decayed and they are incapable of controlled expression. Nevertheless, something about the way they look up at me reveals a cold and savage intent. They hate me. I want them to know that the feeling is mutual. If I had the time and energy I'd jump back down into the crowd and tear every last one of them apart.

Still standing on the roof of the car, I slowly turn around. And there it is. Home.

Torrington Road stretches out ahead of me now, wild and overgrown but still reassuringly familiar. Just ahead and to my right is the entrance to Harlour Grove. *Our* road. Our house is at the end of the cul-de-sac.

I'd stay here for a while and try to compose myself if it wasn't for the bodies snapping and scratching at my feet. I jump down from the car and take a few steps forward. I then turn back for a second – something's caught my eye. Now that I'm down I recognise the car I've just been standing on. I glance at the licence plate at the back. It's cracked and smashed but I can still make out three letters together: HAL. This is Stan Isherwood's car. He lived four doors down from Georgie and I. And good grief, that thing in the front seat is what's left of Stan. I can see what remains of the retired bank manager slamming itself from side to side, trying desperately to get out of its seat and get to me. It's being held in place by its safety belt. Stupid bloody thing can't release the catch. Without thinking I crouch down and peer in through the grubby glass. My decomposing neighbour stops moving for a fraction of a second and looks straight back at me. Jesus Christ, there's not much left of him but I can still see that it's Stan. He's wearing one of his trademark golf jumpers. The pastel colours of the fabric are mottled and dark, stained by dribbles of crusted blood and other secretions which have seeped out of him over the last four weeks. I walk away. I liked Stan. He doesn't pose any threat to me like this and I can't bring myself to kill him just for the sake of it.

I jog forward again. A body emerges from a nearby house, the front door of which hangs open like a gaping mouth. It's back to business as usual as I tighten the grip on the machete in my hand and wait to strike. The corpse lurches at me. I don't recognise it as being anyone I knew, and that makes it easier. I swing at its head and make contact. The blade sinks three quarters of the way into the skull, just above the cheek bone. Kill one hundred and forty-nine drops to the ground and I yank out my weapon and clean it on the back of my trousers.

I turn the corner and I'm in Harlour Grove. I stop when I see our house, filled with a sudden surge of emotion. Bloody hell, if I half-close my eyes I can almost imagine that everything is normal and none of this ever happened. My heart is racing with nervous anticipation and fear as I move towards our home. I can't wait to see her again. It's been too long.

A sudden noise in the street behind me makes me spin around. There are bodies coming at me from several directions. At least six of them are behind me, staggering after me at a pathetically slow pace, and two are more ahead, one closing in from the right and the other coming from the general direction of the house next to ours. The adrenalin is really pumping now I'm this close. I'll be back with Georgie in the next few minutes and nothing is going to stop me. I don't even waste time with the machete now – I raise my fist and smash the nearest corpse in the face, rearranging what's left of its already mutilated features. It drops to the ground, bringing up my one hundred and fiftieth kill in some style.

I'm about to do the same to the next body when I realise I know her. This is what's left of Judith Landers, the lady who lived next-door but one. Her husband was a narrow-minded idiot but I always got on with Judith. Her face is bloated and discoloured and she's lost an eye but I can still see it's her. She's wearing the remains of the hardware store uniform she wore for work. Poor cow. She reaches out for me and I instinctively raise the machete, but then I look deeper into what's left of her face and all I can see is the person she used to be. She tries to grab hold of me but one of her arms is broken and it flaps uselessly at her side. I push her away in the hope she'll just turn round and disappear in the other direction, but she doesn't. She grabs at me again and, again, I push her away. This time her legs give way and she falls. Her face smashes into the pavement, leaving a greasy, bloody stain behind. Undeterred she gets up and comes at me for a third time. I know I don't have any choice and I also know that there are now eleven more corpses closing in on me fast. Judith was a short woman. I flash the blade level with my shoulders and take off the top third of her head like it's a breakfast egg. She drops to her knees and falls forward.

I have carried the key to our house on a chain around my neck since the first day. With my hands tingling with nerves I pull it from under my shirt and shove it into the lock. I can hear dragging foot-steps just behind me now. The lock is stiff and I have to use all my strength to turn the key but finally it moves. The latch clicks and I push the door open. I fall into the house and slam the door shut just as the closest body crashes into the other side.

I'm almost too afraid to speak.

'Georgie?' I shout, and the sound of my voice echoes around the silent house. I haven't dared to talk out loud for weeks and the noise seems strange. It makes me feel exposed. 'Georgie?'

Nothing. I take a couple of steps further down the hallway. Where is she? I need to know what happened here. Wait, what's that? Just inside the dining room I can see Rufus, our dog. He's lying on his back and it looks like he's been dead for some time. Poor bugger, he probably starved to death. I take another step forward but then stop and look away. Something has attacked the dog. He's been torn apart. There's dried blood and pieces of him all over the place.

'Georgie?' I call out for a third time. I'm about to shout again when I hear it. Something's moving in the kitchen and I pray that it's her.

I look up and see a shadow shifting at the far end of the hallway. It has to be Georgie. She's shuffling towards me and I know that any second I'll see her. I want to run to meet her but I can't because my feet are frozen to the ground with nerves. The shadow lurches for-ward again and she finally comes into view. The end of the hallway is dark and for a moment I can only see her silhouette but there's no question it's her. She slowly turns towards me, pivoting around awkwardly, then begins to trip down the hall in my direction. Every step she takes brings her closer to the light coming from the small window next to the front door, revealing her in more detail. I can see now that she's naked and I find myself wondering what happened to make her lose her clothes. Another step and I can see that her once strong and beautiful hair is now lank and sparse. Another step and I see that her usually flawless, perfect skin has been eaten away by decay. Another step forward and I can clearly see what's left of her face. Those sparkling eyes that I gazed into a thousand times are now dry and she looks at me without the slightest hint of recognition or emotion. I clear my throat and try to speak…

'Georgie, are you…?'

She launches herself at me. Rather than recoil and fight I instead catch her and pull her closer. It feels good to hold her again. She's weak and offers no resistance when I wrap my arms around her and hold her tight. I press my face next to hers, fighting to ignore the smell of her decay.

I don't want to ever let her go. This was how I wanted it to be. It's better this way. I had known all along that she would be dead. If she'd survived she would probably have left the house and I would never have been able to find her, but I'd have never stopped looking. We were meant to be together, Georgie and me. That's what I kept telling her, even when she stopped wanting to listen.

I've been back home for a couple of hours now. Apart from the dust and mildew, the place looks pretty much the same as it always did. She didn't change much after I left. We're in the living room together now. It's almost a year since I've been here. Since we split up she didn't like me coming around. She never usually let me get any further than the hall, even when I came to collect my things. She said she'd call the police if she had to but I always knew she wouldn't. That was just what *he* told her to say.

I've dragged the coffee table across the door to stop her getting out and I've nailed a few planks of wood across it, just to be sure. She's stopped attacking me now and it's almost as if she's got used to having me around again. I tried to put a bathrobe around her to keep her warm but she wouldn't keep still long enough to let me. Even now she's still moving around, walking round the edge of the room, tripping over and crashing into things. Silly girl! And with our neighbours watching too! Seems like most of the corpses from around the estate have dragged themselves over here to see what's going on. I've counted more than twenty dead faces pressed against the window, looking in.

It was a shame we couldn't have worked things out before she died. I know I spent too much time at work, but I did it all for her. I did it all for *us*. She said we'd grown apart and that I didn't excite her anymore. She said I was boring and dull. She said she wanted more adventure and spontaneity and that, she said, was what Bryan gave her. I tried to make her see that he was too young for her and that he was just stringing her along, but she didn't want to listen. And where is he now? Where is he with his bloody designer clothes, his city centre apartment and his flash car? I know exactly where he is – he's out there on the streets, rotting with the rest of the masses. And where am I? I'm *home*. I'm back sitting in *my* armchair drinking *my* whiskey in *my* living room. I'm at home with my wife and this is where I'm going to stay. I'm going to die here and when I've gone Georgie and I will rot together. We'll be here together until the very end of everything.

I know it's what she would have wanted.

He calls himself Skin, though his name is actually Scott Weaver. He'd never admit it but, despite all the bravado and bullshit, he's as scared as hell. Skin is what he used to beg his friends to call him. It's the name he used on forums and in chatrooms, the tag he left scrawled onto the sides of buildings and bus shelters. Skin is sixteen and like many other similarly alienated and disenchanted adolescents, he has a grudge against the rest of the world because he's convinced the rest of the world has it in for him. His frustrations have been building and his problems festering for months now, and each day he has felt himself getting closer and closer to breaking point. Three weeks and two days ago, however, much of that pressure was inexplicably released. Three weeks and two days ago, the rest of the world died.

In the long hours he'd subsequently spent alone, Skin often thought back to how it began. It was a Tuesday morning, and his parents had been giving him hell because he'd only just come back in from being out all Monday night. He didn't know what their problem was. He'd been out with a few friends and they'd lost track of time, so what? They'd had a few drinks, so what? They'd done some drugs (nothing heavy, but his parents didn't need to know that), so what? His dad had gone on and on about how this was the time of his life where he needed to be putting more effort in, not less, then he and Dad had started yelling and swearing at each other and that had made Mom cry, and that had made Dad even angrier. Christ, they didn't ever see his point of view. More to the point, they didn't want to. They judged him by the way he dressed, the music he listened to and the people he hung around with, nothing else. His dad hadn't spoken to him for almost a month when he'd had his first piercings. Fuck, if only they'd known about the stuff he'd had done in the summer just gone…

He'd been trapped in the kitchen with them both, trying to find a way out of the argument without letting them win, when it happened. One minute they were both in full flow – Dad screaming at him for being a bloody waste of space, Mom crying into her tea and yelling at Dad to stop yelling – the next they were dead. Both of them. Facedown on the kitchen floor.

The death of his parents (and, apparently, the rest of the world) was the moment it all finally began to make sense. Until then Skin's life had been increasingly fucking miserable, and the tedium showed no sign of relenting. He'd flunked his exams and left school, only to then be forced to enrol for re-takes at college. And his girlfriend had left him. They'd been together on and off for eight months when Dawn ended it. She said that he'd bullied her into having sex. She'd said that he kept asking her to do things she didn't feel comfortable doing. It was her fault, the fucking tease. She was the one who dressed like a fucking whore all the time. Jesus, she was the one who'd been sat there in a fucking corset, tight black mini-skirt, torn fishnets and knee-high PVC boots when she'd told him that she didn't want to be with him anymore. He'd lost his virginity to her pretty early on in their brief relationship and his imagination had run away with him since then. He'd already discovered that he'd been the only virgin in the relationship and that had made him feel like he had something to prove, or that he had some catching up to do. Skin had always imagined that first sex would have been this incredible event, the undisputed highlight of his young life so far, but the reality had been bitterly disappointing. Instead of endless hours of uninterrupted dirty passion, he'd had to settle for a fifteen minute fumble in Dawn's bedroom while her mom went to the chip shop. And half of those fifteen minutes were spent trying to get the bloody condom on.

In the three weeks between Skin splitting up with Dawn and the end of the world, he began to hate her with a passion. He still saw her regularly because as soon as she'd finished with him, she started sleeping her way around his friends, doing more with each of them (if the rumours were to be believed) than she ever had with him.

After everyone had died he'd been terrified for a while (well, who wouldn't have been?) but his fear was short-lived. As the hours passed and his personal safety and apparent immunity to whatever had happened seemed more certain, his confidence soared. He put as much distance as possible between himself and his parents' safe and predictable upper-middle-class home and began to enjoy his new and

367

wholly unexpected freedom. He was king of the world. He could do what he wanted, when he wanted. After a couple of days the bodies had risen, but even that hadn't dampened the sudden euphoria he'd felt at having survived when absolutely everyone else had died. The zombie apocalypse was, as he'd always imagined it would be, incredibly fucking cool.

Skin was invincible. Without doing anything, he'd won.

A lover of pulp horror films (the bloodier the better) and comics, Skin revelled in the filth, disease and decay. As the bodies around him became more active, he actually became more self-assured because he knew he was better than them. As the potential dangers increased, so his excitement and adrenalin levels rose also. He looted shops, taking food, booze, cigarettes, magazines, music and whatever else he damn well wanted. And, in a long-considered and calculated gesture of defiance, he built a base for himself right in the middle of the school he'd just left. He spent days tearing the place apart, ripping the heart out of the place that had caused him and countless hundreds of other kids untold amounts of grief over the years. He'd pissed on the headteacher's corpse. He'd even squatted down and taken a shit in the middle of the classroom where he'd been humiliated and yelled at by his Nazi-like Maths teacher Mr Miller during his last term there. And where was Miller now, he asked himself? Dead, just like the rest of them. Sitting in Miller's classroom with his feet on his desk, swigging scotch, Skin laughed out loud at the irony of it all. And they'd said he'd never amount to anything…

The bodies began to get annoying. The damn things just wouldn't leave him alone. He convinced himself he was the focus of some bizarre kind of hero-worship from the dead, but he knew that wasn't really the case. The merest sight of him would cause a herd of the bloody things to come after him incessantly. And he noticed they'd started to become more violent too, scrapping with each other as they jostled for position. He guessed it wouldn't take much for them to start on him if he gave them half a chance. Skin made a conscious decision to keep out of sight and lie low for a while but, before disappearing from view, he went out looting again. He rode into town on his bike, following the bus route he remembered, heading for one particular shop. He and his friends had spent hours looking in the window on wasted Saturday afternoons, but they'd never made it inside. The shop sold hunting and fishing equipment. He didn't know what he wanted or what he needed, but he took as much from the shelves as he could carry: knives, pistols, rifles and anything else which looked vaguely useful and suitably dangerous. He packed it all onto the bike and rode back to school.

Skin was in charge now. He was unstoppable. He made the decisions and he made the rules, and after a while he decided that hiding away didn't suit a man in his position. He began to move through the bodies with contempt, only running when he absolutely had to. Already knowing he was vastly superior to the decomposing morons all around him, his guns and knives made him feel all-conquering. He carried weapons all the time. He hadn't had to use them yet, but he was ready.

Food became a problem. He'd had some supplies but they'd dwindled down to nothing. With a rucksack slung over his shoulders and a rifle in hand, he walked to the local shopping precinct, half a mile from school. He'd spent many afternoons hanging out there with friends when he should have been in lessons. Missing school hadn't done him any harm, had it?

He crept through the supermarket, collecting whatever food he could find that was still edible. Most stuff had gone off, and the place stank so bad that he almost threw up. He needed to rest and catch his breath before he made the trip back to school and he walked further into the building, eventually emerging from a back entrance. A metal staircase led up to a boarded-up, graffiti-covered flat above the shop. Skin climbed the stairs and forced his way inside. He rested for a while in a damp living room with a mouldy carpet and peeling wallpaper, passing the time with cigarettes and alcohol he'd taken from the store below.

A narrow veranda ran across the front of the flat. Skin stepped outside and looked out over the whole of the dead precinct below him. A large, roughly elliptical collection of run-down shops centred around an oval-shaped patch of muddy grass, it didn't look very different now to how it always had done. There were a few bodies still lying on the ground, but other than that the place looked as grey, lifeless and terminally dull as it always had. Even those bodies which continued to incessantly drag themselves around looked strangely familiar: as slow, vacant and pointless as they'd been before they died. Skin baulked at the idea of ever allowing himself to become like that.

Standing up there, in full view yet untouchable, he felt like some kind of ancient tribal chief looking down on his rotting subjects. Maybe this was his opportunity to show them just how powerful he was? He grabbed his rifle and rummaged around in his rucksack for ammunition. He loaded and took aim.

Can I do this? *Of course you can.*

Should I do it? *Why not, who's going to stop you? You're Skin: no one tells you what to do anymore.*

Does it matter? *Don't be fucking stupid. Of course it doesn't matter. Damn things are dead already.*

Skin lined up a single, bedraggled figure in his sights. He squeezed the trigger slightly and took up the slack. Then he cleared his throat and held his breath as he readied himself to fire. The end of the rifle seemed to be waving about uncontrollably. He wedged the butt deeper into his shoulder, shuffled his feet and re-balanced himself, then located the figure in his sights again. Then he pulled the trigger and fired. The gunshot cracked in his ear, rendering him temporarily deaf on one side, and the force of the shot almost threw him over. He dropped the rifle and rubbed the sore patch on his shoulder where the recoil had dug in. He shook his head clear, then looked out over the precinct. There wasn't much to see at first, primarily because the noise had caused all of the bodies to stagger towards the supermarket, but after a few seconds he managed to locate the one he'd been aiming at. He'd hit it. Christ, what a shot! Half the damn thing's head had been blown away. More importantly, the fucking thing had finally stopped moving.

Skin stood on the veranda and fired another thirty-two times, managing to down another nineteen bodies. He became more used to the noise and recoil of the rifle with each shot, learning how to ride the kick. He learnt how to load and reload fast. Most importantly, he learnt how to get rid of those fucking things below him.

Unchecked and unrestricted, Skin's confidence soared. No one was laughing at him now or trying to tell him what to do, were they? No one was on his back to do this or do that or be home by a certain time or not to wear certain clothes or not to speak in a certain way or not to drink or smoke… Christ, he felt like he could do anything.

He began by getting himself more comfortable. The school had two gymnasiums, housed in a single two-storey building. He moved from his previous classroom hideout and made his home in Gym B on the first floor. Using an old, battery-powered machine, he filled the vast room with music from when he first woke to when he finally fell asleep at night. Fully aware of the effect the noise had on the dead population outside but arrogantly indifferent, he drank and smoked his way through each day. His height above the crowds seemed somehow to camouflage the direction and source of the sound. Although it continued to attract many more bodies to the school, they wandered aimlessly around the campus rather than gravitating around his building.

Skin kicked a football around the gym. He threw empty beer bottles out of the window and watched them hit the bodies below. He spray-painted the bland grey-brick walls. Now and then he took potshots into the festering crowd with one of the guns. He slept, he ate, he got bored. The novelty of his situation began to wear dangerously thin. A person of sound mind and average intelligence might well have been able to rise above the boredom, or put up with it in view of the potential danger outside. Skin, however, although not stupid, was driven by a hormone, alcohol and drug-induced anger. The power he had now was incredible, and yet he wanted more. In spite of all this freedom, he still felt incomplete.

It was late one night when the way forward became clear. *Revenge.* That was what was missing. It was the ultimate expression of his superiority, wasn't it? Hell, why hadn't he thought of it before? Here he was in this incredible position of power, and he hadn't once used it properly. Sure, he'd fired a few shots and got rid of a pile of bodies, but he'd not yet taken out his anger on the people who deserved it most, had he? Christ, he had a string of people he needed to get even with. His parents topped the list, then his ex-girlfriend, then the so-called friends she'd slept with after she'd dumped him, then his teachers… *Fucking hell*, he thought, *what a fucking idiot.* All that time he'd been stuck here in the gym, and those fuckers had been wandering about free.

This was his time. He was in control. Time for retribution.

There would be little satisfaction in just finding these people and destroying what was left of them, he decided next morning as he walked back towards his parents' house through the dawn shadows. *What I need to do is make them suffer. I have to make things as unpleasant for them as they did for me. I have to hurt them.*

His mother and father were still in the kitchen of the house where he'd left them on the first morning. His mother still lay on the ground where she'd fallen, slumped between the now defrosted fridge-freezer and the dishwasher. Her soggy body stank. She was going nowhere, but a whack to the back of her head with a rolling pin removed any uncertainty. Skin's dead father, though, followed him around the kitchen, occasionally lashing out at him with sharp, twisted hands. Skin brushed aside his pathetic attacks and slipped a dog collar and lead from the dead family pet around his neck. He tied his father's hands together with washing line and half-led, half-dragged him the quarter-mile or so back to school. He threw the body into the empty ground floor gym below his den, and watched what was left of Dad scramble around aimlessly for a while. He spat and threw stones at it, then lit a cigarette and blew smoke into the damn thing's face before stubbing it out on his forehead. 'Bet you wish you hadn't been such an uptight fucker now, eh Dad?' he shouted as the corpse came at him again. 'Who's laughing now?'

Skin found Dawn in her bedroom at her mother's house. He slipped the lead around her neck, then tied her to the bed. Before leaving he spent some time going through her belongings. He wasn't sure whether that made him feel better or worse. In her underwear drawer he found the kind of things he'd hoped she'd wear for him, but which she'd obviously saved for his friends. To humiliate the dead bitch he stripped her bare before dragging her back through the streets and dumping her in the gym too.

He'd had a feeling that he'd already seen the bodies of Mr McKenzie, Mr Miller and Miss Charles wandering around the school, though it was getting harder to distinguish between individual corpses. It was while he was searching for them that he came across what was left of an ex-friend (and one of Dawn's recent conquests) Glenn

Tranter. Tranter's face was pretty badly eaten away, but he knew it was him. Although his skin was a blotchy blue-grey, he could still see the tip of a tattoo Glenn had recently had done on his neck, just below the loose collar of his blood-stained school shirt. Another one for the gym.

There was no sign of Mr Miller. Damn, if there was one fucker who deserved a little dismemberment and torture, it was him. It was of some consolation when he found what remained of Mr McKenzie, his dictatorial modern languages teacher, crawling along the corridor outside the main assembly hall. Stupid fucking thing was still wearing the same damn tweed jacket it had worn to school every bloody day for as long as he could remember. He took great pleasure in wrapping the dog collar around the dead teacher's neck and dragging the body twice round the school before throwing it into the gym.

Miss Charles, his twisted, sadistic, sour-faced ex-head of year, had been trapped in the stock cupboard next to her office when she'd died. Skin found her still crashing around the room, half-buried beneath text books and papers. He'd hated this bitch, and she'd hated him too. He tried to drag her to the gym by her long grey hair, but it wasn't strong enough. It kept coming away from her scalp in sickly clumps. Skin resorted to the dog lead again.

Over the course of the next day and a half he gathered together another fifteen bodies. Some of the rapidly putrefying corpses had been people who had wronged him in one way or another. Others were just poor unfortunates who just happened to have been in the wrong place at the right time, plucked from the obscurity of the faceless masses and flung into the gym.

So what do I do with them now?

He pondered the question as he lay on his makeshift bed at the far end of Gym B. Music blared out of the player which he'd now hung from a basketball hoop with skipping ropes. He thought it sounded better like that, although the volume was so loud that getting the right acoustic settings didn't really matter anymore. The room was filled with a haze of smoke. It helped disguise the increasingly noxious stench of death which filled his world.

Tomorrow I'll make those fuckers suffer, Skin decided as he drifted into a nauseous, drink-fuelled sleep. *One by one I'll take each of them apart.*

He didn't move until early afternoon. He woke with a hangover of epic proportions which, he decided, could only be eased by drinking more alcohol. Damn, he was getting low on booze. He'd need to go out and get more soon, but not today. He had more important things to do today.

After he'd taken a piss out of a first floor window onto the heads of the crowd below (and thrown up too – he was feeling particularly bad today) he ambled down to the ground floor gym and opened the door. The twenty bodies he'd shut in there immediately began to move towards him. He pushed his way through them with contempt, shoving them away whenever they came at him. Keen to spend a reasonable amount of time with each body and not be rushed, he built a corral in one corner of the gym with benches and various other pieces of apparatus. The bodies, although still very animated, were also clumsy and their coordination was desperately poor. It didn't take very much to keep them restrained behind vaulting horses, trampolines, crash mats, weight training equipment and anything else he could lay his hands on.

Who first?

He'd had a late start, and getting the gym ready had taken longer than expected. The sun was already beginning to set as he looked across the room at his motley collection of corpses. *Which one of these fuckers has caused me most pain? Which one hurt me most? Which one showed the most complete disregard for me and for everything I ever stood for or believed in or wanted?* It was a close call between two of them. It was either Dad or Dawn. Just because he preferred the idea of messing with Dawn's body (it made him feel slightly excited in an uneasy, perverted kind of way) he chose her. He grabbed hold of his ex-girlfriend's corpse and hauled it over the barrier.

'Okay, Dawn?' he asked, surprising himself with the sound of his own voice. Dawn's dead body lumbered towards him, twisted arms outstretched. For a moment he almost lost his nerve. What was he actually going to do? He hadn't thought this through. He squinted as she came at him, remembering her as she used to be. More specifically, he remembered what it was she'd done to him. Even more specifically, he remembered what it was she hadn't let him do to her. Bitch.

Christ, just look at the state of her, he thought as his dead ex-girlfriend slipped in a puddle of blood or vomit or something equally unpleasant. Over the course of the last twenty-four hours the floor of the gym had become covered with various noxious spillages, both from the corpses and from Skin himself. The corpse dropped to its knees in front of him and then managed to pick itself up again, clumsy feet skidding like a new-born animal. Dawn was an appalling sight but, knowing her strange tastes, he thought she might have approved of the look. Her eyes were hollow and sunken, her skin green-hued and ruptured in places. She had a deep cut on her right shoulder and, in the low light, Skin was sure he could see squirming movement in and around the wound. Was it just blood or decay glistening, or was it something more foul? Maggots, flies or larvae feeding off her dead flesh? Whatever it was, the thought of it was disgusting, too much even for the twisted mind of Skin to handle. The sight of her standing there, naked and practically falling to pieces as he watched her, was too intense. He pushed her back over the barrier and grabbed another body from the other side of the divide. Change of tactics. He'd have to build himself up to his headline acts.

Mr Read! Bloody hell, it was Mr Read, the head of music at the school. He'd almost forgotten that he'd found Read's body. He hadn't set out to get this particular teacher, but he was glad he had him. Now this bastard really deserved to suffer. He was the one who made kids sing on their own in front of the class and play endless bloody glockenspiel solos in his lessons.

Skin hadn't got on with Read, but he had no specific issues with him either, just a generic dislike. He felt sure he could deal with his body without giving it a moment's thought. Maybe the strength of his hate for Dawn, his dad and certain other ex-teachers made it harder for him to do their corpses justice? He just needed practice, that was all. Mr Read's body was the ideal candidate.

What could he do to him? He glanced around the gloomy gym and his eyes settled on a pile of weight-training equipment in the corner. As the body dragged itself after him, moving pathetically slowly, he took a short bar (the kind he'd seen used for single arm exercises) and stripped the weights off it. He was left with a bloody heavy, fourteen inch, chrome plated metal rod. He turned back around to face the body of the dead teacher and swung the bar at its head. He'd expected to feel the impact but he hardly felt anything. It seemed to cut through the flesh like a hot knife through butter, such was the level of the creature's decay. And Christ, look what he'd done! The damn thing's jaw had been ripped right off its bloody face!

Now feeling more confident and in control again, Skin circled the helpless corpse. He was moving at several times its miserable speed, and it had no idea where he was. It staggered around, desperately trying to find him, spinning circles, and he hacked at its legs. He hit the right knee cap, shattering it, and the body crumbled to the ground. This was too bloody easy! He smashed the bar down again, this time coming down hard on its pelvis, feeling bone splinter under the force of the metal.

Whatever tensions, frustrations and fears had been building up inside Skin were released by the therapeutic destruction of the school teacher's body. By the time he'd finished with Mr Read he had all but disappeared, spread around virtually the entire gym. This was really firing him up. It felt good, and he wanted more.

Dad was next.

Hungry, tired and cold, Jackson approached the school.

More bodies.

Something must be happening around here.

What's the attraction? Why this place? I need to rest and I need food. Think I'll take a look around.

Skin dragged his father's body through the creamy, barely recognisable remains of the music teacher. Using skipping ropes which he'd found alongside the weight training equipment, he lashed the corpse's thrashing arms and legs to a wooden climbing frame bolted to the gym wall. His knots weren't particularly good but Dad was weak and couldn't escape.

Just look at the state of you, he thought as he stared at what was left of his father. The thing squirmed on the wooden frame like it had been crucified. *You used to tell me you were somebody I should look up to, and now look at you. You used to tell me that I should aspire to be like you, to do the things you did and to believe in the things that you believed in. Now look at you. A pathetic lump of rotting meat that's about to be destroyed. Now you look at me. I took so much shit from you because of how I dressed, what I did and who I did it with. And why? What was so good about doing things your way? What made your values any better than mine? If you were so fucking clever, why aren't you the one who's stood here now? If I got it so wrong, how come I'm in control?*

Skin had edged closer and closer so that he was now just inches away from his dead father's face. He stared deep into the corpse's cold, black eyes and he hoped, bizarrely, to see a flicker of recognition or emotion. He wanted his father to know what was happening. He wanted him to see and feel everything he was about to do to him. He wanted him to understand and to be able to admit that Skin was right and he'd been wrong.

Nothing.

Stupid fucking thing.

In a fit of temper Skin picked up a metal-framed chair and swung it at his father's remains. Two of the chair's metal legs scraped across the rotting flesh covering the creature's abdomen and ripped it open, practically disembowelling it. Partially decomposed organs began to slip, slide and ooze from the open body cavity and dripped onto the floor under its thrashing feet.

Skin dropped to his knees and watched as what was left of his dad began to slowly fall apart.

It must be somewhere around here. This is where the bodies are heading. Was this a school or a college or something?

Jackson crept around the outskirts of the school campus. Something had definitely happened here. There were far too many bodies for it to just be coincidence. It couldn't have been looters because there'd be nothing worth taking here. Most likely survivors had been using it for shelter. Interesting. He'd only come across a handful of other people in all the time he'd been travelling. He'd found evidence of them having been around and he'd come across their remains when the bodies had got to them before he had, but he'd seen very few actually managing to survive. He'd done his best to keep out of their way. The more of you there are, he'd decided, the more noise you'll make and the more chance you'll have of being caught and killed. Stay alone and stay alive was rapidly becoming his motto.

A door nearby was open. Jackson went inside then stopped and listened carefully to the sounds echoing around the vast, stinking building. He heard the odd distant shuffle and crash of bodies but nothing too ominous. He decided to risk spending a little more time looking around.

Whenever Jackson found a staircase in a place like this, he climbed it. Stairs give you an advantage over the dead, he'd long since decided. The bodies had trouble climbing (although they'd manage it if you gave them long enough and if they had enough of an incentive). Also, the higher you go, the better view you had of whatever's going on around you.

What Jackson saw from the top of this particular staircase confused him. There was a grassy courtyard in the middle of the campus directly below, and it was filled with bodies. In the dark, however, he couldn't immediately see what was drawing them there. He'd come across huge gatherings before, some which had been caused by the most ridiculous of things: a squeaky hinge or rainwater dripping from a broken gutter, for example. Were these bodies trapped? He'd found large numbers of corpses which had managed to get themselves stuck, usually when there was only one way in and out, and those still coming in were preventing the rest from getting back out. He watched the crowd for a little while longer, trying to analyse their movements.

Then he saw it.

There were bodies trapped in a gym on the other side of the grass-covered quadrant. Perhaps the noise of them moving around in there was creating enough of a disturbance to keep the hundreds of surrounding corpses close. It was possible, but unlikely. Whatever the reason, he decided that was where he was going to make his attack. Just a very quick run in and out. Enough to cause a little damage and get a decent fire going. And once the building was properly alight he could concentrate on getting himself sorted out. He was starving. He hadn't eaten for more than a day. There'd be shops nearby. The fire would distract the bodies and when enough of them had come here he'd go scavenging through the shadows they'd left behind.

How to get close? The buildings surrounding the courtyard appeared to be connected. He decided he'd work his way around until he got as close as he could to the gym, then he'd cause a minor distraction and make a run for it. It wasn't going to be easy but he'd done it before. He took his rucksack off his back and scrabbled around inside for the various items he'd need. A small plastic bottle of paraffin and a cigarette lighter. Simple.

The best thing he'd found to use as a distraction was a well dried-out but still mobile body. If he could find one that had been trapped indoors for a decent length of time, that would be ideal. The bodies were always attracted to fire, and if he managed to set one of them alight, its movements would add to the confusion and dramatically increase the impact. Although the infection had originally struck before school had started for the day, he had no trouble finding a suitably emaciated cadaver. The young boy was scrambling around pathetically in the shadows of a second floor classroom. He grabbed the body by the scruff of its neck and carried it back down to ground level.

There's no room for sentimentality any longer, he thought as he held the body at arm's length and doused it with paraffin. Whatever this thing used to be, its character, personality and every other attribute which made it a unique and individual human being died with it on that Tuesday morning, more than four weeks ago. *This thing isn't someone's son, brother or friend anymore, it's just a skin-sack; dead flesh and bone. I'll be doing it a favour. Putting it out of its misery.*

Jackson checked that the door to the grass courtyard was open, then lit the body. He gave it a few seconds for the flames to really take hold before pushing it out into the night. Hordes of bodies immediately began moving towards him, attracted first by the sound of the opening door, then by the brilliant, dancing flames. He grabbed hold of one of the dead boy's arms and dragged it over to the diagonally opposite corner of the courtyard near the entrance to the gym building, then left it. Bizarrely oblivious to the fact it was on fire, it staggered into the mass of corpses which silently converged on it.

Jackson took a deep breath and moved again. He ran back to the door he'd just emerged from and waited, wanting to be sure the distraction had worked before he risked running further from safety and deeper into the bodies.

Perfect. It was working like a dream. The entire mass of diseased flesh was ignoring him and moving towards the bright flames about fifty metres away. Several bodies were burning now. Stupid bloody things. Relaxing slightly, he crept along the wall towards the entrance to the gym. He tried the door but it wouldn't open. Strange. He looked down at the handle and shook it. Bloody hell, it had been barred from the inside.

There wasn't much left of Dad.

Skin had punched and kicked and slashed and ripped and pulled and spat at the remains of his father until very little remained hanging from the wooden climbing frame. There was almost as much rotten flesh on him as there was left on the corpse. Dad's head, neck, shoulders, spine and right arm still hung from the wood, but that was all.

If the destruction of the teacher's body had been strangely therapeutic, then this was bliss. Using climbing ropes and feeling no remorse, Skin had flogged his father's corpse. Half-drunk, stoned and completely out of control, he tore into the body mercilessly. Nothing else mattered. Years of pent up adolescent frustrations were released in the space of a few brief minutes of revenge. He forgot about the other bodies in the gym, and he was so transfixed by the disintegration of his dead father that he didn't see the fires burning outside. Feeling invincible again, he returned his attention to Dawn. Once more he dragged her body over the barrier and out into the middle of the room. He grabbed her from behind (it felt good to do this in front of his father) and ran his hands over her flesh. Her skin felt alternately wet and curiously dry and brittle, but that didn't matter. He gently caressed her still feminine shape as he decided how he would dismember her. In a state of semi-arousal and drink- and drug-fuelled euphoria, he didn't hear the glass smash and the gym door being forced open.

'What the hell are you doing, you sick bastard?' Jackson shouted as he burst into the blood-soaked gym. He shone a torch at Skin who immediately let go of Dawn's body and pushed it away, ashamed.

Christ, Jackson thought, he'd seen some pretty unpleasant things over the last few weeks, but nothing like this… a stupid, fired-up teenager torturing and molesting the dead. He knew that he'd just done something pretty unpleasant to a dead school boy outside, but that had been different. There had been a reason for doing that, but what this kid was doing here was just sick… bordering on necrophilia. Twisted, evil and sick.

Skin stood in front of his crucified father, dumbstruck, feeling like he had the day Dad had caught him wanking in his bedroom. Behind him, the body still twitched. Its head rolled from side to side.

'I…' he began to say, 'I was just…'

Jackson shone his torch around the blood-soaked room, unable to quite believe what he'd found. He glanced back over his shoulder as the bodies from outside began to pour into the building through the door he'd left hanging open. He'd only intended being inside for a matter of seconds. 'What the hell have you been doing?' he demanded. 'Is there something wrong with you? I know what these things are and what they do, but this… this is wrong.'

Skin wasn't listening. How dare this man come into his world and start questioning his actions and decisions. Did he know who he was? Did he not realise how strong he was now? Did he know that upstairs he'd got guns and knives and that he'd killed massive numbers of corpses over the last few weeks? To Skin, Jackson represented everything he despised about the world before the apocalypse. He saw the authority he'd rebelled against and he saw the common-sense and rule-following that he detested. He couldn't let it go on. This man was a threat to his new found independence and freedom. He had to make a stand or it would have all been for nothing. He grabbed the metal bar he'd used to bludgeon the music teacher and ran at him.

'Don't be stupid,' Jackson yelled as the desperate, half-drunk teenager charged. Skin lifted the bar high, ready to strike. With twice his speed Jackson let rip with a single jab to his face, catching him square on the nose and sending him reeling back. He dropped the bar and it clattered loudly to the ground.

Jackson looked around anxiously. By breaking into the building he'd opened it up to the bodies outside and they were now streaming inside in huge numbers.

'Time to leave,' he suggested to Skin who still sat in a heap on the floor, blood pouring down his face. 'Unless you like this sort of thing, of course,' he added. 'Could have yourself a real party now, you sick little bastard.'

Skin couldn't move. Jackson reached out his hand to pull him up but he didn't take it. He couldn't speak. He felt crushed. He watched in silence as Jackson turned and shoulder-charged his way through the dead and back out into the night. There were still a couple of bodies burning nearby. That, coupled with the movement around the gym, was enough of a distraction to enable him to slip away into the darkness.

What about the kid?

Forget him. Stay alone and stay alive.

Skin slowly stood up and stared at what was left of his father. It stared back at him. He stood in the middle of the gym, drenched with blood, completely still and, for a time, ignored by the hundreds of bodies which were now inside.

The room was filling up quickly.

Skin was scared. He needed help. He looked around for Dawn but she'd gone, swallowed up by the faceless crowd. There must be someone who can help me, he thought? With tears of sadness and humiliation running down his face he walked deeper into the gym. He reached the barrier he'd built and looked over the mass of chairs and equipment. In the darkness he could see what remained of his friends and teachers. Over his shoulder an ever-growing mass of cadavers moved closer.

Skin climbed over the barrier and collided with the body of Miss Charles. He had to look twice before he was sure it was her. He began to talk to her. Wiping blood and tears from his face he tried to apologise for what he'd done and how he'd behaved. But Miss Charles wasn't listening. Along with the remaining seventeen bodies of his teachers and his friends, she tore him apart.

Jackson watched from a hillside overlooking the school as it burned. It was a dry night and the fire spread quickly. The whole bloody place was in flames now.

Good.

He lay on the grass for a while, watching as more bodies stumbled past him, heading towards the bright light in the distance, not even aware he was there. When enough of them have disappeared, he decided, I'll go and get myself something to eat.

DAY THIRTY-EIGHT

ANNIE NELSON

After I left the community centre, I came home. There didn't seem to be much any point doing anything else. I had nowhere else to go. That was just over three weeks ago, I think. I'm not exactly sure. It's getting harder to keep track of the days.

I never felt safe in that community centre. The people there used to talk about surviving, but none of them actually did anything about it. There were always people crying, arguing and fighting but no one did anything constructive. When I first got there I thought we might all bond together and make a go of things like we used to if there was a war or crisis, but we didn't. Most people were too scared to even try. You see, everyone had lost someone. Everyone had their own problems that needed sorting out before they tried to help anyone else. Most of them couldn't see the point of trying to pick up the pieces.

I spent most of my time there with my friend Jessie. She said she couldn't ever see things getting any better. I kept telling her they had to, and I said what was the point of thinking like that? No matter how bad things get, you always get yourself sorted out in the end, don't you? It might be a struggle, but you'll always manage it if you think positive and don't give up. I should know. Sometimes my life's felt like one long struggle, not that I'm complaining, of course. Poor old Jessie. She'd always had everything on a plate, and it never did her any good in the end. I lost her when those things got into the building. She tried to get away with the others, but she hadn't got any fight left in her. Don't suppose I'll ever find out what happened to her now. I gave her my address. I keep hoping she'll call…

There were a few people in that community centre who were like ticking bombs, just waiting to go off. It was only a matter of time before what happened, happened. I've never been so frightened as when the fighting started and the doors opened. It was all I could do to keep out of the way. I curled myself into a ball and lay under a table as the room filled up with those horrible, dirty, stinking things from outside. I know that they used to be people and that I should have shown them some respect, but honestly, they were disgusting. They made me feel sick to the stomach. We all have to go someday, but I hope and pray that I don't go like that. I just want to go to sleep one night and not wake up again.

I looked out for Jessie when the building started filling up but she must have already gone. Most people were trying to get out through the back and she was probably dragged out with them. I hope she's all right. I just kept my head low and waited for things to calm down again. I kept as still as I could and watched those horrible creatures as they walked around and around and around the room. My old bones were killing me but I knew I couldn't risk moving. I couldn't let them see me. It must have been the best part of a day before I finally saw a gap in the crowds. I stood up, as quiet as I could, and sneaked out the building. I did my best to stay out of sight but I never expected it to work. I'll never know how I managed to get past them. Maybe they just weren't bothered about an old girl like me?

It was good to get home.

I let myself in, and suddenly everything felt better. I wish I'd just stayed there from the start. It was just like I'd left it. The washing up was still in the bowl, and my clothes were still on the line in the yard.

I collected up all the food and drink I could find, then dragged the mattress out of the spare bedroom down to the cellar. That's where I've stayed since then. It's cold and dark down here but at least I'm home and at least I'm safe. I've got a torch and candles and matches for light and I've managed to find plenty to do to keep me occupied. I'll stay down here as long as I have to. I've got books to read and I can knit and sew if I want to. Shame there isn't any music. I miss the radio. I miss the voices. The radio used to keep me company but I know I have to stay quiet now. If I make too much noise they'll find out where I am. Sometimes I can hear them moving around up there. Sometimes I can even hear them in my house.

Such a shame about all those people in the community centre. Such a waste. You don't have to make a noise and fight and scream all the time to survive. Look at me. I'm doing perfectly well down here on my own, thank you very much. I've lived through wars, terrorist attacks, flu epidemics, water shortages and much, much worse. I've been mugged twice and I got over that, didn't I? The problem with most people is they don't have enough experience of life. I'm eighty-four, and I've seen just about all there is to see. Nothing shocks me anymore.

The trouble with most folk is they want their problems sorted out today, not tomorrow. They've had it too easy with their computers and the Internet and mobile phones and the like. They expect to just flick a switch and make all their troubles disappear, but that's not going to happen, is it? Not anymore. What's happened isn't going to get better overnight. It's going to take time. It's going to take patience. Be quiet and keep yourself to yourself and everything will be all right in the end.

It's very cold today. It's the middle of October by my reckoning. Not sure what the exact date is. Anyway, it doesn't matter. I'm sure I used to have a little oil heater somewhere. Maybe I'll nip upstairs and try and find it later if there aren't any of them about. It might be in the bedroom. I think that's where I last saw it. I need to do something though because it's going to get much colder yet. And the cold and damp won't do my cough any good. I hate it when I cough. When I cough I think they can hear me and work out where I am. I don't want them to know I'm down here.

I keep thinking someone's going to come for me eventually. They'll have to, won't they? They'll have a long list that tells them who lives where and they'll tick everyone off and realise I'm missing. Someone from the government or the army will come and help us sort this bloody mess out.

I hope it's soon. Don't fancy the idea of spending Christmas on my own down here.

I'm doing less and less every day, but I'm getting more and more tired. It don't make any sense. Everything's a real effort. I've got to go out and get some food soon but I can't face it. I keep putting it off.

Keep your chin up. That's what I keep saying to myself. You've done all right so far, Annie.

I'll get by. I'll survive.

ANGEL

It's been over a month now, and the situation shows no sign of improving. It's getting worse out there if anything. He expected that, really. Each day it's getting harder to do this, but he has no choice. If he could, he'd find somewhere safer and lock himself down, sit out the storm, but that's not going to happen. He has no option. For now, it's out of his hands. He has responsibilities.

He readies himself to face hell again. He'd already seen more than his fair share of trouble before the end of everything – the sick, the injured, the dying and the desperate – but never anything on this scale. He's doing all he can, but he's known since that first morning it was never going to be enough.

There's no sign the infection is contagious, and that's something of a comfort. It means he can think more about practicality than protection. He dresses himself like he used to when he went out running in the winter: lots of thin layers, breathable, keep the heat in and the cold out.

He swings the empty rucksack onto his back and stares into space, going over the route he's going to take in his head, making sure he remembers the twists and turns he needs to follow to get there. His route has been planned to avoid the areas where the dead still mass in large numbers, to take advantage of the short-cuts he's discovered over the last thirty-or-so days of scavenging. But even though he always does what he can to avoid them, he knows some contact will be inevitable. It always is. There's always some foul, rotting fucker that manages to get in the way somewhere along the line and, for that reason, he doesn't go anywhere without weapons. Quiet, efficient, deadly weapons. Several blades hang in their sheaths from his belt. He runs with a machete-like knife in each hand, taken from a butcher's shop early on. He's so used to carrying them, they've almost become extensions of himself. He doesn't have to think, he just cuts. He hates what he has become. This endless brutality goes against everything he's ever believed in, but he has no choice.

He's ready.

Time to do this.

He's on the ground floor of the building. It's surrounded as it always is, huge crowds, but there are more of them to the south and east today. The west exit is his best option. He psychs himself up then lets himself out and secures the door from the outside. He can see seven of them. Seven is good. He's had to get through many times that number before now. The longer he waits, the worse he knows his nerves are going to get. He starts running, and it begins again.

His footsteps pounding the road are loud enough to give him away. The first corpse comes at him hard. Despite the fear and the need for speed, he still instinctively tries to look beyond the decay to see who these people were before it happened. This one was a professional man in a business suit. His face is blackened by decay, ruptures and pustules around one eye swelling the skin until it's almost shut, dribbling yellow, pus-filled tears. When he lurches at him he anticipates the dead man's awkward movements and chops down at his neck, slicing through the cold flesh and doing enough damage to his spinal cord to stop him. He kicks the corpse away, yanks the blade free, then runs on.

This one looks older than it probably was. Another bloke, wearing some kind of overalls. He stabs it in the gut with his left-hand blade, hitting it with enough force to shove it back against the wall, then slides the other knife across its throat, virtually decapitating it. The cadaver slumps against him, its innards emptying out through the new holes he's made in its flesh. He shakes himself clean as he avoids the third corpse. Four, five, six and seven go down easy.

Checkpoint.

These short stops are important. They make him feel like he's still in control. He could run the entire distance in one go, but he thinks that'd be a risk. He needs to be careful. He needs to get this right. There's too much at stake to fuck this up. Breathing hard, he stands perfectly still and composes himself, doing what he can to blend into his surroundings, wishing he was back inside and that this was done.

He peers around the corner. *Shit.* Between here and the store, the next street is swarming. He didn't expect it to be like this. Something must have drawn them here. He now has three choices. He rules out the first option – taking the long way around, working his way from building to building. It'd be safer for him, but it'd take time he doesn't have. He's up against the clock as it is. He needs to get back. Option two is to just give up. That's never going to happen.

Okay, option three it is. Straight through the middle of the fucking lot of them. He's done it before, but it's hard. Makes him feel like he used to on the start line of races. Nervous anticipation. Adrenalin rush. He can't believe he used to be able to run for fun. Nothing's fun anymore. Nothing's done for pleasure. If it was he wouldn't be out here now, risking his neck again.

You're procrastinating, he yells at himself. *Just fucking do it.*

Blades gripped tight, he turns the corner and charges at them. He cuts them down at an astonishing rate, like he's harvesting a crop that's been left to go bad. He's not interested in 'killing' them (he still doesn't know how you're supposed to kill something that's already dead), just incapacitating them. He flashes the knives at limbs. He cuts below knees, into necks, across shoulder blades, hacking through muscle, gristle and tendons… anything to slow them down and stop them fighting. He's gradually becoming covered in the same foul brown soup as always – a mix of blood, bile, shit and decay. He tries not to think about it, though the stench makes it impossible not to. The road is littered with body parts now, covered in gore, and that just makes his mission so much harder. He has to divide his attention equally between his attackers, the carnage all around him, and his objective. And at the same time, he has to do everything he can to stop himself from panicking. It's hard not to scream out in horror or disgust. It's equally hard not to just stop and give up. It hurts. *It fucking hurts.* It all takes too much effort, but he knows he has to keep fighting because there are more important things at stake than him. *This isn't me*, he thinks as he shoves a blade between the eyes of a corpse of similar height and build to himself. *How long can I keep doing this?*

But he has to. He doesn't have any choice.

Checkpoint.

A staircase. They struggle with stairs. They're like Daleks in Dr Who. Remember them? Remember TV? They can fall down steps okay, but they can't easily get up. Can't control themselves well enough to climb. The sudden height advantage lets him stop for a second and catch his breath again. To focus.

He looks back down the street he's just run along, and he's impressed and appalled by what he's done in equal measure. It's a fucking bloodbath.

Okay. Nearly there. Last push.

He can see the building he's been aiming for. Back down to ground level, then straight across at the crossroads and he's pretty much there. Getting to it shouldn't be a problem, nor should getting inside. He's worried about what he'll find once he gets in there, but he's probably already had to deal with much worse. Some of the things he had to do during those first few days and weeks… to the bodies of the people he knew, and the girl he'd loved…

You can cry yourself to sleep again when you get back, he thinks. *Get this done first.*

The building he's heading for is tall and narrow. From memory, he wants the second floor, maybe the third. He hopes he can find what he needs there, he doesn't know what he'll do if he can't. He can see that the door is open slightly, but he hopes it's shut enough to have kept the bulk of the dead out. If he gets in there and finds the place full of corpses, he's going to have to look for somewhere else. He can't go back empty handed. He *won't* go back empty handed.

He runs down the steps, then sprints across the street, focused completely on reaching his objective. There are hardly any bodies here, save for a couple which immediately turn and walk towards him, desperately slow, but filled with unstoppable intent. He flashes his right-hand blade at the nearest of them, slicing open its gas-filled gut, but he keeps running, desperate to get inside as quickly as is humanly possible because he knows the more of them that see him now, the larger the welcoming committee he'll have to deal with when he emerges from the building later. In some ways that'd be worse – to get what he needs, then be unable to deliver it. That'd kill him.

Three more, but he runs past them so fast they haven't even realised he's there before he's gone. They look around uselessly, trying to track the sudden blur of movement with tired, empty eyes. And then he's at the door of the shop. It's wedged open by a dead woman's head, and in spite of all his training and all he's seen and done, the crushed skull and broken, bloodied nose makes him feel nauseous.

He screws up his face in disgust as he picks up the corpse and hurls it outside. The door swings slowly shut and he blocks it with a display rack as the first few bodies slam against the glass. Their noise is enough to attract more. He needs to get out of sight, fast. He goes deeper into the dark building and climbs the stairs.

Straight up to the second floor. It's deathly quiet in here, and the space is filled with shadows. The shelves make it difficult to see anything much. He checks the dust-covered signs. This is it. His heart sinks when he detects movement nearby. There's at least one of them up here with him, maybe more. He stands his ground and waits for it to come to him this time, tapping the tip of his blade on the frame of a metal trolley to make a little noise and make the creature move faster. It lumbers into the light and, once again, he's doing all he can now not to look at the person this thing used to be. Much shorter than him, overweight, long dark hair falling in greasy curls around its yellow jowls, it used to be a teenage girl. Its bulging eyes and black, gaping mouth give the impression of madness, though he knows it's incapable of anything other than the most rudimentary of controlling thoughts. Its tongue rolls sickeningly around its swollen lips, looking bizarrely like it's puckering up to kiss him. He used to get a lot of attention from girls this age. It was part of the job, he thinks. It was because he cared. Because he made them feel better.

The body of the horrific thing in front of him has ballooned with the juices and gases produced by decay. She's still wearing a dark blue store uniform polo shirt, but it's too tight now, and he can't see where her breasts end and her gut begins. She has a badge pinned to her top. It says 'My name's Joanne, how can I help you?', and he thinks *sorry, Joanne, there's nothing you can do. I think it's my turn to help you now...*

She comes at him with arms outstretched, a classic pose, he thinks, and he slices across the top of her head like a hard-boiled egg. She stops – looks hurt – then drops to her knees, dead eyes still fixed on him. She falls forward, face-plant, and the liquefying contents of her open skull spill out over his feet. He jumps back, straight into a wall of shelves, and the noise startles him. He holds completely still, listening to the rest of the building. Some movement on another floor, nothing else on level two.

He's clear. Time to get to work.

He slips the rucksack off his shoulder as he paces the floor, working through the department, looking for the right section. And when he reaches it, he fills the bag.

Made it back. Thank fuck for that. It'll be a while now before he needs to go out again. The relief is immense.

Still on the ground floor, he peels off his blood, gore and sweat-soaked clothes and disposes of most of them. The trainers and socks he can re-use. A couple of the undershirts should be okay after a quick rinse with rainwater. The rest he'll chuck away.

He dresses quickly, keen to get back upstairs. He's hungry, and he wants to see if she's okay. He puts on his other uniform, his old uniform, wishing it was cleaner, but knowing it'll have to do. It feels comfortable; as reassuring for him as it is for her. He picks up the rucksack and begins the slow climb up to the top floor.

More tired now than ever, soaked with sweat again, he stops off in the small kitchen and turns on the gas ring to heat dinner. Then he goes onto the ward. 'Hey, Jen, you okay?'

She looks up, and grins that toothy grin. 'You took your time.'

'Sorry about that. It was busy out there today,' he tells her.

'Did you get anything?'

'I got loads.'

He empties the rucksack onto the end of the bed. Jenny grabs at the books with eyes like saucers. 'Oh wow, I really wanted to read this one!'

'Well now you can.'

'Thank you!'

'My pleasure. You start reading, I'll get dinner sorted.'

He watches her, and all the effort of the last hour is rewarded. Jenny is eleven, but she won't make twelve. She's terminal, doesn't have long, and there's no medicine that can help her, save for some pain relief when things get really bad. The best thing he can do – the *only* thing – is keep her busy and keep her shielded from the hell outside until her time comes. He's the last nurse left in this hospital, and she's his final patient, and as long as she needs him, he'll stay on duty.

DAY ONE HUNDRED AND NINETEEN

UNDERGROUND

John Carlton is a twenty-four year old army mechanic who, for the last one hundred and nineteen days, has lived in a military bunker buried deep underground. Trapped down there with him are another one hundred and sixteen soldiers, less than half the base's original compliment. A pale shadow of the highly trained fighting force they used to be, these men and women are desperate and terrified. Backed into a corner with no hope of escape, their command structure has broken down. All order and control is gone. Supplies are running low. Time is running out.

For these people, the bunker has become a tomb. They have no means of escape or salvation, and each one of them is painfully aware just how precarious their situation now is. The alternatives are all equally hopeless: it won't be long before their lack of equipment and supplies renders the bunker uninhabitable, and yet they are unable to leave. The infected air outside will kill them seconds. Furthermore, the dead remains of the population on the surface have, over time, already gravitated towards the base, burying it under literally thousands of tonnes of rotting human flesh.

Inside the bunker, the situation continues to deteriorate day by day, almost by the hour. Law and order is non-existent and every man and woman has to fend for themselves. Rank and position are long-forgotten. Everyone is equal now: all at the bottom of the pile. Self-preservation is all that matters, and comrades are rapidly becoming enemies. The next breath of air that the person alongside you takes, or the mouthful of water they swallow means, ultimately, that there is now less for you.

Whatever decisions these men and women take, they know the end result will be the same. But worst of all, each of them now understands that death no longer carries with it any certainty. The end of their natural lives may just be the beginning of something far worse.

John Carlton is hiding in one of the most inaccessible parts of the bunker. His home for the last two weeks has been a narrow service tunnel. He has only a pistol, a few rounds of ammunition, some meagre supplies and his standard issue protective suit.

Sound is easily carried along the twisting maze of tunnels at the heart of the bunker. Though its precise source is unclear, Carlton knows that trouble is uncomfortably near. He suspects the sounds he's now hearing are almost certainly the beginning of the end. Somewhere in the underground base, intense fighting has broken out.

That's it, I guess. The supplies must have finally run out. It had to happen sooner or later. This base was only ever stocked for around seventy days, and we're way over that deadline. The fact we lost so many men and women in the battle meant that we've lasted a little longer, but I reckon our number's up.

The day of the battle was when I knew there was no hope for any of us. I'd suspected as much since we arrived down here, but until then I'd done my best to stay positive. It was the lack of information that unnerved me to begin with: no hard facts, no definite instructions. I mean, I'd heard stories about the casualties on the surface and what might have killed them, but while we were safe down here with the doors locked, none of it felt real. I half expected to finally go up top and find that nothing had changed, that we'd been part of some fucked-up psychological experiment, something like that. It wouldn't have been the first time.

The battle had already been raging for several hours when we were ordered to get suited up to fight. There was no tactical briefing, because there were no fucking tactics. We'd heard that the enemy numbered hundreds of thousands, and we were told to go out there and get rid of as many of them as we could. If it's not military, we were told, destroy it.

We'd made it as far as the airlock when the retreat began. I've never seen anything like it, and I pray to God I never do again. I only managed to get a faint glimpse outside before the doors were closed for good, but it was like hell on Earth out there. Our boys were trying to get back to base but it wasn't a controlled fall-back. Blokes were just running for their lives. And behind them... Christ, following them into the bunker were thousands of those fucking things. Huge swarms of these bloody monsters that looked like corpses. They were falling apart, barely able to keep going, but you could see that they knew what they were doing. I watched them ripping our people to shreds, trampling them underfoot and tearing at their suits. There was nothing we could do against their numbers. It was like an infinite army, and its soldiers couldn't be stopped because they were already dead.

The commander gave the order to lock-down the base and all we could do was watch as the chambers were sealed. It was fucking heart-breaking to see men and women that I'd stood alongside and fought with being left out there to die. They'd have kept on fighting for as long as possible, I know they would, but the bodies would have got all of them in the end. I heard there were so many of them that they couldn't get the main bunker doors closed. There was too much dead meat in the way to get them shut.

I went back up to the decontamination chambers about a week later with a handful of others to do some maintenance checks. We tried to look outside but it was dark and we couldn't see anything much. We thought the electrics were fucked, but they were still working. It was just that the hangar was full of rotting flesh. They were packed so tight against the doors that the damn things couldn't even move. There were so many of them they blocked out the light.

All that was sixty-five days ago now. Since then I've counted every frigging hour and watched every minute tick past. Hard to believe I've lasted this long. Truth be told, it feels like I've been here ten times longer.

10:17 am.

I just heard gunfire again. Part of me wants to go and find out what's happening, but I'm not going anywhere. Maybe when it quietens down again I'll try. I'm going to have to move sooner or later. I've run out of food.

1:35 pm.

More fighting. More gunshots and more yelling. Bloody hell, I wonder how many others are left alive now? I can still hear their screams in the distance. I keep thinking I recognise their voices but it's just my mind playing tricks again. Can't take much more of this. I'm going to try and get closer. See if I can find out what's happening.

Carlton crawled out of the low tunnel where he'd been hiding for what felt like forever, his joints stiff and aching. He tried to move quietly but, after being inactive for so long, his movements were clumsy and awkward. His protective suit further reduced his manoeuvrability. He kept it on because it gave him an extra layer of warmth and also because he was too scared to take it off. What if the base was contaminated? He had to take a chance and do without the breathing apparatus, though. It was too bulky and it slowed him down. He held his loaded pistol tightly in his hand.

The service tunnel opened out into a second tunnel which was slightly wider. That tunnel, in turn, eventually connected with an arterial corridor which led to the centre of the base. Carlton decided to see how far he could get.

The lighting around him was virtually non-existent – a dull yellow glow from intermittent emergency lamps, that was all – but it was enough. The darkness was helpful. Any brighter and it would have been difficult to remain hidden.

Carlton paused for a moment to get his bearings. The bunker was a large, sprawling construction which seemed to meander aimlessly underground in every direction. Long, empty tunnels connected storerooms, mess halls and dormitories which were a surprising distance apart. If he was where he thought he was, the next door on his left would be the entrance to the kitchens. He crept further along the corridor, pressed tight against the grubby wall, then stopped when he reached the door. It was half-open. He peered inside. No one there.

It was slightly brighter inside the kitchens, and the relative brightness made his eyes sting after days of dark. It was immediately obvious (and not at all surprising) that the whole area had long since been cleared out. The cupboards and storage areas – those he could see from where he was standing – had been stripped.

Carlton was about to leave the kitchen when something in the layer of rubbish under his feet caught his eye. He kicked a pile of plastic food trays out of the way and saw a hand, sticking up through the garbage as if asking for help. Working quickly, he uncovered the body of Lynn Price, the officer who'd been in charge of the kitchens. The poor bitch had a bread knife buried in her right kidney. A large pool of blood had spilled out over the kitchen floor. In places it was still tacky but most of it was dry. She'd been dead for some time.

Nerves threatened to get the better of Carlton. Did he continue to push further into the base, or should he turn around now and scuttle back to the relative safety of his dark tunnel hideout? Hiding was by far the easier option, but he knew it wouldn't have done him any good in the long run. If he didn't find food and water soon, he wouldn't last. He was already beginning to dehydrate. Christ, what he would have given for a glass of ice-cold water right now. The fact he was standing in the middle of a kitchen only made him feel worse. He pressed on.

The kitchen was connected to the main mess hall. Carlton climbed over a stainless steel worktop then through the wide serving hatch before taking a few tentative steps into the deserted hall. It was in just as bad a state as the kitchen. It looked like there'd been a riot here. Furniture had been upturned and he could see the bodies of at least four more ex-colleagues. He was about to check the vending machines in the corner (obviously empty, but still enticingly illuminated) when the sound of another hail of bullets stopped him in his tracks. That was close. Too close. A moment of cautious silence followed, then the sound of heavy footsteps thundering past the mess hall entrance. From his position he saw four figures rush past the door and carry on down the corridor. He waited for a moment, then looked to see where they'd gone.

'Carlton,' a voice hissed at him from out of nowhere. His heart skipped a beat. He spotted a frightened face hiding in another doorway opposite. Who was it? It was difficult to see but he didn't want to get any closer. Wait, was that Daniel Wright?

'Dan? Dan, is that you?'

The figure on the other side of the corridor checked in both directions then crossed over into the mess hall. Wright pushed Carlton further back into the shadows.

'Where the hell have you been?' he asked, his voice just a whisper. 'Haven't seen you in weeks.'

'Been hiding,' Carlton replied, giving little away.

'Sensible move. Best thing to do around here.'

'What about you?'

'I was with a few others. Got into a scrap and I took the chance to duck out and get away.'

'What's happening?'

'We're all waiting to die, didn't you know? Fucking place is falling apart. *People* are falling apart. Half those left down here are already dead, and most of them killed themselves.'

Carlton was silent. Nothing Wright said came as a surprise. 'So what are you doing now?'

'No bloody idea,' Wright admitted. 'Way I see it, there's not a lot any of us can do.'

The conversation was interrupted by the sounds of another fight breaking out deeper in the base. Wright peered out into the corridor again, then quickly pulled his head back inside.

'Anything?'

'Nothing. It's just a matter of time, though. Won't be long before this whole fucking place goes up in smoke.'

More noise. Getting closer now. Wright started to shuffle uncomfortably. 'Where you been hiding then, mate?' he asked. Carlton didn't immediately answer. He couldn't tell him. 'Come on, man,' Wright begged as the noise echoing along the corridor continued to increase in volume. 'Let me come with you. I won't do anything to get you found, I swear. I just want somewhere safe where I can—'

Soldiers appeared at the end of the corridor. More gunshots. A figure collapsed in a hail of bullets. More troops trampled the fallen body as they ran for shelter.

Carlton wanted to run back to the service tunnel, but he knew Wright would follow and he couldn't afford to let him. He had to lose him fast.

'Come on, mate,' Wright begged. 'Please…'

In a sudden flash of movement, Wright drew a knife and held it to Carlton's neck. All Carlton could think about was the suit. *Cut me, but don't cut the bloody suit.*

'I can't…' Carlton whimpered.

'Show me where you're hiding or I'll fucking kill you,' Wright said, his face against the other man's ear.

'I can't,' he said again, and before Wright realised what he was doing, Carlton shoved his pistol up into his gut and fired. Wright collapsed and Carlton stepped over him, wiping dribbles of blood from his precious suit and checking for tears.

He was about to go out into the corridor when another group of soldiers ran past the mess hall doorway, this time heading in the opposite direction to the first, moving deeper into the base again. More followed, then even more. One of the soldiers straggling at the back of the pack tried to grab hold of Carlton and drag him along with him but Carlton squirmed free. 'Get out of here,' the soldier in the corridor screamed at him. 'Get out of here now. They're opening the bloody doors!'

Not caring who saw him now, Carlton ran back through the mess hall, climbing back through the serving hatch and sprinting across the kitchen. He raced back to his hideout as quickly as his tired, under-exercised legs would carry him. He threw himself into the service tunnel, then scrabbled around in the darkness for his breathing apparatus. Hands trembling with nerves, he put on his kit then wedged himself into a gap between two large ducts. He melted back into the darkness and waited.

Five soldiers had fought their way into the decontamination chambers at the entrance to the bunker. Their priorities skewed after weeks of frightened isolation, two of them worked to get the sealed doors open while another three held off other troops who fought to prevent the integrity of the base being compromised. Perhaps the risk of infection had finally passed? The men now struggling to open the doors and get outside genuinely believed this was their last chance.

Whenever the soldiers covering those working on the door saw even the slightest glimpse of movement in the corridor leading to the decontamination chambers, they let fly a hail of bullets. Those trying to stop them didn't stand a chance, such was the position of the doorway being defended. Explosives and grenades were useless too. To use munitions of any strength at this close range would almost certainly cause irreparable damage to the chambers and compromise the base. A few desperate fighters continued to try and prevent the breach at all costs; mostly those who'd been unfortunate enough to have already seen the hell outside, those who'd already fought hand to hand with vast numbers of the unstoppable dead. They'd rather die now than face them again.

It seemed inevitable that the doors would eventually be opened again. It was just a matter of time.

Carlton lay on his back in the tunnel, shaking with fear. The world sounded different from behind the mask; muffled, distant and indistinct. It made him feel even more disconnected, even more scared.

He could hear people dying, their screams echoing through this maze of subterranean corridors and passageways. The noises seemed to surround Carlton, coming at him from every angle.

Then it all stopped.

The chaos was replaced by a sudden silence so unexpected and terrifying that it made Carlton lose control of his bladder. He lay on his back in a pool of his own piss and lifted a trembling hand up to his mask, ready to tear it off. *I should just do it, just get it over with...*

But he couldn't.

Sobbing with fear, he lay still and waited.

The silence had continued for almost two days. In his cramped confinement, Carlton listened intently to the stillness. He was weak with hunger and slept fitfully.

After endless hours of nothing, he finally heard something. Had he imagined it? He held his breath and listened carefully, the rapid thump of his own frightened heartbeat pounding in his ears and threatening to drown out every other sound. What was happening? He'd begun to presume that the all-consuming silence of the last forty or so hours had been a good thing. Surely if the base had been invaded by swarms of decaying bodies he would have seen or heard something by now?

There it was again – the bang and clatter of metal on metal. He had to do something now, he couldn't wait here any longer. Moving slowly, he slid back down the service corridor to the junction with the second, slightly wider passageway. Once there he crouched down on aching knees and listened again, keeping well out of sight. More noise. This time even further away, still unclear and indistinct, random, almost.

Carlton moved forward, then stopped when he reached the next corridor. He could see the kitchen door. The lights were lower than before, only the dull yellow back-up lighting still working. He retraced the steps he'd taken a few days earlier, tiptoeing through the wreckage, doing all he could not to make any unnecessary noise. He stepped over the officer's corpse he'd discovered last time he was here, then slid through the serving hatch and out into the mess hall.

More distant sounds. He primed his pistol, cringing at the uncomfortably loud noise it made, then walked to the end of the hall. He stopped when a figure appeared from a doorway over to his far left. Christ, who was that? The figure wore a soldier's uniform, but it moved painfully slowly, obviously badly injured.

Carlton held his breath, trying not to move for fear of giving away his position. Something was very wrong here. The soldier's head hung heavily over to one side and he seemed to be dragging his feet rather than taking steps. He was now no more than a couple of feet away. He staggered into the dull glow of an emergency light directly overhead, and Carlton recoiled at his nightmarish appearance. What the hell had happened to him? It was as if the life had been drained out of him: his skin was white, almost blanched, and thick, dried blood had dribbled from his mouth, down his chin and onto his uniform. His eyes were unfocused, staring ahead but not actually appearing to look at anything. To all intents and purposes this poor bastard looked dead. Carlton disappeared back into the shadows of the mess hall, and the soldier shuffled past him oblivious.

It had to be the infection. That was the only logical explanation. The integrity of the bunker had been compromised and the germ or whatever it was that had done all the damage outside had been let in. His mind began to work overtime. *If everyone else is infected*, he thought, *then I have to get out of here*. Christ, he'd seen for himself what the dead hordes were capable of when they'd forced the military back and entered the hangar almost seventy days ago. And now he found himself trapped on the wrong side of the bunker doors with, potentially, anything up to a hundred of these bloody things. He had to get out of here. He had to get out right now. He didn't know where he was going or how he was going to get there, but he had to try and make a run for it. He was going to die soon, that much was inevitable, but he wasn't about to let himself be torn apart at the dead hands of former friends and colleagues. As weak and tired and frightened as he was, he wasn't prepared to end his days like that. One last push...

Carlton stepped out into the corridor, the dead soldier still tripping away to his right.

To Carlton's left the passageway was clear. He limped further down the corridor, passing the door from which the body had emerged and eventually reaching a T-junction. Left or right? All the corridors in this damn place looked as grey and disappointingly featureless as the next. Carlton was disorientated and he couldn't clearly remember the way to the control room, but he knew if he could reach the control room he was sure he'd then be able to find the communications room. Once he'd made it there he'd be able to work his way back through the maze of tunnels to the decontamination chambers, and that had to be the area he aimed for. If he could reach one of the chambers then, providing there wasn't still a flood of rotting bodies trying to force their way inside, he'd have a chance, albeit a very slight one, of getting out of the base alive. What happened after that, though, was anyone's guess.

He turned left. Damn, wrong way. Just the door to a ransacked equipment store and a dead end. He retraced his steps, moving with a little more freedom now. All he had to do was... shit, another figure up ahead, and he had no option but to pass. He watched the shabby figure as it tripped towards him and he readied himself to defend against attack. He held up his pistol and aimed it into the other man's face. 'Stop,' he ordered. 'Stop there or I'll blow your fucking head off.'

But the dead soldier continued its lethargic advance, and all Carlton could do was shoot. He closed his eyes and squeezed the trigger and winced as the deafening sound of the gunshot echoed throughout the underground complex, taking forever to fade away. When he dared look again he saw that the soldier's corpse had crumbled to the ground in front of him, the top of its head missing. Crimson red dripped from the grey corridor walls. Carlton was so preoccupied with the bloody mess that he failed to notice another two figures approaching until they'd almost reached the corpse on the floor. Without stopping to consider his actions, he fired off two more shots at close range.

At the end of this corridor was the control room. More through luck than judgement, he'd found it.

Carlton weaved around empty desks and redundant computer equipment. Another body staggered towards him but, rather than waste precious time fighting, this time he simply stepped out of its way and the vacuous thing blundered past. It didn't even appear to have seen him.

Out of the control room now. Another left turn, straight down the corridor to the very end and then right. Jesus Christ, yet another one of them. He shot this one in the face – the passageway was too narrow to take any chances. He stepped over the corpse and pushed through the door into the communications room. And then he stopped. But it wasn't bodies stopping him this time, it was self-doubt. Another couple of hundred metres or so of corridor and he'd be outside the decontamination chambers. Did he really want to do this? Could he do it? More to the point, was there any alternative? Carlton realised his choices now were appallingly grim: stay underground with around a hundred undead soldiers for company, or try and get up to the surface and face the possibility of having to deal with many, many more bodies up top. The thought of getting out of the bunker was the deciding factor. Okay, so it might not be any better (it would probably be much worse) aboveground, but at least he'd be out in the open, if only for a few minutes. *Imagine not seeing the sky again*, he thought to himself. *Imagine dying in this place and never seeing the sun*. His decision was made.

Carlton paused for a second longer to catch his breath, then left the communications room through another exit and ran headlong into a crowd of seven more bodies, all of them struggling to get down a corridor which was only wide enough for two. Instinctively he began to kick and punch at them, either battering them to the ground or dragging them out of the way. They offered next to no resistance as he angrily beat a clear path through.

The corridor ahead was clear now, and he could see through to the doors into the decontamination chambers. Just a few metres further… but there were yet more bodies to get past first. In the doorway leading into the main chamber lay a pile of fallen corpses, blood-soaked and riddled with fresh bullet holes. Bloody hell, the creature at the very bottom of the gory heap was still moving! In the chamber itself more corpses staggered around aimlessly. Doing his best to ignore their disarmingly insistent, clumsy movements, Carlton focused on the open decontamination chamber doors, preparing himself for the expected onslaught of endless thousands of savage corpses, all baying angrily for his flesh.

But where he had expected to see such frantic activity, he instead saw nothing. No movement at all. Complete stillness. Unexpected calm.

In disbelief, convinced his tired eyes must be deceiving him, Carlton pushed away the last of the dumb bodies still moving around the chamber, and walked up to the final door which separated the interior of the bunker from the diseased world outside. He could see that the huge hangar doors were still open and much of the vast cavern was filled with harsh but beautiful sunlight. He looked out at an utterly unbelievable scene, then took a single, very hesitant, step out into the hangar.

The cavernous place was virtually unrecognisable, the air filled with the angry noise of millions of swarming flies and other insects. He carefully put his foot down on the ground, his boot sinking into a putrefied sea of human remains several inches deep. Bloody hell, the whole of the chamber was coated with a layer of stinking, rotten flesh. As he looked deeper into the sickening quagmire he was able to make out features – bones, the remains of clothing, abandoned weapons and armour. And some of it was moving! All around the apparently endless grey-green-red mire he could see occasional twitches of movement.

Overcome by the horror of what surrounded him, and almost forgetting the fact that he was now outside the inner sanctum of the bunker, Carlton moved slowly forward through the once-human sludge. He forced himself to look up rather than down as he dragged his tired feet along. It was easier to scrape the soles of his boots rather than take proper steps and risk losing his footing and sliding deeper into the gore.

Before long he had reached the bottom of the ramp which would lead him back up into the rest of the world. He didn't hesitate to start climbing. No matter what he found up there, it couldn't be any worse than the sickening pit of death he was already standing in, could it?

It was difficult to make any progress up the flesh-covered incline. His boots struggled for grip in the slime and filth. Eventually he dropped down onto his hands and knees and began to crawl, still angling his head upwards so that he didn't have to look at what he was crawling through. He kept moving steadily, trying to think about absolutely anything that might distract him from this slurry of rotting human remains. Whilst generally slippery and creamy and almost liquefied in places, the gruesome mixture was full of brittle bones and pieces of abandoned military equipment. *Don't rip the suit*, he desperately told himself, *for Christ's sake, don't rip the suit*.

He finally reached the top of the ramp. Before standing up he closed his eyes and remembered the lush green countryside which had surrounded the base. It had been the last thing he'd seen before they'd disappeared underground four months ago. Since then he'd been haunted by a lost vision of the blue sky, bright sun and endless rolling hills. He'd thought he'd never get to see it again.

Carlton carefully got up and walked outside. Then he slowly lifted his head and looked.

The sky was just as deep and blue and perfect as he remembered, but everything else... Christ, what had happened to the world? For as far as he could see in every direction the ground had been scarred by battle. Mud replaced grass, there were huge craters and dips where munitions had exploded, trees had been scorched and burned down to blackened stumps. And as for the bodies... God, the bodies... Carlton was completely still, transfixed by the horror all around him. Everywhere he looked he saw more and more of the dead. The withered skeletons of his former colleagues, still wrapped in what remained of their now useless protective suits, lay alongside the others, their corpses frequently entangled, entwined forever with those they'd died fighting. And even here there was still some movement. Subtle and indistinct, but occasionally some of the bodies were still moving: too decayed to get up, twitching where they'd fallen. Bloody hell, hadn't these things suffered enough?

Disconsolate, Carlton finally began to slowly walk away from the underground base.

It was a cold, dry and bright winter morning. The precise time, day, date and season didn't matter anymore, because Carlton knew this day would be his last. Or if not today then it would be tomorrow or, at the very latest, the day after that. He couldn't imagine lasting any longer. If he was honest, he didn't want to.

Months back, when the fighting began, he'd completely failed to appreciate the scale of the battle which raged on the surface. As time progressed he'd heard plenty of rumours and reports, but no one had accurately conveyed the full enormity of what had happened. This endless devastation was hard to comprehend. It seemed to go on forever. He'd walked for hours and yet he was still surrounded by craters, abandoned military machinery and bodies. Endless hordes of putrefying bodies... flickers of movement...

He guessed that he must have covered several miles by the time he reached the outermost edge of the battlefield. It had clouded over and the light had faded but he could see that the number of bodies and the scarring of the land had definitely reduced. A short distance further and the world around him began to appear deceptively normal and familiar. He saw lush green grass, undamaged trees, and even birds flitting about above him. For a few seconds he allowed himself a faint glimmer of hope. Might there yet be an escape from this nightmare? But then, as the first few drops of icy winter rain trickled down his visor, he was reminded of the need for his protective suit. He remembered the germ in the air which had caused all of the devastation, and all illusions of salvation and normality were immediately shattered.

Carlton stumbled through several more fields before reaching a narrow road which twisted through the countryside. For a while he walked along it, instinctively keeping close to the hedge at the side of the road should anything be coming the other way. The longer he walked, however, the louder the silence around him became. He quickly accepted there would be no car, van, bike or any other vehicle along this road today. Today – for one day only – he was completely alone in the world.

Further down the track, Carlton finally came across a car. It was a small saloon. He stopped and stared at it for a moment. There was nothing special about it, and perhaps that was its strange attraction. It looked so ordinary. In the bizarre world he was moving through, however, what he considered usual was now most certainly not. The car appeared completely at odds with its surroundings. Carlton looked further and saw that it had been parked on a patch of gravel next to a gap in the hedgerow. It was a drive. Curious, he took a few steps away from the road and saw that he was in front of a house. It took him a while to be able to properly distinguish the outline of the building. Once typical and ordinary, today the house looked subtly different. Its garden was unkempt and overgrown, and he imagined this was the first sign of the building being swallowed up by the countryside, reclaimed. Its windows were opaque with cobwebs and dust. Carlton stood and stared for a while longer before moving on.

Another house, then another and then another. Soon he found himself in the middle of an empty village. It was perfectly still – like a freeze-frame – and uncomfortably eerie. Several buildings on one side of the village had been destroyed by fire and were now little more than charred black outlines of their former selves. The rest of the silent shops and houses looked dirty and neglected like the first house he'd seen. He stopped in the middle of the road and thought about calling out, but what good would it do? What if he found someone? For a moment his heart leapt, because there had to be survivors, didn't there? But then reality hit home. What could they do for him? More to the point, what would they expect him to do for them?

Carlton continued to walk until he could go no further. He followed the road as it trailed back out of the village and dragged himself along it as it wound up and around the side of a hill. The earlier rain had passed and the world was now drenched with bright winter sunlight again. The sun was well on its way down towards the horizon, a huge incandescent orange disc now. The lone soldier watched its descent with fascination and a fond sadness, knowing he probably wouldn't be here to see it rise again tomorrow.

At the top of the hill, the exhausted man clambered over a wooden stile, then sat down at the top edge of a steep field. There were a few sheep at the bottom of the field, and from where he sat he could see cows and horses in the distance. His eyes were tired and his vision was beginning to blur but he scanned the horizon constantly. It occurred to him that from up here he couldn't see a single trace of man. It would be there if he looked hard enough, but he didn't want to. Buildings, roads and everything else seemed to have been absorbed back into the land. Carlton felt an overwhelming sense of alienation and isolation, like he no longer belonged here, but at the same time he was glad he'd been given this final opportunity to see the world once more.

It was getting dark. One last thing to do.

Carlton unclipped his pistol from its holster on his belt and checked it was loaded. He'd planned this. He'd spent all afternoon thinking about it. He wanted to remain in control to the very end, to deny the infection one last victim and at the same time ensure his death was as final as it should always have been.

Nervous, shaking with cold, he pulled off his face mask and slipped the end of the pistol into his mouth. He pressed it against the roof of his mouth, gagging as he shoved the oily metal to the back of his throat, then paused.

Should it have happened by now?

He sucked in cool, clean air through his nose, too afraid to take the gun out of his mouth just in case the infection caught him before he was able to fire. He'd heard his former colleagues in the bunker talking about a germ which struck and killed in seconds, so why hadn't it got him? He'd heard about people spitting blood as they were asphyxiated, so why couldn't he feel anything? Was it over already, or was the air here clear? He couldn't believe that – the last soldiers in the base had been infected just a couple of days earlier.

But the seconds continued to tick by…

The only explanation, he finally decided after several minutes had passed, *is that I must be immune.* He almost laughed, choking on his pistol. All that time! All those unbearably long and painful days, weeks and months spent down there underground and I could have walked out at any time!

Another minute had passed. Still no reaction.

Carlton took the pistol out of his mouth, shook his head and laughed out loud. A perfect end to the day, he thought as he grinned and lay back on the grass. The air was sweet. It tasted good.

Just a few more minutes, he thought.

Carlton looked up into the sky, the first few stars starting to appear, and he thought about his family and friends and all he had lost. He thought about the nightmare of being buried underground and how he'd had to battle through the reanimated bodies of his dead colleagues to get outside. He thought about Daniel Wright, the soldier he'd killed in cold blood just a few days earlier, and the others he'd subsequently fought. He thought about the fact that right now, he might well be the only man left alive.

Carlton thought about the aching in his bones. He thought about his appalling physical condition, the dehydration and malnourishment. He thought about how much effort it would take now to find food and clean water, and how much of a struggle it would be to try and make himself well. The village he'd walked through earlier would be the most sensible place to start. He thought about all those empty, dead buildings and the distance he'd have to cover to get back there. He thought about the cold and the oncoming winter and how hard it would be to survive. He thought about the effort everything would take now and whether any of it would be worth it. He thought about being alone, about doing all of this by himself. No one to talk to when things got tough. No one to share the highs and many lows with. No one to hold him at the end of each day and tell him he'd done good, and that they loved him and they were proud of him.

Carlton enjoyed the next hour. He lay on the grass and dozed and daydreamed until the light had all but disappeared and the clear sky above him was full of stars. *Millions of stars*, he thought, *just one man*.

Calm, composed and completely sure, he slipped the pistol back into his mouth and fired.

JOE AND ME

When I look around the school yard at the other kids' parents, I can't help wondering if their lives could be more different to ours. I see the same faces here day after day, all of them so absorbed in their individual problems and routines, never stopping to think about anything outside of their own little worlds. Sometimes I picture Joe in his class, talking with his friends about what jobs their parents do. One's dad might be a cop, another a bus driver. Sally's mom is a lawyer, and Kyle's dad owns a store. I imagine the teacher going around the room, asking each kid in turn. And then it gets to Joe, and the class falls silent. *My dad stays at home*, he tells them, *but my mom's a brilliant scientist. She's going to save the world.* The teacher tells him to stop telling lies while the rest of the class piss themselves laughing.

Thing is, it's true. Gillian Huxtable – my wife, Joe's mom – is doing exactly that.

Joe appears in the doorway, almost the last one out as usual. He scans the yard then catches my eye and runs over, weaving through the mass of other kids trying to get away from school. He might only be seven, but my little man looks so grown up. He digs deep into his rucksack and finds a carton of juice, then throws the bag at me and races off after one of his friends.

He's waiting for me when I get down to the gate. He always is.

'You okay, Joe? Had a good day?'

'Pretty good,' he says, breathing hard from the run.

'What did you do?'

'Just stuff,' he answers, shrugging his shoulders, and I know that's all I'm going to get. Doesn't matter. He's happy. I know he'd tell me if anything was wrong. We talk a lot, Joe and me.

We stop at the store to pick up some food. I let him choose what we're having for dinner, then grab something else for Gill and me when he's not looking. Neither of us are big on processed chicken bites.

Joe disappears as soon as we get to the apartment. He does this every day after class. He calls it his 'me time', though Christ knows where he picked that phrase up from. I don't mind. Gives me chance to cook before Gill gets back. She said she'd be home just after five.

I delay dinner because Gill's usually late but, when it gets to half six, Joe and I eat. He's hungry. It's not fair to make him wait any longer.

'Where's Mom?' he asks.

'Gone to the circus.'

'Really?'

'No, just kidding. She's still at work.'

He shoves more chicken into his mouth. 'That's okay though, isn't it,' he says, mouth too full, 'she's doing important stuff.'

'She certainly is.'

'And no one else can do it, can they?'

'Not as far as I know. Your mom's a clever lady. One of the cleverest people I've met. Far cleverer than me.'

'But you're clever too, right?'

'Suppose. I passed all my exams. Mom took more exams than me though.'

'So you got beaten by a girl?'

'Not beaten. It's not a competition. And anyway, it's not *a* girl, it's *the* girl. Your mom is truly gifted.'

'And she's going to save the world?'

'That's what she keeps telling me, and if that's what she says, then that's what she'll do.'

'Will we see more of her when she's done?'

'I expect so.'

It's gone nine by the time Gill gets home. Joe tried to stay awake to see her, but he's spark out. She carefully opens the door and creeps into the apartment like a kid back late from a party they weren't supposed to go to. And the first thing she sees is me sitting there like a parent about to hit the roof. For a second she looks concerned.

'Sorry, Simon,' she says, kicking off her shoes and draping her coat over the back of a chair.

'It's all right,' I tell her, and I mean it. She's under a huge amount of pressure right now. As long as she's okay I don't care what time she comes home. There's a weight of expectation on her shoulders and I can barely imagine how it must feel. 'You hungry?'

'Starving.'

I get up and stretch, feeling guilty because I fell asleep in front of the TV just now. I warm her dinner in the microwave, pour her a glass of wine, then take it all through. She's waiting at the table, her head in her hands.

'Thank you. You had a good day?' she asks, yawning.

'Fine.'

'Joe okay?'

'Yeah, he's okay. He tried to stay up but didn't make it.'

'I didn't know I was going to be this late.'

'You say that most nights.'

She smiles with resignation, and reaches across and squeezes my hand. 'I know. I'm sorry.'

'Tough day?'

'You could say that. I can't seem to get it through to those dumb fuckers that if they want results, I need to be left to get on with the work. Interrupting me every couple of days for progress reviews and demanding endless reports won't help anyone, you know?'

'I know, but this is the military we're dealing with don't forget.'

'I don't know which are worse, the morons in Defence or the politicians. I hate them all the same.'

'You're getting there though, right?'

She nods her head and drinks more wine. 'I think so. They want everything delivered yesterday. They don't seem to understand how long something like this takes. I can't work any faster, and I'm not working more hours.'

'There aren't any hours left to work.'

'You know what I mean, Si. It would help if I wasn't surrounded by grunts all the time. If they thought more about the process and less about the end result we'd probably have fewer arguments and we'd get there much quicker.'

'You think they're getting annoyed because you're moonlighting?'

'I'm not moonlighting. You have to stop saying that.'

'Okay, but you are using their funding and resources to develop something that's not for the military.'

'It's a double-edged sword. Same overall process, two very differ-ent applications.'

'Try explaining that to your grunts.'

'I have, believe me.'

'I can see why they might get pissed off, though. All that cash they've thrown your way, and you have the audacity to actually want to *help* people, not kill them?'

I stop talking when she puts down her fork and glares at me. 'Are you deliberately trying to wind me up?'

'Yes. Is it working?'

'Beautifully.'

'Good. I love it when you're angry. Have I ever told you how sexy I think you look in your lab coat? I wish you'd order me about the same way you do poor old Alfie.'

'Don't even get me started on Alfie. He drives me to distraction. He's a stereotypical science nerd, you know? Great ability, fantastic qualifications, but no common sense. I don't know how he functions in the real world. Do you know what he did today?'

'No, and I don't want to. Finish your dinner, drink too much wine, then come to bed with me.'

It's hard to sleep when you haven't done a lot all day. I used to feel incredibly guilty, but I'm slowly getting used to it. It's just the way it has to be for now.

It's late and I can't sleep. I look across at Gill lying next to me. She was out the second her head hit the pillow. Things won't always be this way, but I know it's how it has to be for now. *You're a kept man*, she teases me daily. *Make the most of it. Enjoy it while it lasts.*

Joe loves coming to the lab. Gill was gone by the time he woke up this morning. When she called at lunchtime and told me it was going to be another late night, I decided to pick up the kid from school and bring him straight over here so we can all spend a little time together. *If the mountain won't come to Mohammad, etcetera etcetera.*

The lab always reminds me of something out of a David Cronen-berg movie. This downtown area is ripe for investment and redevel-opment, and it looks like something's finally happening. There's a lot of construction traffic and signage around that wasn't here last week. It's about time.

The building itself looks like little more than a dilapidated shell from the outside, appearing almost on the verge of dereliction, and I guess that was half the appeal. You'd never suspect that anything with the potential to be world-changing could happen in a shit-hole like this. If you asked anyone where the major scientific developments were being made in this city, they'd all point you in the direction of the gleaming glass and metal spires at the high end of town. They couldn't be more wrong. Those places are filled with bankers and other people who think they're important but aren't. *This* is where the real advances are being made.

We park the car and I walk Joe down the dingy back-alley to the building entrance, gripping his hand tight just in case. With tall blocks on either side, it's dark here even in daylight.

The lobby of the building smells of piss, stale-beer, and other things I don't even want to think about. The lift's temperamental and Joe never feels safe in the rattling metal cage so we take the stairs to the top floor. He runs on ahead, leaving me behind, carrying the pizza. I can hear his footsteps thumping on the steps and occasionally I see a flicker of movement or a glimpse of his shadow so I know he's okay. There's no one else here. Three of the four floors are empty, and on the top floor there are PIN codes and biometric codes and good old-fashioned traditional locks and bolts preventing unauthorised access. Gill can't afford to take any risks. This entire place can be locked down quicker than you can say 'lock it down'.

He's waiting for me on the gloomy landing, leaning against the door, waiting for me to enter my PIN. We go through, the four, high-pitched bleeps and the clunk of the locking mechanism announcing our arrival. And here's where things change. Beyond this corridor and the next strengthened door is another world. The lab cost a small fortune to design and install, and no expense was spared. In effect it's a hermetically-sealed shell which was dropped into the top floor of the existing building. Within it are office, living and meeting spaces, and two further, even more rigorously sealed inner units. Gill and Alfie sometimes have to handle seriously dangerous shit in there. They can't take any chances.

A second PIN and a retina scan and we're almost inside. Light floods through the inch thick safety glass, spilling into the corridor.

'I saw your number,' Joe says.

'You shouldn't have been looking. Don't tell Mom.'

He laughs. 'Can you fix it so it takes pictures of my eye?' he asks as I lean into the camera.

'You're too short,' I tell him. 'You're only just tall enough to reach the handle. You need to grow first.'

He punches me and I push him through the door. Gill spots him straight away. 'Hey you!' she shouts, and he runs over. He jumps up and wraps his arms around her. I check the doors are locked behind me then go through, passing Alfie who's working at a desk strewn with papers.

'Evening, Simon,' he says, glancing up from his computer screen for the briefest of moments.

'You okay, Alfie?'

'I'm fine,' he replies with his typical, Vulcan-like lack of emotion. And that's it. Conversation over.

'You okay to take a break?' I ask Gill. She's already sitting on the sofa with Joe in the rest area. I take the pizza over and Joe dives in. 'How are things? Had a better day?'

'Much better,' she answers. 'No generals or bureaucrats to deal with today.'

'Generals?' Joe says, puzzled. 'Generals are soldiers, aren't they?'

Gill looks over at me before answering. 'That's right, honey.'

'Why soldiers?'

'There are lots of people interested in what we're doing here.'

'I know that, but why soldiers?'

Sometimes Joe acts older than his years. Most kids would just accept there are soldiers involved somewhere along the line and leave it at that. Not our boy. He needs more.

'There are some nasty people in the world, you know that, don't you?' Gill says.

'Of course I do. What's that got to do with it?'

'Can you remember what I've told you before about what we're doing here?'

'Not really. A little…'

'Okay, so you know when you get sick and you go to the doctor, what happens?'

'Time off school?'

'That's not what Mom means,' I interrupt, and Joe flashes me a quick grin.

'Medicine,' he says.

'Exactly,' says Gill. 'Right now, if you need medicine, the doctor can give you a pill or a capsule, maybe even a jab.'

'I don't like needles.'

'I know you don't. Neither does your dad,' she continues, winking at me. Joe gorges on his pizza as Gill explains. 'You know how you sometimes hear about diseases going crazy? It happens in other countries usually. Pandemics. Have you heard that word?'

'Don't think so.'

'You remember last year when half your class was off with a cold at the same time?' I ask him.

'I remember.'

'Well a pandemic is like that but much, much worse. Lots of people getting really sick at the same time.'

'Sometimes the reason that happens is because we can't get enough medicine to enough people,' Gill says, 'either because it's too expensive or too dangerous. So what we're doing here is trying to find a way of giving those people their medicine and making them better without having to give them pills or shots. Does that make sense?'

'I think so, but how else can you give it to them?'

'In the air,' she explains. 'That's what we're trying to do. Just pump it into the sky so it can make everyone better at once.'

He chews on his pizza and nods thoughtfully.

'Your mom's pretty smart, isn't she?' Alfie says, finally coming over and helping himself to a slice.

Joe nods. 'I still don't get why there were soldiers here though.'

Gill looks across at me again. How much do we tell him? How much does he need to know?

'The world can be a rough place at times, son,' I say. 'People fall out and start fighting.'

'Don't patronise me, Dad. I know about wars.'

'Never mind that, when did you find out what patronise means?'

Gill takes over. 'So our soldiers try not to start these fights, but they have to do what they can to look after people like us, don't they?'

He thinks about what she's said. 'So they want what you're making so they can spread bad medicine, is that it? To sort out all the bad people who start all the fights?'

'That's one option,' Alfie says with his usual lack of tact. Gill jumps in quick.

'Sometimes bad people try to use diseases to make innocent people sick. They're terrorists, Joe. You've heard that word before, right? What we're doing is making something that'll stop those germs from working. Kind of like a shield. It'll stop the bad stuff getting through. Understand?'

'Think so.'

'Sure?'

'Yep. I need to pee.'

With that he jumps up and disappears into just about the only other room he can get into here without a PIN code or military-level clearance.

'You think he's okay with all of that?' I ask Gill.

'Joe's a smart kid. He can tell when someone's avoiding answering his questions. Best to tell him straight.'

'He'll probably talk at school.'

'I'll get him to sign a non-disclosure form.'

'I'm serious.'

'So what if he does? To be honest, Si, I bet he already has. Thing is, no one will believe him. He could give them the address of this place and it wouldn't matter. Anyone coming here would take one look and think he was making it all up.' She looks up as Joe comes running back over and reaches for another slice of pizza. 'Did you wash your hands?'

'Yep,' he says, though he probably hasn't. Gill pulls him close and holds him tight.

'Enough about my boring work, what have you been up to today sunshine?'

I drop Joe off at school first thing then run a few mundane errands, trying to avoid going back home because I know there's equally mundane stuff waiting there that I don't want to do. I missed a call from Gill while I was filling up the car. I'm in the neighbourhood, so I drive over to the lab to see her. There's a car I don't recognise parked in the alleyway next to Gill's and Alfie's. Unusual plates. Dark windows. Sinister looking.

'Who the hell's this?' some stuffed suit demands when I get upstairs and let myself into the lobby area of the lab.

'This is my husband, Simon,' Gill tells him. She looks flustered and angry.

'And he has full access to your research and facilities?' the suit continues, talking about me as if I'm not here.

'No, though he does have some limited access,' she tries to explain. 'Simon sometimes helps out with processing and data entry, and occasionally transcribes my notes. It's all authorised. He has the right clearance levels and he's been background checked.'

'Does the General know about this?'

'I haven't made a point of telling him, but he appreciates we need some level of administrative support. Look, Simon and I have a son. Simon looks after him so I can work full-time. I'm here all hours so it just wouldn't be feasible not to allow—'

'I'm not happy about this.'

I'm conscious that I'm standing in the middle of this discussion like a spare prick at a wedding. I offer the guy my hand, but he doesn't react.

'This is Mr Jenkins,' Gill says, 'one of General Nicholls' team. He was just leaving.'

That explains it. I'm starting to think I shouldn't have come here. Maybe that was why Gill called, to tell me to stay away? I should have checked first.

'I'll get out of the way.'

Even from the living space on the other side of the lab I can still hear everything. Jenkins' voice is naturally loud, and Gill is clearly exasperated. I try to talk to Alfie but he stays focused on his work, not wanting to get involved.

'This is just symptomatic of the kind of issues we're having with your approach here.'

'But does it matter? If you're getting results then—'

'We're not getting results though, are we?'

'We're just a few months away from finishing this now, Jenkins. Years of progress and it's just a matter of weeks before we can give you everything you've—'

'Save your breath, Dr Huxtable, we've been through this before. You know our position now. We'll talk again tomorrow when you've had time to consider the options.'

And with that he's gone. Gill walks him down to his car. I watch from the window as he disappears, then wait for her to return. She seems to take forever coming back up to the top floor.

'What was all that about?' I ask.

'They're shutting us down,' she says, in tears. 'They're pulling our funding. We're so close, Simon, but it's not good enough for them. They think they have enough experience and data to take the project on in-house.'

'So what are you going to do?'

She slumps down into the nearest chair. 'How much did you hear?'

'Not much.'

'They've given me an ultimatum. I can walk away from all of this, or I can go and work for the General on his terms. Not much of a choice, really.'

'You didn't answer my question. Those are the options they've given you, but what are you going to do? What do you *want* to do?'

'I can't go and work for the military, Si, I just can't. The second I sell out and jump in bed with them exclusively is the second the rest of my research dies. The vaccination applications, the humanitarian aspects of what we're doing here… all that will be forgotten. Oh, sure, they'll tell me otherwise to keep me sweet, but we both know it'll happen. I can't turn my back on what we've been doing here, Simon, you know I can't.'

'You knew this would happen eventually though.'

'But we were so close…'

'So what happens next?'

She sighs and looks up at the ceiling. 'I've only been able to keep working because the military were bankrolling us. Without their cash I'm screwed. I mean, they'll give me a pay off and as long as they've got the research Jenkins says they'll negotiate on these premises, let me stay a while longer…'

'So do that. How much longer do you need?'

'How long's a piece of string?'

'Well are we talking weeks, months or years?'

'Six months maybe. A year at the outside.'

'And can we do it? Can we afford it with what they're giving you?'

'No way. I've got maybe a third of what I need.'

'What if I went back to work? Then there's the equity in the apartment…'

'It's a possibility.'

I think carefully before I ask my next question. I'm not sure how she'll take it. 'And are you completely sure you can't work with them? I mean, you've been working on your stuff without them knowing since you started here. Couldn't you just carry on?'

She shakes her head. 'Not that simple. The General has made it very clear that I'd be part of a team under his direct command. I get the impression I'd have to account for every second of my time. I just know I wouldn't be able to work on anything but the military applications of the project.'

'You're sure about that?'

Gill doesn't answer. She gets up and starts pacing the room, tears flooding down her face now. I move towards her but she pushes me away, not wanting to be touched.

'Why can't they see?' she sobs. 'My work has the potential to save thousands of lives, millions even, but they're not interested. Profit and politics comes first. They're too busy starting wars to realise how pointless what they're doing really is.'

'You'll never change them. It's a mind-set. It's why the fuckers with all the guns keep telling us they work for the Department of *Defence*. Bastards.'

'I can't do it, Si,' she says, finally relenting and reaching out for me. I hold her tight, her body rocking in my arms as she sobs. 'I can't turn my back on my research. I couldn't live with myself if I don't see it through.'

'Then don't. Tell them to stick their job and keep working here. We'll find a way.'

Considering the economic environment, finding work was pretty easy. So far it's mostly been cleaning, bar work, or flipping burgers alongside people half my age, but they all pay and I've been able to juggle them around Joe. Selling the apartment has given us a temporary financial cushion, but it also seems to have increased the pressure on Gill. It's been a struggle since we moved into the cramped living quarters in the lab. More than that, she knows that once the money from the apartment has gone, that's it. We've nothing else to fall back on.

At least Joe gets to see more of his mom now. Shame the three of us don't get to spend as much family time together as we'd like. The novelty's definitely worn off, and Joe gets left alone in front of the TV more than either of us would like, but I keep telling myself that this is only temporary. It's been almost three months now. It'll all be worth it when Gill gets to present her research.

She had to let Alfie go. Truth be told, that was probably a good thing and it was partly my suggestion. This place is our home now, and it didn't feel appropriate having him around so much. To be honest, I think he was glad to leave. We made it easy for him, and he hinted he had something else lined up. It means I've been having to take up some of the slack, of course. I feel like a glorified secretary a lot of the time, typing up Gill's notes, documenting her findings.

Things are different when I look around the school yard now. Now I feel like the rest of the parents: tired and irritable, struggling to make ends meet. Of course if the teacher went around the class and asked, Joe would still tell them all his mom's busy saving the world. I don't know how much of what's going on he's picked up. He's a bright kid, though. He knows we're stressing, and he also knows sleeping on a camp-bed next to your parents on the floor of a science lab isn't how most kids his age spend their time.

'Hey Dad!' he shouts as he runs over, pushing his way through the crowds.

'Hey you!'

I grab his hand and take his bag.

'Where are we going?' he asks.

'Home.'

'You mean the lab?'

'Yep.'

'Can we go somewhere else?'

'Like where?'

'The park? Please, Dad.'

'Believe me, Joe, there's nothing I'd rather do. Sorry, though, not tonight.'

'Why not?'

'Because I've got work.'

'Again?'

'Again.'

'You're always at work.'

'At least it means you get to spend time with your mom.'

'I'd rather spend time with you.'

'Don't say that. Do you have any idea how much Mom loves you?'

'Nope. She's always working.'

We stop walking and I crouch down so I'm at Joe's eye-level. 'Don't talk like that, sunshine. Mom and I love you more than anything else in the world.'

'I know *you* do.'

'Mom does too.'

'She doesn't show it. I hate it when you're not there, Dad. It's like I don't matter anymore. She's always tired and cross. When I ask her to do stuff with me she just gets mad and shouts, then she gets upset when I get upset. I don't like it.'

'I'll talk to her.' We stay staring at each other for a few seconds longer. 'What do you want for dinner, champ?'

He shrugs his shoulders. 'Burger, maybe?'

'Burger it is.' I grab his hand and cross the road to get to the nearest place. Giving my son a treat is the very least I can do. I'm going to spend most of the evening flipping burgers for other people. Why shouldn't Joe get one too?

It's late when I get back, but Gill's still working. I was hoping she'd have stopped and spent the time with Joe, but I know she hasn't. She barely looks up when I say hello. I strip and shower, then make us both some coffee. 'Thanks,' she mumbles, barely lifting her eyes from the computer screen.

'We need to talk,' I tell her.

'What about?'

'About Joe. About us.'

I've been dreading this all night. At least now she's listening. She takes off her glasses and rubs her eyes. 'I knew this was coming.'

'Doesn't that make it worse?'

She's still distracted by the numbers on the screen. I switch the monitor off and she slumps back.

'Gill, stop. Listen.'

'I'm listening.'

'I was talking to Joe before work. He's struggling.'

'I'm struggling too…'

'You're thirty-two, he's eight. Did you talk to him tonight?'

'Didn't see much of him.'

'Is that because he wasn't in here, or because you were too busy to look?'

'Both… Shit, I don't know. What am I supposed to do, Si? I can't stop working. We don't know how long we've got left before the money runs out, and if I stop now it'll all have been for nothing. I can't give up on this… you know what's at stake.'

'I know, I know. Believe me, Gill, I know exactly where you're coming from.'

'So what are you asking me to do? Make a choice?'

'No… yes… Christ, I'm not sure. Something's got to change, that's all I know. Joe's our responsibility. He should be our priority.'

'It's not that simple.'

There's an awkward silence. I sense she wants to get back to work but it's late. Too late.

'Come to bed, Gill.'

She reluctantly gets up and I hold her. At first she just stands there, then slowly she melts. 'I'm sorry,' she whispers.

'Don't be. It's not your fault. It's an impossible situation. We all know how important what you're doing is.'

'I'm stuck between a rock and a hard place. Damned if I don't, damned if I do.'

'It's not as bad as you're making it sound.'

'Isn't it? From where I'm standing it looks that way. From here my ultimate choice looks simple. I have to choose between my son and everyone else. You're asking me to make an impossible decision.'

Some days it's hard fitting everything in, other days it's a breeze. Thankfully, today is one of those days. I dropped Joe at school first thing, then worked the cleaning job through until early afternoon. That's me done for the day now. I've got a night off, and I'm going to convince Gill to take a break too.

I have to slam on the brakes and give way when a car races out of the mouth of the alleyway alongside the lab. Was that Alfie? He's gone too fast for me to see, but I ask Gill as soon as I get up to the top floor.

'Yes, it was Alfie.'

'What did he want?'

'To confess his sins.'

'What?'

'The little bastard jumped straight into bed with the General and Jenkins, didn't he.'

'You thought he might.'

'I'd hoped he wouldn't.'

Something's not right here. Something's seriously wrong. Gill's seething.

'So what's happened?'

She sweeps her arm across the desk in rage, sending papers flying, then kicks her chair across the lab. She thumps the wall, and manages to trigger the containment protocol in her fit of temper. She panics when she realises what she's done, but she's too angry to think straight. Warning lights flash and the alarm starts to sound. The secure doors slide shut and bolt themselves and air hisses, sealing off one of the inner labs. She shuts it all off quickly enough, thumping her PIN into the override keypad, then leaning against the panel so the system can scan her retina. She leans against the wall as everything slowly resets, breathing hard.

'Talk to me, Gill.'

She's still too angry to talk. Then, finally, she speaks. 'Alfie came to tell me he'd walked out in protest. The fucking idiots have launched.'

'Launched? Launched what?'

'What do you think? The military have triggered the ADP.'

'ADP?'

'Airborne Defence Program. That's what they're calling it now.'

'And does it really matter? They beat you to it, so what? You can just keep working on your research and—'

'But they can't have fully tested it. They haven't had time. Alfie's no fool, he tried to warn them, but they still went ahead and did it.'

'It's early days though. Can't you just—'

'It's self-replicating, Simon. They've engineered a variant that's self-replicating. Jesus, in a couple of days it'll have spread every-where. It'll be all over the fucking planet.'

'And will it work?'

'Probably. Alfie seems confident.'

'But you knew they'd do this eventually.'

'You're missing the point. Everybody will be breathing their stuff in. It means all my work is wasted now. None of it's worth a damn anymore.'

'I don't understand. How can that be?'

'Don't you see? Christ, Simon, think about it. The stuff they've pumped into the air is based on pretty much the exact same princi-ples as my airborne vaccinations. By the time I'm ready to go pub-lic, the ADP will have such a hold it'll neutralise the vaccines before they've even had chance to start working. I'm fucked. They have total control over the air we breathe. All of this was for nothing.'

This stuff was Gillian's life's work, but it wasn't her life and I needed her to see that. We'd both lost sight of what matters and had let ev-erything get out of balance. In a strange way, I thought the loss of her research might help us get things back on track. I convinced her to take some time away from it all, that maybe things weren't as bad as they looked. Whether she genuinely agreed with what I was saying or just wanted to shut me up, she left the lab and came with me to get Joe from school. Once I'd got her away I said we should make a night of it. She instinctively found a hundred reasons why she shouldn't, but I wasn't listening. It'll all look different once you've taken a step back, I told her.

The expression on Joe's face when he pushed his way out through the school door was priceless. I couldn't remember the last time we'd picked him up after class together. Come to think of it, apart from sleeping, I struggled to think of anything much we'd done together as a family for months.

We've been out for a couple of hours now, and Gill seems a little more relaxed. We walk home together through the park, taking the long route back to the lab. Joe runs on ahead, kicking through the first fallen leaves of early autumn.

'Money's not an issue. Seriously. I know it's been tight, but once the lab's been broken up, we'll be back on an even keel again.'

'Who said anything about breaking up the lab?' she says.

'Sorry, I just assumed.'

'Assumed what? That I'd roll over? That I'd just give up on all that work without a fight?'

'No, that you'd be ready to move on. That you'd come back to your family. We need you, Gill.'

She stops walking and I stop too. Joe looks back, a huge smile on his face. Her shoulders slump.

'Okay. You're probably right. I have a few loose ends to tie up first.'

'Cool.'

'Do you remember Grant Jefferson?'

'Think so.' I don't, but I tell her I do to keep the conversation moving.

'I spoke to him last week. He said there's a teaching position at the university if I want it.'

'Sounds good.'

We walk again, taking a pathway which branches right and runs between two football pitches. There's a junior match in progress on one of the pitches. We walk behind a row of parents all screaming encouragement at their kids. Joe stops to watch.

'You like to play football one day?' I ask him.

'Sure,' he says before running off again.

'This could be us,' I say to Gill. 'This *should* be us. We should be enjoying our time together. Enjoying our son. He's taken second place for too long.'

'I know, but you have to believe me, it's not because I didn't want to be with him. I love him more than I can tell you, it's just that…'

'Just what?'

'Just the responsibility. You know, I thought I was doing something that would make a real difference. Christ, how naïve was I?'

'Not naïve, just honest. Genuine.'

She takes my hand – first time she's done that in ages. 'It really hurts though, Simon, and I don't think you can understand how much. I had such an incredible opportunity, a chance in a lifetime to make things better, and it's all gone so horribly wrong. All I've done is help create something that's put everyone at risk, you, me and Joe included. We're probably breathing it in right now. Our son's lungs are probably full of the manufactured shit that I helped create.'

'Some things are bigger than us though, Gill. Hate to say it, but it's true. Since they first heard about what you were doing it's been you on your own against the whole damn government. What hope did you really have? You're a person with feelings and emotions… a wife, a mother, a daughter. Them? They're just power-hungry, emotionless bastards. It's time to forget about the rest of the world and focus on us. Focus on Joe and me.'

'You're right,' she says, wiping a tear from her eye, thinking I haven't noticed. 'We're just little cogs in an overcomplicated machine that's going nowhere. I was stupid to think any different.'

'So you'll take a break from all of this?'

'I'll take a break. Like I said, just give me a few days to tidy up the loose ends.'

Gill picked up through the course of the evening. Her mood steadily lifted, and she once again became the woman I fell in love with and married, not the high-profile, world-changing scientist she thought she had to be. It was good to have her back.

Joe settled quickly once we got home. Once he was asleep Gill and I drank wine and fucked on the floor of the lab, exploring each other's bodies with a ferocious excitement I'd started to think we'd lost forever.

On Sunday Joe got sick. Just a twenty-four hour stomach bug which had been working its way through his class, nothing more serious. He asked his mom if she could use some of her 'air medicine' to make him feel better, then spent most of the day either throwing up or sitting on the toilet. We've kept him home today, just to let him get it out of his system. He's keeping Gill company as she starts packing stuff away. It's just another day at the office for me: the cleaning job first, then on to the burger bar around noon. Days like this will be few and far between soon. Once things are back on track I'll be able to cut down. We'll find ourselves a new place and settle down again.

I spoke to Gill on my way between jobs to check how Joe was doing. She sounded genuinely happy. I think a major part of it is relief now she's severed her ties with the military. She was even talking positively about her research again. She says she thinks she might still be able to adapt the vaccination dispersal technology. To be honest, I don't care. As long as she's okay, that's all that matters.

The burger job turned into a double-shift when one of the stupid kids who works there called in sick. It's late now, and dark. I can see the lights of the lab even from a distance. The other buildings in the neighbourhood are in darkness, and the top floor of our building stands out against the gloom of everything else. We definitely need to get away from here. I pass the construction site and wonder how long it'll be before they come knocking at our door to pull the place down. That'll force Gill's hand if nothing else.

I park the car and jog to the door. The dark plays tricks on me here and makes me feel nervous. I'm thankful for the layers of security which keep the lab isolated from everywhere else. I check no one's watching, then slip inside.

I'm getting paranoid. I've been thinking all kinds of stupid thoughts all afternoon. It's only now she's stepped away from them that I've realised what a risk Gill was taking by continuing her humanitarian research while she was working for the military. They could make things really unpleasant for her – for *us*. It wouldn't take much to seriously piss off the wrong people and make enemies of those she reluctantly accepted as friends. All they'd need to do is dig up something one of us did in our student days, one of the many rallies we went on, the marches against capitalism and corporate greed… A few words to the people in the know, maybe a cash bung to someone who used to be close, and before you know it Gill's a terrorist: a threat to national security, no longer the future Nobel winner I still believe she is. She's been walking a fine line. I want her away from all of this.

The heavy door swings open then shuts behind me, blocking out the last of the traffic and city noise. In its place is the familiar quiet of this old building; the creaks and groans, the low machine hum coming from the top floor.

It would be quicker to walk but I'm tired and I call the lift. I wait for it to work its way down to ground level, then get inside and slide the metal lattice door across. It judders into life again and I lean back, thinking of bed. It's been a long day. Hopefully tomorrow will be quieter.

I step out onto the landing, then stop. It's dark. Darker than it should be. The corridor is quiet. I enter my PIN, scan my eye and let myself in, then stand in the small lobby area. There are fewer lights on in the lab than usual. Is something wrong with Joe? That seems a far more likely explanation than Gill having switched everything off to get an early night. I can hear the TV.

'Gill? Joe? Where are you?'

I head straight for the cramped living area we've claimed as a home, flicking on more lights as I go. The TV's on, but neither Gill or Joe are there. I go further into the lab, and as I approach the main area, it immediately becomes clear what's happened. One of the inner labs has sealed itself off. Shit. Gill must have tripped it. It's always been over-sensitive. Damn, I bet that's exactly what's happened: the containment protocol has triggered and they're both stuck inside. I go to the small window and look in but I can't see either of them. I rap my knuckles on the glass but it's too thick and they can't hear me. Stay calm. I can deal with this.

I sit down at the control desk, trying to remember the log-on details Gill gave me for when I helped her document her work. I shake the mouse and tap the space bar and the terminal immediately comes to life. Gill's still logged in. There are windows open all over the screen. I can't make sense of most of them.

Between this computer and the next is the mic I've seen Gill and Alfie use to talk to each other when one of them is working in the inner lab. I drag it over, press the button on the base, then cough, not wanting to startle Gill or Joe. Then I speak, and I can hear my muffled voice inside the lab. 'Gill? Gill, are you in there?'

No answer. I try again. Still nothing.

Don't panic. I can sort this out. We've talked about this happening before. She's shown me where to find the emergency instructions and troubleshooting guides. I tell myself over and over that it's probably just a system fault… just a malfunction.

There are CCTV cameras controlled by another computer. I fluff my password twice, then manage to get in on my third attempt. The dark screen flickers into life. The display is split into quarters – different CCTV images of what's happening inside both of the inner labs. I scan each of the pictures, and in the lowest corner of the bottom right image I see her. Oh, Christ, it's Gill. She's sprawled across the floor, and she's not moving. I get up and run over to the glass again and strain to see more. I can see one of her feet sticking out at an awkward angle to the rest of her body. What the hell happened here? Some kind of accident? I hammer on the glass but I know it won't do any good.

My hands are shaking with nerves as I sit back down at the keyboard and try to sort out this mess and get into that lab to help my wife. I find the camera controls and manage to zoom in on her face. The black and white images are pixelated, hard to make out… is that blood? I click the intercom button again. 'Gill! Answer me, Gill!'

The static hiss of an empty channel. No reply. Then finally something.

'Daddy?'

Joe's voice sounds huge through the loudspeakers. I cycle through the CCTV images again, desperately looking for him. 'Where are you, sunshine? Come to the window.'

Then I see him. He's been hiding in the corner behind a cabinet, and he only becomes visible when he starts to move. He stands up slowly, then runs across the room, giving his mom as wide a berth as possible and knocking over a tray of instruments which fill everywhere with ugly, distorted noise. I look up as he slams against the glass, face ashen white with terror, standing on tiptoes so he can see over the sill. I carry the mic over to the window. Joe's hammering against it now, tears rolling down his cheeks.

'What happened, Joe?'

His amplified voice fills the room. 'All the doors locked on us, Daddy. I couldn't get out.'

'What about Mommy? What happened to Mom? Did she have an accident? Can you try and get her to talk to me?'

His whole body judders as he sobs. He gives his mom a sideways glance but he can't bring himself to look straight at her.

'She's not moving, Dad. The doors all shut and she couldn't get them open again. She got angry and shouted at me. She was on the computer, trying to make something happen, then...'

'What, Joe? What happened?'

'She started coughing. It got really bad, real quick, Dad. I didn't know what to do. She started bleeding. She threw up blood on the floor, Daddy.'

My mouth's dry. Can't think what to say. She's dead. I know already that I've lost her. I have to get in there. Have to get Joe out. Have to get help.

'Daddy, can you get me out? Please, Daddy...'

'I'm going to go and find out how. Give me a minute.'

I press my hand against the glass, as close as I can get to his, then go back to the desk. I start scanning the screens and menus, looking for the release to get him out of the inner lab. There's nothing obvious. No instructions. Jesus, there must be something. I remember Gill used to use a PIN, then a retina scan...

Wait.

It hits me like a hammer-blow.

Why did the lab go into lockdown? Shit, what went wrong in there?

Joe's crying over the loudspeaker, and the noise makes it impossible to think straight. He's still straining to look over the bottom of the window.

'Wait a sec, sunshine,' I say, trying to keep myself together and not let him pick up on my nerves. 'I'll have you out of there in no time.'

I nudge the sound down to concentrate. Have to try and focus. I go back to the terminal Gill's logged onto so I can access her notes and recordings, the way I did when I used to transcribe them for her.

I compare the files and times on one screen with the camera feeds on another, then reverse the recordings. For a few seconds I'm frozen, watching my wife come back to life as the footage runs backwards in double-time. I spool back to just before she gets ill, then go back a little further still. I can only bear to watch a few seconds before I have to switch it off. I can hear her choking. She grabs her throat. She's trying to speak, but her noise is drowned out by Joe's terrified screams.

'Almost there, Joe,' I tell him, glancing up at his saucer-like eyes, staring at me in abject terror. 'Won't be long, okay?'

Rewind again. Watch again. What was she doing? She was supposed to be disassembling the lab, but she looks like she was still working on stuff.

I've gone back several hours on the cameras now. Gill's sitting at a workstation in the inner lab. Joe's lying on the floor next to her, reading a book. Everything looks normal. And then I find her corresponding log entries, and I play the file. Her voice fills the room.

4:03pm.

My analysis of the ADP is complete. As usual, the military science division have fucked it up. This is one of the reasons I couldn't work with them. They've tried to run before they could walk, and they've overlooked a couple of major flaws. Makes me glad I got rid of Alfie. He should have spotted this.

I can't leave this project as it is. I can't leave the entire world breathing in this military-grade shite day after day. I can't have it on my conscience.

I left myself a way out, and it's time to use it. There's a way to alter the structure of the ADP at base level. If it still works, it'll neutralize itself – see itself as a threat, almost. The self-replication traits the military strapped on means that a chain-reaction should then take place. In effect, if I've got this right, the ADP will eliminate itself and we'll be back to square one. It's a safeguard I had in place from the very beginning.

My god, is that what happened? That would explain it... she did what she thought she had to do to eradicate the program, only for it to react. She used to talk about it as if it was intelligent sometimes. She said it could adapt, that it would target hostile germs.

441

Another loud sob from Joe focuses me again. I fast-forward the CCTV, watching Gill move around the lab at double-speed. She dashes around the place, stepping over Joe who lies stationary on the floor under her feet. Then he gets up and he's sick everywhere. I thought he would have got rid of that bug by now. Gill stops what she's doing to clean him up, and for a moment all I want to do is watch the two of them together. A mom and her son. Not a scientist. A mother. She sits him on a chair across the room and fetches a bowl.

Fast forward.

They're laughing again. Both of them look calm and relaxed.

Fast forward.

5:25pm.

Perfect. I took an air sample contaminated with ADP and added my re-engineered variant. The results have been exactly as I'd expected, gradual ADP decay. After fifteen minutes the sample showed hardly any trace of ADP remaining. Kiss this, General Nicholls. Wish I could see the old bastard's face when they tell him his new 'peacekeeper' has disappeared.

Gill leaves the lab then returns a short while later with a cup of coffee.

Fast forward.

Stop.

A sudden change. Gill's up again. Checking screens. Moving frantically from terminal to terminal in the lab. I pause the film and check her log-in again, desperately scrolling through the entries to match with the time on the CCTV footage. Got it.

6:13pm.

Something's not right. Something's very wrong here. The two strains of the ADP appear to both be reacting to something, but I don't know what. There's a third element in here. They're combining… mutating…

Christ, it's Joe. It's his sickness bug.

The voice recording ends. Back to the CCTV. Gill bundles Joe up in her arms but, before she can get him out of the room, the lab locks itself down. The camera shakes with the force of the doors double-locking themselves. On the screen, Gill drops Joe then clutches at her throat.

'Daddy, get me out,' Joe says, his amplified voice echoing around me. I can't take my eyes from the screen. Gill's on the floor now, thrashing helplessly, unable to breathe.

Then she stops.

'Daddy,' Joe screams again, the desperation in his voice clear. His cries force me into action.

'I'll get you out,' I tell him, wiping tears from my eyes, then pressing my hand against the glass, covering his. I try the door overrides, but they won't respond. The status manager says there's been a breach... that the lab can't be re-opened until it's been decontaminated. I don't know how to reset the system. I'll have to break in. 'I'm going to get some tools, Joe. I won't be long. I'll get you out, son, I promise.'

I take the lift down to the basement, the sound of his sobbing still echoing in my ears. I run over to the construction site, desperately looking for anything I can use to smash my way into the lab. There's a van parked out of the way as if someone was trying to hide it. I break a window and manage to scramble into the back, its triggered alarm deafening me. In it I find a pick and a lump hammer. I take them both and run back to our building.

The lift cage rattles and judders as it climbs back up. And as it slowly approaches the top floor, all I can do is lean against the wall and think about Joe and Gill. The initial panic starts to fade slightly and I start to consider my options with a fraction more clarity. Should I contact the military? I dismiss that idea almost before I've finished thinking it. I can't take that risk. Who knows what they'll do. If whatever's in there killed Gill, then they'll take Joe and run tests on him, lock him up in another lab and I won't be able to do anything to help. I can't let them. I could try Alfie, but I don't trust him either. No, I have to do this by myself.

The lift stops and I slide back the door.

I stop when I'm halfway down the corridor.

Jesus Christ.

A sudden realisation makes my legs go weak with nerves. Gill was talking about whatever it is that's loose in the lab being self-replicating. Can I risk breaching the seal and letting it out?

'Daddy, get me out.'

Joe starts screaming again the moment he sees me.

'How do you feel, son?'

'Scared. Really scared.'

'Do you still feel sick?'

'A little. Need to pee.'

'Use the sink.'

'I can't.'

'Just do it, Joe.'

I watch helplessly as he walks across the lab, occasionally checking back over his shoulder to make sure I'm still there. He drags a stool over to the sink, then kneels on it and pees into the sink like I told him. He tries to wash his hands, but the water's dried to a dribble. Everything's shut down in there. Joe looks tired. He comes back over to the window, dragging his feet.

'You okay?'

'Really hot. Tired.'

'Sit by the air vent.'

He does as I tell him. 'Nothing coming out.'

My worst fears are confirmed. The inner labs are hermetically-sealed rooms. Nothing's getting in or out. There's no air in there. Total lockdown.

Joe's distracted, staring at his mom's corpse again.

'Don't look, son.'

'I'm scared, Daddy. Get me out. Please, Daddy, get me out.'

Whatever it is that killed Gill, it hasn't affected Joe. Is it over, or is he somehow immune?

It's late. I've gone through all of Gill's files and all the manuals and system guides I can find, but I've found no answers. I can't make sense of any of the data, but then again, I don't need to. All I know is my wife is dead and my son is trapped. If I let Joe out, there's a chance more people might die, but what else can I do? He's my responsibility. I'm all he has left.

I remember Gill's words from a few nights back. She talked about having to make an impossible decision: having to choose between our son and everyone else. And now I find myself facing the exact same choice, and for the first time I can fully feel the enormous weight of pressure Gill had been struggling with all this time.

I'm standing at the window again. Joe's sitting on the floor next to his mom. He's stopped crying. He looks like he's struggling to stay awake. With effort he glances up and sees me at the window, his eyes locking onto mine.

What do I do? I can't let him die.

I put on a face-mask from one of the hazmat suits Gill and Alfie sometimes wore, then grab the pick and start swinging it at the wall. The window and doors are strengthened; my best bet is to try and hammer my way straight through the brickwork. In a momentary gap between blows, I hear a voice.

'That you, Daddy?'

It's Joe. Just a whisper. Barely alive.

'Stay right back, sunshine,' I shout, my voice muffled by the mask, not knowing if he can hear me. The plaster crumbles. Wood starts to splinter. Bricks shift. My muscles are already burning with effort but I know I can't stop until I have him in my arms again. 'I'm coming to get you, son.'

'Where are we going, Dad?'

'Away from here. I'm going to try and take you to Pop's house, okay?'

'Okay. We going to keep these masks on all day?'

'For a little while. Just until we're sure it's safe.'

'What about when we need to eat.'

'I'll think of something.'

'What about Mom?'

Hard to answer. Hurts too much. 'When you're safe with Pop, I'll come back and look after Mom.'

'What do you mean, look after her?'

'I'll tell people about the accident. Tell people what happened.'

'Are you going to get into trouble.'

'No, Joe. It'll all be fine.'

I start the car and drive away from the lab. The side roads are clear, but the traffic's backed-up on main street. We can't go any further. It's the middle of the night, for Christ's sake.

'What's wrong?' Joe asks.

'A crash, I think. Wait here.'

I get out of the car and pull my hood over my face so people don't get freaked out by the mask. Looks like a car's gone into a hydrant. Jesus, is that someone lying in the middle of the road up ahead? And now I see that most of the other cars in this traffic queue have crashed too, like they've just run into each other. What the fuck?

I walk a little further forward then stop when the guy behind the wheel of the car I'm next to thumps against his window. He's hammering on the glass. I pull him out and try to help but there's nothing I can do. He's choking. He writhes at my feet and spits blood over my boots.

More people are collapsing now. Everywhere. All dying like Gill. It's spreading.

I have to get Joe away from here.

I manage to turn the car around and find another route out of town.

'What's happening, Dad?' Joe asks, strapped into his booster seat behind me.

'Don't know,' I lie.

'Those people were getting sick like Mom.'

'That's why we have to keep our masks on.'

'Shouldn't we help?'

'We can't.'

I put my foot down and drive out of town. And now ours is the only car moving. I look at Joe in the mirror and I picture him still trapped in the lab with Gill, waiting to die. I know I did the right thing. It's just Joe and me now.

'We still going to Pop's?'

'That's the plan.'

'Will Pop be okay?'

'I hope so.'

Billions died in less than twenty-four hours.

WHO'S WHO

Many of the stories included in this collection are separate to the characters and events featured in the five **Autumn** novels. Here is a brief summary of those people and situations which do figure in the books.

AMY STEADMAN is not a named character in the novels, but she appears in **Purification** as the creature on the other side of the airfield fence which grabs the recently reanimated corpse of Kelly Harcourt. *'Eight weeks ago this had been an intelligent young clothing store department manager with a bright future ahead of her. Now it was a mud-splattered, half-naked, emaciated collection of brittle bone and rotting flesh. Unlike the majority of the seething crowd, however, this one was beginning to exhibit signs of real control and determination.'*

JIM HARPER, **HARRY STAYT**, **BRIGID CULTHORPE**, **PETER GUEST** and **KAREN CHASE** are among the first survivors to settle on the island of Cormansey in **Purification**. Harry goes on to have a major role in **Aftermath**.

JACKIE SOAMES, **JACOB FLYNN**, **GARY KEELE** and **JULIET APPLEBY** are four of the survivors based at the airfield in **Purification**. Jackie is their self-appointed leader, whilst Gary is their reluctant pilot.

SHERI NEWTON, **SONYA FARLEY** and **DEAN MCFARLANE** (**Innocence**) are survivors in the group sheltering in a university accommodation block in **The City**. The mall where Sheri worked security is where several key characters meet for the first time after a run for supplies.

WEBB and **CARON** both appear in **Disintegration**. Caron goes on to play an important part in **Aftermath**.

PHILIP EVANS is the lone survivor discovered by Michael and Emma in **Autumn**.

KIERAN COPE and **JACKSON** both play major roles in **Aftermath**.

KATE JAMES and **ANNIE NELSON** are both survivors who remained in the community centre after Michael, Carl and Emma left in **Autumn**.

KILGORE has a large role in **Purification** after managing to escape the battle outside the military bunker.

BREAKING POINT takes place between the end of **Autumn** and Michael and Emma's appearance in **The City**.

BEGINNING TO DISINTEGRATE follows two groups of survivors through the early days of the infection, and explains how the group sheltering in the derelict block of flats came together at the beginning of **Disintegration**.

UNDERGROUND occurs in and around the military bunker two months after the catastrophic events of the beginning of **Purification**.

Also by David Moody

the acclaimed **autumn** series
www.lastoftheliving.net

"A head-spinning thrill ride"
Guillermo del Toro

www.thehatertrilogy.com

TRUST
DAVID MOODY

"Trust is a slow-burner and all the richer for it. The layers of characters and details of the story play out perfectly when matched with an ending you're not likely to forget. It's also an outstanding novel, delivers in more ways than one, and is worthy of a place on the discerning fan's bookshelf. 10/10."
— **Starburst Magazine**

www.trustdavidmoody.com

If you are the original purchaser of this book, or if you received this book as a gift, you can download a complementary eBook version by visiting:

www.infectedbooks.co.uk/ebooks

and completing the necessary information (terms and conditions apply).

www.ingramcontent.com/pod-product-compliance
Lightning Source LLC
Chambersburg PA
CBHW020922020726
47495CB00002B/311